PASSION'S STORM

"Are you still cold, honey?" Trace asked softly.

"No." Oh, the way he said 'honey'; it drifted over her like a soft caress.

"Then why did you shiver? Were you thinking about the storm?"

Addy nodded. That was as good an explanation as any, and as close to the truth. There was *another* storm building at the moment, but it had nothing to do with the tempest raging outside the covered wagon.

"It's just about over."

She licked her lips nervously. "Are you sure?"

His hands stroked her back, and his voice rumbled like the thunder over the plains when he finally answered her question. "No, I'm not sure. The storm may never end."

His hands massaged her shoulders, then cupped the back of her neck. Excitement coursed through her body. He was going to kiss her, and she could hardly wait . . .

HEARTFIRE ROMANCES

SWEET TEXAS NIGHTS   (2610, $3.75)
by Vivian Vaughan

Meg Britton grew up on the railroads, working proudly at her father's side. Nothing was going to stop them from setting the rails clear to Silver Creek, Texas—certainly not some crazy prospector. As Meg set out to confront the old coot, she planned her strategy with cool precision. But soon she was speechless with shock. For instead of a harmless geezer, she found a boldly handsome stranger whose determination matched her own.

CAPTIVE DESIRE   (2612, $3.75)
by Jane Archer

Victoria Malone fancied herself a great adventuress, but being kidnapped was too much excitement for even Victoria! Especially when her arrogant kidnapper thought she was part of Red Duke's outlaw gang. Trying to convince the overbearing, handsome stranger that she had been an innocent bystander when the stagecoach was robbed, proved futile. But when he thought he could maker her confess by crushing her to his warm, broad chest, by caressing her with his strong, capable hands, Victoria was willing to admit to anything. . . .

LAWLESS ECSTASY   (2613, $3.75)
by Susan Sackett

Abra Beaumont could spot a thief a mile away. After all, her father was once one of the best. But he'd been on the right side of the law for years now, and she wasn't about to let a man like Dash Thorne lead him astray with some wild plan for stealing the Tear of Allah, the world's most fabulous ruby. Dash was just the sort of man she most distrusted—sophisticated, handsome, and altogether too sure of his considerable charm. Abra shivered at the devilish gleam in his blue eyes and swore he would need more than smooth kisses and skilled caresses to rob her of her virtue . . . and much more than sweet promises to steal her heart!

Available wherever paperbacks are sold, or order direct from the Publisher. Send cover price plus 50¢ per copy for mailing and handling to Zebra Books, Dept. 3110, 475 Park Avenue South, New York, N.Y. 10016. Residents of New York, New Jersey and Pennsylvania must include sales tax. DO NOT SEND CASH.

Santa Fe Fantasy

JUDITH STEEL

ZEBRA BOOKS
KENSINGTON PUBLISHING CORP.

ZEBRA BOOKS

are published by

Kensington Publishing Corp.
475 Park Avenue South
New York, NY 10016

First printing: August, 1990

Printed in the United States of America

This one is for you, Daddy

And I would like to make special mention of my two grandmothers, both in their nineties, wonderful ladies who have been pioneers in their own rights.

Prologue

Boston, 1849

Addy Montclair wiped her damp palms on her dress. She scowled as she looked around the office. What was keeping everyone? When the door suddenly opened, she jumped to her feet, smoothing the wrinkles from her long, full skirt and giving her lustrous brown curls a quick pat.

Timothy Sharpe, the Montclair family lawyer, stepped into the room. He turned and swept his hand before him, ushering through the doorway the person accompanying him.

Addy's bright hazel eyes rounded as she stared, astonished, at the new arrival. *This* was cousin Delilah? This tall, assured, well-tailored woman was the short, timid, frumpy little cousin she had known as a child? No, it couldn't be!

Mr. Sharpe broke the strained silence that had settled over the dimly lit room. "Delilah. Adeline. I'm sure you two are glad to see each other. How long has it been? Eight years?"

Delilah held out her hand toward her cousin. "Ten years, Mr. Sharpe. Ten long years. How are you, Addy dahlin'?"

Addy hesitantly extended her hand. After all, it wasn't polite to refuse a gesture of friendship. And she, too, remembered how long it had been since she and her family had last journeyed to Virginia.

"Hello . . . Lily. I'm all right, I guess. Glad you were able to come."

Timothy Sharpe directed the two ladies toward the pair of chairs drawn up before his desk. If he noticed the furtive glances Addy shot at Delilah, he paid no undue attention to them.

"I know the two of you have a lot of catching up to do, so we may as well get business matters out of the way." He shuffled through a tall stack of papers in the middle of his desk.

"Now, as the sole remaining survivors of the Montclair estate, the two of you will inherit equally the money, investments, and business properties."

Tilting his chin, he peered over the rim of his spectacles at Addy. "Your father maintained Delilah's estate upon his brother's death, to insure her trust."

Addy nodded. She was well aware that her Uncle Elias's bequest had had a great deal to do with her own father's success during the past few years.

She begrudged Delilah nothing. Except the fact that the young girl had refused to come north to live with Addy's family after her father passed away.

They could have had ten years of growing up together, and shared fun and companionship, instead of ten lonely years raised as only children.

The lawyer's voice interrupted her pensive thoughts.

"For the past five years, Adeline's father invested heavily in the trade between Missouri and New Mexico Territory, bringing a tidy profit to the estate. However, he also made several unwise choices and lost a great deal of his assets."

The cousins looked at each other, surprise and concern evident in their expressions.

Mr. Sharpe hurried to reassure them. "Please don't misunderstand. You both still have your homes, and a healthy sum of money in your respective accounts, enough to keep you comfortably for a number of years—with careful management."

Addy was the first of the two women to speak.

8

"Why wasn't I told of this? Father would have—"

"Yes, perhaps your father *would* have mentioned it, if he hadn't thought he could recoup his losses through the freight company. And he was doing so, quite nicely, before he . . . he and your mother were . . . taken from us."

Addy's fingers curled around the arms of her chair, gripping the polished oak with such force that her long, manicured nails dug small arcs into the varnish of the hardwood. Unable to sit still a moment longer, as rekindled anger surged through her chest, she leapt to her feet.

"Before they were *murdered,* you mean. Whatever got into Father, anyway? He assured us that there was no danger involved, that the Indians valued their trade as much as the Mexicans—otherwise, Mother never would have gone with him."

"My dear, if your father hadn't believed your mother would be safe he would never have let her accompany him. You know that."

Delilah reached out a hand, but drew it back as suddenly. Her voice trembled. "Those dirty, cowardly savages." She sighed. "I have a letter from your mother, Addy. It was written about a week before. . . . Well, she sounded so excited and thrilled with the adventure of her journey. I really believe she was where she wanted to be."

Addy spun around, a sharp retort on the tip of her tongue. She swallowed it. Delilah was right. She had received a letter, too. Her mother had never sounded so happy.

"Ladies, if you don't mind, I would like to continue."

Addy slumped back into her seat, massaging her forehead as she listened to the lawyer.

"The point I would like to make is this: It would be in your best interests to keep the freight company in operation. I can hire a capable manager to take control of the business, and—"

9

Delilah bounced in her seat. "Ooh, I know just the person. My husband, Jubal, is in Independence right now. He's been over the Santa Fe Trail several times. I'm sure he would be more than happy to supervise the company."

She took a deep breath and narrowed her eyes as she looked to her cousin. "For us, of course. He would run it for *us*. In fact, I've been thinking of joining him — why, I could even keep the records. We could send the reports back to you, Addy, and you wouldn't have to worry about a thing."

Addy contemplated her cousin's almost-too-eager announcement. Delilah didn't sound at all like the scared recluse Addy had grown accustomed to from the letters she'd received — although, if she remembered correctly, she hadn't heard a word from her cousin for over two years. It *was* possible for a person to change, she guessed.

"I don't know, Lily. That would be an awful imposition on you and your . . . husband. By the way, just when did you get *married?*"

Delilah flushed and averted her eyes. "Um, I've, *we've,* been married almost a year now. I was certain I wrote to you about it. It was a small ceremony. You know me, I don't get along well around a lot of people."

Addy nodded. Yes, that sounded more like Lily.

Delilah's eyes then sought her cousin's. "It wouldn't be an imposition at all. I know Jubal would be hurt if we didn't take advantage of his knowledge."

The impatient lawyer cleared his throat. "Well, what do you say, ladies? Shall I find someone to help you, or will, uh, Mr. Wilkins do?"

Addy glanced at the frowning man, then at her cousin. She smiled for the first time in weeks.

"I think we'll be able to handle the arrangements, Mr. Sharpe. Let's go pack our bags, Lily. *We're* going West."

Chapter One

"Addy, dahlin', what *are* you starin' at?"

Startled, Addy gasped. Her hand fluttered over her chest. "Lord, Lily, how do you move so quietly? You nearly scared me into the river." She blinked. Her eyes stung. How long *had* she been gazing toward the railing?

When Delilah only smiled, and was herself caught up by an attraction on the deck of the steamboat, Addy exhaled a long-suffering sigh. She and her cousin had enjoyed a fairly pleasant trip — so far — but if she heard one more "Addy, dahlin'," she would be tempted to violence.

Eyes drawn forward once again, her heart leapt to her throat, beating with a rhythmic cadence that curled her toes. It dawned on her that she'd been staring at one particular spot, and the man who had been the focus of her undivided attention had suddenly turned to face her. The air left her breast in a loud *whoosh*.

She gritted her teeth when the same hissing sound escaped Delilah's parted red lips. Had the woman no shame? She was married, after all, and wasn't free to be so conspicuously open with her admiration.

"My God, Addy. He's gorgeous. No wonder you didn't hear me callin'."

She barely heard her cousin's breathless words. From the moment her eyes had collided with those of the man under discussion, Addy had been unable to tear them away. She tried, but it felt like she could fall into those sparkling deep blue pools and drown

11

more swiftly than if she fell overboard.

Blushing from the roots of her hair to the tips of her toes, she waved her handkerchief in front of her in an effort to stir the air and cool her heated body.

Dear Lord, what had she done? Had she really been caught staring raptly at a complete stranger? And from the look on the man's face, he'd enjoyed it.

Behind the undulating hanky, she whispered, "Hush, Lily. You don't want him to hear you."

Delilah smiled seductively, though she could well see that the man's eyes were trained elsewhere. "Who cares, dahlin'? He knows the effect he has on women. Why, look around. Every person wearin' skirts is as besotted as we are, if not more so."

Realizing that she and her cousin were, indeed, aboard a public conveyance, and not in some secret dream hideaway, Addy dragged her eyes away from the tall, blond Adonis. She glanced around in utter embarrassment.

Thank heavens, no one seemed aware of her wanton behavior. Every female eye was, as inconspicuously as possible, directed in the same moonstruck fashion at the well-proportioned gentleman in the form-hugging blue uniform.

Her eyes retraced their path. They widened with amazement and apprehension when she discovered he still watched *her*. The faint flush that had engulfed her body kindled to flame as his gaze seared her from the high-buttoned collar of her silk dress to the lacings of her small, dainty shoes.

She glared at him, indignant that he should take the liberty of ogling her in public.

Then he had the audacity to wink. Her mouth gaped open. She was horrified. Fury lent impetus to her feet as she swirled around, stumbling over her bulky petticoats in her haste to leave his brazen presence. Her hand shot out to grab Delilah's arm on the way.

Dragged by her cousin into the nearest open door-

12

way, Delilah hissed, "See? I warned you. You would have been much better off back in Boston, where you wouldn't be exposed to ruffians unaccustomed to using their manners, if they had any to begin with."

Addy snapped back, "Well, what about you? *You're* a lady. What are *you* doing here?"

Delilah sniffed. "I'm a married woman now, Addy. I'm not completely innocent in the ways of men."

Marching as swiftly as possible, without loosening her grip on her resisting cousin, Addy huffed, "Just because I'm not married, doesn't mean I'm ignorant, Lily. I know a little about men."

Her face flushed anew at the falsehood. Well, she *had* had one kiss—one brief peck on the corner of her upper lip from Augustus Moreland. But it hadn't inspired the butterfly sensations she'd heard other girls rave about after such doings.

The chaste kiss certainly hadn't had the effect on her body that just a look and a wink from the good-looking soldier had produced. She pouted. Was there something wrong with her?

During her moment of hesitation, Delilah jerked away and stood, blocking Adeline's path of retreat.

"It's not too late, you know. There's still time to go back to Boston before you get hurt."

Addy's back stiffened. Her eyes flashed beneath a thick fringe of dark-brown lashes. "You sound awfully positive that I will regret this trip. Just what do you think will happen, Lily?"

Delilah stepped to one side and leaned against the wall as the boat gave a slight lurch.

"Why, nothin' in particular. I just can't see you gettin' on well there, is all. From everything Jubal's said in his letters, it's no place for a genteel woman such as yourself. I don't want to see you get hurt. That's all I meant."

Addy admonished herself. Of course her cousin hadn't intended to sound so threatening. It was only Addy's overactive imagination at work. Ever since her parents' untimely death, she'd behaved quite uncharacteristically. It was disconcerting.

In fact, if Timothy Sharpe hadn't said almost the same things to her the day before she left Boston, she probably wouldn't have thought a thing of Delilah's warning. As it was, she still smarted from the man's angry outburst—he'd actually had the presumption to say that she would come crawling back to Boston, to him, begging on her hands and knees for him to *wed* her.

Oooh, it made her mad all over again. How mortifying, that the man her father trusted enough to name as her guardian should suddenly make such an outlandish proposal. He had even intimated that, because of her gentle breeding, she wouldn't survive the trip from Independence to Sante Fe.

At the time, she hadn't seriously decided to make the overland journey, but after his callous boast, she was bound and determined to take the first caravan to Santa Fe. The faraway town must be grand indeed, if what she'd overheard on the boat was true. Some even referred to Santa Fe as "Paradise." Now she could hardly wait to get there.

Yes, she would show Timothy Sharpe and Delilah and everyone else that she wasn't the pampered "dahling" they all expected to cave in at the first hint of hardship. She was a Montclair, wasn't she? If her mother could do it, and like it, so could Addy.

She looked over to say as much to Delilah, but her cousin was gone. Addy turned and looked behind her, and again down the hallway. Now why had she run off like that? Addy shrugged, rubbing a trembling hand over her eyes.

As she took a step forward, intending to go to her room, she swayed, bumping into a hard, unyielding object that immediately reached out and gripped her shoulders with long, strong fingers.

"Oh, Lily, I thought you'd left . . ." Her words trailed to an open-mouthed gawk when she looked up

14

into the soldier's dark blue eyes. His blond mustache quirked up amusedly as his slim lips opened.

"Are you all right, ma'am?"

"Er, pardon?" She stammered. His teeth were perfectly straight and white.

"I thought you were going to fall. Are you ill?"

"N-no." He smelled clean and . . . *masculine* — of soap and cigars and the fresh outdoors.

"No? You look awfully pale."

The mustache lifted at the corners. Was he making fun of her? He had winked at her on deck. Now he laughed. She sniffed indignantly and hissed, "Thank you," as she turned her back and marched stiffly away, hoping all the while that he had as foolish a look on his face now as she must have had on hers earlier.

The *nerve* of the cad! For a minute there, she'd almost lost her head.

Later in the afternoon, after taking a restful nap, Addy prepared to meet Delilah for supper. Her heartbeat had at last returned to normal; the unsettling experience with the handsome soldier forced from her mind.

Tomorrow morning she and her cousin would leave the boat at Independence and never lay eyes on the outrageous man again.

Her stomach knotted as she recalled the tremors that had rippled through her entire form that afternoon. No wonder women were scarce in the West, if all of the men were so insufferably impudent.

As Addy walked out of her cabin, her full skirt caught on a splinter in the doorway. Moaning, she turned to free herself, backing into the passageway, carefully pulling her petticoats and skirt along with her. A few gentle swipes of her hand down the soft green wool smoothed a tiny pull in the material. She sighed with relief.

With a deep breath she spun around, in a hurry not to be late. "Oof!" The air rushed from her lungs as she bounced off a solid steel wall.

"Well now, ma'am, it appears we're making a habit of running into each other."

Addy blushed furiously as the maddening soldier steadied her as he would a clumsy child, then stepped back to give her petite figure a thorough going-over with his dancing blue eyes.

That was definitely *not* a look he would give a child. She hunched her shoulders, for the first time in her life self-conscious of the fullness of her bosom and the revealing manner in which the soft wool clung to her generous curves.

"You certainly look lovely this evening, ma'am."

His deep voice rumbled seductively in her ear. Goose bumps rippled over her flesh. She shivered, glared at the man, and lifted her chin to a hauty angle before swishing off grandly down the hallway.

The nerve of the oaf, speaking to her so familiarly. And what was his inference? Had she looked dowdy this morning?

"Well, pardon me all to Hell," she heard him say. "Most *ladies* at least know how to say thank you when they're paid a compliment."

The vibrancy of his remark echoed behind her, stinging her very soul.

Tears stung the backs of her eyes. It was the first time she'd ever been accused of *not* being a most well-mannered young woman.

She walked faster, unable to muster the courage to apologize for her rude behavior. Couldn't he see that she wasn't used to men behaving in such a forward manner?

She'd never been confronted by a man of his like before, and she hadn't the faintest notion of how to handle herself, let alone *him*.

Maybe Timothy Sharpe and Delilah were right. Maybe she should have stayed in Boston.

The next morning, as the steamboat docked at the Independence wharf, Delilah rushed by Addy, leaving behind a cloud of perfumed air.

"Wait for me, Addy. I forgot my hat."

Addy opened her mouth, intending to give her cousin an affirmative reply, only the woman was already out of hearing. She shrugged her shoulders and leaned back against her cabin door, grateful to be in the shadows, out of the hot, morning sun.

Suddenly, the air about her became charged. The bare flesh at her neckline and on the backs of her hands tingled. Her eyes were drawn, as if by magic, to a lean figure descending the walk to the dock.

The fellow stopped, midway down the wooden plank, and it seemed she could see the muscles beneath his snow-white shirt tense. His head cocked to one side, as if listening for something. Then he turned. Deep blue eyes glittered as they sought, and found, her.

She sucked in her breath, wishing desperately to be absorbed into the solid wood at her back. Her knees turned as weak as rainwater when he flicked the brim of his hat in salute. The rapid thump of her heart caused her to feel unusually light-headed when he flashed his teeth in a wicked smile.

And just as she felt that at any moment she might slide to the floor in a smoldering heap, he turned his back and walked to a waiting stagecoach.

Her hand clutched at the throbbing pulse in her neck. She took a couple of long, deep breaths. And he was gone. Just like that!

A deep sigh escaped her trembling lips. *What a relief.* Now maybe her senses could return to normal. He had only been a momentary lapse in what would continue to be a well-ordered life of common sense and self-discipline. It could happen to anyone.

"Addy! There you are. Come on. Jubal's waitin'."

When Addy hesitated, Delilah literally dragged her from her stupor. Addy had to snap out of her reverie or fall down the gangway.

At the end of the planking stood a heavy-set, middle-aged, balding man, whose face was wreathed in what Addy considered to be a thoroughly counterfeit smile. His lips were properly curved, but his eyes settled on Lily and herself like a starving cat's would a pair of crippled mice.

"Jubal, dahlin', I've missed you so."

Addy hung back as Delilah gave her husband a hug and kiss. She shuddered. The man gave her a strange feeling. . . . His skin was pale and sickly-looking. A sudden glimpse of the handsome soldier's tanned, vibrant skin flashed in, and quickly out of, her mind.

Her eyes narrowed. *Soldier.* Now she knew what had been different about the man this morning. He hadn't been wearing his uniform.

Gold flecks sparkled as her eyes softened and she mused on. He was surely the most handsome man she'd ever seen in those snug-fitting leather breeches and the clean white shirt. So lean and muscular and powerful. It took her breath away just thinking of him.

"Addy, come on down here, will you?" Lily finally reached out and grabbed Addy's hand, pulling her forward.

"Jubal, this is my cousin, Adeline." Delilah beamed proudly as she hooked her arm through her husband's.

"Addy, this is my husband. Isn't he something?"

Addy swallowed the first words that threatened to spill from her twitching lips, and mumbled, "Oh, I . . . have to admit, he's everything you said, and more."

She held out her hand and fought to keep from jerking it back when Jubal's soft, clammy fingers touched hers. His lips were cold on her flesh, and

18

made her skin crawl until he finally lifted his head. Hiding her hand behind her back, she wiped it down her skirt.

Addy hoped she murmured all the correct responses as he led them to a waiting carriage. She wished she could dislodge the unsettling feelings of disquiet she experienced in Jubal's presence.

For the sake of the freight company, she would have to get over this awful first impression. After all, she'd had a weird sensation upon seeing Delilah too, but it had dissipated as they reacquainted themselves during the long journey to Independence.

In the seat across from the happy couple, Addy was surprised to hear Jubal say the Montclair company would start a caravan to Santa Fe the following day. He said the time for travel was late spring to early fall, and since it was already the end of May, competitors had the advantage.

"Tomorrow? Did you say the caravan is leaving tomorrow?"

Jubal smacked his lips, causing his jowls to jiggle. "No other choice, if you ladies want any income from Montrose Freight this year. Don't you fret, little lady. Ever since my Delilah wrote to tell me you all was comin', I've been workin' like Hell.

S'cuse the language, darlin's, but we're not used to bein' in the company of fine ladies out here."

Delilah cocked her head and glowered meaningfully at Addy.

"Anyway, I've put together a large supply of goods for trade in Santa Fe. Might as well get on with it an' get 'em there, don't you think?"

Addy gulped and nodded her head. Tomorrow. That didn't give her much time.

"What will I need to take, Mr. Wilkins, I mean, Jubal?" Since he *was* her relative, by marriage at least, and they would be spending a lot of time together, Addy supposed it was "friendlier" to call him by his first name.

Jubal sputtered. His eyes bugged out. "You? *Haw! Haw!* That's a good one. Delilah, your little cousin's a real joker. You two will get along real fine while I'm gone."

Delilah frowned, proving to be an unexpected ally in Addy's cause. "Why, Jubal, dahlin', I do believe that bein' without the influence of 'real ladies' has addled your mind. Don't you remember? When I wrote to tell you we were comin' to Independence, I also mentioned that we'd be goin' on to Santa Fe with you."

Jubal's face turned a blotchy red. His mouth opened, but no sound came out. His breathing was labored.

Addy swallowed nervously. When she'd made up her mind in Boston, the journey to Santa Fe had seemed like a wonderful adventure. Now that she was actually en route, she saw the folly of her bold actions. What did she know about the freight business? What did she know of the kind of men who would risk their lives to make such a dangerous trip? What did she know of the wild country through which they would travel? What did she know of her own constitution?

What if she . . . couldn't do it?

Trace Randall scowled as the men inside the stagecoach snickered.

"What ya gawkin' at Randall?"

"Yeah, ya leave a little gal a pinin' fer ya again?"

"How many wenches it take ta satisfy a stud like you, Randy?"

To stop their incessant ribbing, Trace ducked his head back into the coach. He'd long ago lost sight of the girl standing in the shadows of the boat, anyway.

His dark-blue eyes glittered as he shot each of his three companions a direct warning. He hunched his shoulders and slid down in the uncomfortable seat, pulling the brim of his hat low over his eyes.

His lips twitched slightly as the men continued to guffaw about his considerable reputation as a "ladies' man." Trace Randall remained implacable.

"Aw, hell, Trace. Whyn't you talk to us fer a while? Tell us what's happenin' in St. Louie."

Trace shifted his position to rest the back of his neck on the slim layer of padding. "Later, boys. I'm tired."

"Yeah, an' I bet we know why, eh, pard?"

"Ya been dippin' the candle late ever night. Huh, Rand?"

A chorus of loud laughter followed the jests, but Trace Randall calmly crossed his arms over his chest and tilted his chin down. He was too busy picturing images of the delectable little piece on the boat to pay attention to the simple-minded banter of his friends. Besides, he was getting tired of their constant commentary on his affairs. He liked women, and women seemed to like him. Why did everyone have to give him such a hard time?

His lips thinned into a hard line. Just because he *liked* a woman, didn't mean he allowed himself to become involved with one for any length of time. He had too much to do yet to be encumbered by a helpless female.

But just as the thought entered his mind, brilliant brown eyes with dancing gold sparks surfaced, as well as images of long, brown hair that shone, even in the shade.

He grinned. She'd been so angry. Her little nose had tilted jauntily in the air, high creamy cheeks flushed an engaging rose-color. And the way that bow-shaped mouth puckered when she compressed her lips—it was a sight to behold.

He inhaled deeply and tried to relax—so his body wouldn't suffer so many jolts and bruises during the rough ride, he told himself.

But when his stomach remained knotted and his

21

loins continued to ache, he knew the unexpected way he had reacted to the tiny, doll-faced woman would cause him countless hours of discomfort.

Damn! What was it about her that made him unable to put her from his mind? He never thought *this* much about the women he bedded, let alone one who he imagined thought his days on earth were spent slithering around on his belly.

Sighing, he straightened up in his seat. There was no use even trying. He would get no rest this day. Picking up his rifle, he poked the man next to him.

"I'm going on top. Close the door after me, will you?"

He threw the carbine ahead of him, then reached up to grab the iron railing encompassing the roof of the rocking stage. The muscles in his arms bulged, straining the soft cotton that covered them, as he easily lifted his long body up and over.

Air. That's what he needed. Lots of fresh air to clear his muddled brain.

Chapter Two

Early the next morning, as she balanced precariously on the walk in front of a large general mercantile store, Addy's eyes rounded with surprise.

"Damn your flea-bitten hide! You jackassed son of a jenny. Get up there!"

There always seemed to be something going on in Independence Square. Today, everyone's attention was directed toward the comical scene of a monstrous bearded man shaking his fist at a miscreant little mule. Addy allowed herself an unabashed grin. Excitement that had bubbled close to the surface for the past two weeks spilled forth in a rush as she rubbed her hands together with unsuppressed glee.

She was going to Santa Fe! Really going. It had taken Lily, and her own persuasive cajoling, the better part of the evening to convince Jubal to take them along. He had *finally* capitulated, albeit with many reservations.

She didn't know what Lily had whispered in her husband's ear, but when Jubal frowned, and her cousin smiled a sweet, innocent smile, Addy knew the tide had turned in their favor.

A sudden thundering of hooves drew her interest as a herd of mules and oxen were driven into the square amid a billowing cloud of dust.

One team of mules, which had stood quietly while being harnessed to a light carriage, suddenly decided to enter the melee. They took off in an instant, bucking and kicking and braying their devilment at the top of their lungs. The driver raced behind, clinging tenaciously to the long reins until he tripped and was dragged along the ground on his belly.

Chains and harness clinked and rattled. Mounted men raced after the recalcitrant animals like avenging demons.

Addy laughed out loud. Since it wasn't a very lady-like thing to do, she quickly covered her mouth, hoping no one had noticed.

Everywhere she looked, similar scenes unfolded. She held her sides as tears of joy trickled down her cheeks, smudging the caked dust. This would be such a fun trip!

"Addy! Whatever are you doin'? No self-respectin lady would be caught dead standin' out here watchin such a display." Delilah's voice was high-pitched and strained.

Addy sighed, supposing she should be ashamed of herself, but at that precise moment a man, trying to control the fractious team in front of the walk, uncer-emoniously clamped his teeth onto a rearing mule's ear. The mule's eyes rolled and its feet stomped a staccato beat on the packed earth as the man held his position. Addy giggled.

"Adeline Montclair, your momma and poppa would roll over in their graves if they could see you now. Come inside this minute! Don't you have to make more purchases before we leave?"

Addy let Delilah lead her into the store. She knew she should be better prepared, but what did one take on a long wagon journey into the desert West?

"Did Jubal tell you what we would need, Lily?"

Delilah snorted. "Huh! No. I've never known him to be so pigheaded. He said if we wanted to risk our health, not to mention our lives, by takin' this trip, it was *our* business. He wants no part of it."

Addy turned away. Her teeth ground together until her jaws ached. How she disliked Jubal Wilkins! Now for the first time, she wondered how her cousin could have fallen in love with such a disagreeable man.

24

She plucked at a piece of lint clinging to a fold of her skirt, refusing to meet Delilah's eyes. "What do *you* think we'll need? Blankets, and food, and things like that?"

Delilah nodded. "I suppose so. At least I know our luggage is on one of the wagons. I saw it bein' loaded myself. And those poor beasts pullin' the wagons. You should see it all, Addy. The wagons are piled *so* high with trade goods." She held up one hand, to emphasize the amount being taken. "I don't see how they can carry so much."

Addy looked through a window as the men continued to load box after box onto the bed of a huge wagon. It was amazing, all right.

She frowned, scratching the tip of her nose. If every spare inch of room was filled with merchandise, where did the men ride and sleep? And of uppermost concern in her mind—where would *she* ride and sleep?

A familiar tremor shook her knees. What had she gotten herself into? She'd never undertaken anything so dangerous, or so . . . exciting. What if she made a complete fool of herself?

Her chin lifted. At least she'd have *one* good story for her grandchildren—provided she lived long enough to find a man suitable to wed!

A pink flush stained her cheeks. She grimaced as her stomach fluttered. Wouldn't Timothy Sharpe have kittens if she returned home with a tall, blond, good-looking soldier? She shook her head. Now where had that thought come from? Why couldn't she get rid of the vision of the rude man on the steamboat?

She was grateful to be drawn from her musing when Jubal Wilkins pushed his way into the store and bellowed, "Get a move on it, ladies. We pull out in exactly two hours. If you're not ready we'll leave without you."

Addy turned to glare at the overbearing man, and

25

missed the negligible nod of Delilah's head in Jubal's direction.

Jubal looked directly to Addy. "The hotel's keepin' your room open, little lady. All you gotta do is—"

Addy stopped him before he could say the words she had been thinking herself. "No, I am not going to stay in Independence, Mr. Wil . . . *Jubal*. I intend to go to Santa Fe, and I will be ready to leave when you are."

The fat man's lips quirked. There was an unreadable glint to his eyes as he responded, "We'll see. We'll sure see about that, little lady."

As he turned and left the store, Addy shivered. Now she'd gone and done it. There would be no turning back.

Addy and Delilah were the ones to wait impatiently for the greater part of the day. It took the rugged, sweat-stained men that long to get the animals accustomed to harness and yoke, and the ten wagons loaded to Jubal's satisfaction.

The women sat on the steps of the mercantile, their stack of neatly wrapped parcels looking lonely and forlorn against the peeling paint of the siding.

Through the long hours of watching the back-breaking labor of Jubal's men, Addy'd had a persistent feeling of unease in the back of her mind. She couldn't help but think that Jubal had given in too easily inside the store.

Around midafternoon, they finally heard a weary voice call out, "Catch up!" Then a stronger, "Catch up!"

The driver of the wagon in front of them finished tying a hitch and shouted, "All's set!" Addy jumped. The same reply echoed down the line of nine wagons.

Several drivers climbed onto their wagons. Other men flipped and cracked their whips as they walked alongside their oxen.

A ruddy-faced, scarecrow-looking individual drove up in a black carriage pulled by a team of two mules. He pointed to Delilah. "Mr. Wilkins sent me to get you and your things, ma'am. Show me what's yours, an' I'll load up."

Delilah's mouth fell open. She watched the thin young man clamber to the ground, then cast apologetic eyes to Addy.

"B-but what about my cousin? Where does she ride?"

"Don't know, ma'am. My orders was to pick up Mrs. Wilkins. That be you."

Addy's heart sank along with all the color in her face. She really shouldn't be surprised, she thought. She'd expected something like this. Well, maybe not *exactly* like this. What had Jubal said? Her room was still available at the hotel? She sank back onto the step.

"Addy, dear, I don't know what to say. I can't imagine what's gotten into Jubal. He's always been so sweet and kind."

Delilah stood in the dust in front of Addy, her bright eyes glistening as she wrung her hands.

Addy looked dejectedly at her kid-covered feet. Her voice was low and husky. "Don't fret over me, Lily. From what I've heard, you haven't spent that much time around your husband. There are probably a lot of things you don't know."

She bit her tongue when Delilah's face fell. *Shame on me for acting so hateful,* she thought. Though her arm felt as weak as pudding and her hand shook slightly, she handed Delilah back a parcel she'd borrowed to lean against. After all, this misunderstanding wasn't her cousin's fault. Jubal was the one trying to discourage her.

"I'm sorry, Lily. I didn't mean that. You go on. I'll . . . think of something."

As she reluctantly watched a suddenly perky Deli-

27

lah point out her purchases and climb aboard the enclosed carriage, Addy's back straightened. She absentmindedly scratched the tip of her nose with her forefinger. Actually, she felt relieved that there wasn't room for her in the Wilkins' carriage. But where did that leave her?

A large man she'd seen prowling through the loading area shouting orders and commands rode by at a brisk trot. He stood in the stirrups and looked over his shoulder, yelling, "Stretch out!"

She flinched as bullwhips snaked out and popped in unison. Exuberant shouts filled the air. The blood throbbed through Addy's veins in a rush as she slowly rose to her feet.

Was she going to sit idly by, like some pathetic ninny, or was she going to Santa Fe?

As the first monstrous wagon, drawn by six yoke of oxen, creaked past her position on the step, she tentatively reached out a hand. The driver either didn't see her, or ignored her.

The same happened with the next wagon, until a sense of desperation possessed her, making every small movement seem exaggerated and jerky.

The next wagon was a smaller one, pulled by two teams of mules. She stepped into the street. Dust hung over her like a cloud. She choked. Her eyes pleaded.

A bent, gnarled individual handled the reins. He craned his head over the sideboard and spat a mass of brown liquid between crooked yellow teeth.

The glob splatted into the dirt, creating its own little cloud. Addy blanched and quickly danced out of the way.

She crossed her arms over her bodice when the old-timer's eyes casually surveyed her with a considering gleam in his rheumy old eyes.

He stopped the wagon in front of her. She backed up so fast she caught her heel in a rut and plopped onto the step.

He cackled, obviously amused. "Ya wanna ride, or not?"

Addy frowned. Her eyes shot up to look into the red beard, sprinkled with gray frost. She hardly saw his mouth move as he spat again. She winced as the goo plopped at the edge of the step.

"Uh, me? Are you talking to me?"

She could have sworn his eyes sparkled, but then figured she imagined it as he closed them, nodded, and lifted the reins.

"So be it. But this here's the onliest wagon that's got any room a'tall for yore personals."

He pointed a curved finger to her small pile of packages. She frowned, quite bemused.

The old man shook his head and flicked out his whip. "Giddap, you mangy bags a bones. We got us a ways to travel."

The wagon had only just started off when Addy yelled, "Wait! I-I'll go with you."

She waited expectantly, but the old man didn't make a move to get down and help with her packages. She sighed. Picking up the smallest of the paper-wrapped parcels, she asked, "Where shall I put these?"

He shrugged. She imagined she heard his joints creak.

"Anywhere's there's a place."

She walked to the back of the wagon. The wheels on the thing were as tall as she. The top of the wooden bed was so high she couldn't see over. And this was one of the smaller wagons! Panic assailed her. The old man would go off and leave her if she didn't hurry. But where were the steps? How did one get into this contraption?

A muttered curse resounded from the next wagon. She turned her head and tried to hide an embarrassed blush as a heavy-set, leather-clad man stalked over to her remaining parcels. He wrapped his thick arms around the bundles and Addy held her breath,

29

knowing he would crush every neatly wrapped item.

When he threw them all into the wagon and held out his hand for the one she held, she grinned and shook her head. He stared at her with dark, knowing eyes. Finally, thoroughly intimidated, she handed it over with a hand that visibly trembled, much to her dismay.

Her voice squeaked, "Thank you."

He scowled and tossed the parcel over the tail.

Fright rooted her to the ground when the man's voice boomed loud in her ear.

"Yore gonna be sorry for this, Scratch. The boss done said . . ."

The cackling voice of the old-timer sounded wonderfully sweet to Addy when he shouted, "I heerd what the boss said, Efren. I ain't deef. You jist mind yore own business, an' quit actin' like some ole lady."

The man called Efren looked Addy up and down with a contemptuous air that caused the hairs to ruffle on the back of her neck. She pulled herself to her full, slight height of five feet, four inches and mustered the courage to glare right back.

Efren sneered and flicked the brim of his hat with the back of his hand as he turned to leave. "You watch out you don't slow us down none, woman. Could be, you'll be the death of us all."

The dire words hung over her head like a black shroud. She took a long, deep breath, contemplating the idea of racing to her safe hotel room as fast as her tiny feet could carry her.

"Ya comin', or ain't ya?"

She swallowed the wad of cotton in her throat and stuck out her chin. Flouncing her skirt around, she marched to the side of the wagon.

Her newly found bravado faded quickly in the face of her next endeavor, that of climbing up and into the wagon box. Her faint sigh evaporated into the muggy afternoon air. Sweat trickled down her back. Alarm over being irrevocably left behind shimmered beneath her downcast lashes.

"Ahem." The old man cleared his throat to gain her attention.

She raised her eyes. Was he going to tell her to get away from the wagon so he could get on about his business?

Her hazel eyes turned golden with hope when she saw his gnarled hand reach over the side.

"Grab hold, gal, an' put yore feet on those spokes. I won't let go of ya. Climb on up here. You kin do it."

Indecision warred with renewed purpose as she looked at the long, crooked fingers and the slanted spokes of the wheel.

"I-I don't know if I can."

The old man snapped, "I done promised to help ya. If'n ya don't want ta try, ya best stay put, cause ya'll need more spunk'n ya kin muster ta make this trip."

He didn't pull his hand back. Addy shivered and slowly extended hers. He was right. If the minor obstacle of boarding the wagon could stop her, she might as well remain in Independence.

She looked over her shoulder and found several pairs of impatient eyes focused in her direction. The handlers of the remaining wagons were anxious to get rolling, and she was holding them up.

As she lifted a dainty foot, her hand was grasped by surprisingly strong fingers.

She gulped and stammered, "B-but my ankles . . . Those men, they're all watching. They'll see . . ."

The rough hand began a steady pull on her arm. "They'll see more'n that when I turn ya over my knee, gal. Quit yore dadblamed stallin' an' climb aboard. This ole ship's a leavin'."

Addy amazed herself by how quickly she maneuvered the wheel. She was almost into the wagon when she looked up and saw the man's face clearly for the first time. It was seamed and weathered.

When he grinned, the yellowed teeth appeared to wink at her. And he smelled—like tobacco and moldy, unwashed clothes. She sniffed daintily and plunked her tender derriere on the hard-plank seat.

She compressed her lips into a straight line, her eyes glaring into the afternoon sun. This was worse than she expected, but better than being left alone in the hot, dusty street. Why, the old man had even dared to threaten her! Of all the beastly men she'd seen today, he was, by far, the worst.

Suddenly, the wagon lurched into motion. Addy jerked backward and almost fell from her precarious perch. She shot a furious glance at the driver. His jaw worked monotonously up and down, and before he finally spat a huge mouthful of slimy juice, she was sure his hair-covered lips twisted into a sly grin.

She glanced quickly around. Thank heavens no one else seemed to have witnessed her clumsiness. She glowered at the old man.

"This is not a funny situation, Mr. . . . Uh, Mr. . . . ?"

He glanced at her and shrugged his bony shoulders. "Ain't no 'Mister' here, gal. Name's Scratch. An' yore shore right. Ain't nuthin' funny 'bout a green-horned, innocent little gal like you agettin' herself kilt."

Addy had heard just about enough about how she had made the wrong decision. And she was still mad over the callous treatment she had received at Jubal's hands. She rubbed the end of her nose and straightened her spine as much as the rocking bench would allow.

"I have every right to be here, Mr. . . . uh, Scratch. This was my father's company. Now it's mine. Well, half mine. I *am* going to Santa Fe."

Scratch chewed his tobacco with a vengeance, smacking his lips with each motion. "Ain't no place fer a woman. Don't make no mind what ya say."

She frowned, and opened her mouth to issue a sar-

32

castic retort, but had to take quick hold of the seat to avoid pitching from the wagon when the right front wheel hit a deep hole.

"Ouch!" She plucked a long splinter from her thumb and immediately placed the injured appendage in her mouth. Realizing she was once again being subjected to Scratch's odd grin, she placed both hands in her lap, covertly cradling the sore.

The wicked old fellow. She knew he had run over the hole on purpose!

They had traveled only a short while when Addy sighed deeply. "How far have we come? Will we go much farther today? Isn't it getting close to dusk? I thought we had to make camp before dark. Why didn't we stay in Independence and get an early start in the morning?"

"Gal, I'd near forgot a woman's questionin' nature. Tis a pure delight. Yes'm, tis."

She sat stiff as a board and pouted at his gleeful teasing.

He spat and slapped the near mule with the reins. "Giddup, Bartholomew."

Then he rubbed his chin, and scratched an itch under his coat. "We'uns always get off late on the first day, cause o' gettin' the dadburned contrary critters used to the harness. Even if'n we only go three, four mile, the stubborn cusses'll be easier to handle. Don't fret, gal. We'll be a stoppin' in a couple o' hours."

"But it will be dark soon. Then how will you know when to stop? How can you tell where you are? The teams won't see where to step. Won't they get hurt, or break a leg?"

Scratch let out a whoop and slapped his leg. The closest mules started, and Addy nearly toppled from the seat.

"Gal, yore gonna make this here trip plumb interestin'. Yessirree!"

Addy snapped her jaw shut so hard her teeth clicked. How annoying! Just see if she asked the old

. . . old . . . *codger* anything ever again.

They rode on in silence. It had long since turned dark when Addy's empty stomach grumbled its displeasure at being left hungry.

"We're most there, gal. We'll be a makin' camp 'round that next bend."

She squinted and strained, but could hardly see the team in front of the wagon, let alone some distant bend.

She had promised herself not to question him again, but the words were out before she could stop herself. "How do you do it, Mr. Scratch? How do you know these things?"

This time the old-timer didn't laugh at her. He took out a plug of tobacco and bit off a chaw before he answered.

"I come out here when I was no more'n grasshopper size, gal. Everthin' I know now I was taught by some'un who didn't mind my darned fool questions an' my taggin' along ahind ever footstep. Ya make mistakes, ya do some things right, but ya *learn* somethin'. An' when ya do those things day after day, they become a second nature, 'special if'n it means a dif-f'rence 'tween seein' the next sunrise."

When Scratch fell silent, Addy turned to look at him. It was hard to visualize the man at a younger age, without the wrinkles and whiskers, cleaner, with groomed hair. She had a feeling his life had been far from easy.

In fact, she imagined he'd just spoken more words at one time than he ever had before. The way his face fell, it looked like he'd drained himself with that long dissertation.

"Maybe *you* won't mind *my* darned fool questions, then. Or my following you around so I can learn some of what you know. Will you, Mr. Scratch?"

The silence dragged on for so long that Addy wondered if she had made a mistake in thinking he might be willing to help her.

34

Finally, his head turned in her direction. She knew he stared at her, studying her sincerity.

At first she wasn't sure, but then distinctly heard him say, "Nope."

She sighed and allowed her body to relax for the first time since climbing aboard the wagon. She would make this trip, and survive, and *enjoy* it, if it was the last thing she ever did.

Addy was surprised by how quickly and efficiently the men unharnessed their teams, set up camp, and began the evening meal. Though it was closer to midnight than dinnertime by then seemed to be of little consequence.

Jubal appeared to have accepted the fact that she was going to Santa Fe, one way or the other, and graciously allowed her to make as much room as possible in the back of the baggage wagon for her personal use.

Delilah gave her a grin and conspiratorial wink when she stopped by long enough to invite Addy to join them for supper. Most of the mule-skinners and handlers ate around their own campfires, but Jubal always hired a man who, besides driving the carriage, could cook a good meal on the trail.

Addy smothered a smile as she glanced across the way at Jubal's ample girth. Somehow, she had known the man would eat well, under any conditions.

Their meal consisted of fried ham, biscuits and coffee. Addy "made a hand," as she'd heard Scratch say earlier, with the best of them. The food tasted marvelous, cooked and eaten out of doors, over an open fire.

After they had eaten, activities around the camp waned. Bedrolls rustled close to the fires. Addy squirmed and held her chilled hands before the flames.

At last she caught Jubal's attention. "Um, Jubal, I

35

was wondering . . . Where will *I* sleep?"

She looked around the small clearing, and at the dark, forbidding outline of trees. What sort of provisions for beds did they have out in the wilderness?

Jubal took hold of a simpering, fluttery-eyed Delilah's hand, and brushed Addy off like an annoying flea.

"I thought I told you to use whatever room you could find in that wagon. That's as good as it's goin' to get out here, little lady. You should be grateful, at that. Most everyone else sleeps on the ground."

With that less-than-subtle rebuke, he turned and started toward the comfortable carriage, pulling a shrugging, apologetic-faced wife along behind.

Left alone, Addy turned uneasy eyes toward the dark wagon on the outskirts of the camp. She seethed anew over Jubal's brusque behavior. Had the man no heart?

Then she thought of the bugs, and all manner of crawling animals inhabiting the brushy ground, and shivered. Maybe she was lucky after all.

Well, sitting and wishing wouldn't change anything. She got up and walked in the forbidding wagon's general direction. An owl hooted nearby. She jumped. Tears burned the backs of her eyes.

This was silly. She'd been alone for a long time. Yet it wasn't like being *alone*. She'd had friends, and had known each servant like they were members of her family.

But this was different. She was in an unfamiliar, vast countryside, amid a group of strangers, some of whom were actually hostile toward her.

As she neared the tail-end of the wagon, her steps faltered. Her heart, which thundered erratically, resumed a fairly normal beat. She reached a shaky hand up to her mouth to smother a sob.

The tail had been lowered, and a stool placed close by with a lantern and several matches. Her parcels were stacked in a small, neatly cleared space just

36

large enough to spread her blankets. Even her trunks were within easy reach.

Scratch. There wasn't another soul who could have done such a kind thing—not even her cousin, Delilah. A few of the tears she'd fought trickled down her dusty cheeks when she found a fresh bucket of water by the left wheel.

She headed for the nearest clump of bushes as she regained her composure. Maybe she had another friend after all. Including Delilah, that made two.

Rubbing the tip of her nose, she stilled her trembling lower lip. Scratch's help and Delilah's moral support—that was all she needed.

Returning to the wagon, she leaned against the weathered wood, hugging her arms about her as she looked West, into the dark shadows. Then why did she feel so lonely and frightened, and so empty?

Morning came too early. Addy felt she couldn't have slept longer than fifteen minutes before the sound of the rousing camp awoke her.

She swallowed a fast breakfast of bacon and biscuits. She was told they would take more time to cook at noon, when they released the stock to rest and graze.

When Addy first saw Scratch, she couldn't be sure, because of the heavy beard, but she thought he blushed. His eyes met hers for only a brief second, then he ducked his head.

If she hadn't suspected before, she knew now. Scratch was indeed the person who had seen to her welfare.

She walked over to him with a timid smile and shining eyes. The old man backed up several steps. She followed and stood on tiptoe, giving him a light peck on the cheek. Instinct prompted that she not say or do another thing to further embarrass him.

She continued on to the wagon and, with a deep

breath, managed to climb onto the seat all by herself. Once she was situated and had her skirt adjusted, she allowed herself a surveying glance of the assembled line of wagons.

She breathed deeply, then let out a long, satisfied sigh. She was proud of her accomplishments. She'd lived through the night, and had conquered the wagon. Her eyes gleamed with excitement. She was ready for whatever the venture had to offer. Her friends back in Boston would be astounded to see the dainty, delicate Adeline Montclair today.

The remainder of the day, the night, and the following morning proved uneventful—Addy settled into the expectation of dust and gradually increasing heat and humidity. She saw her cousin only once or twice that next morning, when Delilah deigned to stick her head out of the close carriage for a breath of equally stuffy air.

The caravan was in the process of crossing a small creek bed. Eight of the wagons had made it over in fine order, but the ninth had veered too far to the left and bogged down in a deep hole. The extra hands were at the rear of the train, helping to get the heavy wagon rolling again.

Addy moved back into the covered wagon to look through one of her trunks for a fresh handkerchief. Scratch sat up front, calling to the driver ahead.

Everyone was relaxed. No trouble, of any kind, was expected for another hundred miles, since American expansion and civilization had driven the Indians West of Council Grove.

That was why, when the shots rang out, they were so taken by surprise.

Chapter Three

Addy ducked when she thought she heard gunfire, but then breathed a sigh of relief. The men were getting the caravan moving again. They cracked their whips with more enthusiasm than usual, that was all. She was such a ninny, always looking for trouble, or something to be afraid of.

She looked out the back of the wagon, then wished she hadn't. The driver of the wagon following them threw away the reins and clutched his chest. A red blossom of color suffused his shirt and trickled between his fingers.

It was his stunned, disbelieving expression when he looked down and saw the blood on his hands that precipitated Addy's first scream. She covered her eyes and turned her head away when he toppled from the high bench.

Then a bullet ripped through the canvas, hissing past her ear. She screamed again and frantically thrashed through the load of boxes and trunks, trying to escape the terrifying sounds of bullets, shrieking animals, and human howls of alarm and pain.

Through her hysteria, she heard a shout.

"Get me my rifle, gal. Hurry! Do you hear me? Gal, get up here!"

Addy turned glazed eyes in the direction of the authoritative voice. She saw Scratch, holding his shoulder, a pained expression on his grizzled face. She opened her mouth to scream, but his eyes bored into her, calm and steady. She gulped.

"Come on, gal. You kin do it. I'm short o' bullets

fer my pistol. Get me that rifle. Now!"

She nodded and crawled forward with stiff, disjointed movements. When she reached the gun, her hand hovered over the forbidding-looking weapon.

Another volley of shots rang out. Scratch yelled, "C'mon, if'n ya don't wanna die a'fore ya reach Santa Fe."

Her fingers curled around the cold iron barrel. She flopped over a stack of parcels to shove the big gun into his outstretched hand. His firm nod and quick use of the rifle reassured her. She crawled behind the seat to peer out between the bench and the floorboards.

A bullet lodged itself with a *thunk* into the closest board, sending a spray of splinters into her skirt. She yelped and ducked back, but not before she saw a ragged-looking Indian, with fierce, painted features, staring from a distance into the wagon. He seemed to take aim directly at *her*.

"Scratch, there's another one! In the trees to your right!"

Then she fell behind a large crate, covering her head with her arms. Her heart beat so rapidly she was sure every Indian within ten miles could hear it and knew exactly where she hid. Sweat trickled down her head and neck, and clouded her vision.

For the first time since the attack began, she faced the very real fact that she could die. Though she had known the risks and dangers involved in the trip, she had never expected her life to be in any actual jeopardy.

Had her mother gone through this same experience? She hadn't fully considered the terrifying circumstances of her parents' death. In her mind's eye, she had pictured them dying suddenly, painlessly.

A rough hand shook her shoulder. She jerked back, her hands curled into claws, a feral glint in her eyes. She might be scared witless, but she wouldn't let them kill her without putting up a fight.

Scratch's exuberant voice penetrated her defenses. "We done it, gal. We done whupped 'em good. With my busted wing, I couldn't git ta my gun. Ya done it, gal."

Addy's arms slowly dropped to her sides. She lifted her head. Had she *really* helped? Made a difference? Had her getting the gun saved their lives? Or was he making fun of her cowardice?

She tilted her chin, daring to look at his face. His eyes were clear and quite serious. No hint of mockery seamed his hairy features. She could see his yellow teeth. He smiled at her.

Smile? Scratch was smiling—at her? She straightened up from the hard boards and pushed the locks of hair that had fallen from beneath the bonnet behind her ears. Her chest swelled.

"C'mon outta there, gal. The shootin's over. We ran the bastards plumb back ta the Arkansy."

A few minutes later, she crawled forward, glad that Scratch had gone on to have his shoulder tended, giving her time to herself. She was still trembling. When she reached the canvas opening she craned her neck out slowly, expecting to see the evil face of the Indian behind every rock and tree.

The small caravan camped at the site of the attack. The men spent the better part of the afternoon getting the remaining wagons across the creek. They were evidently heavily loaded, and presented more of a problem than the rest.

Addy and Delilah helped prepare the noon meal, though neither had been of much *real* help.

Jubal paced back and forth between the wagons and the site selected for the burial of the two slain drivers.

Scratch and another man, both with shallow

41

wounds, rested beneath a shade erected close to camp.

Addy's eyes followed Jubal. He was watching a flock of large birds circling gracefully in the distance. She wondered what was so interesting about the sight. Her curiosity grew as his patience waned.

Finally, she turned to Delilah. "I can't stand it, cooped up here, any longer. Want to go for a walk?"

Delilah's eyes glittered for a moment with a look Addy couldn't decipher, but then they changed as she looked toward the mounds of piled dirt by the graves.

"No. Since I am Jubal's wife, and part owner of the company, I feel I'm needed here."

Addy had been reprimanded, but didn't know why. "For heaven's sake, Lily, the funeral isn't until this evening. I don't think anyone will mind if we stretch our legs a bit."

Delilah sighed. "You're right, of course. I guess I'm still shaken from the attack. You go head. I don't feel like it right now."

"Well . . . all right. I won't be gone long."

Normally, Addy wouldn't cross a street by herself, let alone wander into the wilderness. But the attack had made her jittery and unable to sit still.

Besides, Scratch and his friends assured her that the Indians were gone.

"Couldn't a been no more'n a raidin' party, gal. Only saw four, five of 'em, an' we got us two, mebbe three. Cain't figure what them varmints was a doin' this far east. Mighty strange, if'n ya ask me."

The other wounded man, Thomas LeFarge, added, "Scratch's right, ma'am. No need ta be afraid no more. They's run back where they come from, fer shore."

Addy decided to walk off some of her nervous energy. The circling birds looked close. She wanted to see what they were doing, swooping from the sky to resume circling again and again. It was the first time

42

she had seen anything quite like it.

Over half an hour later, Addy grabbed hold of a heavy branch and pulled herself to the top of a rise. She was hot, dirty, and tired. The distance to the birds had been much more than it had appeared. She took a deep breath and looked down into a narrow valley.

Her eyes rounded with shock. It seemed her heart would thump past the confining walls of her ribs.

There was a man, naked, spread-eagled on the ground. Disbelieving, she shaded her eyes with one palm and looked again. Yes, someone was indeed lying there in the valley.

Her stomach muscles fluttered. She wrung her hands. Should she run back and get help? Or should she go down and see if the person was alive? Maybe she could do something to help, now.

She quickly determined that, if the person was dead, there would be no need to run to camp, and if he wasn't, she could hurry back with the information.

Afraid of what she might find, she hesitantly took the first steps that would take her to the valley floor. She tried desperately to keep her eyes on the ground, to watch where she stepped, but her gaze kept straying anxiously to the body.

She approached cautiously, at first only able to see the bottoms of a pair of large feet. She stopped and peeked over the toes. She saw immediately that it was a man, and blushed. In the second that it took her to rush forward, she self-consciously noted the corded muscles on the man's arms and legs, which had been pulled taut and secured to stakes. His torso was long and lean, the upper portion tanned bronze, the lower half baked a hurtful red color.

She had yet to observe any movement from the body.

One of the big black birds circling above let out a raucous squawk. Her eyes jerked to the man's face.

43

She knew him! It was the man from the boat.

Her heart twisted when she saw the ugly wounds covering his body. There was a fierce abrasion on the side of his head, and blood soaked through layers of his blond hair.

She tentatively reached out her hand to touch him. A horrified gasp erupted from her throat as she saw tiny ants scurrying over his eyelids and nostrils. She frantically brushed them away.

The thought that he had not been able to do so himself caused a tightness in her chest she hadn't experienced since she'd learned of her mother's and father's demise. Her hand trembled as she cupped his strong chin and felt the smoothness of his skin.

Suddenly, his head rolled to the side. She jumped and toppled over, barely catching the ground with her hands before landing on her backside. Her palm landed on something round and hard, and her fingers unconsciously closed around it. She put her hand in her pocket, exchanging the object with her handkerchief, which she used to wipe the blood from his forehead and lips before replacing it.

He groaned. She thought she might be sick.

The horrid heathens! How could human beings do such things to one another? She crawled to the nearest stake and tried to work loose the thong binding his wrist. Two of her fingernails bent to the quick and broke, but the tough leather wouldn't budge.

She was frustrated and exhausted, and sweat dripped from every pore of her body. Addy plopped down in a dejected heap. Once she recovered her strength, she had to get help.

But would he die before she returned? Her mind shouted a desperate plea. *Please, Lord, not now.*

Her head cocked to one side. Had she heard something? Or was it her imagination, because she wanted it to be so?

Birds flew from the nearby trees. A gray squirrel

fluffed his tail and scampered to cover.

Lumbering to her feet, her eyes scanned the valley, then returned to the soldier. Was he afraid, too? She stopped and listened. Now she was certain. Someone, or something, was crashing through the thick layer of trees.

It dawned on her that whoever, or whatever, was near, might not be friendly. She shivered with dread and knelt again beside the prostrate man. His presence gave her a sense of comfort, even though he was probably oblivious to any danger.

Finally, the snapping branches and twigs gave way to two riders who emerged from the brush into the valley.

Addy recoiled fearfully. What if it was the Indians, coming to finish what they had started? What would, what could, she do?

The air left her lungs in one giant rush when she recognized Jubal Wilkins' huge form and his large sorrel horse. She jumped up and began waving her arms like a mad woman.

"Over here! Quick! Please help us!"

Her body visibly sagged with relief when Jubal and his man, Rudy, kicked their horses to a faster pace. When they pulled up beside her, but did not immediately dismount, she turned a worried face to them.

"I didn't know what to do. He's tied so tightly, I can't get him loose. Help me . . . Please?"

Jubal shifted his weight and the saddle leather squeaked under the strain. He didn't swing to the ground. Addy watched a deep frown settle over his flushed features. What was the matter with him? Why wouldn't he get down? Jubal's multiple chins quivered. "I can see from here. The man's near dead."

Rudy Potts pulled his gun from his holster and spun the cylinder. "Might just as well put the cuss

45

out'n his misery."

Shock suffused Addy's face and entire body. She felt as though a multitude of sharp needles stabbed her spine. She stepped in front of the helpless body.

"No, you won't shoot him. Unless you shoot me first."

Her chin trembled and she thought her chest might cave in and meet her backbone when Rudy's eyes took on a thoughtful gleam.

What had gotten into her? She wasn't a brave person. And she was no idiot. So what did she think she was doing?

She had never been placed in such a position before. She was fighting for a man's right to survive. A man who had insulted and teased her. . . .

She glanced at the man's bruised, swollen face and her knees shook. Her chest rose and fell unevenly. There wasn't much time. "Jubal, he's a human being, for heaven's sake," she implored. "We can't let him die without at least *trying* to save him."

Her heart picked up its pace when Jubal and Rudy exchanged considering looks. Jubal said something she couldn't hear. She was lightheaded with relief when Rudy twirled his gun and slipped it back into its holster.

"We'll take him back to camp, but he's your responsibility, little lady. You hear me? Can't have no stranger puttin' the rest of us in danger."

Addy gulped and nodded. *Oh, my.* She had never even taken care of a sick pet.

She watched Jubal pull a wicked-looking knife from his belt scabbard and slice through the leather thongs as easily as if they were butter. Her apprehension grew.

What if she caused the soldier more pain? What if she killed him?

Jubal looked at her with narrowed, suspicious eyes, then called to Rudy. "Bring me your blanket. Can't

46

leave a man buck naked in the presence of a . . . lady."

Addy stiffened. He had deliberately paused, slurring the last word. She bit her tongue to keep from making a rude retort. At least Jubal was helping. She didn't want to do anything to make him quit.

A gasp slipped past her gritted teeth, though, when Jubal rolled the injured man roughly into the coarse blanket, then slung him over the back of his horse.

"Stop! You're going to . . ."

She was about to lose all control when Rudy brought his horse up closer to her. He pulled his left foot from the stirrup and held out his hand.

"Looks like *you'll* have to ride with *me*."

She thought of walking back to camp, but did not want to let the soldier out of her sight. She wouldn't put it past Rudy, or even Jubal, to carry out their initial plans and avoid the trouble they thought the man would make.

Addy was a good rider; she had learned when a young girl. Rudy tried to pull her up in front of him, but she swung her hips and straddled the saddle behind him.

It had been a while since she had been on a horse. She thought she might have pulled a muscle in her thigh, but at Rudy's grumbled oath, she stifled a groan and managed to look composed as Jubal reined his horse past with a disgusted scowl meant only for her.

His narrow eyes kept searching the countryside, returning frequently to the stakes and dried blood on the packed earth. He shook his head and kicked the horse's sides. Addy wondered what he was looking for.

She had noticed the inordinate amount of time he had taken while covering the naked man, feeling about, knocking over loose pebbles. Why?

Suddenly, unexpectedly, her face began to feel hot from more than the long hours in the sun. *Naked man. Sculpted perfection.* She had seen, first hand, a man's unclothed body. And it was beautiful. She closed her eyes, embarrassed for herself, for him.

Then she remembered how smooth his face had felt above the short stubble of beard. And she regretted the chapped, cracked appearance of the straight, narrow lips almost hidden beneath the bushy line of hair forming an immaculate moustache.

She raised her hand and traced the tiny, bow-shaped outline of her own lips. They were dry, but not peeling. Once his had healed, what would they feel like if they touched hers? Would they be soft, or rough and hard?

Her wayward musings were abruptly interrupted when Rudy reached back long, bony fingers and patted her knee.

"You'd a been more comfortable up here in my lap."

She flinched and anxiously looked to where Jubal rode, a good ways ahead. "Don't you think we should catch up? We're falling behind."

The change in motion was almost imperceptible, but she knew the horse walked even more slowly than before.

"Aw, what's the hurry? That bastard'll be dead fore we reach camp, anyways. An' if not, he'll wish he was. Why, the boss . . ."

Rudy fell silent.

Addy looked over his shoulder and saw that Jubal had stopped. He glared in their direction. Rudy's horse picked up the pace.

Uneasy with Jubal's eyes boring into her, Addy prodded Rudy—anything to get her mind off Jubal's frowning countenance.

"What were you saying? Something about Jubal?"

"Uh, that's funny. I cain't remember." He shifted

48

forward in the saddle and snickered, "T'wasn't important, anyways."

By the time they caught up with Jubal, Addy could see the camp in the distance. The graves were ready, awaiting the double burial.

Jubal smiled. "Might be puttin' *three* bodies down if this hombre's quit us."

Addy blanched. "He is *not* dead. I just know it."

Anyone that handsome and vital, as she'd last seen him in Independence, wouldn't die easily, she thought.

Jubal shrugged, a smug look on his face. "Well, we'll dump him off with Pedro an' see what happens."

Pedro Alvarez was one of the two herdsmen, and the closest thing the caravan had to a doctor. He carried herbs and knew how to use the native plants to make poultices and medicine. He was the one who had tended Scratch and the other wounded man.

Addy wasn't satisfied.

"I-I'd like you to take him to my . . . er, Scratch's wagon."

At Jubal's surprised and somewhat angry glance, she snapped, "He's my responsibility, remember? You told me that back in the valley."

Rudy giggled and patted her thigh. She slapped his hand away.

He leered at her and added, "That's right, boss. That's what ya said. Heard ya plainer'n a bull frog on a clear night."

Rudy's remark earned him a frosty glare and verbal reprimand.

"Shut up, Potts. When I want to hear your yap flap, I'll let you know."

Jubal turned his cold eyes on Addy. "All right, little lady. You asked for it. You got it."

Addy's stomach muscles fluttered. Could she really handle this?

They rode to the back of Scratch's wagon. Jubal

dismounted and slung the soldier over the tail and into Addy's small bed as if the man was no heavier than a feather pillow.

She slid from behind Rudy before he could offer to help, and promptly landed on her backside when her sore legs refused to support her.

Jubal sneered. "Come tomorrow mornin', I'll be tellin' you I told you so. You can't even take care of yourself, let alone a dyin' man."

She picked herself up, brushing the dust from her skirt and hands. Swallowing hard, afraid that what he said might be true, she gathered all her courage. "Y-You come back tomorrow. He'll be alive." Under her breath she added, "I hope."

As Jubal and Rudy rode off, she heard them mumble something, then break out laughing. She couldn't decide whether to shout her anger, or break down and cry, or do both. One thing was certain—she couldn't stand around feeling sorry for herself. She had a sick man to care for, and he would *live,* if she died in the effort to make it so.

A heavy hand settled on her shoulder and she jumped. "Rudy Potts, you get your . . ."

She spun around, hand raised to give the wily pursuer a much-deserved slap. When she spied the actual culprit, she smiled for the first time during that fateful afternoon.

"Mr. Scratch, you scared me. What are you doing up? Shouldn't you be resting, and taking care of that wound?"

The old man scratched his bearded chin with the fingers of his good hand. "Shuckens, gal, tweren't nuthin'. Bone warn't even busted. I been hurt worse a high footin' it with a fancy . . . er, uh, lady."

Addy blushed and rubbed the tip of her nose.

"What do you know about healing wounds, Mr. Scratch? Bad wounds."

Scratch's mouth turned down. "Wal, I reckon I'se

50

fixed a few in my day. Why? If'n yore hurt . . ."

"Oh, no! I mean, it's not me. I-it's him."

She was so nervous she couldn't think straight. Her hand trembled as she pointed to the tailgate.

Scratch raised his eyebrows and gave her a wondering look.

"Look inside, damn it!"

As soon as the words were out of her mouth, she slapped her hands over her lips. She had never said a . . . one of *those* words before, and she was horrified. Less than a week on the trail, and she was talking like a mule skinner! What would become of her after two months?

Scratch eyed her warily and stepped over to look inside the wagon. A moment later, he lowered the tailgate and was fussing over the unconscious man like a mother hen over a newly hatched chick.

"Trace. Goddamn it, boy. What happened to ya?"

Addy looked over the old man's shoulder. When he pulled the blanket away from the battered body, she self-consciously turned away.

"Mr. Scratch, do you know this man?"

Scratch's mutterings ceased abruptly. His eyes narrowed.

"Why do ya say that, gal?"

She stomped her foot in exasperation, raising a cloud of dust. Why did everyone treat her like she was a dimwitted child?

"I have ears. I heard you talking. You called him by name."

The old man cleared is throat gruffly. "Wal, reckon I've seen 'im afore. Recollect I heerd his name oncet, or twice."

Addy backed up until she could lean her hips against the wagon. "What did you call him, then?"

Scratch's hands were busy as he talked, poking and prodding and examining the wounds. "Seems I 'member 'im answerin' ta Trace. But I cain't swear to

51

it, hear?"

"What's he look like?" She turned to the man and then hurriedly ducked her head. "I mean, what do his wounds look like? Do you think he's going to live?"

"Don't know fer shore, gal. Breathin's purty shallah. Has a nasty knot on 'is noggin. Ain't good, but ain't bad, mebby. Got any clean rags?"

While Scratch cleaned Trace's body, she told him how she had found him and in what condition. She could tell from the way his lips smacked together that he was agitated. For someone who barely knew the man, he seemed awfully upset.

"But now he's my responsibility, and I'm going to take care of him. I am. And he's going to live. He'll . . . be fine. You'll see. You'll all see." She sniffed, and her eyes met the old man's directly. Her lips trembled.

Scratch stared at her.

She gulped and straightened her spine.

A gleam turned the old eyes a shimmery, colorless gray. His beard wriggled as his broken teeth appeared. "Wal, gal, I reckon he might at that."

He turned, and was gone.

Scratch had cleaned the man's wounds and reblanketed Trace, but Addy had absolutely no idea of what to do next.

She glanced around the camp. Everyone was making the most of the delay. Several men repaired harness. Another worked on a broken spoke. No one paid her any mind.

It was a long way up, but she managed to pull herself, and her heavy load of petticoats and skirt, onto the tailgate. The late afternoon was muggy and hot, and the bodice of her dress clung to her full figure.

On her knees, she crawled over the soldier's long legs. His toes stuck out from under the blanket, and once she was comfortably situated on a sturdy box, she reached down and pulled the covering over his feet.

When she did that, she bared more of his broad chest. Now that he was clean, she could better see the corded muscles that lent shape and beauty to his upper torso.

Her hand reached forward. She trailed her fingers over the taut flesh, wincing as she discovered tiny abrasions scattered over the soft, down-covered expanse. The blood was gone, replaced by small, crusty patches coating the jagged tears.

Her heart was heavy. It made her almost physically ill to think of the suffering he must have endured. She leaned over, gazing dreamily at his discolored features, remembering the cocky smile, the rakish tilt of his brow, the brazen way he had looked at her aboard the steamboat.

That time seemed so long ago. She had been shy and embarrassed. Now, here she sat, actually touching him.

All at once, iron-hard fingers closed about her wrist. She was jerked from the box to land on her knees at the man's side. She was nose to nose and staring into a pair of glazed blue eyes.

The voice was hoarse and raspy, and so cold it sent tremors of fear shivering down her spine.

"You don't know me," he said.

Chapter Four

Addy was stunned. This was the last thing she had expected to happen when the man regained consciousness. A smile, an audacious wink, maybe—not this brusqueness . . . this *cruelty*.

"Did you hear me, lady?"

"Y-yes." She swallowed and stiffened. Why had she allowed herself to become so lax, so trusting around this person, who was really no more than a stranger?

When the grip on her wrist loosened she took a deep breath and glared down into his ashen features. "But, I-I don't understand."

Though thoroughly frightened, her heart softened slightly when she heard his labored breathing and weak, unnatural voice.

"You've never seen me before. Now, do you understand?"

The grip on her wrist tightened again. She winced.

"Ow! You're hurting me!"

His teeth ground together as he whispered, "Understand?"

Confounded and intimidated, she decided the wisest course of action was to agree with the crazed man. Obviously, he was delirious with pain.

"All right. Y-yes, I understand. I've never seen . . ."

Finally it dawned on her. He didn't want anyone to know she'd seen him on the boat. But why?

She rapidly recounted the few encounters they had had. What could he want to conceal about those brief exchanges?

"Why? Why don't you . . ."

She realized his eyes were closed then, and her arm free. He had fallen asleep. After inflicting two long, ghastly minutes of fear on her, he slept like an innocent babe.

She rubbed the purpling marks on her wrist, flinching at the soreness. Sighing, she leaned back against a stack of boxes.

Her first inclination had been to crawl across the fellow and make her escape as quickly as possible. But fascination and intrigue had gotten the best of her. She couldn't take her eyes from the tousled hair and relaxed, boyish features.

What was he hiding? Why had he been staked to the ground in the middle of nowhere? She had seen him get on a stage in Independence. Why had he left it?

She blinked, returning to the present, when she heard her cousin's voice.

"Addy? Addy, where are you? The funeral will be in . . . Oh!"

Addy quickly clambered over the sleeping figure and awkwardly worked her way out of the wagon.

"There you are. We've got to hurry . . ." Delilah's voice trailed into nothing when she spotted the blanket-wrapped form.

"That must be the man Jubal rescued this afternoon." She cocked her head to one side. Her brows furrowed.

Addy didn't realize she'd been holding her breath until she gasped, "Yes, it is. Come on. We don't want to keep the men waiting. They think little enough of us as it is."

She knew she should be angry about Jubal's taking the credit for saving the man, but her prominent emotion was *relief* that Delilah didn't seem to recognize Trace as the man from the boat.

Her stomach knotted as they walked toward the empty graves. How long would it take? And what

55

difference would it make if Delilah *did* remember?

All Addy knew was that she experienced a tremor at the thought. Would it put Trace in danger? Or even herself?

The funeral was a subdued affair. As the self-appointed leader of the caravan, Jubal said brief words over the deceased and turned to leave.

Addy shook her head. Was that all there was to it? This morning, two men had been alive, productive members of the train. In a few short moments of violence, they were gone. And this was sufficient burial, Jubal's vague, almost uncaring words?

The rest of the men replaced their hats and started to follow Jubal. They hesitated, then stopped, when Addy's soft, resonant voice permeated the air. Hats were immediately yanked from heads, their brims worried in nervous fingers. Soon, one deep, masculine voice after another joined in the hymn.

When the song ended, Addy stood in embarrassed silence. She hadn't planned to make a spectacle of herself. Would her interference be appreciated, or would she once again find herself the object of the caravan's disregard?

Her wary eyes scanned the men's faces as they quietly filed by. Scratch was the first to return her gaze. He nodded with what she hoped was approval. The others who deigned to glance her way held her eyes with looks of new respect.

She drew in a deep breath and turned to find Jubal and Delilah directly behind her. Jubal scowled and stalked away. Delilah quickly lowered her eyes and shook her head.

"That was sweet of you, cousin, but completely unnecessary. Jubal says the men are used to buryin' their dead with little fanfare."

Addy smiled sadly. "I suppose they are, but I'm not. Even the dead deserve more consideration than

56

that given by Jubal. I'm not sorry." She thrust her chin out in a most belligerent manner.

Again, Delilah shook her head before trailing after her husband. Over her shoulder, she added, "Supper'll be ready in half an hour."

Trace Randall groaned, and groaned louder when he rolled his head to one side. It felt like someone had taken an ax to his head and split it wide open. He tried to open his eyes, but barely managed to create a narrow slit. They burned like hell, like they'd been baked in the sun . . .

Ah, he remembered. His belly knotted and ached as he recalled again the sudden, unexpected ambush on the stage. Though the men had all been well armed, no one had been prepared to defend themselves so close to settled territory.

And because their guards were down, everyone was dead. Not *every* one. Trace Randall was alive.

When he'd been taken away and staked in the valley, one question repeatedly ran through his mind. Why? Why just him?

For what purpose had he been spared? The more he thought about it, the less sense it made, and the harder his head throbbed.

Then from out of nowhere, a sweet, vibrant voice filled the air with song, distracting his attention from his worries and pain. Another memory suffused his brain—that of an angel hovering above him, a tiny halo of sunlight surrounding her head.

At first he had thought her only a dream, until he realized he *couldn't* have died and gone to *heaven*. He might have believed he was dead if she'd been outlined by raging flames.

A picture of the perfect face came to mind. The woman *from the boat*. She had seen him in his uniform. If she said anything, told anyone . . .

He flexed the fingers of his right hand. He could

57

still feel the delicate skin and thin bones of her wrist. His ears rang with her horrified gasp of surprise. The terrible burning sensation in his eyes was his just due for the anguish he had seen in hers.

How he hated himself for the scare he'd given the little thing, but it was for her own good. If only she would keep her promise, and never breathe a word of his identity. Both their lives now depended on her silence.

Another spasm gripped his belly. Damn it to hell! Now he had the added nuisance of keeping an eye on the damned hoyden, along with his other responsibilities. She was trouble. He'd known it from the first moment they'd locked eyes on the steamer. How he'd known, he couldn't explain if he tried. The feeling was *there*, like a gnawing ache in his gut.

On her way to supper, Addy saw Scratch and went to him.

"Uh, Mr. Scratch, I thought you should know . . . The man, Trace, woke up a little while ago."

Scratch reached out his good hand and gripped her arm hard. "He did? When?"

"Just before the funeral. But, he, uh, went back to sleep."

Scratch heaved a huge sigh that jiggled the fringe on his leather shirt. "Now that's plumb good news, gal."

His eyes narrowed. "Did he say anythin'? Mention what happened?"

Addy hid her hands in the folds of her skirt, as if the gesture could protect her from his probing gaze. "N-no, not really."

To change the subject from something she desperately wanted to talk about, but knew she shouldn't, she asked, "Should I take him something to eat? He'll be hungry when he wakes up again."

The old man shook his head. "Naw, don't you

bother with nuthin'. Ole Pedro cooked up a batch of soup, jist special fer us wounded, sickly fellers. I'll see the boy gets hisself some, if'n he comes 'round agin."

She nodded and headed on to the Wilkins' camp. She had hoped Jubal would be too busy to join them, but saw his huge shape already seated near the fire. Just her luck.

"Patient still alive, is he?"

Addy bristled, but forced herself to smile for Delilah's sake. "Yes, thank you, he is."

She was immensely proud of that fact, though his condition was thanks more to Scratch than to herself. She almost blurted out that Trace had even come to once, but decided to let Jubal bask in his own ignorance for a time. He'd learn about Trace's recovery soon enough.

She hurried through her meal, barely tasting the food, and was preparing to check on her charge when the sight of Jubal's smiling face caused her to shudder.

"We'll be unloadin' the baggage wagon 'round daylight."

Silence settled over the small group around the Wilkins' fire.

Addy's eyes widened. Her heart fluttered with dread.

"The baggage wagon? B-but that's my . . . Scratch's . . . Wh-why?"

Jubal picked at his teeth with his dirty fingernails, very calm, very relaxed. "We lost two drivers today. No spare men to handle the wagons. Have to leave two. Scratch's'll be one of 'em."

Addy couldn't believe it. If they moved more cargo into the other wagons, it would cause them to be even more crowded and heavy, leaving no room at all for the injured Trace, or even . . . a place for herself.

When she gathered Jubal's motive she jumped to her feet, legs spread, eyes blazing, fisted hands on

59

her hips.

"Oh no, you don't. You aren't leaving *my* wagon. You said I could use it as long as I needed, and I'm holding you to your word. Besides, Lily and I are the owners of these wagons, not you!"

Jubal's jowls bounced up and down as he opened and closed his mouth in amazement. Before he could say a word, she continued.

"I have two hands. If there's no one else to do it, I'll drive the wagon."

The bluster left her words like wind leaving a billowed sail. The pressure in her chest heightened when she realized the meaning of what she'd said.

Jubal's eyes glinted dangerously. "Oh ho. So you think you can handle a man's job, do you? Well, we'll just see about that. Go right ahead and drive that wagon, little lady. But just you remember that I'm responsible for this outfit. I'm warnin' you here and now, you don't keep up, you get left in the dust. Fair enough?"

Addy's eyes desperately sought out her cousin. She almost lost her composure in the light of Delilah's genuine concern.

"Jubal, dahlin', you can't mean it!"

Delilah stood, taking her husband's arm in her shaking hands. "You know Addy can't possibly drive that big ole wagon. She could be hurt, or even killed."

Triumph gleamed in Jubal's eyes. "I tried to tell you both that before we left Independence, but you refused to listen to good sense. I didn't ask for you to come, just like I didn't ask for the damned raid this morning, but now maybe you can see why I was so set on your stayin' where it was safe. Ain't nothin' else I can do or say. If the little lady wants a place to ride, an' to carry that piece a trouble we carted in today, she'll have to drive. An' that's the way it is."

With an angry glare directed toward both women, he snapped his heavy lips shut with a loud smack and spun around faster than it would seem his bulky weight would allow.

Delilah's mouth, which had gaped open during most of her husband's tirade, closed so fast she bit her tongue.

"Hell! Er, I mean, there's a *hellacious* temper on that man." She turned to Addy and pleaded, "Addy, you can't do it. Please, don't try to drive that wagon. There's no telling what could happen. You've seen how unpredictable those awful mules can be."

Addy gulped and plunked herself down. The realization of what she had let herself in for was more than she could bear. Mules? Dear heavens, she would have to harness and handle those obstinate, cranky animals? All by herself?

A sudden vision of a long-eared jackass, with Jubal's beady eyes and heavy jowls, flashed through her head. She stood by his side, wielding a vicious-looking black whip. She almost smiled.

But then the gravity of her predicament took hold of her. Yes, she would be alone. Scratch would have another wagon to handle. He wouldn't have time to see after her too.

Her hands clenched. She couldn't do it. She knew she couldn't. She and the soldier would be left on the . . .

Soldier! The first time she'd seen him, he'd been in uniform. When he'd left the boat, he'd been in civilian clothing. Could that be it? Was he hiding the fact that he was in the Army?

"Addy, are you listenin' to me? What are we . . . you . . . goin' to do?"

Rubbing the tip of her nose, Addy took a deep breath and slowly stood up. She looked at her cousin and sighed.

"I don't know about you, Lily, but I'm going to Santa Fe."

"But . . ."

"I don't know how I'll manage, either, but I can't

61

let Jubal win. Somehow, I'll make it."

Delilah's eyes glistened as she patted her cousin's shoulder. "I'm so proud of you, Addy. If there's anythin' I can do . . . Well, let me know."

But Addy was already out of hearing as she stiffly made her way back to the wagon. The closer she got, the more her steps shortened. Her heart felt like a heavy boulder in her chest.

She'd never had the responsibility of another person's welfare before. The injured man would be relying on her capabilities, the poor fellow.

Reaching the tailgate, she peeked inside. He was asleep. There was an empty bowl beside the pallet. Scratch had been back after all. And a salve of some sort had been smeared over the man's abrasions.

As she rested her chin on her folded forearms, she gazed wistfully at him. At least he looked comfortable, and seemed to be resting peacefully — for now.

Then she frowned. The pallet. He was sleeping on *her* bed, in her *private* quarters. Now what was she to do? There certainly wasn't room enough for the two of them — even if it was acceptable that they stay together, which it was not.

Looking around the camp, she saw that most of the men slept under the wagons, or near the fire. Her eyes made contact with the black carriage. How nice it would be to sleep inside the conveyance, on piles of soft blankets and fluffy pillows. Addy sighed and figured she was better off than Delilah. At least she didn't have to sleep with Jubal Wilkins.

Well, she couldn't stand around all night and wish for things to change. She gingerly crawled inside the wagon and carefully stepped over the sleeping man to get to her trunk.

The situation wasn't so bad. She could wriggle between the boxes and change into her long flannel gown. And if she slept in her robe, she would be as well covered as if she was dressed. There were extra blankets she hadn't unwrapped yet. Yes, she could manage very well.

While she banged her elbows and scraped her knuckles trying to shimmy out of her many garments, she kept poking her head above the boxes, keeping a watchful eye on Trace.

As outlandishly as the man had behaved aboard the boat, she wouldn't have been a bit surprised to find him miraculously propped on one elbow, with his roguish blue eyes peeping around corners to catch a glimpse of her undressing.

She couldn't decide if she was more disappointed, or relieved, to see that she hadn't disturbed him at all. His eyes were closed, and his chest rose and fell in deep, even breaths.

He never once roused as she stepped back across him, lifting the hem of her gown in one hand, while clutching two blankets in the other. She stumbled when she almost stepped on one of his bare feet, but missed him and crashed into the tailgate instead.

Luckily, the blankets cushioned the fall and she was unharmed, but for the scare she had suffered.

Once outside the wagon, she looked at the hard ground, unconvinced it could be made into a comfortable bed. She squatted down and spread one of the blankets lengthwise, then scooted under the raised base of the wagon. Now she was glad the wheels were so large and the wagon set far off the ground.

She had no more than settled herself on top of the blanket and drawn the other over her when she felt a very hard lump under her bottom. She sat up, reached underneath her, and found the offending rock.

She fished out several more stones from beneath her before she was able to get fairly comfortable, if that was the word she could use to describe her position on the hard, uncompromising surface.

Her eyes finally drifted closed, only to reopen suddenly when she felt something tickling her leg. She screamed and sat up again, nearly banging her head on an axle. She threw the cover back immediately.

There was just enough light from the moon to illuminate a large, long-legged spider slowly making its way up a fold in her gown. She would have screamed again, but was too busy fighting her way from under the wagon to bother.

When she was able to stand straight, she stomped her feet up and down over and over, shaking the hem of the nightgown.

Scratch's familiar voice enabled her to bring her hysteria under some semblance of control. "What's after ya, gal? Ya see an Injun, or a bear?"

The hammer clicked on his rifle.

"Show me whar it be. I'll take keer o' it."

She pointed and yelled, "There! There it is. Kill it. Quick!"

Scratch eyed the critter and laughed. Her face flooded with heat. He laughed so hard he had to hold his sides. She heard snickers from others and wanted to dig a deep hole and bury herself.

Finally, Scratch came to stand beside her. In a low whisper, he asked her, "Ya mean ya near skeerd us outta a year's growth over a teeny bitsy spider?"

She stabbed the ground with her bare toe and flicked at a piece of gravel. "Well, I . . ."

"Listen ta me, gal. There's lots wurse thin's than spiders out here. Yore gonna have ta get used ta 'em."

"I-I know. I really do. It's just . . ."

She ducked her head, so embarrassed she couldn't speak. Back home, one of the servants would have rushed in, taken care of the spider, and calmly left the room, not daring to confront her with her silly fears.

Scratch awkwardly patted her shoulder. "Go back ta bed, gal." Then he added, "How's the boy?"

She flushed anew, swallowed, and took a deep breath. Oh, heavens. What if he'd heard all of the commotion? She'd never be able to live it down. "He was all right a few minutes ago. He's asleep."

"Good."

They stood uneasily for a moment, until Addy cleared her throat. "Uh, Mr. Scratch . . . In the morning, would you . . . ? I mean, I have to drive the wagon. Could you . . . ?"

The old man smiled. "Shore, gal. I'll give ya a hand." He shook a finger at her and grinned even broader. "But jist this oncet, hear?"

Addy nodded, and caught a whiff of stale tobacco and perspiration. It was an odor peculiar to Scratch, and she was oddly comforted by it.

As he retreated to his own bed, she heard him mumble, "Or mebbe twice," and she grinned.

The unfamiliar smile caused the skin on her cheeks to crinkle. She reached up and ran a hand over her flaky flesh, glad for the moment that she didn't have a mirror. She must look an absolute horror.

Picking up the hem of her gown, she marched back to bed. She had to get some sleep, bugs and spiders and all.

She lay down, staring at the wooden slats above her head. Dear Lord, she needed help. *Please,* she prayed, *give me strength.*

The camp was roused before dawn. Addy stretched and rolled to her side, but found her muscles complained when her brain ordered them to move her from beneath the wagon. She winced and groaned, finally inching her way out.

She was sore and stiff from the hard ground. How did the men sleep like that every night? Watching them scurry around, doing their chores, one would think they had rested on soft, comfortable mattresses.

She put a hand to the small of her back and arched, sighing at the snap and crackle of her spine. It felt good, until she noticed several pairs of inter-

65

ested eyes enjoying the outline her body created, even beneath the heavy layers of cloth. Rudy Potts was the one who made her shudder, though.

Immediately, she bent and grabbed the blankets, hurrying to the end of the wagon. Without thinking, she threw them over the tailgate and grabbed hold to pull herself up.

"Hey! What's going on?" came the voice within.

The startled yelp halted her progress. She pulled herself up to where she could just see over the boards.

"Don't hurry on my account," the man said sarcastically. "These damn blankets are smothering me. I'm hungry, and thirsty. But don't hurry."

Addy's concern for Trace's welfare vanished under a quick flare of temper. "I most certainly won't. Of all the rude, ungrateful . . ."

She hadn't realized she'd spoken aloud until his head turned and his oh-so-blue eyes captured hers. They were a cloudy blue, not the clear, deep blue she considered his normal color, but still a beautiful blue. But his skin looked clammy, with a faint sheen of perspiration, as if he ran a temperature.

"My head hurts," was all he said before he closed his eyes and his head rolled back.

She hurried into the wagon, exasperated at herself for getting angry with a sick person. She pulled the heavy blankets from his body and folded them, placing them in a neat stack in the front corner.

Her hand timidly reached out to feel his forehead, lest he suddenly open his eyes to pounce on her, as he'd done the day before.

When her cool fingers soothed his heated skin, he merely sighed. She became braver, moving to kneel by his side.

As she reached over him to the nearest trunk she didn't notice him watching her. His eyes narrowed as he saw again the halo of light behind her head. It came as a relief when he spotted the bullet holes in

66

the canvas, the sun streaming through.

He inhaled a scent as fresh as spring flowers, and was captivated. Then his eyes lowered, and he was lost.

Addy found the cotton cloth. Her intention was to use it to bathe his face with cool water, but when she glanced down, and saw his eyes glued to the fully defined swell of her bosom, her nerveless fingers dropped the white square, directly over his eyes and nose.

He sputtered, "You're trying to kill me. I know it. Go ahead and get it over with."

"Of all the . . . I should have left you staked out in the sun. Maybe I should have let the men put you out of your misery. Maybe then you'd be more appreciative . . ."

Scratch's amused voice interrupted. "Now, gal, what's all this? Trace awake, is he?"

She glared at Scratch and pointed to Trace. "Th-this lout is complaining that I haven't done enough for him. Why, I've—"

The old man reached in and plucked the cloth from Trace's face. When he saw white teeth gleaming up at him, he knew why it hadn't been removed sooner.

"Tut, tut. Don't ya go a raisin' your voice. I done come ta help ya. Go on an' git yore duds on. I'll see after the boy."

Addy frowned at the relief in Trace's eyes. She sniffed and turned up her nose, brushing his unprotected toes with her foot as she stepped over him.

Her mumbled, "Good luck," brought a chuckle from Scratch. She fumed while fumbling through her trunks for fresh underclothes.

She saw Trace watching her and clutched the garments to her chest. Under her breath, she muttered, "A woman deserves some privacy," and earned two chuckles. One was deep and throaty and warmed her entire body.

67

Scrambling through the piled boxes, she literally dove into the hidey-hole she'd discovered the night before.

It was difficult, dressing and keeping an eye peeled on the two men, but she soon saw they were caught up in their own whispered conversation, acting as though they had forgotten she was present, let alone aware of the fact that she was half naked and only a few feet away.

She stilled her movements and cocked her head, but couldn't make out what they said. "Dratted men. They're all disgusting and . . ."

"What's that, gal? Cain't hear ya."

"Uh, nothing. Nothing at all."

"Wal, speak up. These ole ears don't hear as good as they used ta."

She couldn't help but wonder how well he heard when younger, if he could pick up her hushed grumbles now.

"I heard her, old man. She says it's nice to have two wonderful men around to watch after her."

Addy shook her head. Even Trace had heard her. But had *she* heard correctly? Had the man who threatened her yesterday, and griped at her not five minutes ago, actually teased her? It caught her completely off guard.

Meanwhile, Scratch seemed inordinately pleased with Trace's fabrication. "Wal, so tis." As if knowing Addy had difficulty hearing, he spoke louder for her benefit. "I'll be back with the boy's vittles, an' help ya hitch up, gal."

Her bodice buttoned halfway to the neck, Addy looked over the top of the boxes, her eyes rounded in consternation. Trace had awfully good ears. She'd have to remember that in the future. Were his eyes just as alert?

When his head turned in her direction, she ducked down, hoping he hadn't seen how annoyed she had become. In fact, she was so nettled that when his

68

deep, rich voice floated into her cubbyhole, she jumped.

"You can come out. I don't bite—hard."

She waited until she felt the extra blood drain from her face and fumbled quickly with the rest of the buttons. At last, she rolled her eyes toward the canvas roof and stepped from behind the boxes.

Amusement glittered in his eyes. She patted several straggling strands she'd missed when pinning her hair. Her voice quavered. "Wh-what?"

He grinned and her heart thundered to a standstill.

"What, what?"

She frowned. "Why are you laughing?"

He slapped his hand over his chest and winced. "Me? I wouldn't do that."

She saw the bruised and torn flesh on his wrist. Her chest burned under the rapid thump of her heart as it resumed beating.

"I think you would. You're making fun of me."

His lids fluttered closed, shutting away the blue pools that seemed to wash over her like a wave in a shallow pond every time he looked at her. She suddenly had the feeling she'd just stepped naked from the water into a cold wind.

His eyes lazily reopened, overflowing with mischief. They left her face to focus intently on her chest.

She reached up one of her hands to her chest. All color left her face. No wonder he grinned like a boy. "Why didn't you tell me?" She turned her back and readjusted the buttons, aligning them correctly this time.

He sounded tired as he rasped, "And have you think I'm disgusting?"

"I-I . . ." She couldn't think of a thing to say. Yes, he'd heard her, all right. "I don't think . . . Oh, here comes Mr. Scratch. Maybe getting something in your stomach will help your headache."

As she leaned over him, anxiously peering out of the wagon, he grasped her hand. His thumb traced the bruises on her wrist. If she expected an apology for the marks, she didn't get one.

"For my sake, and yours, don't tell anyone you've seen be before."

"I won't."

Then, as if drained of the very last of his energy, his hand fell back to his side.

Addy stared at the man. "I —"

A loud bray and sudden splintering of wood interrupted her.

"Come out here, gal. Get acquainted with yore team whilst I help the boy with his food."

Trace was relieved when Scratch drew the woman's attention away from him, and used the time to look more closely at her.

Damn, she was beautiful! What was a woman like *that* doing on the Santa Fe Trail? Hadn't anyone told her how dangerous it was for a man, let alone a woman?

He glanced at her round, full breasts and his palms dampened. He closed his eyes. This wouldn't do at all. Important business awaited. It wasn't right that a helpless piece of woman-flesh had garnered his attention this way.

But damn, she was beautiful!

Chapter Five

An hour after the caravan had pulled out without them, Scratch helped Addy onto her wagon.

"Jist do like I showed ya, gal. Snap them reins an' get the critters ta fall in a'hind me. Oncet they get in the notion a followin', they won't cause so much trouble."

She didn't have the energy, but Addy managed to nod, indicating that she had at least heard what he'd said. His old eyes glinted, but she couldn't tell if he was proud of the morning's accomplishments or put out with her.

He patted the lead mule, rolled his tongue around his mouth, spat, and wiped the end of his beard on his sleeve. "Let's catch up."

Addy swiped strands of hair from her glistening face with fingers raw from working the heavy leather harness. Clumps of her coiffure were still pinned haphazardly in place, while the rest hung loose around her face and shoulders. Rivulets of perspiration streaked through the dust on her face, which smeared in globs when she brushed her cheek against her shoulder to catch a droplet tickling her ear.

She was hot and tired and irritable and thoroughly disgusted with the entire situation. Inevitably, her thoughts turned to her passenger. She knew she was being unreasonable but she blamed him for all of her problems.

If not for Trace, she might be riding in another wagon, maybe even in the comfortable carriage with Delilah. Her dress would be clean, her hands soft and smooth.

In another few hours the sun would bake every exposed inch of her ivory-hued skin. She might as well be a heathen herself, as she certainly would not look like a lady.

A tear joined the trails of sweat as she swatted at a buzzing fly trying his darnedest to land on her nose.

The wheel mules jumped when the reins touched their backs. They took several steps, which Addy deemed a good sign. Scratch was quite a ways ahead already. During the moments spent feeling sorry for herself, he'd moved on and she had lagged behind.

The wagon lurched forward, paused and lurched again. She grimaced when she heard her passenger moan. Well, she couldn't help it. What did *she* know about handling a team and wagon?

Then, as if sensing they had no direction, the team stopped. Their long ears flicked back and forth.

Oh, heavens! She rubbed her hands together and took a deep breath before gathering the thick leather straps in her tender palms. Raising the reins the way Scratch had shown her, she brought her arms down, slapping the leather against tough, dark hides.

When that action produced only a shake of a head, she repeated the motion, and blushed a bright scarlet as she pleaded, "Get up, mules. Please?"

There was a general stomping of feet, which encouraged her. The muscles in her arms burned, but she snapped the reins again and yelled, "Get up there, mules!"

The harness tightened. Her eyes shone with challenge. She stood to get better leverage, bending her body sharply as she brought the leather down hard.

"All right, you lily-livered beasts, gid up! Hee-aahh!"

The wagon rolled. When the bench seat hit her behind the knees, she lost her balance and plunked onto the hard wood. But she grinned. It was worth the slap on the bottom. The mules were walking.

She laughed and jangled the reins, just to let the animals know she was paying attention.

"Come on, you moth-eaten sons of . . . Ooops!" She exclaimed. She'd almost repeated some of the foul epitaphs she'd heard from the *other* drivers.

Exhilaration flowed throughout her sore figure and she slapped the mules again. They broke into a trot. She jounced up and down on the seat, unaccustomed to the jarring motion.

"Hey! What's goin' on up there. Ouch!"

She pulled back on the reins. The mules slowed. Then they stopped.

Her face fell. She groaned. "No-o-o. Keep going. *Please.*"

Weariness like she'd never known before began to take its toll. She shouted, "Giddup, you sorry excuses for . . . for . . . wolf bait. Yes, that's good. Giddup!"

The team finally strained into the harness. She cried exuberantly, "Yeah! Let's go, fellas. Whooppee!"

The voice from the rear of the wagon was faint, but she thought she distinctly heard, "Thank God."

She screwed her face into a pout. Of all the nerve! Sure he was hurt, and all the bouncing around couldn't be helping him, but she was doing her best. He ought to be grateful.

A bee landed on her skirt and she jumped to her feet, bringing her hands down quickly to brush it off. The mules mistook her gesture for a command to increase speed, but she pulled them back.

"No. Slow down. That's the way. Keep walking."

She kept up a steady flow of conversation with the team, all the while keeping a wary eye out for aggressive insects.

The trees thinned and the heat became more intense. She was thirsty and hungry and wanted desperately to relieve her aching derriere of the rock-hard bench.

It was close to a half hour later when the wagon left the forest altogether and she purposely drew the team to a halt. She couldn't help herself. Before her lay the most awe-inspiring sight she'd ever seen.

Flat land. Grass. Everywhere. As far as the eye could

73

see. The only trees in sight lay behind her. She stood up on the seat and looked, and looked.

Ahead, ruts marked the only sign of human violation. All around her lay the wide open prairie, and it was beautiful in a wild, lonely sort of way. She had the overwhelming feeling of being a miniscule part of a larger design.

A deep, clearly agitated male voice called out, "Hey! What's the hold up? Why have we stopped this time?"

Irritated by the interruption, she poked her head under the canvas and scolded, "Don't call me 'Hey' again. My name's Adeline Montclair, thank you. Just relax. We'll move on in a minute."

"What's goin' on? Who the hell's drivin' this thing?"

Addy held her head high and said more loudly than she'd intended, "For your information, *I* am. And I stopped for a reason. Keep your pants on, for hea'en's sake."

She clenched her jaw shut and ducked quickly back. What in the world had come over her, saying such a thing to a man? Shy, timid little Adeline, who never raised her voice under any circumstances? She was a lady to the end—usually.

The voice was weaker, but she could tell he laughed at her—again. "For your information, I don't have any pants *to* keep on. What do you say to that, Adeline Montclair?"

Before she realized what she was saying, she blurted, "That's all right. You look just fine without them."

"What?"

For an injured man, he'd put a lot of energy into that one word. She smiled. That ought to keep him quiet for a while.

"Get up, mules. See Mr. Scratch's wagon up there? That's where we need to be. Come on. Giddyap!"

The breeze created by the moving wagon felt good upon her hot cheeks. She was grateful.

* * *

74

Scratch and Addy caught up with the rest of the caravan just as it prepared to depart after the noon break. Her stomach grumbled at the thought of missing the meal, as she'd been too nervous to eat much at breakfast.

Her voice cracked when she called out, "Mr. Scratch, I've got to stop. My legs ache, and I need a drink."

Scratch talked for a minute longer with the two men in charge of the loose stock before they, too, left the camp. When he came over to Addy, he held out an ugly strip of something. She frowned and hid her hands behind her back.

"Go on an' take it, gal. It'll fill yore belly."

She grimaced. "You mean, I'm supposed to *eat* that? Wh-what is it?"

She finally reached for it, but crinkled her nose at the strange smell. She wasn't sure she really wanted an answer to her question. The strip was rubbery and dry and nasty-looking.

"It's jist jerky. Dried deer meat. Go on an' try it. Put it in yore mouth an' soften it up some, then tear off a hunk. Chew it right good."

He handed her a full canteen of water. "Keep this here jug with ya. You'll need it later in the day."

"Oh, thank you." She pulled the plug and took a long drink. The water was lukewarm, but tasted like heaven. "What about the . . . Trace? Do you think he'd like a drink?"

Goose bumps erupted over her flesh when a husky voice called, "Damned right I do. I'm dyin' back here."

Scratch chomped his tobacco and grinned. " 'Magine he is, at that. Whyn't ya give 'im some?"

"Well, I need to . . . I mean . . . I think I'll walk over that rise a ways. If that's all right," she added hastily. She didn't want to burden Scratch, after all he'd already done for her, but she couldn't bring herself to see Trace right now, either. It was humiliating, the way he taunted and made fun of her.

The old man spat between his teeth.

Out of habit, Addy hurriedly moved her skirt away, then shrugged at the futile effort. He'd never hit her yet. Besides, what difference would a little tobacco juice make, when added to dirt and, more than likely, manure.

Scratch rubbed a spot under one sweat-stained arm and cackled, "You go on, gal. 'Magine the boy'll need ta take a walk hisself."

She blushed and turned away. Butterflies and grasshoppers fluttered out of her way as she stumbled past clumps of wildflowers and knee-high grass.

When she returned, it was in time to find Scratch helping Trace back to the wagon. Trace's arm was hooked over Scratch's bony shoulder, a blanket loosely wrapped around his narrow hips, nearly obscuring the halting steps he took.

She stopped near the back wheel and watched as Scratch lifted the grim-faced Trace into the wagon. Her heart throbbed with the pain of knowing how he must hate being so helpless.

Her eyes sought the ground so that, just in case he looked, he wouldn't see that she felt sorry for him. Instinctively, she knew he would resent it.

The knowledge was immediately confirmed. "Hell, old man, I'm sorry. I'm no better off than a babe."

"Shucks, boy, 'tain't nuthin'. You'll be up an' 'round in no time a'tall. Kin ya help 'im get comfortable, gal? I gotta water them mules."

"Uh, sure. I guess so." She hesitated, until Trace looked toward her. Then she sauntered confidently to the lowered tailgate.

"What do you need?"

Trace thought the sway of her hips as she neared him was seductive. He knew she was nervous and trying not to show it. Inwardly, he cursed the fates for her fear, but there was nothing he would do to change things. He couldn't afford to be the cause of her coming to harm.

He'd had nothing to do but think all morning, and he had come to the conclusion that *someone* knew who he

76

was and what he was after. He'd been kept alive for a reason, and he couldn't get the notion out of his mind that he'd been purposely left for that someone to find.

His eyes raked over Adeline Montclair. Someone had found him, all right, and she leaned toward him like a scared rabbit that would bound away in an instant if he so much as growled at her.

He rubbed his chin with a hand that trembled with weakness, and quickly hid it underneath the blanket. Let's see . . . What had been her question? Oh, yes.

"What do I need? Well . . ." He let the word trail off as he thought of what all she could do for him, then grinned when she blushed. Innocent. Ah, innocent. How very intriguing.

"Well, how 'bout somethin' under my head, for a start."

Addy glanced around the wagon. The blankets she'd stuffed in the corner caught her eyes. Silently, she took one in hand and placed it by his barely covered hip. The one he had used for a cover had come unwrapped and lay bunched, mainly around his legs.

She gulped and tried to figure out how to climb into the wagon and still maintain her dignity. When a brown hand opened in front of her, she darted her eyes to his intent face.

"You can take it. I won't let you fall."

She was immensely grateful for the offer, but argued perversely, "How can you say that? You're so weak you can barely get up and down, even with help."

His fingers flexed. She saw the muscles tighten all the way up his bare arm. Though his hand shook slightly, she had no doubt that he would not let go of her. Not in a million years. So why was she afraid?

Finally, knowing she wasted valuable time, she let him help her. His fingers grasped her hand, and she hated to think what could have happened to her delicate bones if he'd grasped her at full strength.

She wasn't sure if he actually held on longer than was necessary to assure her safety, or if she imagined it. As it was, her fingers tingled when he released them, and she quickly reached for the coarse blanket.

Gently lifting his head, she rolled the blanket to make a thicker pad, and propped him up.

He sighed when she laid him back. "Thank you. That's better."

She looked into his blue, blue eyes, dragged her gaze away until she focused on the broad expanse of muscled chest, then anxiously tore her eyes from that gorgeous spot. Confused, unable to decide *where* to look, she stared at her hands, folded demurely in her lap.

"How did you find me, Adeline Montclair?"

His deep voice rumbled over her like waves washing against a rocky shore. She shivered and looked at him. "Pardon me?"

"When I was staked . . . Well, I wondered how you managed to find me?"

"Oh. It was after the caravan was attacked. I kept watching Jubal, my cousin's husband. You haven't met my cousin, have you? Delilah and I . . ." She blushed when he frowned.

"I'm sorry. Mr. Scratch would probably say I tend to get off the subject now and then. Anyway, Jubal was looking at the sky, at a bunch of circling birds. He seemed real nervous. I was curious, and decided to see what they were doing. I'd never seen birds like that before. They were big and black, and had such ugly heads."

Trace reached out and touched her soft cheek—just to get her attention, he told himself. "Excuse me, but you're strayin' from the story. What happened when you found me?"

She rubbed the end of her nose, and he stifled a grin at her childlike gesture.

"Sorry. When I first saw you, I didn't know what to do. But then, when you were alive, I knew I'd have to go for help. I couldn't untie the leather. It was too hard and tight. Wouldn't budge . . ."

He sighed. "Did you go back to get help?"

Animated with the retelling of the tale, her eyes glittered with excitement. "No. I didn't have to. Jubal and Rudy, Rudy's Jubal's second in command, found me . . . us . . . first."

She stopped abruptly and frowned. It wouldn't change matters to tell him how she'd had to convince the men to bring him along, rather than kill him. Besides, she'd told Jubal he would live, and she'd been right.

The smile she turned on Trace made his stomach feel like he'd been kicked by a team of stubborn mules. Sweat beaded on his forehead, and it had nothing whatsoever to do with fever or sunburn.

"Guess I was lucky, huh?"

Addy's eyes rounded. Had he read her mind? Then she relaxed. "Yes, you are fortunate to be here." She smoothed a wrinkle in her dress.

When he looked at her like that, with those big blue eyes, funny sensations rippled through her body. She felt . . . anxious, and uneasy. She darted her eyes around the wagon, then peered outside. She sighed.

"Here comes Mr. Scratch with the team. We'll be leaving soon."

Hesitating, she met his ardent stare. "I'll try to be more careful this afternoon."

His fingertips brushed her arm. "You haven't hurt me. Not really. How long have you been driving the wagon?"

She gulped and blushed. "Since this morning."

"What? What in hell's the wagon master think he's doin'? Lettin' an amateur drive . . ."

"Listen here, mister! Don't you dare shout. If it wasn't for my volunteering to drive, we'd both be stuck at the last camp. One of these days, someone's going to teach you to be grateful for what you have, and—"

"Hold on, younguns. Cain't leave you two alone fer a gol durned minute 'thout ya holler like a litter o' spittin' tomcats."

Trace's face turned a mottled red as he glared at

79

Scratch.

"You're damned right I'm hollerin', old man. The very idea of allowin' this . . . this . . . *woman* . . . to drive a damned wagon. Why, she's never—"

Addy put her hands on her hips and thrust out her chin. Before she could reply, Scratch stepped in.

"That's enough out'n ya, boy. If'n ya'd ruther walk, jist say so."

Scratch chomped his tobacco so hard Addy heard it squish between his teeth. Her stomach churned noisily.

Trace sank back, exhausted and exasperated by his weakness. "Guess I don't have a right to complain. I'm beholden to both of you."

He closed his eyes, intending to reopen them to apologize for his foul behavior, but found he didn't have the energy.

Scratch motioned Addy to go on to the front of the wagon.

"The team's hitched. We'll ketch the rest o' the train afore sundown. Yore doin' fine, gal, jist fine."

Addy glowed under the praise. When she looked down at the sleeping Trace, she sniffed and turned her back, mumbling so only he could hear. "At least *someone* appreciates me. Wicked soldier. I knew you were trouble."

As she awkwardly clambered over the cargo, she stopped for a minute to rub the flesh on her arm where his fingers had last touched her—so tenderly, so gently.

The exertion of the afternoon took its toll on her. An exhausted Addy peeked into the wagon as the last rays of the setting sun sank beneath the barren horizon.

Trace had not awakened to eat the evening meal. She was loath to disturb him, but carefully reached inside to pull the blanket over his chest and arms.

Her feet were braced on the lower rim of the tailgate as she leaned precariously over the gate itself. Balancing as best she could, she lifted the top fold of material from his lower belly.

Her hand was suspended in midair, fingers clutching the coarse wool; she closed her eyes and took a deep breath to still the sudden trembling in her arm.

Lord, he was handsome. Again, the strange flutterings overtook her insides when she gazed upon his near-naked form. Her palms turned clammy. She tottered backwards as her knees threatened to buckle, but reopened her eyes in time to steady herself.

His deep, even breathing reassured her that he slept soundly. She released the breath she'd held, relieved that he seemed to be comfortable, and climbed down from the wagon.

Settling herself on the ground, she leaned against the frame of the big wheel. Somewhere, someone played a harmonica. The haunting melody drifted over the camp as dusk turned to darkness. The moon had yet to rise and lonely shadows loomed eerily from all directions.

She wrapped her arms around her legs, resting her chin on her knees. It was the first time she'd had, since the journey began, to sit and think. But her thoughts made her extremely uneasy.

Why was she here, really? Was she *that* interested in learning the business side of the Santa Fe trade? Or was she a spoiled brat, satisfying a sudden whim? If Timothy Sharpe hadn't been so adamantly opposed to her coming, and then Jubal . . . Why, she might still be in Boston, and certainly not farther than Independence.

But no, she had to act stubborn and willful, and here she was, in the middle of nowhere, at least another two months of hard traveling ahead of her, with no civilization or conveniences to look forward to until Santa Fe. What kind of a fool was she?

Addy brushed a leggy insect from her skirt and shivered. This was all so unnecessary. She felt the dry, chapped skin on her neck and lower arms. So unnecessary. And if she wasn't mistaken, the smell of sweat she whiffed every now and then was coming from under

81

her own arms.

Unaware that she was no longer alone, she started when her eyes focused on a pair of scuffed boots and dirty brown trousers. Their owner's knees bent and Rudy Potts' scraggly, bearded face filled her vision.

She winced as his whiny voice intruded over the melancholy strain of the harmonica.

"A purty woman shouldn't be sittin' in the dark alone. Ya need a *man* ta keep ya comp'ny."

"Mr. Potts . . ."

He leered at her. "Call me Rudy."

"Mr. Potts, I'd appreciate it if you left me alone. I enjoy the peace of being by myself, thank you."

He moved his hand toward her, but she shifted out of reach. Her nose twitched at the foul smell of his breath. Even in the darkness, she saw things moving in his beard. How could Jubal stand to be around someone, or something, like Rudy Potts?

"You're playin' games with the wrong man," he snarled. "You ain't no diff'rent than any other woman under them fancy duds."

She took a deep breath, releasing it in a huff when he edged back a ways.

But he wasn't through with her yet. "See if I ain't right, lady. Another day or two, an' you'll be beggin' me ta pay ya some attention."

He stood over her. She turned her head aside, digging her shoulders and back into the spokes, wishing the wheel would magically move between herself and the awful, threatening man.

She was grateful the clods of dirt he kicked onto her skirt and bodice were the worst indignities she suffered as he turned and stalked from her sight.

Her entire body trembled. She had never *liked* Rudy Potts, but she had never been afraid of him — until now!

Should she tell Jubal and Delilah about . . . about what? What had he actually done? Nothing. Just talked. He hadn't made any *real* threat.

No, she'd wait. Jubal would probably only laugh and

82

tell her it was her imagination, and remind her again that she had no business on the trail.

She would do what Rudy had accused her of, play a game — a waiting game — and keep her eyes on him. All she had to do was stay close to camp and near other people. He wouldn't dare make advances in plain sight of his boss and companions. Would he?

The next afternoon found the caravan preparing to cross a deep creek before making camp for the night. Addy's eyes were wide and troubled as she looked at the steep banks. It was impossible for her to comprehend how the poor teams could make the descent into the creek bed without being crushed by the heavily laden wagons.

And, of course, if the team and wagon went, so, too, went the driver. Her hands trembled at the reins. The mules, sensing her fear, shook their heads and stamped their feet impatiently.

Hers would be the last wagon to make the crossing, and she was glad. Maybe most of the other drivers would have too much to do to stand by and watch her make a fool of herself.

She'd been so proud of the way she had handled the team thus far. They had actually kept up with little problem. Well, other than her own physical problems. She rubbed her blistered hands gingerly down her skirt to wipe off the excess moisture.

Pain from the broken sores caused her to wince and grind her teeth. She'd noticed the drivers all had gloves, but she'd been too embarrassed, or too proud, to admit that gloves were one item she had neglected to purchase. Hadn't even *thought* about them, really, as they were the last things she had expected to need.

She reached over her shoulder to finger the rip in her dress. The form-fitting bodice allowed little room for excessive movement. When she'd had to take hold of the reins too quickly, the seam connecting her sleeve had torn asunder.

She jerked up her head as snapping whips, creaking wood, and shouted curses alerted her that the first wagon was braving the creek. Instead of watching to see if everything went all right, she closed her eyes. She would know soon enough, without having to witness it.

She heard crumbling dirt and rocks and then a splash as the oxen entered the water. Her chest heaved. Thank heavens! Now, they had the long pull up the other side.

She leaned back against the canvas, seeking the small cover of shade. Soon, distant "Hurrahs!" were carried back on the breeze. One down.

She looked overhead and gauged the position of the sun — something she'd seen Scratch do often. At this rate, it would be dark before her turn to cross.

Sure enough, it was dusk when she halted the mules at the top of the bank. Her hands shook, and her heart thundered so loudly that she barely heard Scratch call her name.

"Jist a gol durned minute, gal. Let me git the boy out'n there. Any of that load shifts, an' it's liable to fall on top o' 'im."

Addy pursed her lips. Oh, sure. They were worried about Trace. Well, what about her?

The hairs on the back of her neck stood on end when she heard Trace voice the same question.

"Why's the woman still driving? This is a dangerous crossing. Doesn't the wagon master know any better than to let. . . ?"

A low mumble cut off the rest of what he was saying, and no matter how far Addy leaned and craned her neck, she couldn't hear the remainder of his sentence.

But she did hear Scratch's muttered, "Mr. Wilkins' orders. The gal drives, or the wagon stays."

There was more mumbling. She was certain of only two words — "Hell!" and "Damn!".

She narrowed her eyes. The curses had come from Trace. Dratted man! She'd show him a thing or two.

She was getting pretty good at driving this old wagon.

At a signal from Jubal, she raised the reins. Then she hesitated before bringing them down, gently. When the mules took their first steps, she tightened her fingers around the straps until her knuckles turned white and her nails bit into her palms.

She dimly heard Scratch yell, "Brace yoreself, gal. Put yore foot up an' give them critters a steady hand."

Finally, as the wagon swayed and dipped downward, she remembered what he was talking about and put one foot up on the running board. She leaned back, pulling on the reins.

The wagon picked up speed, but she kept her balance. Excitement surged through her as they plunged down the slope.

Crack! The sound rent the air with the immediacy of a rifle shot — Addy's foot went right through a split board.

The next thing she knew, she pitched forward, falling between the rear mules' churning hooves and the lumbering wagon.

Chapter Six

Addy curled into a tight ball. The huge wagon rumbled over her, the wheels churning clouds of dust.

She lay still as death. Daring to blink, she flinched when grit scratched her eyes. She gagged and coughed as fine sand ground between her teeth.

Everything was quiet. It all seemed so strange. No birds chattered. The wind was still.

A movement in the corner of her eye caught her attention. Trace was running toward her. He tripped down the steep bank, one arm in the air, the other clutching desperately at the blanket around his waist.

Scratch trailed behind, his hands grasping for, but not quite reaching, Trace. The older man's lips worked constantly. Addy wished she could hear the colorful dialogue that must be taking place.

It was the expression on Trace's face that held her enthralled. He looked so fierce, as if daring anything to stand in his way.

Finally, all she could see were bare legs as he loomed over her. Then the legs were replaced by a pair of concerned eyes.

"Adeline?"

She blinked, and tried to move. *Her* name was Adeline. He was talking to her. But her body wouldn't obey her commands. Until a pair of gentle hands ran up and down her limbs and along her spine and ribs. *His* hands.

"Say something! Are you all right?"

She slowly stretched one arm and touched the wool

blanket. "Y-you need a p-pair of pants."

The hard features softened when he grinned. "Think so?"

When she nodded, her neck ached and she groaned.

"Aw, don't be hurt. Can you get up?"

Her lips quivered. "Sh-sure. I'm not an in-invalid. What makes you think. . . ?"

But when she attempted to unfold her body, it seemed giant straps held her down. With each movement, another ache started in a different part of her. She sank back and lay still.

Bits of dirt and gravel rolled into a pile in front of her. She gingerly tilted her head to see what had caused the disturbance.

"Gal! Ya be all right? By damn, she ain't been runned over, has she, boy?"

The searching hands sprouted tender fingers that poked and prodded her body. She shifted closer to the source.

"I can't find anything broken, old man. I think she'll be fine. Probably just some good-sized bruises."

She sighed. That deep voice was like a balm to her soul. Her eyes drifted closed. Why didn't they ask *her* how she felt?

"C'mon, gal. Let's git ya up an' out'n this here crik."

"Wh-what?" She wanted to stay there forever and never move.

"You've had a nasty fall. Don't you know where you are?"

Suddenly, every muscle and joint in her body throbbed. When she stretched her arms and legs, wincing pitifully with pain, she moaned, "Y-yes. Remember. Fell off wagon. So silly."

As Addy, aided by Scratch, struggled to her feet, she stepped on the edge of Trace's blanket as he, too, rose from the ground.

He came close to losing his cover then, but hastily

bent to retrieve his . . . composure.

Addy smiled, then winced at the pain it caused. "He needs pants," she told Scratch. "It's indecent, the way he flaunts his pretty body."

Addy and Scratch waded on across the narrow creek. Trace stood where they had left him, his eyes slits.

Flaunt? Him? Then he grinned and, finally, laughed outright. What would his friends say when they heard Trace Randall had a "pretty" body?

He sobered. Friends? What friends? They were dead—murdered during the attack on the stage.

"C'mon, boy. I'll help ya up the bank, an' then git the wagon up the other side a'fore . . ."

Feeling an odd presentiment, Trace raised his head. Jubal Wilkins stood at the top of the slope, staring intently down at the immobile wagon.

"Too late, old man."

Scratch frowned and followed Trace's eyes. "Reckon so."

"What's the holdup? This wagon should have crossed half an hour ago." Jubal's eyes searched the two men's faces, then scoured the debris-ridden slope before returning to glare at the staggering Trace.

Scratch wrapped Trace's arm over his shoulder. Trace's energy, in the face of Addy's near disaster, had quickly drained from his body.

"Had a mite o' an accident."

Jubal folded his hands over his belly, waiting for Scratch to continue. When no further information seemed forthcoming, he demanded, "What kind of accident? Where is my wife's cousin?" His eyes shone as they darted around the ground, seeking, not finding.

The large man almost launched himself into the creek when Addy suddenly spoke at his back. "I'm right here, Jubal. You can tell Lily I'm fine. Just a little battered."

Jubal looked back and forth between Addy and the

opposite bank. He cleared his throat. "Uh, ahem, well, that's good."

Then, in a sudden rush to leave, he told her, "It'll be too late to get that wagon out of there if you don't hurry. We can't afford to wait on you to cross tomorrow."

Addy's back straightened, though it caused her a good deal of pain. "Don't worry about us. We'll be out of here in no time."

She gulped and released a long breath when Jubal finally turned and left. The wagon sat in the middle of the creek. The mules stood hipshot, resting, enjoying the feel of the cool water over their tired legs.

It would behoove her to watch what she said from now on, she thought. One day, she wouldn't be able to deliver on her rash promises. Then where would they be?

"C'mon, gal, ya be lolly-gaggin' long 'nough. Take keer o' the boy whilst I git that wagon out'n there."

The concern in his eyes as he watched her agonized movements belied the harshness of his tone, and Addy was grateful.

Trace sat on a flat stone, his back against the bark of an oak tree. Addy sank down next to him. They watched in silence as Scratch skillfully maneuvered the team and wagon up the steep slope.

Addy soon found her eyes wandering to the broad, lightly-furred expanse of Trace's bare chest. The waning sun glinted off the silky blond curls. Though the day had been long and hot, he still smelled good — of the clean outdoors. She sniffed. A faint hint of Scratch's tobacco, the smell of which she had become quite fond, lingered in the air.

Suddenly she climbed to her feet. The aches and bruises were replaced by a tingling sensation deep in the pit of her stomach. She glanced at Trace and saw that his eyes were closed. Wandering to the nearby bushes, she was amazed to find wild raspberries and gooseberries. Her mouth watered. The berries were

89

appealing even though they were obviously not ready to eat.

A group of tiny purple wildflowers caught her eye. While she bent to see if they smelled as pretty as they looked, something long and slender slithered from beneath the leaves and crawled over the tip of her shoe.

Addy's eyes nearly popped from their sockets. She screamed and jerked upright. Too paralyzed with fear to run, she watched in horror as the rest of the snake slowly wound over her foot.

All at once, she felt herself being shoved aside. As she staggered back, she saw Trace take her place, a huge rock held above his head. She closed her eyes, prepared for the sound of the stone smashing the flesh of the abhorrent creature. Finally, when all remained quiet, she slowly raised the lid of one eye. She gasped. Her eyes shot wide open.

Everything within her vision faded into the background except the sight of Trace's bare body. The blanket lay in a sagging heap around his ankles.

Her first reaction was to snap her eyes closed, but they peeped open again of their own accord. And she couldn't help but marvel anew at the absolute beauty of the man. His body was whipcord lean. Why, even his . . . buttocks . . . were hard and muscled. She covered her mouth with her hands in time to smother a sigh.

The sound of the rock falling on dirt startled her. Her eyes darted upward to find him staring at her. Then his head dropped out of her line of vision as he ducked to cover himself.

She opened her mouth but no sound came forth.

Trace was at no such loss for words. His fingers gripped the edges of the blanket until his knuckles turned white; he almost wished they were wrapped around the damnable woman's neck. This was all her fault, after all. If she hadn't screamed like some wild, crazy Indian, he'd still be sitting peacefully on his

90

rock, his modesty intact. Hell, now she'd seen him naked as a newborn babe, and he felt almost as helpless.

He took a deep breath and shouted, "Hell, woman, what's gotten into you? You scared the livin' daylights out of me! What got you so all-fired frightened?"

Her finger shook violently as she pointed to the retreating serpent. She stammered breathlessly, "Sn-snake! I-it was on . . . my . . . foot."

Completely exasperated, he shook his head and muttered, "Tenderfoot."

She frowned. Why was he upset with *her*? It was the snake that had started the trouble. She could have been killed. Just thinking about the danger she'd been in was almost enough to make her forget the sight of his bare backside — almost. She pointed at him, trying to dredge up a semblance of anger. "Listen, you . . ."

Trace, who had been impatiently pacing through the tall grass, stopped and turned on her. "Hell, can't you tell a harmless snake when you see one?"

Addy sniffed. "N-no! I'm not in the habit of associating with snakes." She glared at him and mumbled under her breath, "Until recently."

He speared her with sharp eyes, then issued a long-suffering sigh. The best way out of this situation would be to pretend nothing had happened — at least concerning the dropped blanket. What could he say, anyway, that wouldn't make matters worse? The snake was entirely the safer subject.

"Adeline, you're goin' to have to quit screamin' every time a little bug, or even a gopher snake, or somethin' else that's not goin' to hurt you, crosses your path. If you're *that* scared, you shouldn't be here."

Her body ceased shaking and stiffened "How dare you preach to me in such a manner? Any person in their right mind would be afraid of a snake.

Why . . ." She snapped her jaw shut. What was the use? She talked to a man who was anything but rational.

In a softer tone of voice, Trace added, "Just try to control yourself. It could be dangerous, for *all* of us."

She couldn't meet his eyes. She felt so silly. Of course, he was right. What if there had been Indians close by? She could easily have alerted them to the caravan's presence.

"I-I'm sorry. It won't happen again."

She could have kicked herself when her voice cracked. Why couldn't she be strong and brave like . . . Her stomach knotted. Like what? Like the other women in Trace's life?

She studied his profile as he looked toward the wagons. With his looks and build, she didn't try to fool herself into thinking the man hadn't known a lot of women.

It was another area in which she felt inadequate. She barely knew how to behave around men. Her eyes glistened. Around half-naked men, especially.

When he looked over at her, he frowned, and she withered inside. How she must disgust him. She was afraid of crawly creatures, and was out of her element here in the desolate wilderness. She'd probably behaved in ways a true lady would be ashamed to admit.

Then she watched, round-eyed, as his hand extended toward her. A warm feeling coated her breast. Her eyes questioned, even as her body responded. She let him take her small, cold hand inside his large, warm grasp.

"Let's get back to the train. The old man's waving at us."

Her heart thundered until she thought her chest would burst when he allowed her to help him. Rather than buckle under his weight, she seemed to grow in height and strength. A pink glow suffused her cheeks.

Trace stole sly glances at her when he thought she wasn't looking. Damn, she was beautiful. His insides contracted when he remembered hearing her scream. Any infirmity he'd felt at the time had been left in the dust as he scrambled to her rescue.

She was so slight and delicate, like a grand young woman who sat in a fine parlor, wearing expensive gowns, holding court with scores of young swains.

He scowled. Why should the thought of other men wooing her bring such a bitter taste to his mouth? And why did holding on to her fragile hand stir him so? She was *nothing* to him.

Just because she had accidentally stumbled across him in the wilderness, had probably saved his life . . . He stopped in mid-thought. His mind tripped over itself as he suddenly fought to recall something she'd said earlier. Something about allowing someone to put him out of his misery. What had she meant?

His fingers squeezed her hand in preparation of asking just that. He heard her gasp at the same time he encountered a sticky wetness on her palm. All questions fled his mind as he halted abruptly and turned her hand up to the light.

"God, woman. What have you done to your hand?"

She tried to jerk her hand away, but couldn't. "N-nothing."

"Hold still!" he commanded, then bent his head. The late evening held little remaining daylight to see by.

"Hell, they're blisters! What'd you do, drive the wagon all day without gloves?"

Addy blushed and yanked her hand again, to no avail. "I-I don't own a pair of gloves."

"Of all the stupid things! You came on a trip across hundreds of miles of the roughest country west of St. Louis, and you didn't bring gloves?"

She stumbled as he started walking, dragging her along like a troublesome child. She tried to stomp her foot and throw a fit, but it seemed he'd had a sudden resurgence of energy, and she had to almost run to keep from falling.

Before they reached Scratch, who was standing on the outskirts of the camp, Trace started shouting. "Look at this, old man. Can you imagine anyone bein' so dumb? Look at her hands, for God's sake!"

Addy shot daggers at Trace and intended to finish the subtle murder with vicious words, until she gasped with pain when Scratch's rough fingers grazed her tender palm.

Trace's chest rose and fell with frustration. Damn! Those soft little hands could be scarred for life. She didn't deserve to be treated so callously.

His eyes roved over the camp, seeking the pompous ass who claimed to be the wagon master of this pathetic caravan.

When he finally spotted the heavyset Jubal, the man was sitting with his neatly coiffed wife, partaking leisurely of the evening meal. Trace glared with distaste at the man's huge gut. It would make an easy target for his first punch.

Just as Trace started to take a step toward the Wilkins' fire, Scratch cleared his throat. Over the top of Addy's head, the old man shook his shaggy mane. He cocked his head in the opposite direction.

"Boy, git yoreself over to ole Pedro's wagon an' fetch me some o' that ointment fer these blisters. Now."

Trace blinked, but bunched his blanket tighter and obeyed. Behind him, he heard Scratch say, "An' ask 'im fer an extry pair o' britches. That *purty body* o' yourn's gittin' a mite weary on these ole eyes, 'specially when ya cain't seem ta keep a holt o' that there blanket."

Trace's steps faltered. But the old man's chuckles didn't deter him from his purpose. He just straightened his back, hitched up the rough wool until he winced, and marched smartly away, only daring to breathe again when the sound of Addy's giggles faded into the distance.

Damned tenderfoot! She should consider herself lucky for having glimpsed his naked hide!

Later in the evening, Trace lay in the back of the wagon, his arms behind his head, as he listened to someone playing a sad-sounding tune on a harmonica.

His eyes had nearly drifted shut when he heard humming from beneath his bed. He stopped breathing to hear better, and was afraid to move lest the lulling sound stop.

Without a doubt, he listened to Adeline Montclair. Just thinking of her brought a sudden surge of desire to his loins. He lifted one knee to ease the pressure from the too-tight denim pants he'd borrowed from the skinny Dead-Eye Dolman.

All Pedro'd had were wide cotton trousers that fell off his hips and reached no farther than below his knee caps. Dead-Eye had even given him an extra shirt, but he had yet to wear it. All he needed now was a pair of boots, or moccasins.

Trace rubbed his clean-shaven chin. It was Scratch's turn to hunt tomorrow. If the old man brought back a deer, or antelope, Trace could use the hide to make his own footwear.

The humming faded with the end of the song, and with it his sense of calm. The anxieties again began to creep in. It bothered him that Adeline headed blindly into a country where few white women had ventured. She had no concept of the hardships and dangers ahead.

He thought of the incident with the snake and shuddered. What if it had been a rattler? She could be dead, or dying, this very minute. His insides turned cold. It had happened to many a man, and woman, too. So why did the thought of one more casualty, namely a Miss Adeline Montclair, make him so anxious?

The canvas rustled to his right, and he nearly came off his pallet. He hadn't heard anyone approach. His senses were becoming numb from the inactivity of recent days. He would have to watch it—his carelessness could be deadly.

"Oh, I'm sorry. Did I wake you?"

Her voice was as sweet as ripe peaches and he sighed. "No. I was listening to the song. Kinda sad, wasn't it?"

She shyly ducked her head as she stepped across him, then instead of answering his question, smiled and said, "You're wearing pants." To herself, she added, "And are they ever tight." He might as well be . . . naked, she thought.

Trace cleared his throat. "One of the men had an extra pair. Do I look . . . decent . . . now?"

She tried to keep her eyes from straying to his bare chest and arms, the muscles of which bulged and strained his flesh in their flexed position of supporting his head. Her face and neck felt suddenly very warm as she remembered seeing even more of him bare.

She stammered, "Uh, I-I suppose," beneath his intense scrutiny.

"May I ask you a personal question, Adeline?"

Her eyes narrowed as she sat down on the nearest carton.

He wondered if she would even answer.

Finally, in a husky voice, she said, "You can ask."

"Why are you going to Santa Fe?"

She drew in her breath. It wasn't what she'd expected, but was maybe even more difficult to answer, since she had yet to resolve the issue within herself. She gave him the excuse she felt most comfortable with.

"My father built this company. When he and my mother were murdered by the Indians, he left the business to my cousin and myself. We want to keep it going."

"Couldn't you have turned it over to someone experienced in the trade and run it just as well from Independence?"

"No, I don't think so. Besides, I . . ."

What else could she say? Should she admit that she hadn't really *wanted* to make the journey? Tell him that she was hardheaded enough to antagonize two different men who insisted she *not* go? Hadn't even Trace suggested it would be too much for her?

No, she was too embarrassed to admit the real truth.

Trace noticed her hesitation and prodded, "Besides, what? You want the adventure, right?"

She gulped and nodded. "I've certainly had plenty of *that*, haven't I?"

He managed a grin, though he was so tired he had to fight to keep his eyes open, even in such stimulating company. But he did say, "Take care, Adeline. Take special care. I'd surely hate to see you hurt."

Her shoulders slumped as his eyes drifted shut. She believed he was sincere—that he was concerned for her welfare. So why all the secrets? What was it that he didn't want anyone to know?

A shiver vibrated up her spine. She was worried. Couldn't help but be. More for *him*, though, than for herself.

She tapped the worn pair of gloves Scratch had given her against her knee. There was something sinister brewing. She just wished she knew *what*.

Several uneventful days elapsed. Trace was able to be up more often, and his wounds were healing nicely. Today, he had even sat up front beside her for a short time, and she had enjoyed his company immensely—more than she would admit.

Now they camped for the night after crossing another deep creek. Two wagons had sustained breaks in equipment, and they would take the next day off for repairs.

Addy looked down at her stained dress. While the men worked on the wagons, she would do some much-needed laundry.

She shook her head and dust formed a small cloud around her shoulders. Visions of a bath in the creek formed in her mind. Images of cool water trickling over her scalp and gritty flesh caused her to lick her lips in anticipation.

Glancing furtively around the group of wagons, she decided to wait until nearly dark, after the men settled down for the evening. Then she could enjoy a bath at her leisure.

Trace was resting in the wagon when she pulled herself inside. She took a deep breath and stepped carefully to avoid waking him. Once she reached her trunks, she spread the skirt of a dirty dress and piled the clothes to be washed inside its wide folds before choosing clean ones to don after her bath.

With her arms full, it was not as easy to slip past the sleeping man. Just when she thought she had made it safely, she stubbed her toe on a loose board and tripped over his leg, kicking him solidly in the shin.

"Huh? Who is it?" Trace was groggy and barely able to make out the shadowy form hunched at his feet. Damn, his leg ached.

Addy quickly assured him, "It's only me. I'm so sorry. I accidentally tripped over you. Go back to sleep. Please."

He squinted his eyes. What in the world was in that bundle she carried? He yawned and nodded. For once, he wouldn't disturb her privacy, he thought. She would appreciate that.

Her heart arose from the pit of her stomach when she saw his eyes close. The empty feeling it left had to be caused from hunger, she thought, not disappointment that he hadn't bothered to ask what she was up to, or where she was going, or even if she'd had a nice evening.

Anger formed a lump in her chest for no explainable reason. She couldn't control her hasty flounce from the wagon. Her hips swung wildly as she swished her way into the woods with her unwieldy bundle.

Stumbling over dead limbs and exposed roots, she kept walking until she reached the edge of the steep bank. The slope was more vertical here than where they had crossed the wagons, but this was the way she wanted it. There would be less likelihood of someone accidentally discovering her.

Addy chewed her lower lip. The only way she could see to get to the creek was to back down, holding to anything she could get her hands on that wouldn't move, too, and pulling the laundry behind. Her passage was clumsy and awkward at best, but she was proud of her ingenuity when her feet finally hit flat, solid ground.

She had to decide whether to wash herself or the clothes first. If she took a bath and donned fresh attire, it would get wet and dirty again when she washed out the rest of the bundle. So, clothes first.

Soon, all available bushes and lower branches were pressed into service. Dresses, petticoats, and numerous "unmentionables" were spread to dry in the light breeze.

Then she began to remove each article of what she wore, soaping it, rinsing it, and adding it to the others as she went along. She couldn't bring herself to bathe in the open with absolutely nothing to cover her body, so she walked to the water's edge wearing her pantalets and chemise.

She stuck out one dainty foot, dipping her big toe quickly into and out of the swirling water. It wasn't cold, not too cold, anyway, at least right there by the bank.

Looking to the left, then to the right, then behind her, she placed her whole foot into the water and splashed it around. She smiled. She'd never been allowed to wade as a child. It was fun. When both feet were submerged, she kicked and sent a spray of droplets onto a pile of rocks.

Something tickled her ankle. She froze. A scream built inside her constricted throat, but she swallowed it like a child would swallow an ill-gotten chunk of candy. Her wild eyes darted downward. She sighed. Nothing more than a willowy weed.

A pleased grin lit her features. She was learning.

Mud squished between her toes as she waded to the middle of the creek. The water barely reached halfway up her calves at the deepest point.

All right, she was in the creek, had her soap. Now what? She looked warily down. What did one do in a low, cool stream to get one's body wet and, more importantly clean? And one's hair? She looked along the length of her fairly short body into the clear ripples. The water was still a long way down.

Ever so slowly, she bent her knees. The water lapping at the thin cotton covering her behind was colder than she thought, and she jerked straight up again.

Taking a deep breath, she decided there was no help for it and sat right down, hugging her arms around her middle. She gasped at first, then tried to relax. Once actually in the water, it wasn't so bad, she thought. The water came up to her waist.

She waved her hands, slapping and splashing the water, like a small boy she'd once observed taking a bath at a friend's house. Memories of the past, of her oh-so-protected childhood, in which she'd never been allowed to play in mud puddles, or get grass stains on her freshly starched clothes, flooded her mind. She shook them off. This was not the time, nor the place. She would not let anything disturb her peace now.

Suddenly, her head snapped to one side. What was that? What had she heard? She listened. Nothing. Her breath hissed between her clenched teeth. For a minute there . . .

A movement caught her eye. There, by the bank. It was a round, furry little creature that appeared to be washing its paws. Why, it looked like a woodland bandit with that dark mask around its eyes.

Her brow furrowed. Could that tiny animal have made the sound she just heard? She shrugged. The animal's presence offered the only explanation.

Chapter Seven

Addy tried to enjoy her bath, but couldn't relax. She continually cast wary glances to each side of the creek. The raccoon had suddenly skittered away, and she had the strangest sensation; it was as if the rocks had eyes, and the trees arms and legs, and everything was moving closer and closer.

Finally, too uneasy to sit still any longer, she stood upright.

Her foot slipped and she waved her arms madly to keep from splashing back into the water. The breeze bit into her flesh, quickly cooling the large droplets left clinging to her body, until her skin was awash with goose bumps.

She shivered, then flushed a bright scarlet when she looked down and saw the outline of her pebble-hard nipples through the damp cloth of her chemise.

The hair on the back of her neck stood on end as her eyes began a wild search of the bank and her drying clothes. What if someone *was* watching? What if they saw . . .

She lifted her feet awkwardly, sloshing through the current. As she approached the bank, she tossed the soap upon the grass and twisted the water from her hair.

Tiny rivulets dripped over her shoulders, forming small trails along her spine and over her taut breasts. She looked from her wet undergarments to the change of clothes she had brought, and again scanned the small clearing.

No, she'd be darned if she would take the time to

change completely now. But it wasn't as easy as she thought it would be to pull the dry material over her wet body and underclothes. The dry garments adhered to the wet ones, and made getting dressed troublesome.

Her head had barely poked through the waist opening of her dress when she heard a twig snap, then another. And each alarming sound was closer than the one before. She struggled faster, paying no heed to the several occasions when the cloth ripped.

"Damned dress," she muttered. She gasped and blushed. Her arms finally found the dress's armholes and she sighed. Her eyes darted guiltily as she pulled her bodice together.

There was another loud snap and she swung around. Her eyes focused on the spot where the noise had come from and her heart stopped in mid-beat. It was a scary creature. A two-legged beast. In her opinion, she'd have preferred snarling bears and snapping wolves. At least she knew what to expect from wild animals. She was never sure with Rudy Potts.

The man's faded brown eyes took in her disheveled appearance as he licked his fleshy lips. She shuddered and hastily finished buttoning her dress before gathering her belongings.

She glanced hopefully over her shoulder for a means of escape. A large boulder filled the small clearing all the way to the water. To her right, a line of trees met the face of a cliff.

She cleared her throat in an attempt to swallow her fear. There was no other way back to camp but past Rudy. She took the first step, then another. With a deep, albeit unsteady, breath, she attempted to push past the rat-faced man. It would be all right. She had handled him before.

He wouldn't budge. His lips curved into a sneer as he grabbed for her arm, nearly upsetting the lopsided bundle of clean clothes.

"What's the hurry, girl? I just got here."

She clutched the clothes tighter to her breast. "I-I need to get back . . . Scratch will be looking for me," she stammered.

Rudy snickered. "Naw. He's all wound up in a big poker game. An' he's winin'. Nope. Won't think 'bout ya for quite a spell, I'd say."

Her heart pounded rapidly, skipped a few critical beats, then raced with trepidation. "Trace . . . uh, Mr. Randall, will be hungry, then. I've got . . ."

Rudy stepped so close she could smell the fetid odor of whiskey on his breath. She blanched and backed away. He followed. Soon, she found herself against the huge, unyielding trunk of a cottonwood.

"No-o-o. He's sleepin' like a baby. I checked a'fore I come a huntin' ya."

She turned her head, wincing when several long strands of her hair caught beneath the rough edges of bark. He leaned his body into her, pinning her in place, trapping her arms, which were still wrapped around the all-but-forgotten clothes.

Sucking in her breath, she rasped, "I'll tell Jubal."

He laughed, a harsh sound that grated on her ears, scaring her even more. "Won't do ya no good. He's too busy cozyin' up to his little wife. 'Sides, wouldn't believe ya."

With an ever-increasing sense of despair, she figured he was probably right. Jubal didn't like her much, anyway. Why would he believe her over his right-hand man?

In a desperate attempt to escape, she shifted her weight, dropped the heavy bundle of clothes, and opened her mouth to scream.

Anticipating her action, Rudy's thin form never wavered. His knee pushed between the opening her legs presented, trapping layers of skirt until she could hardly move her lower body.

At the same time, his chest filled the space the clothes had occupied, crushing her breasts. One of his hands was large enough to effectively cover both her mouth and nose.

Addy's eyes widened, their hazel depths dark with loathing. She couldn't breathe — couldn't move. Into her heart thundered the formidable recognition that she was completely at Rudy Pott's mercy.

If she could have, she would have snorted her disgust at the thought. *Mercy!* As if the man knew the meaning of the word. Then her mind clouded, her thoughts running together. A faint lethargic feeling took hold of her limbs. He was killing her, and there was nothing she could do to stop him.

All of a sudden, his hand moved. Enough to uncover her nose, but still pressing her lips into her teeth until she tasted her own blood.

His whiny voice squeaked in her ear. "Ya daren't scream, girl, cause I'll tell the rest of the fellers ya enticed me down here, teasin' me with your long bath, tauntin' me with your nekid body. They'll all want a turn at ya, too."

Of all the stupid thoughts to cross her mind at such a time, she thought — she was indignant over the fact that he hadn't admitted she was fully clothed while taking her bath.

He snickered, causing her flesh to tingle. "I done told 'em 'bout us, ya know?"

She squirmed, shaking her head until he finally released her mouth. She gulped huge breaths of air and hissed, "Us? What do you mean, 'us'? I don't like you, Mr. Potts, not one little bit. Surely you must know that? Now, release me. At once!"

He ran his free hand over her bosom. "Yore settin' me atremble, girl, ya surely are." Making gruesome smacking sounds with his lips, he said, "Ya got big titties fer a little woman. I like my women ta have big titties."

She gasped and opened her mouth, only to quietly close it. Tears of frustration welled in her eyes, some spilling over to blend with the damp tendrils of hair clinging to her cheeks. Her stomach churned until she thought she might be sick.

The beast was correct when he stated she wouldn't—couldn't—scream. What would happen if the whole caravan were to be drawn by her cries, and they actually believed Rudy's insane claims? She would be labeled a tease and a . . . a . . . woman of loose morals.

Rudy's tongue flicked over her ear. She shuddered. Her mind raced. She might not yell out, but there had to be something else she could do.

His hand moved from her chin to her cheek. She ducked to escape his blubbery, wet lips, and without taking time to consider the consequences, clamped her teeth into the fleshy part of his hand.

He cried out and backhanded her across the mouth.

Her head reeled. She felt faint. Hope of release drained from her. No matter what she did, she couldn't free herself from Rudy's painful grasp.

He lowered his head, making deep, guttural sounds in his throat. She pulled her lips back in a feral snarl and spit. Then she closed her eyes and waited for his swift retaliation.

And she waited. Suddenly, his oppressive weight lifted. Miraculously.

What she saw when she opened her eyes caused her to gasp and fold her hands over her heart. Trace! Trace was there. How? She watched in stunned silence as his bare arm swung back. His fist slammed so hard and fast into Rudy's face that she barely witnessed the movement. The smaller man yelped and staggered backward.

She held her breath, knowing Trace was in no condition for a lengthy fight.

Rudy regained his balance and squared his stance, ready to charge. But when Trace raised his right hand, Rudy saw that he held a pistol, pointed directly between his eyes.

The smaller man squinted, as if his mind had a hard time registering the fact that he had lost the upper hand. His eyes narrowed as he slapped his thighs. He froze. His fingers curled into fists. His eyes darted nervously around the clearing.

Trace could read the indecision in Rudy's eyes. The varmint knew Trace was weak, and was calculating his chances. There'd been a lot of men of Rudy's caliber during Trace's years in the West, cowards who would push around women and weaklings, but who turned tail and ran when confronted with someone bigger and stronger.

Trace calmly looked down the barrel of his gun and cocked the hammer. Sure enough, Rudy held up both hands, palms outstretched, placating. He backed away. When Rudy reached the fringe of trees, Trace grinned as the weasel spun and crashed through dry limbs and decaying brush. His curses drifted back to the clearing on the soft breeze.

Trace's voice was thin as he yelled after Rudy. "Go ahead, run, mongrel. And don't bother the lady again."

Then, before Addy's astonished eyes, Trace's bold stance all but crumpled. He doubled over, holding his right hand next to his chest, his breathing deep and labored.

She rushed to him. "Trace! Are you all right? What happened?"

But he wouldn't allow her to touch him. Painfully, he straightened and glared at her. His hand hurt like hell, and he felt weaker than a kitten, but none of it detracted from the fury of seeing Rudy pawing Addy.

His chest rose and fell mightily with each angry inhalation. It felt as if he could explode. His hands unconsciously clenched into fists; he winced at the strain it caused his right wrist.

His eyes bored into her, backing her up a step with their force. The little idiot! Didn't she know better than to wander around the woods alone? And at night, no less? She needed to be taught a damned good lesson.

His eyes glittered with more menace than Rudy Potts could ever hope to inspire as he snarled, "Well, hell, looks like I interrupted somethin'. Did I, Adeline? Should I have waited? Maybe another ten minutes, or so?"

She gaped at him. Just what was he implying? She backed away another step and shook her head, though the gesture was concealed in the deep shadow of the tree.

In contrast, the stars shone brightly overhead as Trace advanced. "Did you like what Rudy did to you? Did you enjoy the feel of his hands when he . . . touched . . . you?"

He gritted his teeth. A pang of intense jealousy suffused him, and just a little guilt. He'd been close enough to hear her gasp of pain, knew she'd been frightened out of her wits, but he couldn't stop. She had to learn what could happen to innocent little girls without sense enough to watch out for themselves.

She inhaled sharply when she found herself once again with her back to the tree. She watched as Trace's long, graceful fingers reached forward and touched the soggy material outlining her breasts. But rather than instant disgust and revulsion, she experienced a warm current that radiated throughout her body.

Her eyes rounded with surprise. She shivered as a tingle vibrated down her spine. Where Rudy had hurt and abused her, Trace's touch was gentle. Rudy had taken pleasure from her fear, whereas Trace just took . . . pleasure. She blinked as the expression on his face softened the ferocious gleam in his eyes.

Her knees trembled. She'd wondered what it would feel like to be caressed and touched — like that. And when his head tilted, and his lips found hers, it was with an intensity that caused her to moan with pain as the tender abrasions inside her mouth stung.

Trace immediately eased the pressure of the kiss, irritated by the rush of desire and longing that overwhelmed his good sense and his ability to walk away from the woman. With that easing, though, her lips became more mobile, following his lead, not allowing him to stop.

This was a mistake, and he knew it, taking the tenderfoot under his wing. She was none of his business, and better left that way. Besides, she had already proven to be the bundle of trouble he'd predicted days ago.

But as he teased her soft, pliable mouth, and his fingers wove into the thick mass of silken hair, he relented a little, thinking that she might not be such an inconvenience after all. She was little and helpless, but definitely a woman.

What had begun as a "lesson," turned out to be a learning experience for them both. Trace discovered a throbbing pain in his chest that he'd never felt before when holding a woman. Addy found out her dreams had been nothing when compared to the reality of kisses from a live, extremely virile man.

Their breaths mingled on a long sigh when Addy found the front of her body pressed to Trace's hard length, rather than her back to the scratchy, uncomfortable tree. His was a much nicer pillar to lean upon.

Suddenly, she stiffened and brought her arms from about his waist. She pushed against his chest. Dear Lord, what had she done? Was she no better, after all, than Rudy professed? — to go from one man's arms into another's?

Trace reluctantly let her go, though he was stunned by the look of horror on her beautiful features.

"What is it, Adeline? What's wrong? Did I hurt you?"

She covered her lips with shaking fingers. "N-no.

109

You didn't hurt me. It's just . . . uh . . . th-this is highly improper. We shouldn't be here . . . alone. I-I mean, someone might get the wrong, uh, impression."

He scowled. "Oh, I see. It's all right for you to be *alone* and attacked by some lunatic, but you can't stomach being here *alone* with me? Is that right?"

Addy started to nod, but then stood, unmoving, a look of utter devastation in her expressive eyes, which were such a bright green they would have rivaled the newly unfurled leaves if seen in the light of day.

Her heart fluttered and sank, as if on a dying breath. He wouldn't understand her alarm. While she would have fought Rudy with every ounce of strength she possessed, she now found herself having to guard against her rising feelings for Trace.

Fighting was the last thing she would do if he took her in his arms and tenderly kissed her again. It was *herself* she had to contend with, not *him*.

Trace was unaware of the battle raging inside the taut woman. All he knew was that he had been rejected, and he was consumed by a myriad of uncharitable thoughts.

"Well, this is a fine turn of events, isn't it? Let me tell you something, tenderfoot. The next time you get yourself into a boiling kettle of water, you can damn sure get your . . . self . . . out. I'll not be burned a second time."

Trace stomped off, stopped, rubbed the back of his neck and turned around to face her. "Pick up your garments and get the hell back to camp. I'll follow and see to it no one . . . inconveniences . . . you again tonight."

She opened her mouth, ready to pour out her sorrow and gratitude, but choked over the words when she saw the angry set to his jaw. The bullheaded creature probably wouldn't accept her apology, or explanation, anyway. So be it.

She rubbed the end of her nose, then gathered the

110

pile of once-clean laundry that now lay scattered in the dirt and dry grass and who knew what else? She pursed her lips when she saw the smudges and wrinkles on each item. After everything else that had gone wrong that evening, now all her hard work had been for nought.

Thinking she frowned at him, Trace folded his arms over his chest and angrily scanned their surroundings. The moon had finally put in an appearance, illuminating parts of the area and eerily shadowing the rest.

His eyes narrowed as his gaze focused on one particular boulder. His body tensed. He gave an imperceptible nod of his head in the direction of the massive rock.

Then he squared his shoulders and trudged after the winsome woman hautily marching before him. His lips twitched. She was something else, this Adeline Montclair.

Once she reached the safety and haven of the wagon, Addy recalled she hadn't asked Trace how he had managed to find her. She dumped her clothes over the tailgate and turned.

Her mouth opened and closed several times. Her eyes glittered with indignation. The beast was gone. Just like that! He had disappeared.

While Addy stood fuming over Trace's high-handed behavior, her cousin sat inside the closed carriage, her head bent close to her husband, her voice a hushed whisper.

"I don't understand it, dahlin'. What keeps going wrong?"

Jubal's tone was gruff and raspy as he tried his best to keep his reply just as low-spoken. "Can't explain it either, sweetheart. But don't worry your pretty little head, hear? It'll happen. Next time."

Delilah pouted, "That's what you said the *last* time,

111

dahlin'."

Another quiet conversation was taking place along the bank of the creek, in the shadow of a large boulder.

"It is good to see you, Eagle Feather. I have been too long in the land to the East and have missed my Comanche brother. How have you been, my friend?"

The stout Comanche nodded. "It is, indeed, good to set eyes once again on my brother, Trace Randall. I am well, but the young men of my tribe are troubled."

Trace sighed and hunched his shoulders. "So, you haven't discovered how they're getting the whiskey and guns?"

Eagle Feather's face formed what might have been called a frown before the stoic, unlined features were once again unreadable.

"No. The young ones, they do not trust me. They think of me as a nosey grandmother and stay out of my way. It is difficult, my brother, to keep from turning them over my knee as a white woman does a disobedient child."

Trace's cheeks almost wrinkled into a smile. Though the situation was far from funny, it was just plain amusing to hear the medium-sized man speak of the white man's ways.

For years now, the Comanche and Santa Fe traders had dealt together with little problem. They had all found it to their mutual advantage to keep the peace in the interest of trade.

However, more and more depredations had occurred, mostly by irresponsible young men of the Comanche nation who could not be restrained.

It was Comanche custom that there be no camp police or leadership. A warrior brooked no supervision, except, maybe, in the case of a large-scale buffalo hunt, and then only until the hunt was well under way.

No, Trace didn't underestimate the difficulty of Eagle Feather's endeavors, or his own. Just as many whites were looking to keep the Indians stirred up, for their own personal gains. The troublemakers on both sides were more than one or two men could ever hope to find, let alone stop.

He and Eagle Feather had their work cut out for them.

The Indian's head tilted to one side. He held out his hand to Trace. "Someone stirs. I will find you when the sun has set two times. Maybe one of us will have more information."

Trace shook his friend's strong, bronzed hand. "In two days, then. Go with God, my brother."

"Vaya con Dios, Trace Randall."

Within seconds there was no sound or trace of Eagle Feather's existence. Trace, who considered his own skills somewhat remarkable, shook his head in wonder. He was always amazed by the Indian's ability to come or go virtually undetected.

He chuckled. Since the Comanche were the best horsemen on the plains, they were also a nemesis to unsuspecting travelers, or caravans, who failed to keep a close watch on their stock.

As he made his way back toward camp, Trace's brow furrowed. If his information was correct, and he had no doubt of its source, then somewhere, between Independence and Santa Fe, there was a train loaded with kegs of whiskey and a store of guns and ammunition.

Somehow, he had to find and destroy it before it reached the young Comanche braves. Somehow.

Since the evening before had been so clear, it came as a surprise to Addy to wake up to a dismal, cloudy day. It was a source of amazement to her, how quickly the weather changed on the plains.

She shivered. Yesterday she'd been hot and sweaty; today she was chilled. A drop of rain splattered on the tip of her nose. She supposed she should be thankful not to have the relentless heat of the sun blistering her sensitive skin or burning her eyes.

She stretched and started after the team. Yes, a little rain to settle the billowing dust would be a welcome change.

A little later in the day, she remembered that thought with scorn as she reined her team through a sticky morass of ruts.

She wiped the sleeve of her dress across her brow, unable to tell if the moisture came from her body or the drizzle that had fallen for the past few hours.

Jubal picked that opportunity to lope past her wagon, gleefully shouting, "Get off an' walk like the rest of the men, little lady. Them mules have enough durn weight to haul without havin' to cart you along, too."

When she made a face, he threw back his head and laughed. She looked distastefully from the muddy ground to her soft, laced kid shoes and soggy, but clean, clothes.

Then she leaned to the right and looked up and down the line of wagons. Jubal wasn't teasing. All of the drivers walked, even those who usually rode upon the back of one of the teams. All of the animals were struggling.

As she peered under the canvas, she was relieved to see that Trace rested peacefully. During the night, she had heard him toss fitfully, sometimes mumbling, sometimes calling out, though his words were indistinguishable.

Guilt suffused her; her face blushed a dull red. If it hadn't been for her carelessness, he wouldn't have overtired himself. Now she was afraid he had suffered a relapse.

Taking a deep breath, she stopped the team and clambered over the side of the wagon. Jubal seemed

114

to have forgotten about her passenger. Maybe Trace would get to ride the rest of the day.

The near mule swished its tail, flicking her in the face with it. She tried to avoid the next swipe, but had sunk to her ankles in the squishy ground. Her knees buckled, and she plunked seat-first into the mess.

Her hair fell in her face, and she lifted a hand to brush it from her eyes, leaving a wide smear of wet, brown dirt across her cheek. She looked down at the fresh dress, now soaked through and discolored with mud.

Frustration welled in her chest. A tear pooled inside the lower rim of her eyelid, then spilled forth to trickle aimlessly down her face.

How she hated the dirt, the sweat, the hard work. She hated the cranky mules, and Jubal's ceaseless badgering. And hated . . . Delilah . . . and Trace . . . because they rode in comfort while she stomped through this awful slop.

She sniffed and wiped the back of her hand over her nose before trying to steady herself enough to rise. Hysteria bubbled in her throat when her hands disappeared beneath the mire. It just wasn't fair. What had she ever done. . . ?

Finally, after grabbing hold of a wheel spoke, she was able to pull herself up. Her feet made horrible sucking sounds as she lifted her legs high, and she almost lost her shoes.

The mules strained into the harness and the wagon slowly inched forward. She held to a strap to take advantage of their strength.

When Trace awoke a while later, he couldn't see Addy on the driver's bench and became worried. After Rudy's assault, he imagined any number of things that could have happened to the hapless woman.

He felt the need to get up and see about her. Besides, it was so humid and muggy in the wagon that his clothes clung to his solid frame like a second skin and he couldn't sleep, anyway.

The exertion of the past evening had taken more out of him than he'd thought. His muscles felt like rubber as he crawled forward.

Peeking through the opening in the canvas, he grinned. The grin grew into a smile, the smile turned into a full-fledged chuckle.

"Adeline? Is that you?"

He could hardly stop laughing long enough to call to the scraggly ragamuffin sloshing beside the team. Everything about the woman was brown, from her stringy hair and sodden dress, to every exposed inch of flesh.

All except her eyes. The brown there was flecked with brilliant green that sparked at him with anything but humor.

He composed his features to ask, "What's the matter? What have *I* done?" Then he couldn't stand it, and laid his forehead on the bench and gasped for breath. He'd never seen anything so funny in his life.

When he next deigned to raise his eyes, he couldn't stop staring at the way her wet dress molded to every delightful curve and indentation of her extremely well-shaped and proportioned body.

He licked his dry lips, suddenly wishing for a swig of Scratch's rotgut whiskey. God, she was perfect. Small and thin, but full-busted with a tiny waist and curvaceous hips. Perfect!

Addy had turned her back, continuing the monotonous chore of walking in the syrupy mud. Though she had tried, she hadn't been able to think of anything monstrous enough to call the odious man in the wagon when he had collapsed with mirth.

And . . . she had seen the flare of interest in those deep blue eyes. It both pleased and embarrassed her. She unconsciously straightened her shoulders, totally unaware of how the action outlined her breasts.

She felt the heat from his gaze like hot needles

116

down her spine. Unable to concentrate on watching her step, she let the hem of her gown sag. The next thing she knew, she tripped on the front panel of her skirt and went face-first into a puddle.

Deep, rumbling laughter erupted from the wagon and her entire body burned. Spitting grit from her mouth, she slowly raised her upper body, blinking water and swiping at strands of hair that had fallen over her face.

A heavy weight settled in the pit of her stomach. Her chest felt as if it would crumble under the sudden pressure. Her ragged nails and scraped fingers clinched around a handful of slimy mud. Her knees formed a pool in the muck as she turned, rose to a kneeling position and threw the gooey wad.

Her eyes gleamed with pure satisfaction when she heard a hollow "plop," and a shouted, "Hey!"

The next handful connected with its mark and produced a gurgled yelp from the target. She felt much, much better.

Even the gummy trickle running down her neck and into her bodice couldn't erase the smile from her lips—until she rubbed her hand over the filthy linen plastered to her chest. Then she grimaced and plucked it away from her flesh, hearing the suck of the wet fabric as it was pulled from her skin.

She held her hand out and shook it, wrinkling her nose with distaste. Then a similar, repeated sucking noise assailed her even after she had released her bodice.

Her vision was suddenly blocked by a pair of long, muscled legs, encased in tight, damp denims.

"Uh-oh," she thought.

Chapter Eight

Addy's gaze traveled uncertainly up the boldly defined, extraordinarily masculine physique. She had to force her eyes not to linger. It was still too easy to recall the vision of that body *naked,* and she had enough trouble with the memory when her eyes were closed.

When she glimpsed a patch of splattered mud on the side of his neck and collar, her hand knotted the folds of her skirt. When she saw the caked dirt on his cheek and forehead, she visibly trembled.

But his too-blue eyes glittered with amusement rather than anger when they locked with hers, and she began to breathe easier. His hands were strong, but gentle, when they helped her to her feet.

Goose bumps crept over her flesh when he spoke in that familiar deep, throaty voice. "You've got a good aim, for a tenderfoot. Now, what was that all about?"

She blushed when her foot slipped and she had to lean against him for support. Her heart fluttered wildly. She could easily get used to this, she thought.

Trace had difficulty keeping his face set in a stern expression. She looked so fragile and childlike. Long-dormant emotions stirred in his chest.

He swallowed a lump in his throat and shifted to lean against the wheel. The girl clinging to his arm moved with him, and his body reacted immediately.

How could he have thought of her as a child? The body that rubbed fully against his belonged to a woman — a very soft, feminine woman.

"Are you all right?" His voice sounded strained and he was unsure where to put his hands. He knew where

118

he *wanted* to put them, but there were far too many interested eyes turned in their direction. He sighed. Another time.

Addy had come so undone by the feel of his solid, masculine body next to hers that it took a moment for her to regain her composure.

"Y-yes. I-I'm fine. Just fine." Then she noticed the wet mud that dirtied his shirt front and remembered why he had come down to her in the first place.

She tried to rekindle the anger that had caused her initial outburst, but couldn't keep from smiling. The brown crust on his cheek was really quite endearing.

Before she knew it, she was giggling.

And the giggles bubbled up from deep within her chest. The sound was so low and seductive that Trace shuddered with a hard-suppressed longing to kiss her bow-shaped, tremulous lips.

His voice was a vibrant rumble. "What's so damned funny?"

Her lips quivered. She was tempted to reach out and wipe the dirt from his cheek. Her hand hovered a moment before she jerked it back to her side.

"N-nothing. I'm sorry about hitting you with the mud." The thought of her jealousy over his riding while she walked sobered her immediately. She certainly didn't want him to know just how childish she was capable of behaving.

He cleared his throat and forced his eyes from the rounded outline of her bosom, so clearly defined by the damp bodice. He'd noticed the delectable fullness before, but then it had been almost dark. His eyes could have been deceiving him. They hadn't been. "Well . . ."

Relief flooded his face when he raised his head and looked forward. "We'd better get the mules moving. It looks like they've chosen a place to camp."

Addy dragged her eyes from his rugged features. It was disconcerting, this hold he had over her, but she didn't know what she could do about it.

119

Suddenly, she felt a sting on her arm. Looking down, she saw several thin, dark insects covering the only clean spot on her hand. A shrill buzz whizzed about her ear and she swung her arms in fright.

Trace's voice broke through the irritating noise. "Mosquitoes! I wondered how long it would take them to find us."

The tiny pests were suddenly everywhere. She whirled and blew air from her mouth as they swarmed around her eyes and nose. Panic welled in her chest.

Trace had a mischievous look in his eyes when he stepped away from her. He bent and scooped up a handful of mud. He drew his arm back. She guessed his intent and started backing up, but he was too quick for her. The cold mud slapped into her flesh.

She sputtered, "Wh-why y-you . . ."

"Now, Adeline, it's for your own good. It'll keep the damn things off of you. Stand still, damn it!"

The next handful covered her neck and the open vee of her bodice. They both gasped. She could have sworn his deeply tanned face turned an even darker shade, but he turned away so fast she wasn't sure.

When he bent again, she frowned and followed his example, picking up a watery mass of earth herself. They each hurled their handfuls of mud at the same time, then collapsed to their knees in fits of laughter, wiping mud from their eyes and mouths.

Finally Trace composed himself, stood, helped Addy up, and then pushed her forward, simultaneously slapping the rears of the mules. "Better get moving. They're worse when you stand still."

Addy ducked her head, suddenly embarrassed by her behavior. She was thankful that her embarrassment was concealed by the layers of dried dirt that caked on her face. With her head held high and all expression wiped from her face, she started walking. If only she could conceal the twinkle in her eyes, she thought.

It was soon obvious that even the animals were not

immune to the vicious insect attack. In their haste to escape the mosquitoes, she had to run to keep up, lifting ten pounds of mud with every step.

By the time they stopped to make camp, she was so exhausted that she came close to humiliating herself by sinking to the wet ground in a shower of tears.

The only thing that stopped her was the knowledge that Trace was right behind her. He'd also walked the last few miles. Sweat beaded on his forehead and upper lip. He sagged and caught hold of the wheel, draping his arms through the spokes.

She started toward him. Her hand barely touched his shoulder when his head lifted. His eyes let her know in no uncertain terms that no matter their brief period of closeness in the mud, he would not accept her help, or pity.

" 'Bout time you young'uns turned up. Already got a fire cracklin' an' vittles in the pot. C'mon, gal. Let's get the boy settled. Ya will stay an' eat with us, won't ya?"

Addy hesitated for only a moment. The past few meals she had shared with Delilah and Jubal, and they had been miserable affairs. Even Trace's suddenly surly attitude couldn't dispel her anticipation of enjoying a pleasant supper for a change.

"I'd be happy to join you, Mr. Scratch. If you're sure you have enough."

"They's plenty."

She slapped the back of her neck. The only problem now was the mosquitoes. They were enough to make one lose one's appetite. That is, if one weren't hungrier than two teams of mules.

After dinner she leaned back and sighed, rubbing her full stomach appreciatively. She thought how funny it was that, since undertaking this journey, she'd eaten things she'd never known were edible, and even liked *most* of them.

Back home, she had always been a finicky eater, turning her nose up at some meats, especially those

121

that had come from animals she'd kept as pets, and most vegetables. Out here, she just ate, grateful to have *anything* that would appease her grumbling tummy.

After she and Scratch finished eating, she looked wistfully toward the wagon. Trace had eaten only a little, then had quickly taken off for his bed. Scratch had soon disappeared too, probably to find a game of cards.

She shrugged her shoulders and took the plates to the river, fighting the blasted blood-sucking mosquitoes the whole way there and back. If she heard one more whine in her ear, she would go crazy. Maybe they shouldn't have washed the mud off before supper, she thought.

Then, to make things even more miserable, thunder reverberated through the black night. A sudden streak of lightning illuminated the entire area.

She ducked. Terror shook her slender form as her feet sprouted wings. Even the slight shelter offered beneath the wagon would be a welcome haven.

She was terrified of thunderstorms—had been since she'd seen her father's favorite stallion and one of the grooms struck and killed by a bolt when she was only a small child.

She ran faster. Huge drops of rain pelted her. Soon she was slipping and sliding on ground covered with running water.

She scrambled under the wagon, pulling her sodden skirt in after her, in an attempt to keep it dry, though it did little good. The ground beneath her was wet, too.

Scratching the end of her nose, she remembered that the blankets were inside the wagon. She sat, huddled in a tight ball, shivering as a cold wind froze her thinly-clad, completely soaked body.

At least there was one bright spot, she thought. The darned mosquitoes seemed to have disappeared, for the time being.

122

White streaks suffused the sky, lighting up the night better than a coal-oil lantern. She quaked and closed her eyes tightly with every clap of loud thunder and flash of bright light.

Finally, she bent her legs and lay her head on her knees, burying her face. Bravado was such an ordeal.

Trace awoke at the first loud boom heralding the storm. He had surprised himself and dozed, though still shaken from his encounter with Adeline.

Supper had been torture. He hadn't been able to keep his eyes or his thoughts from her for a single minute. And the worst part of the entire episode was that he had seen the way Scratch watched the two of them. It was like a red-tailed hawk playing with a pair of baby rabbits, giving them just enough space to trap themselves.

Well, he had stood all that he could stand, and left to return to the wagon, where he'd lain in silent agony ever since. His body definitely knew what he wanted, and needed, though his mind was in turmoil.

Troublesome thoughts were plaguing him, threatening his well-ordered existence.

He had never known much love, coming late in life to a sickly mother. And his father . . . He could almost forgive his father now, after all these years. Almost. Lawrence Randall had been a good man, but loved his wife with excessive devotion. When she died in childbirth, it literally broke his heart.

Trace had been reared by a strict grandfather who saw to it he had every necessity in life. Everything any child could want or ever hope to have—except a kind word, a loving touch.

Closing his eyes, he tried to vanquish the disturbing memories of the past from his mind. His head ached, as it always did when he allowed himself to remember.

The storm raged for almost an hour. Every once in a while, he thought he heard a strange sound. He would cock his head and listen, but couldn't make out what it was or where it came from.

Then there was a lull in the weather. The wind stilled momentarily; the thunder rumbled low across the plains. The lightning continued to light up the sky.

There it was again. It sounded like a puppy whimpering. He shook his head. Naw. No one had brought a dog on the trail with them. Wait! This time it seemed more like a sob.

He scooted to the end of the wagon and pushed the canvas outward. Whatever it was was coming from beneath the wagon.

With the next flash of lightning, he was able to scan the camp. No one stirred. All the fires had been drowned long ago. Puddles formed in every depression.

Rain continued to splatter the canvas. Dust motes sifted through the stuffy confines of the wagon, permeating the air with a dank, musty odor. But at least it was dry.

His curiosity got the best of him. As swiftly as possible, favoring his sore muscles, he clambered over the tailgate and knelt, awaiting the next bolt of light.

When the sky again turned into a flickering white-and-blue tapestry, he stared, unbelieving. He blinked, his hand gripping the axle so hard his fingers turned numb.

With the next illumination and rapid-fire series of booms, he leaned forward and called, "Adeline?"

The soft whimpers ceased abruptly. He sucked in his breath when huge, glistening eyes nearly undid him. His chest felt as if a team of runaway horses stampeded across it.

She sat there, shivering, looking at him as if he was some kind of specter. His eyes narrowed and the muscles in his jaw leaped frantically when he ground his teeth.

"What are you doin' under there? Why aren't you inside where it's dry?"

She sniffled. Her teeth chattered so badly she could hardly speak. "Th-this is where I b-belong."

Disbelief filled his being as she timidly turned her head aside. He reached for her, but she was beyond his grasp. Irritation replaced his surprise. What was she talking about? Was she delirious? Did she expect him to accept that she seriously thought that she "belonged" in the cold and rain?

"Addy, come here. Please." Whatever she thought, he had to get her out from under there.

His heart lodged in his throat when her eyes once again found his. They brimmed with unshed tears and . . . Was it *fear?*

"Surely you're not afraid of me. I won't hurt you. I'd never hurt you. Come inside the wagon with me and get warm. You'll catch your death if you stay out here."

Addy weighed his words. She knew he was right. She should get warm. Her joints ached and she was so stiff and cold she could hardly move. And, darn him, he wouldn't hold still. Every time she thought she had him in focus, his form blurred to one side or the other.

No, she wasn't afraid of him. It was her reaction to him that seemed to terrify her. She held a trembling hand to her head, then inched toward him. All the while, a little voice nagged, "You mustn't. It wouldn't be seemly." But the chill was unbearable, and she went despite her misgivings.

Almost to the end of the wagon, she faltered, but discovered her hand was already enveloped by his warm fingers. She shyly lowered her eyes as he helped her out, then inside.

Sitting prim and straight-backed on the nearest box, she watched warily as he knelt on the pallet. She flinched when his hard, blue eyes froze her with an intense glare. She didn't think it was possible that she could get any colder, but she did.

"All right, young lady. I want an explanation."

"Wh-what?" Her big brown eyes grew even larger.

He sounded just like her father used to.

"You heard me. I want to know what you were doin' under the wagon in this storm. I didn't think even a . . . tenderfoot . . . would be that stupid."

And it was true. He'd given her more credit than that. Just what had she been up to down there? Maybe *spying* on him? He shook his head. No, he was being unreasonable. Adeline would never . . .

She interrupted his thoughts, her face flushed and eyes bright with anger. It had taken a while for his words to sink in.

"Stupid? Me? You think I'm an ignorant tenderfoot? Well, I'll have you know, I thought I was being kind and thoughtful to someone who desperately needed my help. If I'd known what an ungrateful beast you really were, I'd have let *you* sleep on the hard ground instead of giving you my bed."

She was so mad she literally couldn't see straight. The ogre's form was blurring again—Why couldn't he stay still long enough for her to at least finish reprimanding him?

The tiny space seemed to swirl about her. Suddenly, she found herself being swooped up into a pair of iron-hard, comforting arms. Her first instinct was to struggle, but it was so nice and warm there, cuddled close to his body.

Just for a minute, she thought. She would let him hold her just long enough to stop her shivering.

Then his low voice rumbled in her ear and her heart fluttered as if a million tiny butterflies were all trying to hide there at once. "What do you mean *your* bed?"

A memory suddenly struck Trace. She'd been underneath the wagon another time. The night he'd heard her humming.

Damn! The truth hit him like a kick to the teeth. He didn't know what to say. All this time he had assumed she was comfortable in the Wilkins' fancy carriage, or even . . . Hell, he'd never really thought

126

about where she stayed at all.

But he sure hadn't figured the prim little Easterner to be sleeping on the ground, all alone, under a dirty wagon. He'd never seen her do a thing to help around the camp, other than hitch and drive her own team. Why, Scratch, or the Wilkins', saw to it that she ate well.

He felt like a cad. He should have at least had an inkling, when she came into the wagon to change clothes, that the space was hers. She just didn't seem the type to . . .

He nearly bit his tongue when she snuggled into him. She was so cold and wet that his own clothes were quickly soaked through, along with a portion of the bed.

Quickly, he moved farther into the wagon and away from the pallet. He stood her on her feet, held onto her shoulders, and shook her a little to gain her full attention.

"Listen to me, honey. You've got to get out of those wet things. Think you can do it?"

She looked toward her trunk. It was only a few feet away. The problem was, her legs felt limp as a wet straw hat. She knew that if she let go of Trace, she would wilt right to the floor.

But she rubbed the tip of her nose and took an unsteady step away, saying, "Sh-sure. Uh, but . . . What was it I was going to do?"

Trace's lips quirked. "Here. Let me help. I'll undo your dress."

Trace approached her, but halted when he found that the buttons ran the length of the *front* of her dress, not the back.

Knowing only that she had to get out of her wet clothes, Addy waited for his help. She knew *she* couldn't complete the chore. Her fingers were numb with cold, and her vision was unsteady.

Trace gulped and reached out with trembling fingers. His brow furrowed. It was the first time he had ever been hesitant to help a woman out of her clothes.

"Hell!"

"What?"

"Nothing, damn it!"

She swayed toward him. The backs of his fingers brushed the cool flesh above her chemise. His hand jerked from the contact. He began at the top, and continued down the length of her bodice.

Once, he felt the fullness of her breasts when she took a deep breath. His gut knotted. He leaned forward and smelled the scent of fresh wildflowers, even more fragrant than usual, coming from her damp locks.

Without another thought, his instincts took over. He ran a hand around the nape of her neck, burying his fingers in her thick tresses, soft and luxurious as strands of silk.

She felt so good, smelled so good, tasted so good. A fact he discovered when he tentatively ran his lips across her cheek.

He pushed the dress from her shoulders, following its descent with his palms, caressing her chilled flesh.

Addy sighed. A warmth built inside her body, beginning at the center and spiraling throughout her limbs, encompassing each and every nerve, until she tingled from head to toe.

Outside, a long, low rumble ended with a loud crack of thunder and a sharp burst of lightning. She launched herself at Trace, knowing that she trusted him to protect her.

Already unsteady, Trace stumbled backward, catching his heel on the wagon's loose board.

With Adeline's arms wrapped tightly about him, strangling him almost, there was no way for him to keep his balance. He tumbled with her onto the pallet, twisting to cushion her fall with his own body.

"Ooooff!" Before he could take another breath, his mouth filled with dark strands of hair.

At first he sputtered and fought to free himself, feeling hemmed in, trapped. Then he smelled her fresh scent and felt her breasts and thighs mold against his chest and legs, heard her gasps of fright and held her shivering form in the tenderest of embraces.

"Sh-h-h. It's all right, honey." He sheltered her head on his shoulder, turning her eyes into the crook of his neck.

"I won't let anything happen to you. I promise."

She could vaguely recall having been very cold. But everywhere he touched her, she felt heat. Her hands were around his waist, and her palms burned. She didn't realize that her fingernails dug into his naked flesh until he groaned.

"I-I'm sorry."

Somehow, the tail of his shirt had ridden up. She liked the feel of satin-coated steel.

The tip of her tongue darted across her lips. There was a slight taste of salt on them from burying her face against his neck.

She felt the steady thump of his heart beneath her breast. Blood sang through her veins, chasing away whatever chill she had felt. It was hard for her to breathe. A languorous sensation invaded her being.

She tried to listen to the voice within her that said that this shouldn't be happening. Her Puritan up-bringing had censured the activity she was even now engaged in. But it was as if she were a moth, and Trace a candle's flame.

When he looked at her with those blue eyes, and his lips curved into a rakish grin, she couldn't remember what it was she shouldn't be doing.

Thunder crashed. Lightning struck near the wagon. She whimpered and pressed closer to him, as if trying to crawl into his very soul.

Trace was lost in the idea of her clinging to him, nestling her curves against him, until he felt her broken nails cut into his tender hide. "Hey, calm down. It's just a little storm," he said gently.

Hysteria bubbled in her voice as she spoke into his

chest. "We're going to die!" She shuddered.

"Where'd you get an idea like that? We're warm. We're dry. All we have to do is stay right here and we'll be perfectly safe."

Tears pooled on his chest from Addy's glistening eyes. He rubbed his hands up and down her back, soothing, cajoling.

"Honest, Adeline, nothin' is goin' to happen to us."

Her hands curled into fists, pinching some of his skin in the process, but she was oblivious to anyone's pain but her own.

"You don't know that for sure. You can't. No one does." Her eyes closed so tightly they hurt, but it hurt Addy more to remember.

Trace was torn. Though he was extremely curious, he decided against pressing her further. She was too upset. Besides, there would be ample time to find out all he needed to know about Miss Montclair before he left the train.

The storm seemed to have no intention of abating, but Addy found herself relaxing a little. There was something about Trace Randall that gave her a safe, secure feeling, like the proverbial "port in the storm."

Her body gradually stopped trembling. Her eyes opened. She lifted her head and looked at him. He stared back. She trembled. The depth and intensity of his gaze was something she well remembered from the first moment their eyes had locked back in Independence.

"Are you still cold, honey?" Trace asked softly.

"N-no." Oh, the way he said "honey"; it drifted over her like a soft caress.

"Then why did you shiver?"

"Uh . . . I was th-thinking."

"About the storm?"

She nodded. That was as good an explanation as any, and as close to the truth. There was *another* storm building at the moment, but it had nothing whatsoever to do with the tempest raging outside the wagon.

"It's just about over."

She licked her lips nervously. "Are you sure?"

His hands stroked her back. She could feel his calluses through the thin material of her chemise. Chemise? Her eyes widened as she suddenly stiffened.

A deep blush suffused her entire body when she remembered he'd been helping her from her soaked dress. It seemed she should be much more horrified from the recollection than she actually was. The sensations his hands evoked were immeasurably pleasurable . . .

His voice rumbled like the thunder over the plains when he finally answered her question. "No, I'm not certain at all."

She blinked and stared dreamily at his lips. "Wh-what?"

He lowered his head and rubbed his nose to hers. "I said, the storm may never end."

"Oh." She snuggled her cheek to his, marveling at the softness of his skin beneath the coarse stubble of his beard.

His hands massaged her shoulders, then cupped the back of her neck. She raised her head to meet his. Excitement tensed her body. He was going to kiss her, and she could hardly wait.

But his lips, when they brushed teasingly against her mouth, his moustache tickling her, enticing her, formed words rather than the awaited kiss. "Relax. You're so stiff a little gust of wind could break you in two."

She sniffed. Didn't the man have sense enough to see what he was doing to her? Didn't he realize that if he didn't shut up and kiss her soon, she would explode into a million tiny pieces the wind could scatter forever? *Break?* She'd show him break.

Suddenly, she pressed her lips to his. Then, startled by her own behavior, she tried to pull back. But it was too late. Trace held her in a firm grasp as their mouths meshed. Her chest expanded near to bursting

131

at the sensual wanderings of his tongue as it teased her lips and traced her teeth before delving deep inside to tantalize the inner recesses.

He rolled over so swiftly that she had no time to protest. All at once, she was on her back, pinned to the pallet by his heavier body.

He chuckled and nibbled at her neck. "That'll teach you, woman. How would you like it if I had you at my mercy and tickled you until. . . ?"

His throat constricted so that he couldn't finish. His face froze at the look she unknowingly gave him. A look that said the idea sounded exceedingly appealing.

This time when his lips took hers, they were hard and demanding. She responded greedily to the heat of the embrace. Astounding feelings rioted through her. She'd never had any idea a person could experience such a varied range of emotions from just kissing someone.

Then she was taken to another level of awareness when his hands touched her — everywhere.

As his palms grazed her breasts, a delicious tingle coursed through her body to settle in the pit of her stomach. An unfamiliar, yet most pleasurable ache began to build in the feminine core between her thighs.

Buttons were undone and pettitcoats pulled aside. Soon, bare flesh met bare flesh — neither of them would have been able to recall just how or when they undressed.

Addy sighed and squirmed her lower body, which brought a muffled groan from Trace. He squeezed his knees between her legs and nestled himself comfortably between them. Though she was a tiny woman, he'd never had anyone fit him so perfectly.

At that moment of intimate contact, she experienced a jolt of trepidation. This was not at all the way she had pictured her first time making love. Of course, her thoughts on the matter were all jumbled and confused, as she had never really heard that much about it from any of her friends. And no wonder! Who could describe something like *this?*

Then he kissed her eyes and her nose and lingered over the lobe of one ear. When his lips trailed down her neck and he licked the throbbing pulse at the base of her throat, she forgot to think at all.

She responded — with a passion that both surprised and pleased Trace. He'd had a feeling a fire was there, buried beneath the trappings of prim and proper Bostonian society.

Yet he'd never imagined such ardor underneath that innocence. It filled him with wonder, and a sense of great tenderness. He held a treasure, and felt responsible for its care and safety.

He slowly took the nipple of one breast in his mouth, suckling gently, laving the tip with his tongue. The other nipple then received the same careful adoration while his hand traced the curve of her hip and one long, exquisite leg.

It seemed he paid homage to a goddess, and it was a rare feeling. Sure, he'd had a lot of women, and though one or two had been special, he wasn't the type of man to lay with any woman just to satisfy his own needs. From the time he'd been a young man, a boy, really, he'd prided himself on assuring that the woman enjoyed satisfaction, too.

But this was different. Adeline was different. *He* was different. And he was utterly baffled.

They came together as a blinding flash illuminated the heavens. Addy wasn't sure whether the white light she saw was a bolt of lightning or her own explosion of ecstasy. Whatever the explanation, neither was frightening anymore.

Oh, there had been a little pain, but it was quickly forgotten amid the agonizingly powerful, wonderful sensations taking hold of her body. And afterward, it was hard to describe the way she felt. Rapturous. Excited. Overwhelmed.

Trace's body partially covered hers, though he held most of his weight with his elbows propped on either

133

side of her. The look in his eyes caused her to blush, though she was certain her body couldn't become any warmer, or more flushed.

She couldn't refrain from shyly asking, "Why are you looking at me like that? I-Is it. . . ? Did I d-do something . . . wrong?"

His white teeth flashed simultaneously with the lightning. Her heart tumbled over itself at his roguish appearance. Several strands of blond hair fell across his forehead and over one eye. But she didn't touch it. She waited.

After what seemed an interminable period, he finally said, "Wrong? Honey, I can't imagine anything more right."

Her breath rushed past her teeth. She hadn't realized she'd been holding it. She reached out to embrace him and her fingers brushed his ribs. He moaned and shifted his body. A giddy feeling enveloped her senses. Why, he was ticklish. The big, virile soldier was ticklish. Somehow, having that secret bit of knowledge, that little part of him that few people would ever know, left her absolutely delighted.

Then her chest expanded. Everything was all right.

So why did he continue to stare? His expression seemed one of amazement. Or was it skeptical? Even fearful?

Chapter Nine

Addy *had* seen fear in Trace's eyes. He was scared—no, terrified—of what he was feeling.

It had been a long time since he'd allowed himself to get so close to another human being, and he was afraid—for himself—for her.

His way of life did not invite the possibility of settling down and taking responsibility for a wife and family. And it was a way of life he had purposely chosen—he was quite content with things as they were.

His mission was a dangerous one. He might, or might *not*, make it out alive. Others had taken the challenge and had died for their trouble. Why should he expect it would be any different for him?

It was the danger and excitement that gave him purpose, after all. He wasn't afraid to die. Because he had been spared once didn't mean he would be so fortunate the next time.

He grinned. Damn, but he loved his work.

Then he scowled. What had gotten into him, to make love to a tenderfooted virgin? What would happen when she went running back to her cousin? The whole caravan would be after his neck, or another part of his anatomy that was very near and dear to him.

Whatever happened, he deserved it. The inability to control his lust was his own fault, no one else's.

But it had been one hell of an interesting night. She was worth every bit of punishment coming to him, and maybe even more.

Addy lay perfectly still, snuggled in the cocoon of Trace's arms. She was afraid to move, lest she break the fragile spell of contentment enveloping her and, she hoped, Trace.

She was still in awe of what had just transpired. It was incredible. *He* was incredible.

Only one thing bothered her. She had enjoyed it immensely *but,* from everything she had heard, a woman *never* enjoyed—*it.* Or wasn't supposed to. It was something a husband had a right, or obligation, to perform. A wife endured . . .

The hair on the back of her neck stood on end. The blood drained from her face. Husband? Wife? Dear Lord, what had she gone and done?

She'd just given away the most precious gift a woman could take to her marriage bed.

Her thoughts turned guiltily to Timothy Sharpe and his almost desperate wedding proposal. Even *he* would not want to marry her now. Not that that bothered her in the least.

But the idea òf *no* man ever wanting her was a little more disconcerting. And as the wiry hair on Trace's chest curled provocatively around her fingers, her eyes misted. Now that she'd proven to be a woman of . . . loose morals, he would surely turn his back on her, too.

Her stomach knotted and twisted until she felt she might be sick. Trace. He was something she had never thought to find in her life. A soldier. An adventurer. The most handsome man ever.

He did not even belong in the same category as Timothy Sharpe! Somehow, she couldn't imagine that man making her feel the way Trace just had. Why, Timothy's hands were cold, his every action precise and calculating.

She wrinkled her nose, unwilling to remove her

hands from Trace's warmth long enough to scratch an itch. She sighed and scooted farther beneath the blanket Trace had pitched over them a little earlier.

There had been nothing cold or calculating about their lovemaking. Her body continued to throb and flush with heat every time she thought about the way his hands stroked and kneaded her flesh, how his lips adored . . . She shuddered at the memories.

"Are you cold, honey?" His words were whispered drowsily as he rubbed his chin in the hair atop her head.

Her throat was dry and she had a hard time finding her voice, but finally managed a "N-no, not cold."

His arms tightened their hold. "Are you still frightened, then?"

"No."

He shifted, brushing his chest lightly against hers. She gasped when the curly hairs teased her taut nipples.

"I didn't hurt you, did I?"

"O-oh-h, no-o-o."

He chuckled. "Then what's the matter?"

"I-I . . ." Her teeth clicked when she snapped her jaw closed. What could she say? That she had liked the things he did to her body so much she wanted more—much, much more? Or that she wondered how long it would take for him to shove her away and tell her he never wanted another thing to do with such a . . . fallen woman . . . like *her* again?

Instead, she gulped, and lied. "Maybe I did feel a little chill."

The wind howled and shook the heavy canvas. She buried her face in his shoulder. "Will the stupid storm never end?"

Innocently, he said, "You'll have to ask Scratch. He's the expert on the weather around here."

Her face flushed so hot she covered her cheeks

with her hands. Scratch! Oh, dear. She'd forgotten about him. He was the only person on the caravan whose respect meant anything to her. He'd done so much to help her. She'd tried so hard to learn, to please him.

What would he think when he found out? What would he say?

She struggled to sit up and started to throw back the cover. Trace's arms snaked around her waist. He nuzzled his face into her side, kissing, licking, tickling her ribs. She subsided in her effort to escape long enough to throw back her head and squirm closer.

"Where were you goin'?"

His breath teased her sensitive skin and she had to concentrate to remember what she had been doing, and why.

"I-I have to get dressed. Someone might come by, or . . . see . . . or . . ."

He released her to lie on his side, one arm bent, his head propped on his hand. A frown marred his face, which he quickly erased before she turned to look at him. His voice was calm and somewhat placating. "You can't go out there now. At least wait until it quits raining."

There was a bright sheen to her eyes as she searched the bedding for her clothes. "No, I can't wait. I've got to leave. Now!"

"Why?"

Incredulously, she snapped. "Wh-why? You know why. I . . . we . . . I shouldn't be here. You shouldn't . . . Together . . . We shouldn't . . . Oh-h, you know what I mean."

She shook her head and grabbed her nearest shoe. The leather was wet and stiff with mud.

Tears of frustration threatened, but she steadfastly kept them at bay. The last thing she wanted to do was cry in front of Trace. It would put her at too

138

great a disadvantage.

Damn! Trace shrugged his shoulders. He'd known this would happen, as sure as he knew the train wouldn't make six miles tomorrow after this storm. Women were so predictable.

"Listen, honey, I know what you're thinkin', but . . ."

She tried to pull her dress on over her head, but couldn't find the arms. Her voice was muffled beneath the heavy material. "How can you know what I think; what I feel? What do you care?"

Suddenly, she felt herself being yanked back on the pallet. Trace's hand fumbled under the skirt of her dress and he threw it over her head so he could look directly into her eyes.

"That's typical of a virgin. Five minutes after the most beautiful experience of a lifetime, and she has to *think*. No matter how gentle or nice a man treats her, we're all brutes who don't know how to *feel,* or *care.*"

Addy sneezed and rubbed her nose. Just how many virgins had the man known, anyway? "So . . . Do you, then?"

He cleared his throat. "Uhm, do I what?"

"Do you care?"

"Well, uh . . ."

Panting, unable to hide her insecurity, she frantically jerked her dress down, the sleeves remaining lost somewhere amid the voluminous folds of material.

"See? What did I tell you? You have no feelings."

He handed her the pantalets that were in a wad, turned inside out.

She blushed and hurriedly stuffed them in a pocket, which she'd mistakenly taken for an armhole.

He stammered, "Of course I-I . . . have feelings and . . . er, care. I care about all my . . ." Oops! He didn't dare finish that line of conversation. She'd slit

139

his throat before morning.

But she knew. She'd already thought it. "Well, thank you very much. I'm relieved to know that you rate me right up there with the rest of your . . . your . . ."

His eyes narrowed to slits. "Whores?"

She swallowed hard, finally stuffing her arms into the newly found sleeves. Her voice was a bare whisper. "That's the word I was looking for, yes."

His fingers bit into her chin. His eyes pounced on hers. "You are *not* a whore, Adeline Montclair, and I don't want to ever hear you say such nonsense again. Understand?"

He squeezed until she winced and nodded.

"That's more like it. You're a fine, passionate woman. There's nothin' wrong with what we did."

Though her head nodded the appropriate response, her heart was devastated. Looking into his blue eyes, she could believe for a moment that she meant more to him than perhaps any woman he'd ever been with — and the thought unsettled her.

There were so many things yet to do. Most importantly, to prove to herself that she had the courage, or in Scratch's words, the gumption, to actually survive this stupid trek to Santa Fe and see to it that her father's business flourished.

Her shoulders rose and fell with a deep sigh as she laughed at herself. Here she was, thinking of reasons why she couldn't get involved with Trace Randall, and he had yet to make the slightest suggestion that she do so. Why, if he knew what she had the nerve to imagine, he'd run so far, so fast . . .

Trace's lips captured hers before she emerged from her own thought. All of a sudden, her heart took over and her emotions ruled her reactions. He made her feel so good, like she deserved the warmth and love he dispensed so freely.

How she wished the feeling could last a lifetime,

but she refused to deceive herself. She knew better.

Trace cursed and grumbled to himself as he slogged wearily through the ankle-deep mud the next morning. His initial prediction of six miles was proving optimistic.

They'd already hitched two teams to each wagon, and three to the heavier ones. He scratched his chin. It was funny how heavy some of the lighter-looking wagons were turning out to be.

His eyes searched the heavens. Clouds hung heavy in the dismal sky. Travel would not improve soon.

Thinking of unpleasant things reminded him of the morning's near disaster with Adeline and Scratch. It had been a close call. If Addy hadn't absolutely insisted on dressing, despite his protests otherwise . . .

A grin split his face and his eyes danced merrily. Oh, she'd had to think fast when Scratch pulled back the canvas at daybreak to find the two of them kneeling on the pallet, her palms still on his chest as she gasped for breath after a long, long, exceedingly sensual kiss.

They were just lucky Scratch hadn't arrived two seconds earlier. He chuckled, and sincerely doubted the old man believed she'd only been checking his heartbeat—to make sure he was breathing all right.

Scratch had chawed his cud for a minute, spat, and replied, "Hell, gal, all ya had to do was ask 'im."

Adeline exited the wagon faster than a cat with its tail on fire, her face redder than any flame he'd ever seen.

Another chuckle rumbled from deep in his throat. And the worst part of it all, his own face had felt just as hot. He couldn't remember the last time he had ever been so embarrassed.

He felt badly for Adeline. She was already consumed by doubts and confusion because of their

141

night together, and the incident with Scratch had only made things more difficult. And he *cared* that she had left before he could reassure her.

He shook his head. Reassure her of what? That he'd at least take the time to stop by and say goodbye when he left, or what? If he wasn't careful, he'd be getting himself all involved. Might even want to hang around and look after the woman, the kind of stuff a man would do if he was thinking of *settling down*.

A shudder shook his otherwise solid frame. Hell, he couldn't afford to let something like *that* happen. She was only a woman, after all.

His eyes automatically sought her out. His brow arched, and a quickening tension gripped his stomach. Even from the back, she was something extraordinary to behold.

Perched atop a large boulder, Addy could look to the east and nearly see the line of trees where they had camped last night. It was noon, and they'd only made three miles. The men and animals were exhausted from the back-breaking labor of trying to roll the weighty wagons through the thick mire.

And if the men were tired, she was doubly so, for she had walked and cracked her whip and shouted at the teams every bit as far and as hard as they.

If it were up to her, they'd stay the night where they were, on higher ground, so if it rained again, the wagons wouldn't bog down before they could get started, like the situation they had faced this morning.

She raised her arm and wiped her forehead on her sleeve. At least the sun was out now, and had been for the last half hour. Though it wouldn't immediately change the conditions, at least it brightened the outlook and would maybe lift everyone's spirits.

Suddenly she was gripped by an odd presentiment.

142

She turned her head and there behind her, in a depression in the rock, lay a huge snake, apparently soaking up the sun the same as she.

Her mouth instinctively opened but her throat was too constricted to emit a sound. She clutched her hands to her chest. A myriad of options flooded through her brain: *Jump! Run! Yell for help!*

But she recalled Trace's reprimand after her last encounter with a reptile. His words echoed in a small cavity of her mind . . . *Harmless snake. Your fear puts the caravan in danger. You shouldn't be here . . .*

Her rapidly pounding heart gradually returned to normal. She blinked. Her eyes hurt since she'd been staring so hard at the unmoving, unthreatening mound of coils.

She took a deep breath and relaxed, though she did scoot slowly forward on the rock. She told herself over and over that there was nothing to be afraid of, that she wasn't scared, but there was no need to sit in the fellow's lap, either.

A deep sigh escaped her purple lips. She mentally patted herself on the back. Calming her fear so handily was quite an accomplishment, she thought, and she was proud of herself.

When she happened to glance up and see Trace approaching, her chest swelled with pride. Just wait until he saw. He'd be pleased with her, too. She *knew* he would.

But her eyes narrowed with concern when Trace paused and looked at her, his eyes widening with alarm. That wasn't at all the look she had expected him to give her.

She sighed with disgust. What *had* she expected, anyway? Who could understand the temperamental nature of a man?

Then, of all things, he drew a gun and pointed it at her. Her eyes bugged out and her mouth gaped open. She heard the whine of the bullet as it whizzed

143

past and flinched when a fine spray of shattered granite pelted her derriere. The lead ball had struck only a few inches from where she reclined.

Outraged, she lunged from the boulder and flew at him before he had a chance to improve his aim. "You simple-minded chowderhead! What's gotten into you? If you wanted me dead, why didn't you just leave me under the wagon last night?"

Her fists pounded against his chest, but she did have sense enough to lower her voice as she mentioned the incident of the previous evening. She was fighting mad, but she wasn't stupid.

Trace reholstered the gun Scratch had scrounged up for him that morning. His fingers cut into her arms as he set her back. "Listen, you little idiot. I never intended you any harm. Believe me, if I'd aimed at you, you wouldn't be alive to make a fool of yourself in front of all these men."

Addy's gaze shot around her. Sure enough, most of the drivers had gathered a ways off and they were all laughing and snickering. Her cousin Delilah stared at her from a distance.

She jerked from his grasp, blushed profusely and whispered, "Don't try to get out of this because we've got an audience. You shot at me! Don't you dare lie about it."

Trace's patience, what there was of it, snapped. His arm shot out in a flash and his fingers curled around her wrist in an iron-hard grip she couldn't break, no matter how hard she fought.

Hoots and catcalls accompanied them as he dragged her back to the boulder.

"That-a-way, stranger."

"Show the filly who's boss."

"Don't take no sass from 'er, fella. Knock 'er 'round some. That shapes 'em up in a hurry."

Addy dug in her heels, but all the good it did was to make two deep furrows in the soggy earth. Finally,

144

he yanked her forward and pointed with his free hand.

"There! That's what I shot at, woman. The snake. Not you."

Her face drained of color when she saw the headless reptile. How had he done that? She gaped at him, awed, stunned by his skill with a weapon. Confusion was all that surfaced when she said, "That's very impressive Mr. Randall, but why the theatrics? What's the big deal over shooting a little ole snake?"

She proudly straightened her back and looked him in the eye. It was important that he knew she wasn't afraid of the . . . Her eyes strayed. *Ugh!* She wrinkled her nose and quickly glanced away from the grizzly sight. A little bullet was capable of wreaking a lot of havoc, even on as large a snake as that one had been.

Trace looked into the sky and raised his hands in supplication. What had he done to get saddled with such an ignorant tenderfoot?

"Don't you know anythin'? That was a rattler. That 'little ole snake' could have killed you!"

Her vision clouded. A shiver ran down her spine, causing her legs to tremble. Her lips quivered as her softly spoken, "Oh," was carried toward him on the gusting breeze.

"Oh. Oh? Is that all you have to say?"

Tears threatened, but she forced them away. She'd be *damned* if she'd let the overbearing oaf see how his words crushed her.

She took a deep breath before scolding, "You act like I'm supposed to know the difference between all these snakes, then say I'm a fool because I don't. Who made you God out here, Mr. Randall? Haven't you ever made a mistake? Didn't you have to *learn* anything when you came to the wilderness? Or did you sprout from the womb already knowing it all?"

This time when the spectators laughed, she sensed

145

a turnabout. They weren't making fun of her. In fact, some of the chuckles resembled nervous giggles, as if maybe they were thinking of their own foolhardiness when they made their first trek into unknown territory.

Trace had the discretion to look away, at anything but Addy's flashing eyes. She was something to behold, she was; with her shoulders thrown back, her loose hair waving in the wind.

His gut tightened and his loins quickened. Damn, but he was proud of her. And the feisty bit of fluff was right. In a sense, he guessed, this misunderstanding was . . . probably . . . his fault. If he hadn't shamed her over the gopher snake, she, more than likely, wouldn't have taken such a risk around the more deadly rattler.

She could so easily have been killed. The thought had frightened him so badly that he shot first, without warning, and then shouted at her. Well, the damage was done. Somehow, he'd have to get back into her good graces.

His grimacing lips lifted into a sheepish grin. He included the rest of the drivers as he shrugged his shoulders and said, "Boys, when the lady's right, she's right."

There were a few assenting nods and several grumbling murmurs before the weary men decided the fun was over and gradually dispersed.

Delilah stepped from behind two burly fellows and daintily picked her way over the sticky ground to stand beside Addy.

"What was that all about, dahlin'? I thought I heard someone say that you'd nearly been killed. And I heard shootin'."

Trace allowed that one woman was trouble, two were more than any sane man dared face alone. He stuffed his hands in the back pockets of his trousers and inconspicuously sauntered down the hill, relieved to make his departure before suffering another dis-agreement with Addy.

Though Addy heard her cousin, her eyes kept straying to Trace's retreating form. The anger she had felt dissolved as suddenly as it had arisen. He had saved her life.

A shudder rippled down her body and she sagged against the big rock. She inhaled a long, calming breath before concentrating on Delilah.

"I'm fine, Lily, but it was a close call."

Delilah's eyes narrowed as she frowned. "My God, dahlin', what happened?"

Addy retold the experience as the two women started back to the wagons. There was an odd light in Delilah's eyes when she hesitated once and stared intently back toward the butchered reptile.

"Uh-oh. We better hurry, Lily. They're rehitching the teams already."

Delilah continued her haphazard steps, lifting the fine folds of her silk skirt to avoid messy puddles. Her voice was strained, even bitter, as she spoke. "Oh, Addy, sometimes I wish we hadn't come on this awful excursion. I'm so sick of bugs and sweat and mud and dirty clothes."

Addy knew exactly how she felt. Though she'd been angry at Delilah lately for practically ignoring, or more aptly, abandoning, her during most of the trip, she understood her cousin's frustrations. Both of them would have made poor companions if they *had* spent more time together.

She paused and stretched her aching shoulders. "I don't know, it's been hard, but it is an experience we'll remember for the rest of our lives."

Delilah snorted. "Oh, pooh. Sure, we'll tell the grandchildren all about our long, boring journey across barren prairies in the company of rude, filthy men."

She looked around the soggy countryside and at

147

the dirt-encrusted wagons, animals, and humans. "Sometimes it's almost more than I can bear. This isn't at all the way I thought it would be."

Addy nodded. "I know. From the tales I'd heard, I thought it would be so romantic and adventurous. Instead, it's been terribly hard labor and more dangerous than I had ever imagined."

"Dahlin', I'm so sorry about the way Jubal makes you work. But he swears it's the only way if you want any privacy. Personally, I don't see that it makes much difference, since you're stuck with that dreadful man. You weren't meant to be a nurse, or a teamster, either."

Addy shrugged. "It's nothing, really. I just should have come better prepared." She refused to comment concerning Trace. It would be like her to say or do something to arouse Delilah's curiosity. And though nothing like last night would ever happen again, she couldn't afford to take unnecessary chances.

Delilah glanced toward Addy and rolled her eyes as they heard the call to "Catch up!" Addy sighed with relief when Delilah quickened her pace, ending the opportunity for further conversation.

The entire caravan was exhausted by the time they made camp. Trace's prediction of six miles had been hard met, but they had done it.

Now, after a meager meal of cold jerky and equally cold and hard biscuits, as there had been no wood dry enough to burn, everyone was scattered about the wagon enclosure, some already asleep, some sitting on their bedrolls, their faces drawn, expressions blank.

As Delilah climbed into her carriage, she paused and waved good night to Addy. The tender gesture warmed Addy's soul. She'd been so lonely, even with Trace and Scratch's company. Delilah was the last

148

family she had left, and she didn't want to lose whatever measure of closeness they shared.

She swatted a mosquito, then stretched her hands over her head. She glanced warily toward the wagon. What would happen when she went in to gather her night things? Would Trace ask her to stay? Expect her to stay? Would he be angry when she told him no?

A familiar form moved from the shadows next to the wagon and blended with the night. If she hadn't been looking, she never would have seen him.

Questions muddled her mind as she watched his stealthy movements. He was headed for the creek.

The camp was quite a ways from the water, made purposely so to avoid the swarms of mosquitoes. It had helped, but the pesky insects managed to find *her* wherever she was.

Her eyes searched the darkness. What was Trace up to? Why was he moving so quietly and, as far as she could tell, undetected by the person who kept watch tonight?

Being naturally inquisitive, she couldn't stand her questions left unanswered. She walked to the wagon and snatched a blanket to use as a cover over her light dress and to give her some protection from the annoying bugs.

It took her longer to follow his weaving path unseen; she was afraid she'd lost him by the time she reached the woods. The night was dark because of the cloud cover, and once in the trees, the blackness was eerie.

She crept forward, stopped, and was about to turn around and go back, when she cocked her head to one side, listening intently.

Aha! There it was again. It sounded like muffled voices. Goose bumps rose on her skin, even though she was too warm beneath the wool blanket.

Following the sound, she moved deeper into the

149

trees. Mosquitoes whined in her ear, but she couldn't free her hands to wave them away. Finally, she paused long enough to cover her head, leaving enough of an opening to hear.

Moving as quietly as possible, she stopped suddenly when the voices came from just the other side of a thick tangle of bushes. She dropped to her knees, for her legs refused to support her. Fear clutched at her throat. What if she were found deliberately listening in to the obviously private conversation?

She had immediately recognized Trace's deep voice, but the stilted accent of the other man was unrecognizable. Closing her eyes, she took a deep breath, contemplating making her presence known before it was too late.

She'd only been curious as to why Trace was slipping around and acting suspiciously. She hadn't intended to eavesdrop. She rubbed the tip of her nose as she wondered what to do.

"Are you certain you were not followed, my brother?"

"Positive. I waited until the camp was bedded down. The man on watch was so tired he was dozing standing up. You know I would never risk your life."

"Yes, you are a good friend, for a white man."

Addy's brows raised in question when the two men laughed. White man? Risking lives? Brother? What on earth were they talking about? Who was the other man?

At least her decision had been made. If they were that worried over being seen together, it would be dangerous to show herself. She'd bide her time and confess her transgression to Trace later.

She gulped. He'd be amused that a mere *woman* had been able to follow him, wouldn't he?

"The young men are nervous. I think they are anticipating another shipment soon. Have you learned

150

anything new?"

Trace's voice was filled with disgust. "No, damn it! If it wasn't for my injuries and slow recuperation, I'd have been out searching days ago. The train I'm with is so small, and everyone so close-mouthed that I haven't even heard where the nearest whore is located."

Addy's face flamed. She heard what sounded like one man slapping the other on the back.

"You have nothing to worry about, my brother. Have you not one of unmatched beauty beneath your very nose?"

Addy frowned. Darn, but she wished she could make heads or tails of their strange conversation! And she wanted to see that odd-sounding man. Something about his voice was very intriguing.

She left the blanket covering her body and reached her arms between the bushes. The branches were thick, but thin and flimsy. It was not difficult to create an opening.

Cautiously, she peered into the small clearing.

Chapter Ten

Addy released the branches so impulsively, they snapped back in her face and she lost her balance. A cry of dismay escaped her lips before she could think to smother it.

An Indian! Trace was standing there, calmly talking to an *Indian*. A murderer. A butcher. Whatever had gotten into him? Had the man no sense?

The next thing she knew, her arm was taken in a hurtful grasp. She was lifted from the ground like a leaf in the wind. Even in the darkness she could see the fire in the Indian's dark eyes.

"Oh . . . my . . . God." She hung limply at the end of the savage's arm. Though she had to be only a little shorter than he, she dangled like a rag doll. The muscles on his arm bulged with tempered strength.

Her eyes felt as if they had sprung from their sockets. She swallowed convulsively. The sharp tip of a knife was barely restrained from cutting into her neck. She nearly swooned from fright.

Then Trace was there. His look of astonishment might have been comical under different circumstances. As it was, with her entire body trembling, she turned pleading eyes to him.

"No, Eagle Feather. There's no need for the knife. I'll handle her."

Hopefully, she turned her wild eyes to the Indian. Would he do as Trace said?

Eagle Feather scowled, but lowered the point of his blade an inch or so to where it at least didn't prick her skin. She took several short, shuddering breaths.

As soon as the Indian lowered her to her feet, she yanked free and ran to hide behind Trace. Her fingers dug into the soft folds of his shirt.

He didn't give her much time to gather her composure before he swung around to shout, "What in the hell are you doin' here?"

She gasped, cringing at the outrage in his voice. The man had just saved her life, but now advanced upon her like a raging demon. She didn't know who to be more afraid of, him or the Indian.

Her feet tangled in clumps of grass and short prickly shrubs as she backed away. Finally, she stopped and pointed a shaking hand toward the shadowy figure at his back, completely ignoring his words. "I-Indian! That's an Indian!"

Deep lines formed between Trace's eyes as he frowned and looked from Addy's horrified face to Eagle Feather's studiously blank features. It came as a relief to Trace to see his friend's relaxed stance. At least he hadn't seemed to take Addy's reaction to him as an affront—yet.

"Your woman is afraid of me." There was a hint of amusement in the Indian's voice.

Trace shrugged. "Sorry, Eagle Feather. I don't know what's gotten into her."

Addy gaped disbelievingly between the two men. It sounded as if Trace was apologizing for her. "You're sorry? You're talking to a savage, for heaven's sake."

Her eyes then turned to Eagle Feather, though they hardly seemed focused. She bordered on the edge of hysteria. "He murdered my parents, and very nearly killed Scratch. Let me go! I've got to get help. If you won't do something about him, someone else will."

The last was directed at Trace as she kicked at his shins and pummeled his chest because he dared to hold her back.

Eagle Feather's heavy dark brows knit into a frown as he studied the frenzied woman. He regarded her as one might a helpless sparrow gutted on the end of

153

a lance.

Suddenly, Addy's fear turned to indignant outrage. She stepped from behind Trace to glare at the scantily clad man.

Her blanket had fallen to the ground during the scuffle. Mosquitoes buzzed around her exposed flesh. She noticed with disdain that the Indian paid them no mind. Of course he wouldn't feel them, she thought, he was just a vicious, uncivilized animal.

With her back held straight, chin in the air, she stared up at the Indian. Actually, he was quite a magnificent sight.

His body was lean and powerful, thick of bone and muscle. He had a broad face, with an aquiline nose and thin lips. High cheekbones gave way to deep-set black eyes. His long black hair was divided down the middle and plaited into two heavy braids. A breechcloth and fringed moccasins were his only attire.

The one feature that kept drawing her attention was a pair of silver rings dancing from his ears. She'd never seen a man wearing earrings.

She winced when the savage laughed and nodded toward her.

"You have chosen wisely, my brother. Beneath the timid kitten lies a stubborn lioness."

It suddenly dawned on her that the Indian spoke perfect English—had spoken once before but she had disregarded it. She cocked her head to one side and regarded him with cautious intensity. How could that be? He was, after all, only an ignorant savage.

And then she realized that it was the second time he had called her Trace's "woman." All other thought was shoved to the back of her mind as she puffed out her chest to vehemently deny that charge, but Trace quickly beat her to it.

"Huh-uh. I did *not* choose the woman. I don't even know why she followed me."

Through the sudden pain Trace's words unexpectedly inflicted on her heart, Addy was certain she saw a sparkle in the fierce black eyes.

"Perhaps, then, if you have no interest in the woman, you would not object if I . . ."

"Wait just a dratted minute. This *woman* doesn't belong to Trace, or any other man. So, there!"

She stomped her tiny foot, though the defiant gesture was probably lost amid the folds of blanket that once again covered her. Startled, she guessed Trace must have put it back over her shoulders while she had been absorbed with the Indian.

She glared at the two men and turned to stalk from their odious presence with as much dignity and haste as possible without tripping and ending up flat on her face. It bolstered her confidence when she didn't hear laughter following in her wake.

Trace threw up his hands and watched her leave. A curious surge of pride enveloped his chest, so that he could hardly speak.

Eagle Feather placed a hand on his friend's shoulder and gently shoved him. "Go after her. There is much danger. We will meet again soon."

Trace glanced gratefully at Eagle Feather, nodded, and took off at a jog after the willful sprite. He caught up with her before she reached the edge of the woods and took hold of her arm, more to give her support and balance than to impede her progress.

He talked as they walked. "Listen, Eagle Feather is a good man. I hope you don't live to regret speakin' to him the way you did." Taking a deep breath of the night air, he continued, "You never answered my question. What were you doin' down there?"

She looked straight ahead, ashamed to admit that she had the nerve to actually follow him. Then her anger resurfaced as she recalled how he had taken pains to reassure the Indian, but not *her*.

Her feet tangled in the folds of the loose blanket when she swung to face him. Heat suffused her face. Drat the man! She would have fallen if he hadn't kept a firm grip on her arm.

But she refused to let any help she received from him interfere with her well-deserved tirade. "How dare you question *my* behavior when *you* were found consorting with a wild savage."

Suddenly, she stopped. Trace almost caused her to tumble to the ground when he kept walking, unprepared for her hesitation. Addy stared at him. A dawning light illuminated the flecks in her eyes until they glowed golden in the night.

Trace sucked in his breath at the sight.

"You! It was you, wasn't it? What did any of us ever do to you?"

The look in her eyes had the same impact on him as a kick in the gut would have. Thoroughly confused, he asked, "What in the hell are you babblin' about?"

"The attack. You led the Indians to us, didn't you?"

He reached out and took her shoulders in a forceful grip and shook her. "You little fool. How could you even think such a thing? Do you really believe I beat myself and then tied myself to those stakes? That's smart, Adeline, real smart."

He released her and stepped back, as if his hands had touched something diseased. She swallowed hard, and nearly choked, her throat was so dry. "Then, wh-why were you with that Indian?"

His face went stone cold, set itself in an unreadable mask. "I can't tell you that."

A stunned, sorrowful expression settled in her eyes and on her face. "Then I have no choice but to go to Jubal. He has a right to know that we all may be in grave danger."

He grabbed her so fast she lost her breath. His hand dug into the back of her neck so hard that she gasped with pain.

"You won't go to Jubal, understand? This will stay between the two of us. Do you hear?"

"And what will you do if I say no?" A lone tear trickled down her cheek.

Trace gulped when the moon, which had peeked from behind a large mountain of clouds, illuminated the sparkling droplet. His voice was husky when he replied, "I don't think you want to find out. Rest assured, if I suspect you've gone to Jubal, or your cousin, or anyone else, I'll see to it that you never tell another tale."

All resistance vacated Addy's body in the form of one giant sigh. She sagged and Trace caught her to him. He winced at the look of utter defeat on her beautiful, forlorn features. It tore him apart to think she believed he would hurt her.

His body stiffened. The truth was, he probably would. He would do anything necessary to protect Eagle Feather, or his own identity. He had to. There were too many lives at stake.

If he could only trust her enough to explain . . .

"Come on, we have to get back before someone misses us. I'm warning you . . ."

"That is not necessary, Mr. Randall. I understand perfectly." She removed the blanket from her shoulders and folded it over her arm. It felt as if she carried the combined weight of all the wagons on her back, so disillusioned was she.

Why? Why was he doing this to her? What was going on between Trace and that Indian? And why couldn't . . . wouldn't . . . he tell her anything? How could she help but believe that he was involved in nefarious dealings with the Indians?

She meekly followed along behind him, stepping carefully to return to camp as quietly as they had left. The camp's guard snored so loudly he woke himself up, and Trace and Addy had to stand perfectly still in the middle of an open, flat meadow, praying that the man wouldn't decide to take his job seriously at that particular time and scout the area.

They were lucky. Within a few minutes, soft snorts

157

and wheezes indicated he had fallen back to sleep.

Trace reached back to take her hand, and led her the rest of the way to the wagon. When she tried to pull away in order to crawl beneath the frame, he squeezed her fingers tightly. She looked at him with imploring eyes, but he only nodded toward the wagon's interior.

She gritted her teeth so hard her temples throbbed. Tossing the blanket in first, she tried to find a foothold, but was so unsteady she slipped.

Finally, Trace grimaced and put his hands around her waist. He was amazed again by how tiny she was when his fingertips nearly connected.

Upset with himself for letting her distract him from his anger over her foolish behavior, he almost threw her into the wagon. Before he could climb inside, she had turned, and he found himself face to face, nose to nose with a spitting she-devil.

"You crude beast! You have no right to force me to stay in here with you. And you could have hurt me just then." There was a whimper to her voice which fueled her anger more than a ton of wood could have.

Trace looked into her flashing green eyes, marveling over how their color changed dramatically with her mood swings. Actually, the only reason he had wanted her in the wagon was to talk.

He wanted to insist that they trade places. His wounds were sufficiently healed, and he'd recovered enough to let her have her bed. In all good conscience, he couldn't have kept the pallet even if he hadn't been feeling better.

Now, however, after her little outburst, she'd presented him with a challenge. He felt he had every right to keep her near, if only to make sure she didn't go running to Jubal with her news of his meeting with Eagle Feather.

Under different circumstances, he wouldn't have expected much trouble from the wagon master, but the business of the attack on the train was still a tender subject. He couldn't afford unnecessary trouble.

He thrust out his chin just as obstinately as Adeline and grinned wickedly. There was no other recourse.

"Don't try my patience, Adeline. You're goin' to sleep right here where I can keep an eye on you."

She blinked and leaned back. "Oh! I-I've never . . ."

His lips curled. "Oh, yes, you have."

She drew back her arm, but he had managed to lever himself inside to secure a strong enough hold to restrain her.

He growled, "That would be a stupid thing to do, honey. Never, ever, try to slap me again. I've never had to resort to thrashing a woman, but if you give me reason . . ."

She sniffed and flopped onto the pallet. "Yes, I'm sure you would, as you have certainly proven to be no gentleman."

A deep chuckle filled the enclosure and Addy shivered. It infuriated her that just looking at him, or hearing the vibrant tone of his voice, was almost enough to melt her anger.

And the closer he got, the more her stomach churned. What would he do to her? Would he take advantage of the fact that she would be sleeping in here . . . with him? Her lips tingled. Would he kiss her? Maybe even. . . ?

She took a deep breath and his fresh, manly scent overpowered the usual stale, musty odor of canvas and boxes. Her eyes drifted closed.

"Get out of that dress. You can't very well rest in those tight garments." Trace flinched. He hadn't intended to sound so gruff. It was just . . . well, the way her breasts filled out the clinging bodice when she breathed deeply. And that *look* that had suddenly come over her. The tight-fitting pants he wore were, all of a sudden, three sizes smaller than they had been.

God, how would he survive the night? He'd seen the stricken expression on her face when he'd ordered her to sleep in the wagon. If the idea of staying with him was that abhorrent, he'd be damned if he ever touched her again.

Then she turned those same huge eyes on him and looked away. Jesus, what had he done now?

Addy tore her eyes from his, wondering how, after all that had happened that evening, she could still want him. Everything she had learned while growing up told her it was wrong. But this wasn't Boston, and she wasn't the same young girl who had left there over a month ago. How she wished life was as simple now as it had been then.

Calmly, she went to her trunk and pulled out fresh night clothes. Then, clutching them to her breast as if they were a warrior's shield, she waded through the boxes to her tiny dressing, or undressing, space.

Once, she dared to peek over the smallest stack of crates and saw that Trace sat on the pallet looking outside. She frowned as she pulled the nightgown over her head. All of the courage she had mustered earlier in the evening seemed to have deserted her.

She had been ready to leave the safety of the boxes for a long time, but still she stood, unable to make her legs take that first step. So many emotions rioted through her that she couldn't determine which one held her stranded in place.

He had scared her tonight, yet she was irresistibly drawn to him. She couldn't make sense of what she felt. It was all so frustrating.

"C'mon, Adeline. You can't hide in there all night. You won't be in any shape to drive the wagon in the mornin' if you don't get some sleep."

She jumped when Trace called out to her. Slowly, timidly, she crawled around the boxes and stepped over to the edge of the pallet.

She rubbed the tip of her nose and looked uncertainly at the small space. Yes, two bodies could fit there, but her particular body was reluctant to place itself in such close proximity to his, especially tonight. He was getting too close, meant too much, and she was too susceptible to the lure of his hands. . . .

When he lay back and stretched full length, then patted the empty space next to him, she sighed and sank to her knees. She might as well get it over with.

She scooted in beside him, stiff, afraid of touching his body with hers. And then she felt oddly disappointed when, instead of reaching for her, he turned his back.

She waited—for minutes, hours, and still he didn't pull her to him, or kiss her, or *anything.*

Later, when she also turned on her side, a pool of tears formed beneath her head, dampening the loose tendrils of hair that served as her lonely pillow.

The next day Addy was in a dreadful frame of mind. She hadn't been able to sleep all night, wondering how Trace had slept so well, and why he hadn't taken her in his arms at least once during the long, long night.

She shook her head, trying to erase the images that popped up at the most inopportune times, of tantalizing kisses, tender caresses, naked limbs.

Suddenly, the mule nearest the wagon kicked at a horsefly. The tug on the reins drew her wandering attention. She wiped her sleeve across her brow. It was hot enough without the added heat of taunting memories.

So what was the matter with her? Why was he not interested in her now? Then it struck her. What she'd been afraid of all along. Once he had conquered the new challenge, his sights were set elsewhere. Well, she should be grateful. It was what she wanted, wasn't it?

161

She rubbed the tip of her nose. Evidently he'd already talked with the rest of the men. Hadn't he told the Indian he couldn't even locate the nearest . . . whore?

Oh, how could she have been so stupid? She'd known better than to ever become involved in the first place. But it had felt so right at the time. And every time she thought about it, she couldn't help but wonder if it would be that wonderful — again.

Though she knew it couldn't, shouldn't, happen a second time, why did that speculation cause her so much pain? Because, she told herself, she cared. No, her feelings ran much deeper than that.

But he was just a man that she seemed always to accidentally run into. She sighed. Yes, an accident. That was the course her life had taken since that first fateful day on the steamer. One misadventure after another.

The double team of mules surged through a deep rut, forcing the return of her concentration to keep the wagon rolling. It was a good thing. Thinking did nothing but get her in more trouble.

Once again, it seemed they had only traveled over the nearest ridge when they stopped for lunch. The oxen and mules were lathered and stood with heads hanging, sides heaving.

Addy unhitched her teams and dropped the wet harnesses beside the wagon. She looked at the mud and sweat-caked leather, and at her red, chapped hands. Even with the gloves, her hands took a beating. The harness needed a thorough cleaning, but she was loathe to tackle it now.

Maybe she'd wait until they stopped that night. Yes, she nodded to herself, later in the evening would be good. The activity would keep her busy and occupy her errant mind.

Her head bent with dejection as her stomach

grumbled. Darn the rain and mud! They hadn't been able to build a fire for the last two meals. Cold biscuits for lunch was not enough to take care of the hunger building deep inside her.

Soft whistling from the rear of the wagon caused her to flinch. And drat that man! He'd taken off his shirt earlier in the morning. She knew he had done it on purpose, to tantalize and tease her with the rippling play of his muscles beneath that gorgeous, golden tanned skin.

A blush heated her neck and face until she covered the warm red flesh with her cool palms. A fleeting grin tugged at the corners of her mouth when she recalled observing, on several occasions, that from the waist down, his flesh was baked red from the sun. Once, that part of his body must have been as white as her own. Again, heat suffused her body.

Then she shook her head. All of her daydreaming was getting her nowhere. Only the ache in her stomach grew more annoying, more demanding. Not even two biscuits and a quart of water were able to fill the void. Her fear was that it was caused from something much deeper than plain old hunger.

When she happened to look around, Trace stood not two feet away. She jumped, wondering if her musing had conjured him from out of nowhere.

He stared at her, his blue eyes boring into her with such penetrating intensity that she hugged her arms about her upper body in an unsuccessful effort to divert a shiver that vibrated clear to the tips of her toes.

His mouth split into a wide grin as if he knew exactly the effect he had on her and was inordinately pleased to see it. She frowned. He leaned closer. A fine sheen of perspiration glinted off his broad chest and shoulders.

She literally dragged her eyes away from his appealing form to stare at the mud-soaked laces on her ruined shoes.

"What's the matter, honey? It's a mite too hot to be cold, isn't it?"

His softly spoken words surrounded her like a passel of marauding Indians, yet settled over her as protectively as a newborn baby's blanket. He was so mouth-wateringly handsome, and she knew that he knew it, too.

Her eyes flashed brilliant green as she shot them toward his grinning face. "The weather's perfect, Mr. Randall. I was enjoying the scenery until you blocked the view. Don't you have anything to do?"

"Aw, Adeline, you wound me. I thought you were goin' to say you enjoyed lookin' at me."

Her heart thrummed madly. She prayed for the strength to govern her own emotions. Just the thought of never again looking upon his magnificent form made her physically ill. How sad her days would be without being constantly on guard for his caustic wit or teasing glances.

A lump formed in her throat, so large and unmanageable she nearly strangled as she tried to reply. She could not find her voice. She almost fainted when he bestowed upon her a wide, engaging smile.

He was so close now that his breath teased the short hair at the nape of her neck. "I was right, wasn't I?"

The flesh on her neck quivered as his finger absently untangled two soft tendrils of hair caught against her starched collar. As if he knew he wouldn't receive an answer to his question, he continued, "How do you stand to wear your clothes so stiff and tight on these hot, muggy days?" His lips whispered against her cheek and she gulped.

"Think how comfortable you would feel if you loosened a few buttons and let the breeze cool your . . . skin."

She cleared her throat. Putting a finger between her collar and throat, she tugged none too gently. "Ah . . . clothes. Tight. Yes. What was the question?"

His lips were only inches from hers. She tried to swallow. His eyes glittered, danced, teased.

"Hey! What the hell's goin' on here?" Jubal's voice sliced through the heavy afternoon air like a dull knife through thick meat.

Trace hissed a curse and leaned back against the wagon, intentionally stuffing his fists as deeply as possible into the snug pockets of his trousers. Damn Jubal Wilkins!

Addy closed her eyes. Her chest deflated as she sighed in resignation.

Today, though, Jubal's scowl didn't frighten her. Her voice did not quaver when she answered her cousin-in-law. "Hello, Jubal. What's wrong now?"

Chapter Eleven

Jubal clicked his tongue. "Wal, now, little lady, I didn't expect such from you." His beady eyes glittered with malice. "Here yore dear cousin was worried sick 'bout yore health, an' sent me to check on yore well-bein'."

He glowered at Trace, then leered at Addy. "Seems my Delilah has misplaced her fears. Yore bein' looked after right fine, eh? Like any common tramp. An' after we were good enough to take you in an' see to it . . ."

The hairs on the back of Trace's neck bristled. He straightened abruptly and cut short Jubal's attack. "Wagon boss or no, you have no right to talk that way to the *lady*." Trace pushed away from the wagon and started toward Jubal when Addy's light touch on his arm stayed him.

"Don't bother. He's goading you. Besides, he'll think what he wants to think."

When the rotund Jubal turned his eyes back to her, she could not stop herself from shuddering. She and Jubal did not like each other. And that fact concerned her. She'd never made an enemy before.

Her voice trembled slightly when she spoke because, deep down, she could not help but be intimidated by her cousin's husband. "You came by for a reason, I'm sure, but I doubt it was to see about my health."

Jubal tucked his thumbs into his vest pockets, rocking back on his heels as he stared down his nose at the quietly wary pair. "All right, if that's the way you want it. We're pullin' out in ten minutes. You'd best keep up better'n you did this mornin'."

Then he pointed to Trace. "An' you, you're lookin' fit enough to ride ahead an' scout aroun' for us. We're gettin' close to Council Grove, an' I don't want no unexpected surprises fore we get there."

Addy gasped. "But he can't. He's not . . ."

This time Trace silenced *her* with a gentle hand. "It's all right." He flexed his shoulders. His muscles were taut from his teasing assault on Adeline. "I could use the exercise." So low that Jubal couldn't possibly hear, he added, "You do certain . . . things . . . to a man, honey."

She swiftly turned her head, thankful that Jubal had moved on before he noticed her red face. That would be all she needed, for him to find confirmation of her relationship with Trace. If one could call their sidestepping and careful parrying a relationship.

It was hard to describe just how she felt about the aggravating man. He was a thorn in her side, yet her only friendly companion besides Scratch. A protector and confidant and, though she hated to even *think* it, a wonderful lover.

And that was one more reason she needed to keep her distance from Trace. He was too . . . dangerous. She couldn't trust her own behavior when she was near him.

She quickly turned to give Trace a piece of her mind about his public display of . . . well . . . whatever it was called. She had to gulp back her words. He stood at the opposite end of the wagon, grinning like the handsome devil he was. And then he sauntered off toward the nearby remuda, but not before he gave her an arrogant salute.

She tossed her head. Let him go. If he thought he'd get away that easily, he was seriously mistaken. Her eyebrows quirked in puzzlement. Trace Randall. He was an enigma she could not unravel. But she would, given the time and opportunity.

With a sway of her hips, she hurried to hitch her mules. Missouri mules she'd heard them called, but Pedro said they had originated in New Mexico and been taken back to Missouri by the early traders laden with riches and goods.

Her mouth twisted and she bit her lower lip to keep from swearing. The harness was tangled. It took forever to straighten it before she could finally stand the mules in the traces.

Then, for some unknown reason, the lead animals became contrary, pulling on the lines before she had the last team hitched. She stepped forward and reached toward one of the mule's noses, drawing her hand back quickly when he rolled his eyes and pranced his feet, jiggling the chains. The other animals shifted nervously.

"Oh, for pity's sake! I'm no more anxious to do this than you are. Now settle down! Jubal'll have all our hides if we don't hurry."

As was her habit of late, she climbed aboard the wagon to wield the reins. From the higher vantage point, she exerted more force and authority, especially when using the double teams. Then, after the mules were pulling well, all she had to do was jump to the ground and walk alongside, flicking the leather occasionally and offering words of encouragement to the straining beasts. The maneuver had worked well so far.

She braced her legs, took a deep breath and shouted, "Get up, mules." The thick leather cracked and snapped along the pairs of brown backs. The lead team surged forward, snorted and reared, causing the other mules to come to a quick halt.

Amid the jerking confusion, Addy hauled on the reins until the teams quieted and again stood steady. Exasperated, she pleaded, "Please, don't do this to me. Giddap!"

Each team awaited the command and lunged into motion, forcing the lead team into the harness. A

168

panicked bray rent the air. The animals raced forward. The wagon was yanked into motion, nearly sending Addy back through the canvas. She tottered precariously, trying to regain control of the mules at the same time.

There was a loud creaking sound, then a snap. She automatically wound her hands around the reins for a stronger grip. All at once, the wagon jolted to a stop. The teams lurched back, then raced free. She felt herself being pulled from the box. Her shins were brought up hard against the wagon as she somersaulted over the front end.

She never had an opportunity to right herself. The reins cut into her wrists. Unable to free herself, she was dragged through the thickening mud and brush and rocks on her belly. Tiny, sharp limbs and pieces of gravel tore at her flesh and ripped her clothes.

Her terrified screams only frightened the mules more as they surged into one tangled, milling mess. For a moment, uncertain, with no direction, they stopped. Then the explosion of a firearm started them running again.

She frantically fought to untwist her hands from the reins. It was as though they clung with a life of their own, like a snake coiling around a fragile branch. Just as she looked up to see the hind quarters of the mules bunch to run, and saw their heads jerk up, eyes white with fear, and felt the first tug on her wrist, a large shadow loomed over her.

She closed her eyes and felt every muscle in her already tensed body quiver. Was this what happened when you died? Did a black cloud settle over you, to wipe the horrendous event from sight and mind?

If so, she was grateful. She really didn't want to know the gruesome details of her fate. She waited for the end to come, eyes squeezed so tightly shut they ached, teeth clenched until the pain in her head overrode the pain that surged through her body.

The clatter of hooves faded into the distance. She

lay stretched along the steaming ground. Tentatively, she dared to peek through one slitted lid.

"God! Thank God! Adeline, honey, I thought I was too late!"

The urgency in Trace's voice sent her heart into wild gyrations. She groaned when he lifted her carefully and turned her onto her back.

"Damn it, honey! Speak to me! Can you hear me? How badly are you hurt? Scratch! Scratch, where are you? Help me!"

A floating sensation possessed her. She was aware enough, however, to know she'd never seen Trace so flustered and agitated.

Couldn't he see she was dying? Soon, all would be peaceful. He wouldn't need to worry anymore.

She didn't die. But soon wished she had. The aching, stinging pain from hundreds of cuts and abrasions gradually replaced her fleeting sense of well-being.

Even a soft tug in the area of her skirt hurt. Her head throbbed when it was lowered to rest on something softer than the caked earth. Her eyes stung when tears pooled at their corners, and her cheeks burned when one salty droplet streaked a narrow path across her face.

The vibrating thunder of approaching hooves caused her to flinch. The mules were returning. She would be trampled! Then Trace's shadow formed a barrier between herself and the oncoming sounds. She sighed and relaxed a little. Suddenly, it was only the rush of heated words that ricocheted through her ears.

"Damn you, Wilkins! What the hell did you think you were doin'?"

Jubal's harsh voice penetrated the buzzing in her head. "I turned the damned mules. What did you think I was doin'?"

Addy managed to turn her stiff neck enough that she could see through her one opened eye. Trace stood in front of Jubal, legs spread, hands fisted on his narrow hips, his tall, lean body taut as a whipcord.

A long blade reflected a ray of sunshine. The intricately carved handle of a knife protruded from his curled fingers.

"I sure as hell wish I knew, you sonofabitch. The mules were already stopped when you fired. If I hadn't gotten to Adeline in time to cut the reins, she'd still be draggin' across the prairie."

Sputtering obscenities, Jubal hauled his ample girth from his heaving horse and nodded toward Addy. "Is she dead? I see Delilah waving. I don't want her to see . . ."

Trace stood still, blocking Jubal's approach. "No, she's alive."

Addy trembled when it appeared Jubal would hit Trace, though Trace seemed almost disgruntled when he didn't. The slight movement of her body made her groan.

"Let me by, Randall. The woman's my relation. I'll see to her."

Trace's eyes glinted and their bright blue hue darkened with a suspicion he knew he could not voice, at least not at the moment, not in front of Addy. He spoke very calmly when he said, "No. If anyone looks after her, it will be me."

Jubal vehemently objected, waving his pudgy hands in the air as he shouted, "You've sure done a hell of a job so far. If I were you, I'd get her back to the wagons where she could at least be seen to and doctored."

He no more than got the words out of his mouth when Scratch and a muttering Pedro, arms laden with small pouches and tins of ointment, rushed to Addy's side. She made a face when the two harried men blocked her view of Trace and Jubal. Their "Tsk! Tsk's" and clucks of sympathy completely drowned out the heated conversation taking place beyond them.

But Addy was too euphoric over the way Trace had taken charge of her to be bothered long. He was so commanding, so forceful. Just as a good soldier was supposed to be. It gave her a warm, giddy feeling.

She blinked, and blinked again. Scratch's features began to dim. His eyes appeared to bob up and down. Though she tried to focus, his beard grew larger and larger, until all she saw were specks of gray and red. Then all went black.

Trace dusted his hands together and stalked swiftly over to the two men hovered around Addy.

Damn Jubal Wilkins to hell.

His knees and ankles still trembled as he walked. He'd never been so relieved as when the mules suddenly stopped running, or so terrified as when he'd seen Jubal's intent to fire the gun. No amount of shouting or threats had deterred the fool.

If he hadn't run for all he was worth, he wouldn't have been able to cut her free in time . . . Well, he didn't even want to think about that now.

By the time he knelt beside Scratch, he had nearly regained his control. God, she'd had a close call. The backs of his eyes burned, and his hand shook when he reached out to touch a wisp of burnished hair that lay matted to her scraped cheek. But at least he was over the nausea that had churned in his gut when he'd looked into Jubal Wilkins' conniving features.

"She done fainted, boy. Cain't think of nothin' better that could'a hap'n'd."

Trace ran his fingers through his rumpled hair. What he wouldn't give right now for a hat. Any kind of hat. Something that had a wide brim to hide his too-close-to-the-surface emotions.

Worry was more than evident in his raspy voice when he asked, "Do you think she'll be all right?"

Pedro did not look up from his cautious examination. And it was probably a good thing, for he missed the speculative glare from Trace's eyes as the younger man leaned closer, wanting to make certain the Mexican didn't get too damned personal with his hands.

"Eez fortunate, la señorita. No eez broken, she arms y legs." He shrugged his shoulders. "No can say, inside. Quién sabe?"

When Pedro leaned back, away from the unconscious woman, Trace relaxed and did the same.

"What can we do for her?" Trace's heart hammered against his rib cage, protesting the sight of Addy's bruised and blood-covered body.

Of all the things to happen. He'd watched for days as the tiny city-woman took all Mother Nature had to dish out. His teeth ground together as he included Jubal Wilkins, and even himself, in the list of bad elements she'd had to battle lately. She had withstood it all, and had not been above putting up a good fight.

His eyes softened and shone. He actually smiled. She hadn't noticed that he'd watched her once when she sank to the edge of a creek bed and gazed at her reflection in the clear water. She had touched the few new sun wrinkles around her eyes. And then she'd stuck her tongue out.

A heavy hand on his shoulder drew Trace's thoughts back to the present situation. "Let's git'er back to the wagon, boy. Pedro done give me some o' his powders. We'uns kin fix'er up good as new."

"Yeah. Yeah, we can, old man. We sure as hell can."

Trace slid his hands oh-so-carefully beneath her back and under her knees, then lifted her smoothly and quickly, as if she weighed no more than a feather pillow. And that was exactly how she felt in his arms—all soft and cuddly.

He couldn't resist rubbing his chin in her silky brown hair as they neared the wagon. When he thought again of how close she'd come to dying, a sharp ache pierced his chest, kinda like how an arrow through the heart must feel, he thought.

Stumbling over his feet, he earned a questioning glance from Scratch. "Damned rock!" It embarrassed him to think this slip of a girl was getting to him, no matter how hard he fought against her.

"Careful with that gal. She be a mite special ta me."

At the old man's admonition, Trace blinked and shot a shocked look at Scratch. The old timer hadn't struck him as one to form attachments to anyone or anything, lest it be his tobacco or mules.

Then he glanced down at the smeared blood on Adeline's face, at her torn clothes, and he saw her stubborn determination and almost childlike innocence. An overwhelming desire flared in his gut. Only it wasn't a lustful feeling. It was an urge to take her to himself, to protect and adore her.

The full realization of what he was thinking struck him between the eyes with the force of a solid-oak post. Sweat broke out all over his body. His knees turned weak as a woman's.

Suddenly, he had another urge, that of tossing the slight figure as far as possible. The collar of his shirt bit into his neck. He nearly choked. *Hellfire!* This couldn't be happening to *him!*

No. Certainly not. He had things to do. A woman would only hold him back, tie him down. Especially a damned tenderfoot. No flouncing skirt, no matter how sweet and adorable, was going to take over *his* life.

"Hurry, old man. Lower that tailgate before I drop her."

Scratch, who had already dropped the gate, turned a baleful glare on the young man. "Then ya give'er ta me, Randall. If'n ya cain't handle that wee mite o' a gal, *I* kin."

Trace couldn't meet Scratch's eye. His arms tightened about the woman. He felt damned ashamed. She'd saved his life, and what was he doing to repay her? Nothing. He'd come that close to actually handing her over to the old man.

His gut twisted until he turned sick at the thought of another man's hands touching her, even if that man was kindly old Scratch.

"N-no. I've got her. Just had a cramp in my arm. That's all."

Scratch's eyes narrowed thoughtfully, but he didn't argue. He climbed into the wagon ahead of Trace and spread out a clean blanket. Then he went to Addy's trunk in search of something to cover her.

His gnarled fingers hesitated over the neatly folded feminine items. He gulped and almost swallowed his tobacco. As if he touched fine china that might crack into a million pieces at the slightest movement, he searched until he found a soft flannel nightgown, then reverently replaced the lid.

A sigh of relief was all that Trace noticed before the garment was suddenly thrust into his now empty hands.

"Want I should he'p ya?"

Trace shook his head, then suddenly raised it as Jubal skidded his horse to a stop near the rear of the wagon and yelled, "Get her as comfortable as possible. We move out in ten minutes."

Trace lunged for the open end of the wagon. "The hell we will. You've seen the shape she's in. We've got to clean her wounds and give her a chance to rest before we move her."

Jubal's eyes bored into Trace and his lips curved into a sinister grin. "We can't wait. Lost too much time as it is. She knows I can't risk these men and supplies over one person. Besides, there's a train or two already in front of us, and several on our tail. If we're gonna get any kind of price for our goods, we've got to go on. It's her company I'm tryin' to save."

"And your wife's. Where is Mrs. Wilkins? Why hasn't she come to check on Adeline?" Trace was beginning to see where Addy got some of her hardheadedness. If someone like Jubal Wilkins tried to order *him* around, he'd balk, too.

Jubal cleared his throat. "Ahem. Delilah has taken to bed herself with a debilitating headache. I didn't want to worry her with bad news, so I haven't, uhm, told her, yet."

"My God, man. Don't you think she'd want to know her cousin is injured and could be dying?"

Beady brown eyes widened with speculation. "Dying? I thought you said she was all right."

"I said no such thing. I only said she was alive."

"I see. Well, is she?"

"Is she what?" Trace purposely played dumb just to anger the wagon boss.

"Dying! Is she gonna die, or not? Speak up, Randall."

Grudgingly, Trace answered, "No. At least, we don't think so. She just seems to have a lot of scrapes and bruises."

Jubal's voice was low. "Then there's no reason to hold up the train."

Trace's face turned as red as the bay horse he'd chosen to ride earlier in the day. "Damn you to hell, Wilkins! I'll not move this woman until she's at least regained consciousness and I'm certain she's not badly injured."

As if he'd been expecting just those very words, Jubal cheerfully told Trace, "That's fine by me. The rest of us are movin' on. Catch up with us at Council Grove, if you're able."

With a vicious yank on the reins, he spun his horse and spurred the beast away before Trace could reply. But over his shoulder, he called, "That means you, too, Scratch, if you want this job."

Scratch clenched his fists until his creaking knuckles turned white. "Some day, I'll take pleasure in rip-pin' what's left o' that bastard's heart right out'n his fool chest."

Trace's eyes glowed with undisguised hatred as they followed Jubal's hasty departure. "Only if I don't beat you to it."

Then they both turned to look at Addy. Scratch studied her beaten features a long moment, then slapped Trace on the shoulder, nearly knocking him out of the wagon.

"Are ya shore this here's what ya wanta do, boy? I s'pect she's gonna be all right."

"Can't take that chance." Though he sounded confident, Trace knew a moment of grave doubt. Was he doing the right thing? By taking it upon himself to remain behind, he could be risking both their lives.

He wiped moisture from the newly formed creases in his forehead. How long had it been since he'd felt this gnawing ache in his gut — like his insides were disintegrating?

A scratchy lump formed in his throat, but he angrily swallowed it down. Since his grandfather passed away. That's how long. When the last person he gave a damn about left him forever alone.

His eyes darted to the wagon. So why all this surge of emotion over the tenderfoot? She wasn't . . . He couldn't . . . *Naw*. He was just concerned about her health. He was returning a favor. He was not afraid of losing her . . .

Foolhardy or not, he was sticking with his decision. The real danger lay west of Council Grove. Yeah, they would stay, he decided.

After watching the gradual display of determination and persistence mold Trace's features, the old timer dug his grimy fingers into his beard and shrugged his shoulders. "If'n that's the way ya want it. Jist be durn shore ya take good keer o'er."

Trace knew the old fella was as concerned about Addy as he was himself. "Don't fret, old man. She's in good hands."

177

Scratch looked down at Trace's hands. The wrists had now healed from the leather burns. "That's what I'm afeerd of, boy."

His expression quite serious, Trace said, "Go on with the train. We'll meet you at Council Grove."

Also suddenly earnest, Scratch promised, "We'll be a waitin' on ya, boy. Ya kin count on it."

"Thanks. That's some consolation, anyway."

The two men shook hands. Scratch stooped to run the back of his bony hand along Addy's soft jaw. "Keep'er safe. That's all I ask."

Trace felt a fine mist in his own eyes when he saw Scratch's wet cheeks. Again he marveled over Addy's ability to get the crusty old loner to care so much about her.

He took a deep breath and looked around the wagon. There were blankets, and cloths could be torn from Addy's petticoats. Scratch had left the medicines. Now all he needed was water.

In two shakes he was back with a bucket of fresh water. He started removing what pieces of clothing still remained over portions of her body.

What could have been minutes, later, his hands stopped in mid air, hovering just above the gentle rise and fall of her lush breasts. He cocked his head. Another jingle sounded from the front of the wagon. Quickly, he pulled his gun and scrambled across the boxes to peer between the ties of the tightly laced canvas.

His chest constricted, as if it had been gripped by an iron fist. He rubbed his forehead with his free hand and holstered the pistol.

Tied to the box were the runaway mules. *Good God!* During his shouting match with Jubal, he'd completely forgotten that they didn't even have a team with which to make Council Grove, let alone move an inch in either direction.

No wonder Jubal's eyes had taken on such a demonic gleam. The man had known full well they would be alone and helpless, with little ammunition or supplies.

Hatred like he'd never known before filled his entire being until his head literally throbbed. Jubal Wilkins better hope he was wearing a gun the next time he ran into Trace Randall. Trace had never killed an unarmed man before, but in Wilkins' case, he was purely tempted to make an exception.

He stared at the mules. Who could have returned them? The train had been gone only a short while, and none of the drivers would've had the time or the inclination to risk Jubal's wrath just to return the team.

Then he spotted a woven band wound around the lead team's harness. He should have known—Eagle Feather! His eyes scanned the surrounding countryside, but he saw nothing. It was a good thing. The wagons weren't *that* far away.

A sigh of relief took a great load from his shoulders. It was comforting to know he wasn't as alone as he'd feared.

A tiny moan reminded him there was still a lot of work left to do. He hated the thought of the pain she'd suffer as he cleaned her poor body, but it had to be done, no matter how long he tried to find excuses to put it off.

His chest rose and fell several times before he turned to scramble back over the crates.

When he stood over her and looked down, a terrible rage trembled through his wiry form. He had felt so helpless, being able to do nothing but watch as she was dragged behind the mules. What could have caused such an accident? She'd hitched the double teams for two days with no apparent problems. What had gone wrong this time?

He grumbled to himself and bent to the task of removing the rest of her clothing. The expensive fabric

179

fell away in pieces in his hand, exposing completely the tiny, fragile woman. As he carefully tended her, he surprised himself. His touch was precise and impersonal as befit the seriousness of the situation.

He was pulling her petticoats and skirt down her long, slender legs when he heard a distinct rattle. Something fell from her pocket and rolled onto the floor. Thinking it might be something important, he felt around the slatted boards and cursed when his fingers encountered the damned loose board.

But he was able to retrieve the small object before he brought his hand up to pick out a long splinter from beneath his nail. He sucked on the throbbing finger, knowing no Indian torture could hurt any worse.

When he finally opened his hand and viewed a round button, his eyes narrowed. It couldn't be! But it was. What on earth was it doing in Adeline's pocket?

He rolled it between his fingers, looking at the hand-carved wolf's head. His gaze then settled thoughtfully on the pinched features of the young woman.

A severe frown knit his brows as he wondered again how she had come to possess a button from his soldier's uniform. Where had she gotten it, and how?

One of the Indians who had attacked his stage and ended up taking him hostage had ripped the button from a jacket found in his luggage. Trace knew. He'd seen him take it. And he had wondered at the time and trouble expended on the task. That wasn't like an Indian. Why hadn't he taken the whole jacket?

If this was the same button, how had Adeline come by it? Did she have some connection to the renegades?

His belly knotted as his pulse quickened. God, he hoped not! How could such a sweet, beautiful, naive girl be a part of such a ruthless . . . ? He shook his head. There was no sense in making himself crazy

180

wondering. He'd just have to wait until he could ask her directly. It might even mean he'd have to stay with the caravan longer than he had anticipated.

In the meantime, he finished removing her chemise and drawers. His breath caught in his throat at the sight of all the nicks and scrapes marring her ivory-hued perfection.

Yes, there were a lot of questions to be answered, and the first would be *why* this had happened.

He dropped the button in his pocket and soaked the cotton cloths in the cool water. He winced when her muscles flinched as he sponged her face and neck. His mind drifted to his grandfather as he tried to take his mind off her pain.

Though he thought he'd never had much feeling for his cold, hardhearted grandfather, after the old man died, Trace had used a good deal of his inheritance to indulge himself in those hand-hewn buttons.

His grandfather's symbol of success had been his obsession with the wolf. His study had been filled with paintings of wolves, books about wolves. He'd even had a wolf's head mounted above the massive stone fireplace. Even the furniture had imprints of paws carved into the oak arms and legs.

Why he had bothered to have the buttons made, he had never been able to explain. He'd just done it. And now it seemed the wolf was back, to haunt him again.

He finished cleansing her body, and rubbed Pedro's ointments into the cuts and scrapes and over the bruises. But as his fingers smoothed across her soft, creamy skin, he found himself unable to concentrate on anything but *her*.

Damn but she was beautiful, even covered as she was with bruises. No amount of marking could devalue the image he would always carry — of her glorious mane of hair, her lustrous skin, and long, perfect limbs. Even with her brown hair smattered with gray and wrinkles around her eyes and mouth, she would

181

still be gorgeous to him.

All of a sudden, he wondered what had gotten into him to stay away from her since *that night* — that incomparable night. He rubbed his hand over his eyes and massaged an aching temple. He knew why. He was stupid.

He was a grown man, damn it, and he had felt as awkward around her the past few days as if she had been his first woman. No time was ever as good as the first. Was it?

Oh, hell, yes! The night with Adeline had surpassed anything he'd ever known before — with *any* woman.

And he was a damned fool to let himself get so caught up with the little snippet of a girl. How many times would he have to remind himself of that?

The corners of his mouth turned up, exposing the brilliant whiteness of his teeth. For a long, long time, he guessed.

Addy had to stifle the urge to reach out and trace the curve of his exquisite lips. She had lain awake for some time, hiding that fact beneath the thick layers of brown, gold-tipped lashes as she watched the conflicting play of shadows in his eyes, the tautness of his features.

Through all his ministrations, his hands remained gentle, though she bit her tongue on several occasions to keep from gasping out her pain when the cloth touched her wounds. But right at that moment, her concentration was centered on what could possibly be going through his mind to cause such visible changes in his expression. It was fascinating.

She felt as though his emotions were laid bare for her to read, but she was blind. Suddenly, she ached clear to the marrow of her bones. Tears pooled in her eyes until she dared not blink.

All of her frailties came to the surface. She had certainly made a mess of things. Whatever she tried to do either turned upside down or into a disaster of

182

gigantic proportions. It would only be right for her to give up now and go home, back to Boston. Let Delilah and Jubal have the business while she slunk home to lick her wounds. Pretend she never came West at all in a futile attempt to make something of herself.

Maybe Timothy Sharpe would still want her share of the estate enough to marry her. Maybe she deserved someone like him — so staid and dull. She sure didn't seem able to handle the rough, exciting life.

It was a shame, too. Even through the extremes of hot winds and deep mud, she had come to love the colorful, serene prairie. For some reason, she felt more alone around the people of the wagon train, excepting Scratch and maybe Trace, of course, than she did in the vast, empty grassland.

A cool hand rested on her forehead and pulled upward, exposing her reflective brown eyes.

"Playin' possum, are we, Miss Montclair? Just how long did you intend to let me worry about you?"

Chapter Twelve

Addy was caught — caught staring at Trace. Normally, she would have been embarrassed. And she *was* aghast, but only because she had been found out, not because she had looked her fill.

Her eyes locked with his. Instead of offering him some inane excuse, she giggled. Her breath hissed through her teeth. The jiggling caused from the laughter created more tears as her aches and pains were reawakened.

They made quite a pair, she and he, she thought. Trace, with leftover welts on his face and upper body from ant bites; and she, who must look like a specter risen from the grave after being dragged across the country behind a bunch of quarrelsome, intractable mules.

"All right, tenderfoot, out with it. What's so damned funny? You were almost killed a short while ago, you know."

Addy quieted and gulped. "Y-yes, I know."

"Then what could you possibly find funny about something as gruesome as that?"

She managed to carefully shake her head. "I don't know. Nothing. Lots of things. You. Me."

Trace frowned. She must have been hurt worse than they thought. Even her brain was rattled. He laid a hand on her forehead. Maybe she had a fever and was delirious.

"Are you in a lot of pain? You don't seem too hot. I can't find anything broken. Tell me what's wrong, honey."

She closed her eyes and was silent for so long that he began to think she had passed out again. His hand reached out to check her pulse; he jerked it back when she finally spoke.

"I want to go home." She continued to lie perfectly still, eyes shut, face expressionless, awaiting his reply.

Would he immediately turn the wagon around? Would he be glad, even anxious, to be rid of her? she wondered.

She opened her eyes, but could tell nothing from his expression. He didn't appear to be happy, or relieved, or sad. Just thoughtful, with his eyes slightly hooded, his mouth pressed into a thin line and little wrinkles between his exceptional blue eyes.

Her heart skipped a beat when his gaze shifted to her.

"Why would you want to do that?" He seemed genuinely puzzled.

Her stomach knotted, her tender flesh was set aquiver. She gasped at the ripples of pain that shot through her. "I-I just . . . think it would be for . . . the best."

He grabbed both of her hands as she reached toward her midsection. "No. Don't touch it. Give the ointment a few more minutes. It will help the pain."

Addy couldn't meet his eyes. She had just realized she was lying beside him, absolutely, completely naked, like it was nothing out of the ordinary, like it didn't bother her a bit, and all she had on her mind was sneaking home to Boston.

"Ahem . . . W-would you cover me, please?"

"I can't, honey."

She shifted, extremely uncomfortable under his studious gaze. "Why can't you? This is . . . is . . . highly improper. And . . . so very humiliating." She ended on a choked sob.

"Yes, I guess it would be. But you certainly have nothing to be ashamed of. Your body is . . . beautiful." He looked guiltily away. *Beautiful* didn't even begin to

185

describe her. From the way she winced and darted panicked glances about the wagon, he wasn't helping matters by speaking so boldly.

She couldn't believe it. It sounded as though he actually understood how she felt. Yet he admitted to enjoying her unclothed state. Her eyes clouded and she became so agitated that she tried to turn over.

His voice was harsh when he commanded, "Don't! Just lie still. I won't cover you just yet, cause you wouldn't be able to stand it."

"Oh." Well, of course. She should have known it was because of her wounds, rather than his *lust*. After all, he hadn't shown the least interest in her since that . . . night.

Trace was glad he had gotten her mind off leaving. She'd caught him by surprise with that little announcement. He hadn't even been able to think quickly enough to come up with any good arguments against her going.

His gut wrenched anew with the lie. All right, so he'd thought of *one,* but he couldn't come out and *say* it. How could he tell her that the thought of never seeing her again hurt a thousand times worse than the pain he'd suffered at the hands of the Indians?

He felt in his pocket for a handkerchief to mop the sweat clinging to his brow. His fingers encountered the button and his body stiffened. How could he have forgotten it so soon?

She *had* to stay! At least until he found out her connection with the button, his torture, and maybe even a shipment of guns.

When he finally glanced down, her eyes were closed and her chest rose and fell in deep, even breaths. She was asleep. Good. Now he'd have time to think.

Whatever reasons he came up with as to why she couldn't leave, they'd better be good ones. If she didn't want to stay of her own free will, he'd have to do something drastic.

A devilish gleam lit his eyes. If he had to, he would.

The wind had come up, drying the ground enough that the caravan made another four miles before stopping for the night.

Jubal swaggered around the camp, shouting commands, issuing orders for the next day. He and Rudy Potts spent a good half an hour with their heads bent close together before he finally opened the door to the carriage.

A disgruntled Delilah grabbed the collar of his shirt and nearly dragged him inside, then slammed the door closed before hissing, "My God, Jubal, what kept you so long? I've been goin' crazy all afternoon an' most the night wonderin' what happened today. Since we never stopped long enough for a buryin', I assumed she was all right—again."

"Damn it, Flo . . ."

"Don't call me that! You know better!"

"All right. All right. Calm down, D-e-l-i-l-a-h!"

She graced him with a petulant sigh and crossed her arms just below her breasts, expertly pushing upward just enough to give her husband a show of bulging flesh. "Go on. What went wrong *this* time?"

Jubal looked around the small space, at the comfortable pads, fluffy pillows, their private store of whiskey and canteens of water. Nothing had been spared in providing for their every comfort.

And why not? They'd had a tough enough life. No need to prolong poverty when they'd struck it rich— thanks to Miss hoity-toity Adeline Montclair and her dearly departed family.

"Jubal Wilkins! Quite your lollygaggin' an' talk to me."

He ducked his head. "Yes, dear. All I can tell you is that the last I knew, she was alive."

Delilah leaned forward. "Was she badly hurt?"

"I don't know."

She frowned. "You don't know? *Why* don't you

187

know, you numbskull? *You're* the wagon boss. You're the one in charge. Why didn't you find out? Why didn't you bring her back here where her only relatives could . . . *take care* . . . of her?"

"It was that damned Randall's fault. By the time I got to her, he was standin' guard like a mother grizzly over her cubs."

"Well, why didn't you *do* somethin'?"

He scrunched up his face. "Quit harpin' at me, Fl . . . Lily. I done all I could. You know we decided to let her get by, or not, on her own. Don't you think it'd be suspicious-like to make a big fuss over her all of a sudden?"

Delilah, stretched out on her stomach across the thick pallet, looked thoughtfully at the man she so hastily married. "Maybe you're right, dahlin'. We don't want to make mistakes at this point. Everythin's worked out so far. It will again."

Dropping ungracefully to his knees, Jubal reached out and unfastened the top buttons down the back of her dress. He followed the unveiling of her milk-white skin with his thick, moist lips.

She moaned and turned over, wrapping her arms about his neck, rubbing her breasts into his chest.

"Hurry, dahlin', hurry! Forget about buttons. We'll do it naked later. Hurry!"

He understood her urgency. His fly was already open. It took only a second to hoist her heavy skirt and petticoats. His mouth hung slack when he found she wore no undergarments.

"God, Flo. If I had known . . ."

With a strangled grunt, he fell upon her. Her legs spread wide and he entered her with a savage thrust. She muffled her scream against his rough shirt, but he still heard her husky whispers.

"Yes, Jubal. Again. Harder!"

While Adeline slept, Trace cared for the mules. He

unharnessed and led them to where they could forage for grass, but be close enough to round up in a hurry if the need arose.

A bleak expression settled over his features. He shrugged his shoulders. The way things had gone lately, he was tempted to tie them to the wagon and not let them get more than two feet away.

He dropped the harness, then bent over to examine the traces and the singletree. After the headlong race, there was bound to be some damage. Falling on one knee, he looked closely at the area where the singletree connected to the wagon tongue with an iron pin.

His jaw clenched until the muscles in his cheek corded and twitched as he traced the jagged edge of a broken wooden spike, the end of which was still jammed into the hole.

The wet weather had caused the wood to swell, otherwise the pin would have fallen out when it snapped, leaving no trace of evidence that a wooden pin had been substituted for the iron one.

He braced his elbow on his bent knee and rubbed his forehead. A sickening sensation roiled through his gut to end up a throbbing ache in his temple. Someone had deliberately sabotaged Adeline's wagon.

He thought back to all of her other "accidents". Had they indeed been accidental? Or was somebody out to kill her?

Good God! Why? And more importantly, *who?*

His anger over Wilkins' stupid trick earlier that afternoon resurfaced. Naturally, he was the first suspect to come to mind, with his sidekick, Potts, a close second.

Maybe instead of calling Jubal out when they met up at Council Grove, he'd wait and keep a cautious eye on him; see what else the sneaky bastard had up his sleeve. He could beat the hell out of the man anytime.

Meanwhile, there was still the problem of getting the wagon *to* Council Grove. He drew his knife as his eyes searched the flat, empty plains, then resettled on

189

the wagon. He needed to find something to replace the pin.

Addy wakened abruptly, and for a moment couldn't remember where she was. When she tried to sit up, and felt the resistance in her stiff, sore muscles, memory flooded and cleared her confused mind.

She sighed. The dream again. It had been so real. Tears of self-pity pooled in her eyes until she blinked them away.

This wasn't the first time she'd had the dream. Sometimes at night, when no one could see or hear, she had cried herself to sleep, missing the softness of her bed, the long, hot baths she had always taken for granted. And clean clothes. What she wouldn't give for a wardrobe full of her soft, sweet-smelling gowns.

And after indulging herself with those recollections, there was the dream. She licked her lips. Her mouth watered as she imagined a table spread wide with Maude's wonderful cooking.

Every morning there were plates of pastries that melted in her mouth with every lip-smacking bite. Lunches were filled with choices of sliced fresh fruit, salads, hearty portions of chicken, ham, or beef.

And in the evenings, seven-course meals impeccably served, even when she dined alone. The delicacy that really stuck in her mind, though, was Maude's steaming cornbread, butter sliding right off the knife to melt in a creamy pool in the middle of the thick square of warm bread.

She groaned when her mind skipped the rest of the food and went straight to dessert. Her favorite was a four-layer chocolate cake with enough icing to add two inches to its height. She could almost taste the smooth chocolate now. She used to dip her finger into the bowl and pull out a gooey glob . . .

No. No! She squeezed her eyes shut. When had dreaming of delicious food turned into a nightmare?

Her stomach growled. Evidently the noisy gurgles were heard clear outside, for Trace immediately poked his gorgeous head beneath the canvas.

"Awake again, are we?" His eyes gleamed with mirth and his voice rumbled when he asked, "Are you hungry?"

She blushed furiously, but answered honestly. "I'm starved."

He pulled himself up into the bed more gracefully than an agile, wild animal. His muscles bunched and flexed, rippling beneath his taut skin. Didn't the man ever wear a shirt?

She swallowed nervously and turned her head away from the sight. She didn't know which would be the most tempting if she could have her choice at the moment — a pan of Maude's cornbread or Trace's lithe body.

The thought of either one was enough to set her juices flowing, and her stomach contracted, drawing attention to that empty void once again.

"Scratch tossed in this sack before he left this afternoon. Let's see . . . Here's a biscuit, and some jerky."

He laughed when she wrinkled her nose. "No good, huh?" Talking around a large mouthful of the tough jerky, he told her, "I've eaten a lot worse, and a lot less."

Ashamed of seeming finicky and hard to please, she held out her hand. He took hold of it and she felt the jolt clear to her toenails. When he then slapped a thick slab of fried meat into her palm, she was disappointed.

"Tell you what . . . This'll keep you busy for a while and" — he grinned — "satisfy the wolf in your belly. Maybe I can come up with something a mite more appetizing for supper."

He rubbed his palms together, then down the legs of his trousers. Glancing uneasily out of the back of the wagon, he leapt to his feet. "Uh, guess I'd better get on it now. It'll be dark fore long."

Her embarrassment abating somewhat, Addy hid

191

the smile stretching her tender cheeks. She'd seen the way his eyes kept drifting to her nakedness. He wasn't nearly as unaffected by her as he'd like to believe.

Then a grim look turned her features into a frown. What would she do? She shouldn't want anything more to do with him. But she did.

He did his best to avoid her, or at least have as little to do with her as possible. But she might be able to change that—if she had the desire, if she stayed around.

She took as deep a breath as her aching ribs and chest would allow. What was done was done. She had *let* him make love to her—had even *wanted* him to. All she could think about for the past few days was what it would feel like to have him love her *again*.

So what if she lived the rest of her life as a lonely old maid? Why couldn't she add a few more memories to keep her days, and nights, interesting? He would be leaving soon. What harm could come from using the time they had left to good advantage?

Now, the hard part would be to convince *him* that he wanted her.

Her excitement got the best of her. She winced when she squirmed to peer outside. Oblivious to her monumental decision, he was muttering and tinkering with the harness.

She smiled. Too sweetly for Trace's good. It would take several days for her body to heal. That would give her ample opportunity to have him on his knees and begging without *her* having to say a word.

Her eyes sparkled. Beware Mr. Trace Randall. I can be a very determined woman, when I *want* to be.

Addy must have dozed longer than she thought, for when she awoke it was to a darkened interior. Her eyes were gritty, and burned when she blinked. She wanted to stretch, but was afraid to.

An orange flicker from between the lacing caught

her eye, and she heard an unmistakable crackling. A fire! How wonderful. Trace had found dry wood.

Her nose twitched. She sniffed and her stomach growled. Quietly, this time, thank heavens. Her head raised several inches, but she couldn't see a thing. What on earth was the man cooking? It smelled heavenly.

"Hey, sleepy head. What'd ole Pedro give you? You've slept like a hybernatin' bear all afternoon."

When her tummy grumbled again, she could have just died. She'd forgotten what good ears the rascal had. A bear, indeed.

She did admit, "I'm just about as hungry as a bear." Her tiny pink tongue darted out to trace the outline of her full lower lip. Trace swayed forward, but caught himself when she added, "Something sure smells good."

"Just so happens, an unexpected visitor wandered across our camp. You like antelope stew?"

She visualized the graceful tan and white animals Scratch had pointed out to her not two days ago. Her throat burned when she swallowed. Then a tantalizing aroma drifted through the gaps in the laces.

"I-I've never eaten ant . . . antelope . . . uh, stew."

"Then you've missed some might good eatin'. Reckon you could try it?"

Her stomach answered at the same time her mouth opened. Trace laughed. She grimaced and conceded, "I could try a little. Just a bite or two, mind you."

But a few minutes later, when he crawled in beside her holding a wooden bowl filled with the savory-smelling concoction, she could hardly wait to try a taste.

Pain shot through her body when she raised her arms to take the bowl. The strain on her shoulders and the muscles in her upper arms while she had been snared in the reins was tremendous. She felt so useless and helpless, she could cry.

Trace must have seen the telltale sheen to her eyes

193

for he nervously offered, "Hold on a minute. Let me help you."

He reached in back of him and pulled out several folded blankets which he propped behind her head. Kneeling beside her, he dipped a spoon into the stew and casually held the bowl beneath her chin.

For a moment, she felt a pang of guilt that she had initially left *his* care to Scratch, but when she saw that he didn't consider her capable of taking a few measly bites of stew without making a mess, her self-criticism quickly turned to ire.

"Open wide."

She clenched her teeth and turned her head. "No. You cannot feed me."

"I certainly can."

"I refuse to . . ."

Exasperated by the woman's swift mood change, Trace scolded, "Look, someone has to help you. Can you feed yourself?"

She sniffed, blinked, and stared down her battered length. Her voice quavered. "N-no."

"All right, then. Open up. I'm tellin' you, this is good."

The spoon nudged her lips until they finally eased open. A drop of warm liquid trickled down her chin, but he caught it in the bowl. She was mortified. And though the meat and wild onions and potatoes were cut into tiny pieces and boiled until very tender, it was difficult for her to chew and swallow. She felt that even a baby was not as helpless as she.

Trace frowned. "I was afraid of that. Here, just eat the broth for now. We'll try the chunky portions again tomorrow."

She closed her eyes as the broth slid down her throat. It was delicious. She could almost forget that she was mad and naked and helpless and had to be hand-fed.

Between mouthfuls she told him, "Uhmm, the stew's . . . not bad."

With a hurt expression on his face, which didn't diminish in the least the teasing glint in his eyes, he shoved another spoonful between her teeth. "Not bad? Woman, if you're demeanin' my cookin' ability, I'll just take my bowl and find someone with better taste to finish it."

He stuck the spoon in the bowl and made a show of moving away.

She nearly strangled as she gulped the last bite he had offered and tried to talk at the same time. "No! Wait. I'm sorry. I'd like some more."

He sat and stared, his brows raised in question.

"Please. Please?"

He shrugged his shoulders and slumped back down. "Well, I guess you can have what's left."

His voice sounded so much like that of a petulant little boy that she grinned. He smiled back.

When the bowl was emptied of broth, she wanted more, but he thought it best to let what she'd eaten digest before stuffing her too full. He still wasn't completely certain of her health, though her seemingly insatiable appetite was a good sign.

"You need to rest. Reckon I'll bed down myself. Probably be a good idea to start watch around midnight."

Her eyes grew large and round. He sucked in his breath. The significance of his words had just struck her.

"I'd forgotten. We're . . . alone . . . out here, aren't we?"

He reassuringly patted one of her hands, and was horrified anew by the tough calluses marring their soft beauty. "Yeah, we are. But don't worry. Just rest. I'll make sure we reach Council Grove safe and sound."

A niggling doubt regarding those confident words squirmed in his belly, but yet he wasn't *overly* concerned. The Indian attack on the wagon train *had* to be an isolated incident.

But Addy was scared. So many things had happened. Freak accidents. Unexplained occurrences. She was afraid — for Trace. What if something happened to him? She wouldn't even be able to help.

Her chest constricted. What had come over her? At one time, her major concern would have been that if anything happened to Trace, there would be no one to care for, or protect, *her*. Yet today, she worried because she couldn't help *him*.

Her fingers curled around his. "Please . . ."

The tenderness in his eyes spread throughout his body. He scowled, even as he consoled, "I'll get you more broth in just a while, honey. I don't mean to be . . ."

"Stay. Please? Stay with me?" There truly was fear in her voice. Fear that he would ignore her plea. Fear that he really didn't want to be any closer to her than he had to be.

Tears threatened and burned the backs of her eyes. What would she do if he left her now, alone, after she had used all of her courage to implore him not to go?

Trace couldn't believe his ears. His heart hammered so loudly his head buzzed. It twisted his insides into miles of knots to think she actually *wanted* his company.

Then his practical side turned thoughtful. Maybe . . . it wouldn't be so difficult after all to get her to stay with the train. Maybe all he had to do was play his hand right.

He shoved that logic into the background as he stretched out beside her. He started to draw her into the circle of his arms, but remembered her injuries. So he lay next to her, and stifled a groan when she snuggled against his warmth.

Later he would try to lay a sheet over her. It could get cold at night on the prairie.

Her voice was no more than a hushed whisper when she said "thank you." But he felt like he could float right up to the heavens.

He turned on his side and nuzzled his chin into her hair, inhaling her sweet, fresh scent, feeling the almost

196

imperceptible touch of her silky skin, hearing the gentle hiss of her breath as she fell into a deep, relaxed sleep.

His hand hovered above her bare shoulder, then dropped. He mustn't think of her luscious body, displayed so openly before his greedy eyes. He mustn't . . .

"Oh, hell!"

Trace blinked. His eyes felt as if they were covered with grit. It was nearly dawn. He'd been on watch for hours. It had been a relief to sit in the cold air, because he wouldn't have been able to sleep anyway, after lying next to the overly-tempting, stimulating Adeline Montclair.

Even as his thoughts drifted to the pleasant subject of the soft, curvaceous woman, the hairs on the back of his neck began to tingle.

Damn it, he'd had this *feeling* for some time, that there was something out there besides coyotes; real coyotes, that is. His head twisted slowly, surveying the camp. The mules were secured to the wagon. The fire had burned out long ago. He'd moved to several different locations. Everything *seemed* in order. Nothing unusual had happened.

He squeezed the bridge of his nose between his thumb and forefinger. Inhaling silently, he took a long, deep breath to ease the pressure building in his chest. The air hissed out in a rush. He cocked his head and listened. Nothing.

Still, he drew his pistol and held it across his legs. Instinct. It had kept him alive many times in the past. Now was not the time to ignore it, especially with Addy as an added responsibility.

His head jerked up. What was that? He stood quietly and listened for what felt like hours. Again, nothing.

He was just about to take a much-needed stretch

when he heard the high, musical trill of a meadowlark. He sank into an immediate crouch and quickly made his way back to the wagon.

The mules fidgeted and stamped their feet impatiently. He peered into the wagon. Addy's eyes were closed, the light sheet still in place. He was glad she'd been asleep when he had covered her. She hadn't felt a thing.

He wiped the moisture from his forehead. It wasn't even daylight, and he perspired like he'd worked a full day. God, he hated the waiting. He wished that whatever was going to happen would go ahead and get it over with.

As if that one thought was the only catalyst needed, the sun began its slow ascent over the ridge. With its first blinding rays Trace heard the rumble of galloping hooves.

He checked his pistol. It was fully loaded. He knelt behind the wheel, then decided to crawl beneath the wagon. It was easier to stay alive if one made less of a target.

The riders were close. Three of them. Spread wide apart. Only one carried a rifle. The first bullet ripped through the canvas. An arrow thudded into the bed directly above his head.

As he took aim and fired, hitting only empty space, he sent up a silent prayer that Addy would have the sense to remain low down and on the pallet. Holding the pistol with both hands, arms straight in front of him, he drew bead on the nearest attacker.

Slowly, with great patience, determined not to waste more ammunition, he squeezed the trigger. The warrior (he could by now tell the riders were Indians) clutched at his chest and rolled off the hindquarters of his paint pony.

A lance buried itself to the end of its flint point in front of him, making a dull, sickening sound as it cut into the damp earth. He cocked the pistol and aimed again. The remaining two were so close he knew he'd only have time to take care of one. The other . . .

Damn! He fired just as the pony's head jerked up. The horse stumbled and pitched to the side. Its rider leapt away unharmed.

He unsheathed his knife and scrambled from under the wagon. He had to keep them from getting inside.

The two warriors, sensing quick victory, pulled their own knives. At least they had honor. They were giving him a chance by using the same weapon he had chosen.

He had a moment to catch his breath as he spread his legs and bent his knees, shifting his weight from one side to the other.

As he swiftly scanned their young faces, his gut wrenched at the glazed, maniacal look in their eyes. *Drunk.* No wonder they had been brazen enough to attack with so few in their party.

Suddenly, his time was up. The older and stouter of the two came at him from the right. Trace parried the thrust of the knife with his own blade and hooked the back of the brave's knee, surprising him, and flipping him to the ground.

Before he could finish the first assailant off, the second jumped him from the left. Trace whirled and cut him on the upper arm. The young warrior snarled and threw his body against Trace before Trace could get his knife back in position.

A large shadow loomed from behind him, blocking the early warmth of the sun. Trace's heart stopped beating for two seconds, then pounded with a dull thud. He was too tangled with the one opponent to defend against both at the same time.

This was it, then. He prayed that Addy had the sense to escape now, while she still had a chance.

Chapter Thirteen

Trace felt an added rush of strength when he heard the wheezes and grunts from another scuffle. Someone had come to his aid. And the initial terror that it might be the foolhardy Addy gave him the power to push his Indian assailant backward enough to get his feet under him.

All thought of anything other than his own battle was washed from his mind when the brave came back at him, slashing at his shins, aiming to deliver a crippling thrust.

He jumped back. The Indian, knees bent, arms spread wide, advanced. Trace waited for him to make the next move. His muscles, unaccustomed to the frenzied activity, began to cramp.

Suddenly, springing with the slightest sign of the customary flash of warning in his obsidian eyes, the warrior came in low, then shot upward. The wide blade knicked Trace's stomach, even as Trace sucked in his gut and whirled, catching the young brave in the back of his knees with his foot.

Blood trickled through the slash in his shirt, which was plastered to his body like a second skin. Sweat nearly blinded him. He was almost caught off guard when the warrior gave a bloodcurdling shriek and dove at his chest.

Trace's hands came up in an instinctive gesture of self-protection. His knife entered the Indian's chest at the base of his throat and grated down through bone and sinew. Dead on his feet, the warrior's eyes glazed, muting their ferocious glare even as his lips quivered and drooped, losing the viciousness of the curled snarl.

The force of the attack had carried them both to the ground. Trace lay stunned for moments before he remembered the second attacker.

Rather than leap to his feet in readiness, though, it was all he could do to crawl to his hands and knees.

The other assailant lay about ten feet away, his head cocked at an odd angle. Trace glanced quickly around the temporary camp, and would have smiled if he had the energy — until the next sight almost gave him heart failure.

Eagle Feather stood near the back of the wagon, one hand gripping the rim of a wagon wheel, the other spread across his heaving chest. Adeline stood inside the wagon, clutching the heavy sheet about her with one arm, while the other made a slow, unsteady circular arc, the handle of a cast-iron frying pan gripped tightly between her clenched fingers.

The Comanche was totally unaware of his danger.

Trace shouted, "Eagle Feather, duck!"

The downward momentum of the heavy pan was more than Addy had the strength to control. Her target easily sidestepped out of reach. The next thing she knew, unwilling to release her makeshift weapon, she was toppling over the tailgate.

Two strong arms caught her before she hit the ground, but her savior was none other than the dreaded savage. She was immobilized with fear. All of the ugly stories she had heard about scalping and mutilation of bodies warred for priority in her brain.

Too weak to fight any longer, she went limp in his arms. A sad little sigh hissed through her trembling lips. Where was Trace? Was he dead, too?

Eagle Feather's eyes were trained warily on the woman lying so peacefully in his arms. Though she was quiet now, he fully remembered the loud cracking of bones when the cooking weapon had slammed into the enemy's head. An inch or two more to the left, and he, too, could have been dead at the hands of the pale-faced squaw.

His dark eyes fairly glowed. He had felt the rush of air as the heavy object narrowly missed his shoulder. His arms tightened on his burden. How he wished he could claim such a woman.

Though he continued to study the lovely, dark-haired creature, his words were directed at Trace. "Good battle, yes?"

Trace stumbled to his feet, gasping, though his quickly indrawn breaths burned his lungs. With what Addy thought was decided unconcern for her well-being, he pointed between the savage and herself, then to the dead man.

"Which . . . one of you . . . is responsible . . . for . . . that one?"

Eagle Feather straightened and stared down his nose at Addy. "I needed no help. I only knelt down to throw my opponent off guard."

Addy regained enough vigor to struggle, trying to extricate herself from the Indian's grasp. She had come to the conclusion that she wasn't going to die immediately, and was nervously assessing the situation. "Trace. Uh, Trace . . ."

Trace was busy looking from the frying pan to the dead brave. He asked Eagle Feather, "Did she do that?"

The Comanche nodded.

Addy, wide-eyed, glanced fitfully back and forth between Trace and her captor. Wasn't Trace going to even try to help her?

She frowned and looked more closely at the Indian. There was something familiar . . . *Of course!* Trace had met this one that night down by the river. But what was he doing way out here?

Though Eagle Feather gazed back at her with an odd glint that she couldn't really make out, his next words were maddening enough to make her forget that she had a healthy fear of Indians.

"The woman does not know her place. You need to teach her the difference between the duties of a man and those of a *woman.*"

Addy was so angry she could do no more than sputter, although she did manage to loose herself from the Indian's strong grasp. The nerve of the man. Why, he made it sound like a woman was hardly a grade above a dog!

Her voice quavered as she responded to the Indian's charge. "And I suppose, when that . . . that . . . *other* savage . . . leaped upon you, his knife raised to come down in the middle of your worthless back, you were in complete control."

Eagle Feather regally nodded.

Trace smothered a snicker.

Addy was shocked into silence.

Her eyes dared a peek at the dead man. They widened, aghast. Color flooded her pale face. Her lips formed a soundless "Oh."

Eagle Feather stalked to the dead warrior and withdrew his elk-horn handled knife from the man's belly, wiping the blade clean in the caked top layer of sandy dirt.

Trace frowned at the navy-blue breechcloth, wondering which poor soldier was the reluctant donor of his uniform. "Know what tribe they're from?"

Eagle Feather examined the poorly made moccasins and the painted markings on the brave's face. "No tribe."

"Renegades?"

The Comanche shrugged.

"They were drunk."

Eagle Feather's face twisted into a scowl. It was the most revealing display of emotion Trace had ever witnessed in the man. So much for the Indian myth of impassiveness.

"I'm sorry."

"Yes, I know you are, Trace Randall. When I get my hands on whoever . . ."

Trace felt the same burning rage that choked his friend. "It's only a matter of time. They can't continue to get away with this forever."

The two men, so different, yet so alike in many respects, stared into each other's eyes. They both heard a moan, and whirled, alert and ready to take on any danger.

Addy had dropped to her knees near the back of the

wagon. Trace was the first to reach her. His hands shook so badly, he barely had time to jerk the sheet back in place and cover Addy's nakedness before Eagle Feather arrived.

"Are you all right, honey?"

"I-I'm sorry. I just . . . felt faint . . . of a sudden."

A proud grin curved Trace's lips. God, but she was some woman. "You were sure brave. Probably used all your energy swingin' that fryin' pan."

He bent down and retrieved the offending skillet, then packed it back inside the wagon.

One glance at Eagle Feather and his nerves unwound another notch. He wasn't at all sure he liked the look in his friend's eyes as the Comanche gazed intently at Adeline. He instantly placed his body between the two, and huskily said to Eagle Feather, "Uh, I thank you for the warning."

Before Trace could react quickly enough, Eagle Feather pushed past him and scooped Addy into his thick, brown arms.

Trace's teeth ground together. That was the second time his friend had held Adeline. What the hell was on Eagle Feather's mind?

Exhausted and totally unable to defend herself, Addy unloosed a strangled shriek at being manhandled by the savage—again.

Eagle Feather ignored her and nodded, first to Trace, then toward the mussed pallet. "The woman needs rest. I will hand her in to you."

Trace tried to hide his anguished sigh as he clambered into the wagon. Damn! He couldn't believe he was actually jealous. And of his own best friend. Eagle Feather was only *holding* her, for God's sake.

As it was, Addy was the one to break the strained silence. "You said Eagle Feather warned you. How? I didn't hear anything. I nearly died of fright." She glared up at Eagle Feather. He sure didn't seem to be in a hurry to hand her over to Trace. ". . . when I saw him coming and thought he was another . . . You know what I mean. And you already had more than you could handle."

She fixed her eyes on him, all innocence, as Trace scowled. More than he could handle? Why, the little tenderfoot. He could've taken on more . . . His moustache twitched with derision. Well, maybe not . . .

Eagle Feather was the one to finally answer her question while Trace was busy pouting. "It is a signal we devised years ago. While most Comanche use the call of the owl, or coyote, we chose the meadowlark. Something different, yet a sound that would not seem out of place."

Addy stared at Eagle Feather, awed by his impeccable speech. He could have gone to any school in the East, even Boston, and held his own in any parlor.

She blinked when he appeared to be waiting. Oh, yes, he'd been speaking to her. Quickly, she responded, "Uh, how very clever." It really was fascinating, the tricks one had to rely upon to survive in the wild West.

After she was finally, and gently, placed on the pallet, she saw the eyes of both men glued to the sheet and the revealing way it draped the curves of her body. She squirmed uncomfortably, her hands fidgeting along a tattered corner of the material. How she'd love to throw the irksome thing off completely.

Oh dear. What a shameful thing to think. She would have to do better at remembering who and where she was. What would the people back home . . . Her lips drew into a thoughtful pout.

Who was she afraid of? There wasn't anyone left in Boston to care what became of her. And why should she give a fig. . . ? No, this wasn't right. What had gotten into her lately, to think and behave with such abandonment?

Besides, she had to think of something to get the two men's attention centered elsewhere.

"How . . . how is it that the two of you are such good friends? It seems rather . . . unusual."

A long time seemed to pass before Trace crawled over to sit on the tailgate. He looked down at Eagle Feather, then into the distance as the morning sun heralded new life to the blooming prairie and its creature inhabitants.

His voice was so low it seemed to drift on a breeze of its own creation. "Eagle Feather saved my life."

The Indian's eyes now concentrated on Trace's strong profile, enabling her to loosen the sheet, at least. But when Trace just sat there, silently contemplating who-knew-what, she couldn't stand it. How dare he prick her curiosity and leave her hanging like that?

"How. . . ?" Her voice sounded shrill, and more shrewish than she intended when the men again returned their eyes to her.

She took a breath and started over. "*How* did he save you? Where were you? Did you know each other before?" Her eyes furtively sought Eagle Feather, standing outside, but close to the wagon. She wriggled closer to Trace and muttered out of the side of her mouth. "I thought Indians killed most white people."

Trace's lips twitched. He'd heard Scratch mutter something now and again about a "damned persnickety she-male and her carnsarned questions." He now knew to whom Scratch was referring.

Whether Eagle Feather had heard her or not, she would never know from his indifferent expression.

"Well, isn't anyone going to. . . ?"

Before she could get wound up again, both men spoke at once.

"It was ten years . . ."

"He was dying . . ."

They looked at each other and grinned.

"As I was sayin', ten years ago, I was just a *tenderfoot* myself." Trace winked at Addy and leaned back against the canvas. "I'd heard the stories about Bill Becknell and the Bent brothers, and about the fortune to be made in New Mexico. So, like many other young men with nothing more substantial than dreams for brains, I started out on the trail to El Dorado, or Paradise, or Santa Fe, or whatever name you want to give it."

Eagle Feather suddenly held up a hand. Trace stilled.

206

When a coyote topped the ridge, saw the small party, and trotted away unconcerned with his nose to the ground, the Comanche relaxed

Trace reholstered his pistol and continued, "I got as far as the second cutoff and couldn't take the time to go on to Bent's Fort. With one canteen and a pouch full of jerked buffalo meat, I set out from the Arkansas River to cross the desert to the Cimmaron."

He stopped and swallowed, a reflex action of remembrance. "Anyway, the first day I ran out of water and my horse went lame. I couldn't take the beast any farther, and I couldn't bring myself to shoot him, so I turned him loose."

"For a while, the next day, I dragged my saddle along, but the sun and heat stole what strength I had. I discarded the saddle, then my bedroll, then my jacket. Somehow, I had the sense to keep on what clothes I wore . . . and I kept the canteen. Wishful thinking, or more dreaming, I suppose."

Addy could hardly picture the competent, resourceful Trace in such a dire situation. Sure, she had been credited with saving him not so long ago herself, but that didn't count. He'd been injured and taken captive against his will.

Scratch's words came back to her, about how one had to learn from one's mistakes. A shudder shook her small frame at the very thought of Trace dying then, of never experiencing the joy or the pleasure he brought her.

Unaware of Addy's tortured thoughts, Trace rubbed a hand over his eyes. Retelling the tale wasn't so easy. His palms were damp and he found it hard to catch his breath.

Eagle Feather took sympathy on his friend, picking up the story from where he'd first seen the collapsed body, allowing Trace to omit details that would offend the woman's delicate sensibilities.

"You were very lucky that day. I could as easily have gone one of a hundred directions. Instead, I saw the tracks of some fool in stiff-soled boots, stumbling across

207

the desert during the hottest portion of the day. I had to find out, who was this crazy person."

Trace snorted. "Thank you very much."

Addy's eyes sparked with interest. "And you two have been friends ever since?"

"Well, it wasn't quite that simple."

"Especially after my blood brother joined the dreaded bluecoats." The Comanche looked back and forth between the two people, saw that the woman wasn't surprised or shocked, and nodded.

Addy could have sworn she saw Trace blush, but he turned his head into the shadows.

"I only enlisted to do what I could to help my friends." He cleared his throat. "I might just as well have gone on wandering, for all the good it's done."

"Your heart is good, Trace Randall. No friend could ask for more."

Addy was lost. When had the conversation gotten away from her? What were they talking about?

Before she had a chance to voice further questions, Eagle Feather tilted his head in the direction of the three dead Indians. "I will take care of our visitors."

Trace jumped from the wagon, winced and doubled over a moment. "I'll help."

As they walked away, Addy heard Eagle Feather decline Trace's offer. "No. See to the woman. She is in great . . ."

Drat! The rest of the sentence faded into nothing as they moved out of hearing. Tired, and still a little shaky from her early-morning scare, she closed her eyes and was instantly asleep.

Trace glanced hastily back at the wagon, but hurried to catch up to Eagle Feather. "You think she's in danger, too?"

The Comanche stopped. "Did you not notice anything unusual about the attack?"

Trace rubbed the short stubble on his chin. "Yeah, I did. But I figured it could have been because they were drinkin'. The first thing that came to mind was that it

208

was an awful small raidin' party to make a head-on charge like that."

Eagle Feather calmly bent over the two closer bodies, then headed toward the one Trace had shot off the horse.

"Nothing about this raid is as it should be."

Trace watched as Eagle Feather searched the man's pouches. His brows drew together when he heard the jingle and clink of coins. "Hell! Gold pieces. Where'd he get those?"

The Comanche's lip curled. "Coins buy whiskey, guns."

"But . . . What use. . . ?" Suddenly, he snapped his fingers. He shook his head. At first, it hadn't made sense, yet, why else would three young braves stage such a daring raid? What if . . . they knew beforehand the wagon was stranded, its occupants impaired. . . ?

And what if someone paid the renegades in gold, knowing full well the money would be returned when the Indians came back to trade for the contraband items? No one could have known about Eagle Feather, or the return of the mules.

The full import of his suspicions nearly made his knees buckle. He thoughtfully rubbed the lobe of one ear as he looked at Eagle Feather. "I have a hunch, my friend, that we may be closer than we ever realized to finding our culprits."

Addy awoke feeling groggy and disoriented. She'd had the most horrible nightmare. Indians had attacked their wagon and . . .

She raised upon one elbow and blearily focused on the frying pan lying just inside the tailgate, rather than in its usual hanging position. As she looked around for anything else that might be out of place, she noticed smears of blood on the corner of the sheet.

She sank back down and closed her eyes. So, it wasn't a dream after all. She'd been afraid of that.

At first, the blood didn't bother her. It seemed she had

209

almost grown accustomed to such sights. But then she started thinking . . . The stains were on a portion of the cover that wasn't even near any of her *own* scrapes. Some faded memory nagged at her.

A rustling at the back of the wagon caused her to gasp and jerk her head in that direction. When Trace gingerly raised himself up and over the gate, it all came flooding back.

"Trace, you're hurt!"

His head came up. "What?"

"Your stomach. You were cut. Don't you remember?"

"Oh . . . Yeah." Actually, he had forgotten. Every once in a while a sharp twinge jabbed his belly, but he hadn't paid it any mind. "It's nothin'."

Concerned by his callous indifference to a deep, or possibly infected wound, she tried to sit up. He was immediately at her side. She reached out and touched the stiff discoloration on his shirt.

He was so strong, dangerous, and exciting. Who else did she know who was brave enough to risk his life against three able-bodied savages? No one, besides maybe Scratch in his younger days. And who would have gone against two of them with only a knife to defend himself? Her eyes literally shone with admiration and . . . an even deeper emotion she wasn't ready to analyze at the moment.

Trace followed the path of her fingers with his eyes and winced when she gave the blood-stiffened material a slight tug. "Maybe I should take a look," he said.

"Wet your shirt first and let it soak. It's dried to the wound."

He cocked his head and grinned. "Thanks ever so much, nurse Montclair."

She sniffed indignantly, but smiled. "Well, even city girls know a little something about dressing wounds. People get hurt, even in Boston."

He gently flicked a spot on her nose that wasn't red or burned. "How do you feel?"

She proudly bent her knees and lifted the arm that

wasn't supporting her a few inches off the pallet. "Better. I'm not as stiff as I was this morning."

"Good. Must've been all the exercise." He was teasing, trying to take the sting out of the bad experience. "If you're able, we'll head for Council Grove in the morning."

He started to peel out of his shirt. Suddenly shy, she forced herself *not* to look away. She blinked in sympathy when she heard his hissed intake of breath as he plucked the spun cotton from the long cut just above the waistband of his trousers.

It was a relief to see the cut was not as deep as the amount of blood lost made it appear. Her own stomach quivered as she watched his hand glide a damp cloth over his hard, washboard belly and lean rib cage.

As his movements slowed and became more pronounced, even tantalizing, her tongue unconsciously circled her lips. She raised her eyes, to find that he watched her watching him. Her hand, seemingly of its own volition, reached out to take the cloth. "Let me help."

She dunked the rag in the pail of water and squeezed it over the wound. Water trickled down his belly and disappeared into his pants. His muscles jumped and rippled. Dipping as far as she could, the thick band scraped the backs of her knuckles.

His chest rose and fell with short, quick pants for air. Her hand trembled. She didn't realize she'd spoken aloud until the words echoed hauntingly in her ears. "You're beautiful."

He moaned. She shook her head as if coming out of a trance and croaked, "Am . . . am I hurting you?"

His bronzed skin turned a deeper shade of brown, with a slightly pinkish tint. He sucked in his stomach and shifted to hide the predictable reaction of his lower body. Whispering, "More than you'll ever know," he reached down to stop the tormenting movement of her hand, and took the cloth into his own, safer, grasp. Then, he bent over and kissed the side of her cheek.

211

The moving gesture came as such a surprise that she caught her breath. For a long time, they stared into each others eyes. If he had taken her body and made glorious love to her, it wouldn't have touched her soul as deeply as that one little kiss.

Her whole body tingled. When? When would he touch her again the way he had that night? That one wonderful night?

She sighed, disappointed when he raised glazed eyes to the canvas and hurriedly left the wagon.

They started after the caravan the next morning. In the distance, Eagle Feather sat regally upon his mustang and raised his hand in farewell.

Addy had slipped into a loose-fitting nightdress, and had even lifted one arm high enough to pull a brush through her hair. Every once in a while, she'd look up to catch Trace peeking at her, craning his neck to see over the crates. Her heart beat a lively jig against her breast, and her pulse throbbed as if she'd actually performed the dance.

At least traveling was easier than they had expected. The mud had dried considerably during their brief stopover. Addy wasn't sure if she was glad or disappointed.

If they made Council Grove the following day, as Trace predicted, then their time alone was drawing to a close. She would be embarrassed to admit it, but she had enjoyed having him all to herself.

Once they were back with the wagon train, everything would change. She'd have to sneak glances and feel guilty, or afraid, if they were found together.

Her face flamed. Not that she had to worry. So far, the brotherly peck on the cheek was as close as he'd gotten to her. Why couldn't she be grateful that he wasn't lusting after her, forcing her to. . . ?

Force? Now that was a laugh. In this particular instance, the tables were turned. *She* was the one doing the lusting. Gently, she scratched the end of her nose. What had happened? Had she done something wrong? Granted, she wasn't very worldly or wise, but . . .

A long, sad sigh hissed through her teeth. Trace. She shook her head. Who would have thought that timid, prim little Adeline Montclair would fall for a devil-may-care adventurer? And wouldn't her old beaux laugh if they knew it was *she* who'd been spurned?

The day seemed to drag on forever before Trace finally decided to make camp. He stopped on a knoll beneath two large cottonwoods. The wind gusted, and though a creek was nearby, the mosquitoes and bugs were not as bad as usual.

"Hope you're not tired of antelope stew."

She licked her lips. "As a matter of fact, I've come to look forward to it."

Trace dragged his eyes away from her perfect bow-shaped mouth in time to keep from burning himself as he started the evening fire. "You sound like you're surprised. Just wait till you taste buffalo."

Grimacing slightly, she leaned over the gate, trying to figure out how to get it lowered. Trace was there in a second, scolding, "I wish you'd let me help you."

His attentiveness disconcerted her. She plucked at the lacy neckline of her gown. "You have more important things to do."

He reached past her, picked up a blanket and spread it in front of the rear wheel. When he turned back to lift her down, she waved him away. "I'm not a baby. I can . . ."

She was in his arms before she had a chance to finish. One would have thought her scrapes were on her backside from the searing his arms gave her flesh, even through two layers of cloth.

"Humor me. The way you're recoverin', you'll be flittin' about on your own soon enough. Take advantage of my kind nature while you can."

She ducked her head so he wouldn't see the despair in her eyes. She'd like to take advantage of more than his kind nature. The confusion and hurt inside her breast rivaled any physical pain she'd suffered.

Trace's arms tightened. Truth be told, he looked for any and every excuse to be near her, and now that he had her in his arms . . . Hell! Why couldn't he find the nerve to outright ask her about the damned button? It should be so simple . . . Put his lips together and . . . No, not kiss her, *talk*, just talk to her.

Blood roiled through Addy's veins until she felt lightheaded from the rush. She wrapped her arms about his neck and dreamily inhaled his masculine scent of leather and sweat and dusty earth.

When he finally set her down on the blanket, she was tempted to reach out and stop him from leaving. He even hesitated, giving her ample opportunity. But she couldn't. She'd been too brazen and bold as it was. Perhaps that was why he had been so . . . so . . . reserved . . . and withdrawn.

Sitting still was torture. There was nothing to do but watch Trace as he knelt close to the fire. The sight was anything but hard on her hungry eyes. The orange glow from the flames caressed his lean jaw, giving his tanned cheeks the look of fine-grain mahogany.

Trace couldn't keep his eyes from straying in Addy's direction. She was exceptionally lovely in the moonlight. Her pale skin was almost translucent, her eyes so wide that a man could lose his soul in their hypnotic depths.

Until the fire burned low enough to cook over, Trace had needed to find something to keep his mind, and hands, busy. Taking off his shirt, he went to the pail of fresh water he'd just fetched from the creek to wash off the grime.

He gulped several large, cooling mouthfuls from the dipper, then poured the rest over his head and shoulders. Rivulets of water trickled down his neck and chest.

Addy's eyes widened appreciatively as he turned facing the fire. Light reflected from the glistening droplets dangling like golden crystals from the curly hair coating the smooth, bulging muscles of his chest. He brushed at the clinging beads, at the same time sending a shower of water from his shaggy blond mane as he shook his head. His eyes glanced toward Addy and narrowed seductively at the obvious pleasure she derived from ogling his body.

The stew was barely warm when he ladled out enough for two portions and went to sit beside her. He couldn't stay away any longer, though he cringed inside to think he was so weak where she was concerned.

Addy accepted her bowl and smiled. His stomach dropped into his moccasins before bouncing back.

Her lashes lowered demurely, her voice was no more than a husky whisper. "Thank you. This is almost like a picnic."

His Adam's apple bobbed in his throat. "You, uh, like picnics?"

Her eyes lit up brighter than the flames dancing along a dry twig, cheeks blushing with a rosy iridescence. "Oh, yes. I used to love them." Then her face fell. "It's been years . . . You know, I remember once, Lily and her mother came to one. We were so very young."

He had no control over his response. "Bet you were a beautiful little girl. And Delilah, too."

"Things were different then. My parents were full of life and vigor, and were so much in love." She paused for a moment, lost in memory. "Who would have thought pudgy, ugly, little Lily would grow up to be so trim and gorgeous?" Stuttering through a nervous giggle, she continued, "I'm sorry. Shame on me for saying such a thing about my cousin. But even my father used to say . . . Well, he would be surprised. He would."

"She'll never hold a candle to you," he said so softly he could have only thought it, then turned away, embarrassed, when she jerked her head around to stare at him with a hundred questions in her eyes. Damn! Yes, he had totally lost control.

"Want more stew?"

"Pardon me? Oh, no. No. I'm fine. I-I thought . . . Uhhmm, never mind." She sighed. His voice had been so low a moment ago that she wasn't sure she heard correctly. Did he *really* think she was prettier than her

215

cousin?

Her eyes left the deep cleft in his chin to pierce each bright red mark within sight on her battered body. No, he couldn't look at her, say such a thing, and *mean* it.

She felt the brush of his knuckles as he took the bowl from her fingers. Her hand jerked as if she'd been burned from a dozen sparks. Instead of backing away, though, he sat the empty bowls to the side and scooted back to lean against the wheel, his shoulder brushing hers. "It's a pretty night." Only his eyes weren't looking at anything but her.

"Yes, it is."

She remembered something about stars and a moon, but right now, all she could stare at were his long, lean legs stretched out beside her own. Her bare toes curled, hiding themselves beneath the hem of her long gown. Her heart beat erratically as her blood turned the consistency of slow-moving lava.

The next thing she knew, she was tucked under his strong arm, leaning her head against his shoulder. Suddenly, she asked, "How is your stomach?" Oh, she could have bitten off her tongue. There she went again, boldly jumping into the frying pan. That wasn't at all what she had been thinking. Or was it? That hard, muscled belly; his smooth skin . . .

He cleared his throat, glad he'd had the presence of mind to slip his shirt on before warming the stew. If only the buttons didn't feel so constraining, like his circulation was slowly being cut off. Why? Why did she have to be injured now, when they were all alone? Just the two of them, the coyotes, and a brilliant moon. "Fine. How's yours?"

He became so caught up in staring at the way the soft flannel clung to the outline of her full breasts that he forgot he'd even said anything until she replied, "Fine. Really. I'm not nearly as sore . . ."

Her eyes sought out the compelling line of his lips and roved upward, locking with his. Was this the time she had been waiting . . . agonizing for? Would he take her

216

in his arms and make love to her?

Their heads tilted at the same time, bringing their lips together in a searing kiss that lasted what seemed like a lifetime. One of Trace's hands touched the outline of her breast. She gasped. Her body was on fire—for him.

He thought he had hurt her. He guiltily tamped the embers smoldering in his gut, surprising himself that he even made the effort. Hell, was it possible that in his concern for her well-being, he gave little importance to his own bodily needs?

"God, honey, I'm sorry."

She saw the change in his eyes, the consternation on his finely sculpted features, and felt as cold as if a bucket of water had been dashed over her head. It was all she could do to force out, "I know." And she did. She understood.

His voice was loud and gruff and it was all he could do to keep from shouting, "Damn it! I can't make love to you." And it was all the more frustrating because he knew she was willing. There was certainly no question that *he* was. But he didn't dare. It was just too soon and she would find it painful. That wasn't what he wanted for her. She should like it, and want *more*.

Her throat burned as she fought back tears at his rejection. "I know." Yes, she knew he didn't want her. It broke her heart.

Chapter Fourteen

Addy leaned back against a box marked HAND TOOLS, trying to find a comfortable position in which to cushion her backside against the bump and sway of the wagon as it jolted over the rutted terrain. The mud had finally dried, but the trail had been made almost impassable by the weight of the earlier wagons.

Her gaze was drawn to the steadfast driver. How could the man appear so relaxed and easygoing after putting her through a night of pure hell? Her chagrin only increased as she stared daggers at his impossibly straight back for the hundredth time in the past half hour.

She didn't think she had gotten one wink of sleep. Damn the man! She covered her mouth in shock, even though she had only *thought* the dratted curse. See what he had caused? He was driving her to maddeningly unpredictable behavior.

Trace shifted his rump on the hard bench and rolled his shoulders to relieve the strain. He knew Adeline watched him, for he felt the prickly sensation of a dozen sharp needles piercing his back.

What was *she* upset about? *He* was the one suffering this morning. The continuous ache in his groin doubled from the pressure of the tight pants.

He tilted his head to scratch his cheek against his shoulder, then flicked the reins. If the mules would only pick up their pace, they could all be in Council Grove in time for supper.

Stretching his right leg to ease a cramp, he allowed himself a brief moment to consider his actions of the

218

previous evening. His throat became drier, and his stomach tightened. No matter what he'd like to believe, his reaction to the woman was fast becoming an embarrassment.

His manhood hardened at the very thought of her. And he knew good and well that the reason he hadn't made love to her last night was because he *cared* for the woman. Hell! How had *that* come about?

He'd like to think that he had reservations about her. The button burned a hole in his trouser pocket. But all suspicion, *everything*, completely slipped his mind when he held her in his arms.

His hands trembled, causing the mules to step uneasily in the traces, jiggling the chain. "Easy now. My fault."

God, what was with him? He had even gone soft on the mules! How could one slip of a girl disrupt his mind, his life; Hell, even his sexual prowess? He could hardly wait to arrive at Council Grove and turn the minx over to Scratch. Only, if that was the case, why did his chest get that peculiar feeling, like it had been crushed by a heavy mallet?

Late in the afternoon, Addy wiped the perspiration from her face and neck and between her breasts. She grumbled when the wagon jolted to a stop.

Trace soon appeared at the tailgate and climbed into the hot, damp, canvassed shade. She winced at his red-tinged cheeks, nose, and forehead as he tenderly wiped the sweat from his face with his sleeve.

"We're almost there." He closed his eyes and leaned against a support rib. If he didn't get a hat, the sun would cook him alive.

Addy leaned forward, craning her neck, bubbling with curiosity. He pointed through the front opening. "See that long line of trees in the distance?"

She nodded.

219

"That's it. That's Council Grove."

Wonder and disappointment warred for possession of her splendid features. Blood throbbed through his veins until his fingertips tingled. He'd never felt so attuned to a person in his life.

She stammered, "Th-that's it? Just trees?"

"What were you expectin'?"

Her voice took on a soft, little-girl quality. "I-I don't know. I guess I thought there would be a town . . . buildings . . . *something*."

He shook his head, knowing how tough the trip would be for her. "Sorry. But there is a cute little creek running through the middle of it."

"Oh, boy." Then feeling ashamed by her outburst, she asked, "Why would anyone stop there? From the way you all talked, I thought Council Grove was someplace . . . special."

"It is. There's lots of good wood—oak, hickory, walnut—to make repairs to the wagons. There's fresh game. You can wash clothes in the creek. Small groups of travelers wait there until more wagons arrive to form a large train with more men and guns. It gets dangerous from here on."

She flashed him a surprised look. "You mean it can get worse?"

His eyes softened as they worked down her flannel-clad form. A grin curled his firm lips. She thought she might swoon as it made his lean features so attractive.

"Maybe not for you. But the things you've gone through won't happen again for another hundred trains."

"I can't say as I believe that."

He was close, only a foot away. Her body swayed, but she caught herself. No, she wasn't going to make a fool of herself again. If only her body wasn't so tingly and . . . sensitive. Even the light-weight cloth of her gown teased her flesh, causing her to squirm with undeniable desire.

220

Trace couldn't take his eyes off her agitated movement. His hands literally itched to touch the blasted woman. How could she sit there so innocently, her hair loose, hanging seductively down her back, and her body, that sweet, delectable body, hardly concealed beneath the thin layer of material? Didn't she have any idea of what she did to him, as a man?

His eyes narrowed as her tongue darted out to moisten her lower lip, leaving a wet, enticing sheen that begged to be kissed away. Maybe she *did* know. Maybe that was why . . . He shook his head. No, she was exactly what she seemed—an innocent. Ah, but he alone knew what a passionate, vibrant nature lay buried inside that prim exterior.

"Well, *ahem,* I guess we better get moving. If the caravan is still there, we should be just in time for supper."

Addy swallowed and nodded. If? What would Trace and she do *if* they had been left behind?

Reading her mind, he said, "Don't worry. Scratch said he would be there waitin'. I think he'll keep his word."

Her eyes were as big and soft as a fawn's when she gazed at him. He shifted uncomfortably on the seat when he read her trust as clearly as the sun glinting off a brand new gold piece.

God, what he had done to deserve it? He wasn't used to looking after anyone but himself, and now this tenderfoot woman stared at him as if his every word and act were the gospel truth.

He took the quickest and most difficult means to get himself away from her disturbing proximity. But as he stepped over her legs, he stumbled on the loose board and had to catch himself. His hand clutched her shoulder. His palm filled with soft, luxuriant hair and fragile bone.

Suddenly, the starch left his legs and he sank to his knees by her side. He ran his fingers into the thick mass of hair, cradling her delicate head in his hands. His eyes

221

darkened until they gleamed black in the shadowed interior of the wagon.

He saw the same naked desire clearly etched in the depths of her eyes, so wide and luminous they shone almost gold. His head dropped and his lips easily captured hers. Her body arched, pressing her breasts against his chest. Her taut nipples seared his flesh like two small branding irons. She opened her mouth to him and he plundered its warm, inviting softness.

But he drew a deep, shuddering breath and pulled away, leaning his forehead against hers. He sucked in great gulps of air in an effort to clear his head before it was too late.

When she moaned and covered her stomach protectively, he knew he had done the right thing.

After the passage of several long minutes, he struggled to his feet and continued to the front of the wagon. Addy weakly lay her head back against a wooden crate, its hardness providing a welcome contrast to the silken feel of Trace's fingers. *Damn him!* The curse felt so good in her mind that she savored it as she would a gooey piece of rich chocolate.

That was the *last* time she would *ever* humiliate herself by acting like a wanton fool. The next time he tried to touch her, she would cut off his hands with a dull ax.

The closer they got to Council Grove, the quicker the mules' pace became. Trace ran the back of his arm across his forehead and nearly jumped from the wagon when Addy spoke from directly behind him. Now he was even losing his hearing.

"How much farther?"

He raised his chin, using his nose as a pointer. "Yonder a ways. Won't be long now."

"Good. My bottom's so sore . . . Uhmm, I mean, I'm anxious to stretch my legs."

He glanced over his shoulder to where she knelt behind the bench, then covertly sneaked several peeks until she realized what he was doing and clutched the neck of her gown.

Finally, he looked away, but his big grin told her she hadn't reacted quickly enough. Ooohh, the beast! She was imagining several different methods of wiping the silly smirk from his handsome face when she cocked her head. "What's that?"

His eyes narrowed as he scanned the area, alert for possible danger. "Where?"

"No. What's that I smell?"

He inhaled and shrugged his shoulders. "Probably wood."

She clapped her hands. "I bet it's campfires."

Trace stared at her. God, she was beautiful, with her hair brushed behind her ears, her cheeks so rosy, and her eyes lit up like twin candles . . . He had half a mind to stop the team and crawl back there with her.

"Oh, look! There's a wagon. And another. And there's Lily. No, there are two other women. It's not our group at all. I wonder who they are? Do you suppose they're going to Santa Fe, too?"

"Well, I . . ."

"One's carrying a baby. But look, they're so thin. I wonder where their husbands are? It's dangerous for them to be left alone, isn't it?"

"I think . . ."

"My goodness, look at those wagons. They're not the same as ours. I wonder why? Where is Mr. Scratch, Trace? I don't see him yet."

Trace stopped the mules and tied the reins around the brake handle before turning to face her. He put his hands on her shoulders to keep her from bouncing out.

"Settle down a mite, will you? I already told you that smaller parties stop here and stay awhile. We're likely to pass several camps before we find ours." Under his breath, he added, *"If we do."*

She squirmed, trying to escape his restrictive grasp

and see past his muscular body. It had been so long since she had seen another woman besides her cousin.

"Can we stop? Can we find out who they are and where they're from and where they're going? I can see . . . Oh, dear. They look so ragged and . . . hopeless. I wonder what. . . ?" Her words faded as she got a really good glimpse of one of the women. She nearly gasped aloud at her bleak features.

Trace's hands tightened. Though his lips remained curved, his eyes mirrored the women's pain. "We need to keep goin' now, honey. Besides, you're not even dressed."

Her mouth turned down into a disappointed pout. She looked at her thin, wrinkled gown. It was just a like a man to use logic and appeal to a woman's vanity.

She ducked from his grasp and went back to scavenge through her trunks. By the time the team was moving again, she was back up front with a large shawl draped over her shoulders.

Resigned, he helped her to take a seat on the bench, looking on with indulged patience when she smiled and waved as they trundled past the staring women.

The next group they passed was a ragtag assortment of wagons and carriages. No women were visible, and the men had a preoccupied air about them. When they ceased their chores and watched the new arrivals, their eyes reflected a distant, inner excitement.

"Gold hunters."

Trace startled her out of her wild imaginings. She'd been putting her own names and places to the people, making up stories of their pasts and what their futures might hold. But she had never thought of *gold*. "What did you say?"

He jerked a thumb back toward the miners. "Bunch of crazy dreamers on their way to California to make their fortunes plucking gold nuggets from the ground."

She turned and peered around the canvas to catch a last look. The men didn't seem crazy to her. And if find-

224

ing gold was *that* easy, she wouldn't mind trying it herself.

Her attention returned to Trace and she forgot all about the others when he exclaimed, "That looks like our people over there across the creek."

She followed his gaze and breathed a sigh of relief when she spotted Scratch's bent, leather-clad figure. And there was Jubal, off to the side of the creek.

But she didn't allow her eyes to linger long before returning to Trace's grim countenance. The muscle in his cheek jerked. Why was he suddenly upset? She had thought he would be glad to be back with the wagon train.

Her teeth clicked as she snapped her jaws shut. At least now he wouldn't have to be *alone* with her; wouldn't have to fret that she would make indecent advances upon him. That should make him very happy. She straightened her sagging shoulders and held her chin at a haughty angle.

At that moment, a woman ran from behind the big, black carriage. "Addy? Oh my God, it is. Addy, thank goodness you're all right. I've been worried sick, dahlin'."

Trace's features hardened, causing Addy to blink, astonished, as his eyes turned to blue ice and his jaw clenched into a rigid line. She'd never seen him look so . . . so . . . dangerous.

She had no more opportunity to think about his strange reaction as she was suddenly flanked by her cousin, Mr. Scratch, and even the little Mexican, Pedro.

"Jubal told me all about your terrible accident. I was afraid you wouldn't be comin' back to us at all. You poor li'l dahlin'. Why, just look at you."

Before Addy's feet touched the earth, she was turned into Delilah's firm embrace. She grunted and winced when her healing wounds were pinched and scraped.

"Forgive me, dahlin'. I'm so thrilled to see you, I just

225

forgot you're injured. Really, I've been beside myself with grief and worry, prayin' y'all would reach us soon. My Jubal's done his best to delay our leavin', you know."

All the while Delilah prattled on, she looked over Addy's shoulder at Trace. It was the first time she had been close enough to get a good view of him. She abruptly stopped talking, released Addy, gave her perfectly coiffed hair a subtle pat and eyed him from head to foot.

"Haven't we met somewhere before?"

Addy sucked in her breath.

Trace shrugged. "I'm sure I would have remembered if we'd been introduced, ma'am."

The look in Delilah's eyes was enough to prove she was unconvinced, but the matter was temporarily dropped as Scratch moved her to one side and gently placed his arm around Addy's shoulders.

"Welcome back, gal. We, ah, we'uns shore missed ya."

Tears glistened in Addy's eyes as she gazed fondly at the old man. "I-I missed you, too, Mr. Scratch."

The old timer cleared his throat and wiped a finger under his nose before turning to the Mexican, who was just opening his mouth to speak to Addy. "Wal, c'mon, Pedro. What're we standin' 'roun here gawkin' at? Got us a passal o' chores that won't fix theyselves 'thout us."

Pedro looked back over his shoulder as Scratch led him away, just in time to catch Addy's sympathetic grin. He sent her a gap-toothed smile and waved.

Delilah took her arm and started walking her toward the carriage. Feeling suddenly low in spirits now that her time alone with Trace was *definitely* over, Addy was grateful for the concerned attention.

She didn't see the suspicious frown on Trace's face as he watched them go away together. He spun around to see to the mules, and came face to face with Jubal Wilkins.

"I see I made the right decision. Nothin' seriously wrong with the little lady after all." Wilkins inspected one of the new indentations on the nearby sideboard

226

caused from a wayward arrow.

Trace's fingers curled into tight fists, but he took a deep breath and gradually eased the tension from his hands. "No. She improved rapidly with a little rest."

"Looks like you ran into trouble."

"Naw, not really."

Jubal traced the splintered wood with a finger. "Then what's this?"

"That? Aw, I was just doin' some target practice an' got careless."

Jubal frowned. "So, you didn't have any trouble . . . findin' the team or anything?"

Trace shook his head and hooked his thumbs into the back pockets of his trousers.

"No trouble followin' our trail?"

"Nothin' I couldn't handle."

"That's good. Glad to hear it." Jubal stared questioningly at the side of the wagon, then smoothed his fat sideburns.

"Well, I guess you can pull your wagon in behind Dead Eye's. Just turn the mules loose and fetch a fresh team when we pull out day after tomorrow."

Trace flicked his fingers in a mock salute.

Jubal walked off a ways, then turned to eye Trace with new awareness. Almost as an afterthought, he said, "You did a good job with my dear little cousin-in-law. Thanks."

"Anytime."

And while Trace studied Wilkins' retreating back with great deliberation, Delilah asked Addy, "Where have I seen that man? I suppose I should've paid more attention to your fella before now."

Addy snapped, "He's not my fella!"

"Well now, dahlin', you should've mentioned that to Jubal before Mr. Randall up an' made off with you like some maraudin' bandit. If I wasn't already taken, I'd be inclined to give you some competition."

"Lily, I haven't the slightest idea what you are

227

getting at."

Delilah leaned closer. "Then let me explain, cousin of mine. *You* are an attractive, unattached lady. Your Mr. Randall is an exceptionally handsome bachelor." She rolled her eyes and licked her full lips.

"Lily!"

"Oh, yes, as I was sayin', I'm afraid your poor reputation is quite destroyed, dahlin'. Ripped to shreds. Nothin' but tattered bits and pieces. You know what I mean?"

Addy blinked. Damn Trace Randall. And damn Delilah, too. She didn't have to sound so smug and . . . gleeful.

She turned her head and stared when Delilah kept right on talking, as if there weren't a thousand disasters to confront. When had everything in her life turned into such chaos? When was the last time she'd had peace of mind?

"You know, it's not at all like me to forget a name or face. I wonder . . ."

"Why, it certainly is like you. You've always had a terrible memory. Remember when we were little, you were constantly forgetting the name of your favorite doll? She was so pretty and had such a lovely face. I bet you don't even remember her now."

Delilah stumbled to a standstill. "Ah, m-my doll? Why, I declare . . . Uh, I guess you're right, dahlin'. I just can't seem to think . . . uh . . ."

Addy stared at her cousin for a long time, but Delilah looked away. The speechless woman fluttered her soft hands and glanced around the camp. "Oh dear. Would you look at that, dahlin'? The fire's burned down and nothin's been put out to eat. Sit down and rest yourself. I'll . . . uh, oh, never mind."

As Delilah scurried around the fire, doing little or nothing, Addy found a comfortable place to sit. She was so terribly tired, and new aches seemed to crop up and take the place of those that had faded every time she moved.

Her mind was abuzz with so many questions and worries that she couldn't decide what to think about first. She finally shook her head. Oh yes, she could. What if Delilah remembered Trace from the boat? What if she mentioned his soldier's uniform?

A little niggle of fear inched down her spine. What was Trace hiding? What was he up to that was so dangerous? Or was he merely trying to frighten her into silence? If so, why?

Her chest constricted. It felt like an iron fist gripped her heart. Could he be using her for some reason? Was getting close to her, making her want him, part of some awful scheme?

Her head throbbed and she closed her eyes. She should rest. Maybe she could make better sense of things later.

Now, all she knew was that it was nice to be back with her only family, even if Delilah couldn't remember the name of the doll. Who cared, anyway? It was only a doll, and it had been a long, long time ago.

The next morning, Addy tried to convince herself that she wasn't worried, that she didn't care where Trace was, or what might have happened to him. But she couldn't resist searching the small camp for just one glimpse of his tall, graceful figure. She'd had him to herself just long enough that it concerned her that she hadn't seen him since last night at dusk when they had both stopped and just stared at one another.

For a moment, his eyes had darkened and she knew his arms were going to reach for her, but Scratch had chosen that time to interrupt, remarking, "Thar ya be. Jist wanted ta see how ya all be doin'."

Addy had snagged both hands into her shawl. "Uh, fine. I-I'm lots better."

Trace had slid his hands into his back pockets, pulling

the worn cotton shirt taut across his wide shoulders and muscled chest. She had gulped deliciously at the rawness of his voice when he told Scratch, "Yeah, me, too."

"Good. Right proud ta hear it. Kin I he'p ya, gal?"

Addy had been glancing from the wagon, to the thick copse of trees not too distant, to Trace, wondering if he would ask her to take a walk. When Scratch held out his hand to help her into the wagon, she took a step backward until Trace had said, "Where's the card game tonight, old man?"

"Down ta ole Pedro's wagon. Wanna take a hand?"

Addy held her breath.

"Naw, don't have nothin' to play with. But I'll watch. Still a bit early. Don't think I could sleep anyway."

"What?" Addy's mind had screamed. Then furious with herself for disregarding her earlier vow to stay away from the insolent rogue, she had gratefully allowed Scratch to help her inside where she ended up crying herself to sleep.

So why couldn't she concentrate on something, anything, besides that wretched Trace this morning? Why did she insist on torturing herself?

Two riders entered the camp from the west end. Her head perked up, and her heart fluttered fitfully when she spotted Trace.

He and Scratch pulled up in the middle of the circled wagons. Behind their saddles rode the carcasses of animals that resembled deer, but were larger and colored a rich rusty-tan with small horns that appeared to be coated with velvet.

Several men put down the harness they mended, or wood they were using to shape extra spokes and wagon tongues. They helped lift the heavy animals to the ground.

She blanched and nearly lost her breakfast when she saw they had already been gutted, but before she could turn away, Trace caught her eyes and motioned her over.

230

Unwilling to embarrass herself by appearing squeamish, she took a hearty breath and gamely started forward. However, she stopped several feet away, not feeling it necessary to stand *too* close to the poor beasts.

"You've got a treat comin' tonight, hon . . . Adeline." Trace bit back the endearment he'd become so used to uttering and glanced warily around. No one seemed to have heard his slip of the tongue.

Addy had noticed, though. Breathlessly she asked, "Wh-what are they? Deer?"

"Look a lot alike, don't they? No, they're elk. Wait till you taste the meat. You're goin' to love it."

She wrinkled her nose, doubtful that she could take one bite of anything so beautiful. Why, those big, brown, sightless eyes seemed to stare right through her — reproachful, accusing. She gagged and quickly turned her back when the men brandished knives and began skinning back the hides.

"Uh, excuse me. I-I forgot . . . something . . . at the wagon." She beat a hasty retreat, ignoring Trace's shouted, "Hey, Adeline. Wait!"

Before Trace could follow, Scratch said, "Here's the hindquarter ya wanted. Whatcha gonna do with it, boy?"

Trace's face warmed. "I know of someone who needs it worse than we do." Defensively, he added, "Is that all right with you?"

Scratch spat a brown trail of liquid into the dust and cocked his head to one side as he considered the younger man. "Yep. Reckon so." Then he dug his fingers into the slick leather covering his backside, cackled, and walked away muttering, "Gol durn young un's nowadays. Cain't ask a durn question 'thout . . ."

Trace shook his head, grabbed the reins of his horse and headed back the way he and Addy had driven in the day before. When he reached the last of the wagons, he hesitated, then called out, "Hello the camp. Anybody about?"

231

There was a movement at the back of one of the wagons. A thin, gray-haired woman peeked around the tattered end of the canvas. "What ya want?"

Trace held up the bloody haunch. "I brought some meat."

The woman's eyes lit up, then turned dull as she asked, "Why'd ya do a thing like that?"

He knew better than to trample on the woman's pride. He said, "My friend and I were lucky this morning. We killed more than we needed, so we divided it with several other groups down the line. But if your man's already provided, I'll . . ."

"Wait. You wait just a minute."

Her head disappeared. He could hear feminine voices arguing. A baby whimpered. Finally, the woman climbed from the wagon.

"Reckon you ought'n made the trip for nothin'. Ain't no man here. He were took from us week past. Reckon we can swap for the meat. What you be needin'?"

He had already taken note of the terribly poor surroundings, and knew anything he took would be missed. His eyes lit on a crate partially hidden beneath the wagon. There was a good felt hat on top of some neatly folded items.

"Those your, uh, husband's?"

"Yep. We're waitin' for some'un headed back to Virginny. Ain't got no use fer a dead man's poss'bles." Her faded blue eyes suddenly narrowed as she gave him a purely speculative once over.

"You an' my man be of similar size. Peers you could use a shirt what covered you in one piece. An' mebbe a bigger pair of britches."

Trace's face colored for the second time in one morning. For a man who, heretofore, thought he was immune to embarrassment, it was becoming an all-too-familiar state.

He and the woman dickered a while, and when he left, in possession of a change of clothes, the hat, and

232

two neck scarves, he was pretty proud of himself.

Knocking softly at the back of Addy's wagon, he looked inside, then all around. No sign of Adeline. Good. That would give him a chance to change.

He had just stripped from his clothes when he heard a stifled giggle. One great lunge took him to the row of boxes, where he found a cowering, wide-eyed Adeline with both hands covering her grinning mouth.

Bare-assed naked and outraged, he shouted, "You little minx! Were you spyin' on me?"

She scrambled to her feet and stood nose-to-chest with him. Her voice was smooth as whipped cream when she replied, "Don't flatter yourself. I was busy looking in my trunk and didn't have time to make myself known before you paraded in here and started to undress faster than a hungry monkey could peel a banana. Besides, it's not like I haven't seen you before."

With a saucy shake of her head, she squeezed past a stunned speechless Trace. She did glance back once, raising a distinctive brow, before winking and disappearing.

Trace stood in all of his naked glory. Slowly, he grinned. "Damn!"

Chapter Fifteen

When Addy again saw Trace, she stood as still as a tree without a breeze, while her eyes traveled at their leisure. She started at his low-crowned, wide-brimmed black hat, past his gleaming eyes and twitching mustache, to a checkered bandanna tied jauntily about his throat.

His broad chest and wide shoulders were encased in a light-blue cotton shirt, tucked into a pair of black trousers that fit him better than the ones he'd been wearing, but were still tight enough so as to leave little to the imagination as to that . . . tantalizing . . . part of him.

A wide leather belt circled his lean, narrow hips. She followed a trail down his long, elegant legs to the brown leather moccasins. Somehow she wasn't surprised that he'd kept the worn footwear in preference to a pair of stiff boots.

As she continued to gawk, he strapped on a holster and gun. The belt rode his hips like a snug glove and the holster caressed his thigh with the familiarity of a woman's warm touch.

Her face blanched, then flooded with embarrassing, telling color. Had she really reflected on such an indecent notion? Oh yes, because her fingertips burned with the imagined sensation.

Trace frowned past her shoulder at the same time she heard her cousin's dulcet tones near her ear. "I swear, dahlin', you've completely thrown aside your genteel manners. Why, as I recall, this is the second time I've caught you gapin' at a man . . ."

Delilah sounded much too thoughtful and considering for Addy's peace of mind. She swung around to find her cousin raptly eyeing Trace. "For goodness sake, Lily, you can't say I haven't seen *you* doing the same."

She turned and started walking in the opposite direction, hoping Delilah would follow, which her cousin did, reluctantly. "Yes, but . . ."

"Look, isn't that Jubal waving at us? Now he's pointing at you. Wonder what he wants?" Addy released a pent-up breath. This was one time she was actually glad to see Jubal.

Delilah made a face. "Who knows. Sometimes he can be so . . ." She shrugged and made a dismissive gesture with one fluttery hand. "I'd better go see what the man's up to, I guess. Will you be comin' to supper, dahlin'?"

"No, not tonight. Mr. Scratch is showing me how to cook elk stew and bake biscuits in a dutch oven." Addy's eyes shone with excitement at the prospect.

Delilah had started toward her beckoning husband, but stopped abruptly, a look of pure horror on her pretty face. "Adeline! How could you! Come with me right this minute. You're goin' to eat with us, an' . . ."

Addy stepped back as if she were afraid Delilah would physically force her to go. "But, Lily, I *want* to do this. I *asked* him to show me."

"Oh, my Go—!" She pressed her lips together as she looked guiltily about. "It's that man, isn't it? You're tryin' to impress him. You're bendin' over backward to stoop to his level of . . ." Her blustery speech dwindled at Addy's defiant glare. "Well, I see there's no reasonin' with you. The next thing we know, you'll be down at the nearest creek beatin' your garments on the rocks like some squaw."

"How do you know I already haven't? If I'm going to wear clean clothes, *someone* has to wash them."

"You've never dipped a hand in wash water in your entire life."

"You'd be surprised. It's quite a simple task to learn. You must try it sometime."

Delilah lifted her chin until her nose pointed to the evening sky. "You couldn't pay me enough."

"I never offered."

"Harrumph!" Delilah turned on her heel and rushed toward a glowering Jubal.

Addy set her hands on her hips and grinned. She hated to think her cousin was mad at her, but she couldn't help feeling a perverse pleasure at having stood up for herself, for once.

In fact, she felt so good that she didn't even flinch when an arm shot out and yanked her behind the solid cover of the nearest wagon. Long, tapered fingers wrapped about her upper arm.

"What were you two talkin' about just now?"

She bit into her lower lip. "You'd never guess."

Trace bent his head close to hers. "I'm not in the mood for games, woman. She knows who I am, doesn't she?"

Addy's moment of lightheartedness faded abruptly. "No . . . I mean, I don't think so. Not yet."

"But she *thinks* she knows me." It wasn't so much of a question as a resigned statement. Addy just nodded and tried to break away from his painful grip.

Trace leaned against the wagon, his mind far away, though he did relax his fingers as his palm smoothed up and down the red marks his hand had left on her arm. His other hand raised to repeat the movement, holding her immobile with the tormenting caress.

Addy's head reeled as the tiny hairs on her arms stood out from the friction, awaiting, anticipating his next touch. To keep from succumbing to his absent fondling, she said, "You look quite dapper today. Where did you get the new clothes?"

His voice was a deep rumble, and his hands slid over her shoulders to encompass her slender throat, his thumbs resting in the hollow at the base of her neck. Her pulse throbbed madly against the warmth of his fingers as he related the story of his trading the meat to

236

the women that Addy had taken such an interest in.

Her eyes narrowed. He had done that? It was a lovely, thoughtful gesture. And Trace was responsible? All on his own? She tilted her head and looked at him — really looked at him. Though she had known him in the most intimate way a woman could know a man, she felt that she didn't *know* him at all.

Watching her eyes, the way her pupils dilated, how the gold flecks sparkled and floated in a sea of changing hues, Trace stifled a groan as his belly constricted and his manhood swelled to such a point that even the looser-fitting trousers became uncomfortable.

Suddenly, he grabbed her hand and headed toward a thick copse of trees. Once beneath their dense cover, he drew her up to one wide trunk and leaned her against the smooth bark.

How he wanted this woman. If he didn't do something soon . . . From his pocket, he fished out the button and held it up. It was hard to see in the dim, speckled light, but he shoved it beneath her nose.

"Do you know what this is?"

Out of breath and ready to scold him for his rough maneuvering, she frowned and peered closely. Whatever it was, was intricately carved and detailed. "No, but it's pretty. What is it?"

"You don't recognize it?"

She shrugged and tried to remember ever seeing anything quite like it. "No."

She glanced up, met his eyes, and was taken aback by the severity of his gaze. The blue shards pierced her, probing to the depths of her soul.

"Think, Adeline. It's important."

A shiver quaked her spine as his fingers dug into her wrist. "I-I don't know anything about it. Honest. Why, Trace?"

"I found it when I undressed you after the accident with the mules. It must have fallen from a pocket or something."

"Well, I don't . . ." She strained her back against the solid trunk, to put some distance between them, but it didn't work. His body followed hers.

Wait! Now that she thought about it, there was something . . . "Was it green?"

He quizzically arched one brow. She almost lost her tenuous train of thought. "It's gold."

"No, silly. The dress. Was it the green muslin?"

He tried to think. Hell, he never paid any attention to what a woman wore. Unless, of course, they wore nothing at all. Then he remembered how a tiny row of lace on the collar outlined her slim neck, and the way the fitted bodice cupped her breasts. The color had given her complexion a rosy glow and brought out red highlights in her hair. "Yes, it was green."

"Let's see . . . I think I wore it the day I found you." She wrinkled her nose. "Yes, I think I remember now. I fell backward and my palm landed on something round and hard. I don't think I ever looked at it, though. Maybe I put it in my pocket. I don't really know."

Trace listened carefully, analyzing every word, every nuance of her speech. He detected nothing evasive or any attempt to distort the truth. "But you think you found it where I was staked?"

She nodded, an extremely solemn expression on her face and in her gold-brown eyes.

And he believed her. It sounded logical. The button had probably been left as a signal, or sign of some kind. But for whom? And why?

Addy shifted, bringing her body in such close proximity that Trace felt the brush of her bodice against his forearm. The scent of wild flowers filled his nostrils and he looked down to see the gentle rise and fall of her breasts. Only, as he watched, it seemed her breathing became more agitated.

He grinned. The attraction was mutual. He disturbed her every bit as much as she did him. So he leaned closer, pressing her firmly against the tree,

238

blocking any movement other than to bring her flush to his body. Sparks ignited between them brighter than the flickering glow of a thousand lightning bugs.

Her voice was a breathless whisper. "Trace? What's so important. . . ?"

His mouth stopped her. He kissed her long and hard. "It's *not* important, honey. I just wondered. That's all."

"But . . ." Again he claimed her, thrusting his tongue between her sharp little teeth to ravish the protected softness. A low moan rumbled in her throat and he responded by hugging her to him, fitting their bodies together in perfect unison.

Addy's mind whirled with jumbled thoughts and confusion as her body throbbed with heat. Why was he so ardent all of a sudden? For days, she'd longed for this and he had acted aloof and distant.

She tensed and started to pull away, until his hands cupped her buttocks and lifted, pressing her femininity to his male hardness. Her breasts slid up his torso, teasing her nipples to taut peaks. His lips nibbled the sensitive lobe of her ear, while his warm breath caressed its inner recess. Her muscles sagged into a quivering mass of limp limbs and melting bones, erasing all thought of protest.

"Come with me, honey." He stepped away, catching her elbows when she swayed toward him. His eyes were dark, shimmering pools.

Her breath came in shallow gasps. "Wh-what? Come where?" She was disappointed. Why had he stopped?

"We're too close to the camp. I know of a little place down by the creek." He leaned forward and whispered, "It'll be you and me and the stars, lovin' in the moonlight. It's been so long. Please."

She couldn't believe he had actually asked. Couldn't he see how much she wanted him, or feel the heat turning her flesh to. . . ? She couldn't stand it any longer. "Y-yes. Let's go."

It seemed only seconds elapsed before Trace stepped

from the dense woods into a small, grass-carpeted clearing. The moon-dappled glade was surrounded on three sides by dark, thick trees and on the fourth by the bubbling creek. The water sparkled with bright ripples that disappeared into inky pools.

"It is enchanting."

"I thought you would like it."

"You mean . . . you had planned . . . all along . . . to bring me here?" Her heart overflowed with hope and joy. Maybe he cared for her after all.

Rather than answer with words, he knelt and laid her onto the soft grass. He stretched out beside her and gazed down into her luminous eyes, which glowed more brightly than any of the stars. His chest swelled with emotion.

"Adeline, honey, I need you." How inadequate his words seemed! If he didn't take her soon, he would explode from wanting her.

She answered by putting her arms around his neck, drawing his head down for her kiss. It was sweet and gentle and tender and drove him to near madness.

His fingers fumbled with the buttons down the front of her bodice. Each time his knuckles brushed bare flesh, she moaned. He'd never felt so clumsy, until she ran her palms down his back and whispered, "You're wonderful."

All of a sudden, he felt as if there were nothing in the world he couldn't do with ease and grace as long as she was in his arms. His desire for her was all-consuming.

Their clothing was shed quickly and pushed to the side. The long days and longer nights of dreaming and fantasizing ended as their bodies met and their flesh melded in the rush to touch and explore and learn anew the intricacies of the other—what he liked, what she craved.

Perspiration slicked their bellies and thighs. She slid easily along his length as he pulled her up to nip and tease her nipples. He drew one succulent globe into his mouth, laving the tip with his tongue until she quivered and moaned her need.

Her body came alive with exquisite sensation, blossoming like the most delicate of flowers beneath the warming rays of the sun. He twisted until she rested atop him. His eyes gleamed almost black as he hissed, "Take me inside, honey."

Her eyes widened with question. His hands pulled her thighs to either side of his narrow hips. She felt the gentle nudge of his manhood at her moist opening. Instinctively, she wriggled, enveloping him with warm softness.

He groaned and thrust up his hips, holding her thighs with both hands. Addy sighed as he slid firmly and deeply into her.

Trace moved his hands to her shoulders and supported her weight as she leaned over him. Slowly he lowered her upper body until he could suckle hungrily at the twin delights dangling before his ravenous lips.

His hips raised and lowered rhythmically. She caught her breath and concentrated on keeping time. Soon, her body took control, and she soared with the knowledge that she could so easily master her brave soldier.

He conquered her defenses, unknowing that she gave them up willingly. Her eyes drifted closed as an explosion of bright light rocked her senses. She met his every thrust as he bucked beneath her and her thighs gripped him — hard.

Later, after their breathing returned to a semblance of normal, her head dropped to his chest. His arms wrapped about her back, holding her so tightly that she couldn't have moved if she wanted to.

She was perfectly happy to rest, their bodies still joined, one heart beating against the other. She had never been more relaxed or content. Trace was a very special man. She would give her life, her soul, to sleep nestled to his comfortable side the rest of her days.

But as most idyllic situations must end, so did she

241

know this time would be over. She sighed with distress at having to move her languorous limbs, but they had been gone a long time. Someone might miss them and become suspicious.

Trace also knew they had to get dressed and return, but his arms refused his command to release her. He kissed her nose, her chin, her eyes until she cried out, "Stop! Please. I can't take anymore."

He grinned, then nipped at her ear.

Surprised, she shifted and gasped with astonishment. He burgeoned inside of her. She responded with a quickening sensation of her own.

She chuckled and smiled down at him. "We can't. We've got to go . . ."

His buttocks contracted and he wriggled his hips seductively. "Oh! Gosh, can we do . . . that . . . again?"

In one swift, sensuous movement, he rolled, pinning her to the ground. Her eyes widened as he began to move slowly, sensuously. Her head rolled back to give him room as his lips devoured her neck. When his penetration deepened, her legs spread wide, then drew up to hook her heels behind his thighs.

With her second release, she would have loudly moaned her delight if he hadn't covered her mouth with his, mingling their cries of pleasure and fulfillment.

"Oh-h-h-h my-y-y." Her words were drawn out over a series of rapidly expelled breaths.

"Wh-what, honey?" Trace, too, had difficulty speaking, but managed better than she as he turned to his side and nestled her into the crook of his body.

"Oh-h-h, i-it was glorious."

Trace's eyes were dark and unreadable as he gazed into the starlit sky. "Yes, it was."

As they walked back to camp, Addy couldn't seem to keep her hands off Trace. She touched his arm and pointed to an owl silhouetted on a dead branch. Her hand brushed his as she coyly swished her skirt.

She was so happy she thought she could die right then and have no regrets. Trace had filled a place in her life, in her heart, left empty after the loss of her family that not even Delilah could fill.

She felt loved again. And *she* loved. Although he had never said anything to indicate it, he *had* to love her, didn't he? Could a man truly do the things to . . . with . . . a woman, that he had done, and not care—at least a little?

A frown furrowed her brow. Delilah's accusations about her reputation worried her. Of course, he had never said he loved her, had never mentioned marriage, but surely now . . . A tiny, niggling fear clutched at her insides as she considered something else. A baby. There was always the chance that their union could have produced a . . . child.

She swallowed a mouthful of cotton. It wasn't as if she hadn't thought about it before, but what if he really did not want her, other than for the obvious purpose? She studied his profile from beneath the shield of her thick lashes.

He was so handsome. He could have any woman he desired. So why assume he would marry her? Sadly, she concluded she would be doing a lot of wishful thinking and hoping during the next few weeks.

Trace smiled and basked in Addy's attention. He'd never known the fun of . . . whatever this was. The closeness. The sharing. It seemed he'd always resisted the attraction of well-bred young ladies, as they had a tendency to cling to a man.

But from the first day he had seen Adeline, something about her had drawn him. He didn't know if there was such a thing as fate. Didn't care. Just knew he had to do something about her fast, before she changed his thinking, his whole life.

Then he stopped so quickly that Addy, lost in her thoughts, collided with his wide back. He gazed intently toward the big fire in the center of camp. She tried to follow his eyes to see what had startled him, but it was too dark.

"What's wrong?"

"I think we've got company."

"Who? I can't see anyone."

"There, on the other side of the fire. A big man with a long beard, and two smaller fellows, all dressed in buck-skins."

She looked hard and finally discerned several blurry outlines that could resemble men. "How can you see that far?"

"Just a will to stay alive." His head tilted to the side. "Like knowin' when you're bein' followed."

"Been huntin' ever'where fer ya, boy." Scratch halted abruptly and glanced back and forth between the two young people. He scowled.

Even in the dark, Addy blushed, knowing he had to have seen her flushed cheeks and kiss-swollen lips. She turned slightly, hoping he wouldn't look at her more closely.

Scratch glared at Trace, who stood his ground with cool assuredness. Addy wished *she* could be so calm.

"We got visitors, boy. Say they be sharin' a mite o' news soon's they et their vittles." He glanced at Addy, but she continued to look the other way.

Trace's voice was harsh and brittle when he commanded, "Go on ahead, Adeline."

She blinked and raised her arm, wanting desperately to run a finger along the trim line of his moustache. But she didn't dare, not in front of Scratch, or anyone.

"Hurry. I'll be here if you need me—us." He added the latter term when Scratch took a menacing step toward him.

She gave him a last endearing glance, wondering how he could change so quickly from a gentle, almost loving man, into a cold, suspicious . . . soldier. Furtively, she looked at Scratch, then started toward the circled wagons, tripping now and then over clumps of low brush and rocks. She hadn't stumbled when she was with Trace. Why be so insecure now? Resolutely, she drew her shoulders back and stepped bravely into the ring of light.

When the people gathered around the fire stopped talking and turned to stare, she lost some of her nerve.

"Addy, dahlin', there you are. We've been lookin' for you."

She turned toward Delilah and started to smile. And then she saw him, behind and to the side of the three strangers. Rudy Potts. All of a sudden, it came to her, why the past few days had been so enjoyable. She hadn't had a run-in with the despicable Mr. Potts.

Though she and Trace had been away for a few days, she couldn't remember Rudy being in camp even before her accident.

About that time, Trace sauntered casually into the light with Scratch close behind. He leaned against a wheel, hooking the heel of his foot onto a spoke.

Addy couldn't help the nervous darting of her eyes as she looked from one face to another around the fire. Only two stared back. Scratch and Rudy Potts.

The only word she brought to mind to describe Scratch's countenance was *sorrowful*. She ducked her head as a rush of guilt flooded her being. But however much she wanted to be a wonderful, perfect person in his eyes, she knew it was an impossibility. She loved Trace. What she had done tonight, she would do again if given the opportunity. Her chin gradually raised. She would not feel guilty—not now.

But her confidence wavered when she glanced toward Rudy. He had such a knowing look to his eyes, like he knew something, and she ought to. She shivered and turned her attention to the strangers as the big man finished his cup of steaming coffee, but not before she looked toward Trace to see if he had noticed Rudy, or his reaction. He hadn't. He intently watched the new

245

arrivals.

"Thankee, folks. 'Preciate the hospitality," the big man said.

Jubal put down his own cup. "Glad to have your company, men. Always good to talk with someone comin' from the direction we're headed."

"Yep. That's a fact," the older of the other two visitors said.

"Purdee fact," the other parroted.

The bearded man rubbed his full belly and belched. "We jist came from Bent's Fort. Got some news you folks'll be in'trested in hearin', I reckon."

"Yep. Interestin'."

"Purdee in'trestin'."

Addy leaned forward, ready to hear whatever the man had to say. Only he didn't say anything. He just sat there, rubbing his fat paunch.

"Don't reckon any y'all got a chaw on ya?"

Addy looked to Scratch. He didn't offer.

Jubal was the one who finally produced the square of tobacco.

"Thankee. Right kind of ya."

The man bit off a large chunk and worked it around in his mouth before handing it to his friends. Addy thought she'd go crazy. What was he waiting on now?

"Don't reckon any'uns got a jug?"

Again Addy looked at Scratch. Again he didn't offer. Again, Jubal came through. She figured it was probably a good thing, as it wouldn't make much sense to deny the possession of something as all-important as medicinal shine. Even *she* had learned that much on the trail.

Addy interlaced her fingers, then twiddled her thumbs. All right. Come on. What was so important that every man was in camp, patiently waiting and listening?

"Ah, this is right nice. So relaxin' ta be with friends 'round a warm fire."

246

"Yep. Right nice."

"Purdee nice."

The big man held out his hands to the flames, though everyone else was too warm to sit anywhere near the fire. "Wal, now, things is purty quiet near the Fort. But me'n Six Toes Hank 'n Arnold, here, come 'pon some in'trestin' sign 'bout fifty, sixty mile west."

Addy wanted to tear her hair out when he stopped, took a long swig of the firey liquid, and passed it around again. Then she decided to pull *his* hair out, one greasy strand at a time when he loosed another disgusting, belly-rolling belch.

"Peers a bunch of traders on the way to Santy Fe was bushwacked an' they wagons burned. Ever' last piece of wood gone, nuthin' but ashes."

"Yep, nothin' but ashes."

"Purdee ashes."

Addy contemplated tying the two smaller men's tongues together, but figured she missed her chance when the bearded man shifted to a more comfortable position close to the warmth of the fire.

"Was mighty strange. T'weren't no trace of any goods. No pick heads, bits 'n scraps of iron, nuthin'."

All was quiet. Most of the men looked directly into the flames, losing themselves in the flickering depths as they absorbed the bad news. But not Trace. Addy saw how he kept his face to the darkness, always studying the shadows.

The palms of her hands turned sweaty in the cool of the evening. Fifty or sixty miles was a long ways away, but the information seemed to bother Trace. If it worried him, it worried her.

All at once, Jubal stood, slapping his gloves against his thick thighs. "That does it. We pull out at first light."

Addy's lower jaw dropped, leaving her staring in open-mouthed wonder. The man was crazy. These three men had come in telling him about a massacred caravan, and he was anxious to follow in the same footsteps, or ruts, as it were.

Trace spoke up. "I thought you were goin' to wait for more wagons. This is too small a party to go on alone."

She silently watched as Trace's eyes narrowed and glittered with an unreadable expression as he stared at Jubal. For a moment, she thought she'd read mistrust, or even more surprising, a real hatred there, but it was gone so quickly she was probably mistaken.

Shaking her head, she chastised her contrary way of thinking. Just because she was frightened, didn't mean she could make *everyone* into a "bad" man.

Jubal's face was flushed with excitement when he finally responded to Trace's accusation. "Yes, but things have changed. There were only two trains ahead of us when we left Independence. Now, we could at least be the second traders to arrive in Santa Fe. And with the Indians bein' restless nowadays, who knows? We could be the *first*."

Chapter Sixteen

Trace stretched and yawned as the group around the fire quickly dispersed. There was much to be done before they left in the morning, but he couldn't seem to find the will to do anything at all.

Then, suddenly, he was spurred to action — he made a mad dash for the concealing cover of darkness when he spotted Scratch determinedly heading in his direction. He wasn't near fast enough to elude the old man.

"Hold up, boy."

He did, but he continued walking away from the wagons. He had a feeling he knew what was coming. "What do you want, old man?"

Scratch fell into step beside him. "Wanna jaw with ya, that be all."

"You're here. Go ahead. If you *have* to."

"Durn right I have ta. What ya mean by bringin' the gal back lookin' like . . . like. . . ? Ya know."

"Lookin' like what? Listen, I've got a lot to do . . ."

Scratch grabbed his arm. They were far enough away from camp that he felt he could talk freely. "Ya knowed durn well. Her hair mussed, her eyes sparklin' like two fires, an' her face, an' all. Like a woman looks after she's been . . . Ya know."

Trace had the good sense not to try to lie his way out of it, but he was angry at the old timer's scolding him like he was some naughty little boy. "So, what's your point?"

The little man straightened his back, looking a bit pained as he did so. He shook a crooked finger under Trace's nose. "I knowed ya a spell, but I be warnin' ya ta

249

take ker 'roun' the gal, boy. She be right fine. I might be old, deaf, an' near blind, but I ain't stoopid. An' neither is ever'un else."

Trace stuffed his hands in his pockets and hunched his shoulders. "I've no intention of hurtin' her."

"Oh? Ya gonna marry up with 'er?"

"No! I mean . . . She'd never . . . I've . . . She wanted it as much as me. There's no need to . . ."

Scratch spat. The thick glob landed on the toe of one of Trace's moccasins. Some soaked into the dry leather; the rest made a dark stain in the dust. "Ya be a bright boy. We'll be seein' soon 'nuf if'n they be a *need*."

The old man started to hobble off, then turned and shook his head. "Ya'll do 'er right, or answer ta me."

Trace kicked the soiled moccasin into an anthill, coating wet leather with a thick layer of dust. As he watched Scratch leave, he continued to kick at the ground, over and over. "Damn!"

The next several days took their toll on man and beast. Jubal pushed them hard, making up for the time lost because of the rain and repairs. It was hot and humid. They were swarmed by vicious hordes of green flies that were not picky when presented with meat so decorously arranged before them. Addy had thought the mosquitoes bad, but the flies were horrid.

She had been feeling much better lately, had done a few chores and walked beside the wagon several miles a day. Soon, she would be back to her old self.

Jubal had actually been nice the past several days, telling Trace to wait until Addy had the strength to handle the team before taking over the scouting duties.

Once, though, she had heard Trace mumbling under his breath, something about, "I'll be long gone before Jubal'd sees the day . . ." Then he had seen her and whistled as if nothing were amiss.

But she had fretted ever since. He was planning to

250

leave. She'd known he would. But when? Would he tell her? Or would he up and vanish, charging out of her life as quickly and with as much drama as he had appeared?

The only scenery was rolling prairie. The tall hardwoods had been left behind at Council Grove, and the only trees to be seen were cottonwoods, and then only alongside larger creeks and in river bottoms.

Days were long and monotonous, filled with hard work and little of the romance and excitement she had expected. It seemed that all they accomplished was to walk and stop, walk and stop. That wasn't the way she had first imagined the trip.

She had hoped to see more of Trace and had wanted to talk with him, learn more about him. How he grew up and where. All the things a woman in love wanted to know about her man. Yes, she now knew that the emotion she felt every time he looked at her or touched her, or when she just thought about him, day and night, was love. It was exhilarating and terrifying.

Though he was quite solicitous and offered a helping hand now and then, he avoided her whenever possible. In fact, she would be willing to wager he hunted excuses to stay away from her. It drove her crazy.

The only thing that kept her hopes alive was the way his eyes burned into her when he thought she wasn't aware of him. She had caught him watching several times. Her body responded quickly and quite embarrassingly.

Finally, after an interminable length of time — it could have been a week, ten days, or longer, she had lost all track of time — he called to her to join him on the seat. "You're goin' to like our next camp."

She sat primly beside him, smoothing the ever-present wrinkles in her skirt. It felt good to be able to wear clothes again, though sitting so close to Trace caused her skin to tingle as if she was as naked as a mule without its thick hide.

Her eyes fastened on his long fingers and the way

251

they caressed the slender leather reins. "Hhmm? Where are we?"

"Cottonwood Creek is just ahead. I imagine we'll camp there tonight and cross tomorrow mornin'."

She looked at the sky and saw the sun was only about halfway down the western horizon. "If it's so close, why don't we cross today?"

He grimaced. " 'Cause, at this time of year, there's always a lot of work to be done clearin' deadfalls and uprooted timber from the banks."

Pausing, he flicked the mules with the reins. "You'll like it. It's pretty there."

Addy couldn't help but wonder why he had bothered to call her up to tell her about Cottonwood Creek. He had been so reticent lately, and this hardly seemed important. Yet the blood rushed through her veins as she clasped her hands tightly in her lap. He had thought enough about her to want to impart information that would please her. It was *something*.

They continued on in silence. As the wagon jostled over the rough ground, she bumped against Trace's shoulder. His thigh brushed her hip. She tried to concentrate on the flat ground and its thick carpet of grass. Tiny flowers added a colorful violet contrast to the green, but she was more attuned to his sharp intake of breath when one of the wheels dipped into a depression and she nearly landed on his lap.

Off to their right, a wagon pulled into view. It wasn't unusual for a caravan to form double rows. Sometimes the large trains traveled in lines of four abreast to cut down on the dust settling over those in the rear.

Trace's arm suddenly shot out, directing her attention to tall stands of cottonwoods interspersed with drooping willows. She had a terrible time concentrating when he showed her thickets of plum, gooseberry, and raspberry, as his forearm grazed her breasts and she jumped as if burned.

She managed to sigh, "You were right. It is quite

252

lovely."

Then, as Trace's body remained stiff and tense as he craned his neck to see around her, she glanced over to the other wagon. Scratch was driving his team. When he saw her looking, he scratched his beard and grinned.

Several more days went by, during which time Addy kept hearing the mention of a place called Big Cow Creek. It seemed the men were dreading its crossing.

She now handled the team, and grinned to herself, proud that she had regained her health so quickly. Even Trace had seemed surprised when she insisted on taking over so he could get about his own duties. There had been a definite look of what she hoped was admiration, or even respect, in his eyes that morning that caused her to have a jaunty spring to her steps.

A rider slowed and mockingly tipped his hat. She glared until he barked a nasal sound that was probably supposed to be a laugh, and rode on. She shivered. That awful Rudy Potts had better stay away from her or . . . or what? What could she do? Beat her small fists on his bony chest and scare him to death?

She saw Trace in the distance talking with Jubal. She eyed his firearm with longing. With the threat of Indians, and Rudy, always on her mind, she wondered if he would be willing to teach her to shoot it sometime?

"Probably not," an inner voice taunted. "Women are too dumb to play with men's toys." Lord, spare her from the superior male, but it seemed that was all she ever heard, even back in Boston — especially back in Boston. Women there were to be looked after and pampered, and Heaven forbid if one had half a mind of her own.

As if he knew she was thinking of him, Trace rode back to her wagon. "We'll be campin' on the next rise. It'll take the rest of the day to make preparations to cross the creek tomorrow."

"Is this the one they call Big Bull Creek?"

253

"Big Cow Creek," he corrected.

"Well . . . bull, cow, it doesn't make much difference." She was already cranky from the turn her thoughts had taken, and now he had the nerve to correct her over something as trivial as . . .

"Makes a *big* difference to the bull, and the cow." He raised and lowered his brows in a very knowing manner.

Her cheeks burned. "You're getting off the subject completely."

He leaned in the saddle and hooked a finger under her chin, tilting her reluctant face up until she looked him fully in the eye. "No, ma'am. I'm talkin' about somethin' that's on my mind night and day."

"Oh." Her eyes couldn't stay still as they devoured his features. She had thought she'd seen handsome men before, but they all paled in comparison to the bronzed, virile male whose deep blue eyes literally touched her soul.

She even caught a whiff of his tantalizing masculine scent. She had never seen him leave camp to bathe, but he always had that faint hint of soap and leather, even on the hottest days. It was almost inhuman of the man.

Trace saw the hungry flare in her eyes. His hand dropped from her chin so fast one would think he'd been scorched. She frowned until he snapped, "Damn, woman, you drive a man crazy." *And cause nothing but trouble,* he silently reminded himself as his eyes darted around, searching for her ever-present watchdog, Scratch.

As protective as the old man had become of the tenderfoot, he wouldn't put it past the old codger to pull a gun on him next.

A smile brightened Addy's face. He had just paid her a compliment, hadn't he?

"Rest up tonight. It'll be a long day tomorrow." He took a long, deep breath to regain at least a bit of his usual composure. One more conversation about bulls and cows, or the birds and the bees, and he'd toss her in the back of that wagon, Scratch be damned.

"W-will I see you . . . later?"

His eyes turned wistful, then went blank. She could have screamed. Why did he always have to hide his feelings?

"Not tonight. We'll be workin' way past dark."

"Oh."

She watched as he rode down the line of wagons. He sat a horse so elegantly and controlled the animal so masterfully. Why wouldn't he practice those same skills on her? She blushed anew at the thought of his masterful expertise in one particular area. Well, perhaps he *did* practice, some.

As it turned out, Trace was right. The men worked very late cutting loads of tall grass and carrying piles of brush to lay across the creek. The banks weren't all that steep, and it wasn't that wide, but there was soft mud. Lots of it.

Because of the mud, they had to form a makeshift bridge to roll the wagons across. They also worked on extra harness as, on occasion, trains had to use as many as eleven yoke of oxen, and even more of mules, to cross one wagon.

And that evening, Scratch showed her how to make "hoe cake" with cornmeal, flour, and water. Though she was nervous about cooking for the men, as they certainly didn't have time to do it for themselves, she couldn't resist asking how the little cakes came by their names.

He spat, grinned and pushed the tobacco to one side of his cheek. "Use ta be, traders'd slap the flat side o' a hoe in 'ter the hot ashes an' pour the fixin's onta the hoe. Cooked right nice thatta ways."

She eyed him warily, unable to tell if he was spinning another of his yarns. "Personally, I'd prefer a skillet."

"Yep, an' ya'd be right lucky ta have'un."

Her eyes widened. "Oh. Oh! I see." And she did. She was grateful to be making the trip now, in 1849, rather than several years earlier. There were so many more conveniences these days.

The next morning, Addy was amazed that the crossing turned out to be every bit as bad as the men had feared. She had awakened at first light and was still the last to get her wagon ready. By the end of the day, they had only traveled four miles because of the precarious crossing. No matter how much grass and brush they had hauled, the wheels on the heavy wagons sank to the hubs in the sticky mire.

Now she knew why they trailed along so many extra animals. All of them had been put to use and hitched to form more teams. It had been a sight to see and was something she would remember to tell her grandchildren on dark, stormy nights — she hoped.

The next fording was at Walnut Creek. The banks and bottom consisted of hard sand — the drawback was that the water was very deep. Scratch had told her it was a good place to bathe, and she was anxious to get there. Using a shallow bucket of water and small washcloth were as nothing compared with dunking one's whole self into cool, clean flowing water.

Jubal had ridden through earlier announcing that they would cross before making camp. It didn't matter how easy or difficult crossing a creek proved to be, she couldn't help being nervous.

Now Trace sat his horse on the other side of the creek, encouraging her on. She whipped up the team and they splashed into the swirling water. Her eyes grew larger and larger as the water rose higher and higher.

When it covered three-quarters of the wheel and was still getting deeper, she darted frightened glances toward the opposite bank. She gulped nervously and held the reins with hands that clenched so tightly her knuckles ached.

Trace stood in his stirrups and motioned her on. When he smiled, she took a deep breath and flicked the reins. The water seemed to have leveled off, though she

256

waited to feel the cold, damp liquid seeping into her shoes at any minute.

Just when she thought mules, wagon, goods, and one hapless woman would be stuck in the middle of the creek, the wagon lurched upward as the mules found the incline leading out of the water.

She pulled the team to a halt next to the wagons that had gone before, waiting for the command to "circle" for the night. Mosquitoes swarmed once again and she was slapping at her exposed flesh like crazy when she heard the first shout.

Suddenly, Trace rode up to the rear of the wagon, leaping through the opening from the back of his horse. "Adeline, isn't there a box of medicine in here somewhere?"

She wasn't so sure about the title "medicine", but she had seen bottles labeled as such in one of the boxes. "I think so. Somewhere near my trunks. Why?"

His voice was muffled, but she thought he said something about Efren, and hitting his head and water. Then there was the creak and scream of nails as he pried open the lid.

"Trace, that stuff won't do any good. You need . . ."

He shouted up to her, "This will deaden the pain for as long as it takes."

She blinked and closed her mouth, swallowing her next protest. *As long as it takes?* That sounded awfully final.

Efren. He was the man who had given her so much grief that first day when Scratch had been nice enough to stop for her. She hadn't liked the man at first but, lately, he and the others had treated her more kindly — with the exception of Rudy.

Regret filled her heart as she made her way from the wagon. She stood at the edge of the creek, shading her eyes from the sun's reflection off the smooth surface of the water.

A small band of men stood with her, silently watching

257

the group bent over the still form across the way. When they saw a blanket being drawn up to cover Efren's face, a collective sigh echoed over the water with the softness of steam rising on a frosty morning.

The rest of the crossing was a somber experience. No one could believe that someone would be hurt, much less killed, during this simple crossing.

Later that evening Addy took her bath, with Scratch standing a distant, though vigilant, guard. She put on her best black wool dress, as the men had asked her to sing at Efren's burial.

Most of the drivers were already gathered beside the deep grave, wearing clothes that appeared damp from a recent wash, their hair slicked back with grease and water. Just as with the first funeral Addy had attended on the trip, they all twisted the brims of their hats through nervous fingers as they shuffled uneasily, more comfortable with their four-legged critters than all gussied up for a somber *occasion*.

Jubal and Delilah followed behind Trace. Delilah's eyes were red and swollen. Addy wondered if her cousin had become well-acquainted with the deceased during the journey. The thought made her more sad. Poor Delilah. They both had so few people in their lives now.

After the words were said and Adeline began to sing, Trace fidgeted until he could stand still no longer. He remembered hearing her beautiful voice when he was so sick he could barely move, just after being found and brought to the caravan.

He felt the same sensation now as then, wondering if he had died and gone to Heaven. That piece of Heaven now stood directly in front of him, almost within an arm's length, but he held his clenched fists tightly to his sides.

Angry with himself, with Adeline, with the whole crazy world, he bent to retrieve the bottle of *medicine* that was almost ninety-nine percent alcohol. He might as well put it back, for it had served its purpose. Efren

258

hadn't been in much pain when he died.

He shook his head. God, what a freak accident. He hadn't seen it happen, but Pedro had told him Efren's wagon had veered to the right. The front wheel had hit a hole. As Efren fell forward, he cracked his head, and somehow caught his shirt on the wheel as it rolled through the water. He had been dragged under the water and run over once before anyone could stop his team.

Trace warded off a shiver. The funeral was over and he needed to get to the wagon and out before Adeline returned. He hurried on his way, but couldn't keep from thinking about the accident. He guessed if it was your time, it was your time.

And it made him think twice about Adeline. Maybe, when a person found someone who was right for him, maybe someone like Adeline, he ought to reach out for her while he had the chance.

Brooding, not paying attention to much in particular, he stepped toward the medicine box and tripped over the same loose board he'd cursed for weeks, nearly dropping the bottle in the process. Determined that the damned thing wouldn't be the cause of his downfall yet, he replaced the medicine, then knelt to take care of the board once and for all.

His fingers slid under the broken wood, scraping his knuckles on something hard and solid about an inch below the flooring. He mumbled a oath and brought his hand to his mouth where his teeth pulled at a long splinter.

He cocked his head, forgetting the sting of pain, as he stared at the floor. Why was there another board that close beneath the rest? A deep frown creased his forehead. He ripped up enough flooring to see into a false bottom.

What he found deepened his scowl. If it wasn't the missing shipment of Army rifles, his name wasn't Tracer Jeoffrey Randall. And it had been under his nose

259

the whole time — in Adeline's wagon.

Fury such as he'd never known ate at his guts. The lying, conniving little witch! If he listened hard enough, he could still hear her sweet, angelic voice raised in hymn. The hypocrite. How could she be responsible for the deaths of hundreds and pretend that the loss of one man actually meant anything to her?

He didn't believe he'd ever felt as betrayed as he did at that moment. God, she had played him for a fool all this time. He'd even believed her story about the damned button.

In a flurry of movement, he replaced the floorboards, re-covering the crates of guns. He didn't want to risk her finding out he was wise to her — yet.

Storming from the wagon into the woods, he needed to vent his rage before coming face to face with the damnable woman, or he might strangle her with his bare hands.

His fingers curled at the thought, but he forced it aside. No, her punishment had to come more slowly than that. She had to suffer as others had suffered, as he was suffering now.

Addy had expected to find Trace when she returned to the wagon. He had left the funeral, had headed in this direction. Addy was disappointed. She had hoped to talk with him.

She changed into one of her older dresses. It was so hot and still that, for the first time, she left off some of her petticoats. The freedom she felt was instantaneous and marvelous.

Goodness! Was shedding one's underclothes tantamount to shedding one's inhibitions? She smiled at her silliness, amazed that she could find anything humorous at such a devastating time.

It almost seemed life was unimportant out here. People came and went and died, and everyone continued about their business as if nothing out of the ordinary had taken place. A solitary tear rolled aimlessly down her cheek as she wondered if anyone would miss her if she were gone.

She coughed. Her throat was parched from the singing. Going to the pail for a drink of water, she was surprised to find it almost empty. Scratch or Trace usually filled it for her, but Scratch was mourning with his friends, telling stories about the dead Efren.

Her nose wrinkled. Some of the tales weren't very nice. She'd overheard one or two on the way back to the wagon.

Oh well, it wasn't far to the creek. Though she'd been warned about prowling about in the dark this far from civilization, what was a person to do if her men were out of hand?

She picked up the bucket and started for the creek, thinking it was time she began acting like a pioneer. She bet the women on the other trains didn't sit idly by while their husbands or sons fetched for them.

She straightened her back as she walked with firm, proud steps. No, they would pitch right in and do any chore that needed doing then and there. Maybe Trace would be proud of her for seeing something that needed to be done and handling it herself.

When she reached the creek, she filled the bucket, then set it to the side while she stretched and inhaled the clean night air. The moon was only a small sliver in the black sky, but the stars twinkled merrily as she gazed into the welcoming heavens.

The slight sound of a rolling pebble caught her ear. She felt a presence behind her. She smiled. Trace had probably seen her leave camp and followed, to make sure she was safe. A sly gleam suffused her eyes as she thought, "From everyone but him."

She took a swaying step backward. Her eyelids drooped seductively. Maybe they could find some time to spend together tonight. Somehow, she didn't think

Efren would find it disrespectful.

When his hands came under her arms and cupped her breasts, she sighed with pleasure until he cruelly squeezed the soft flesh and pinched her nipples—hard. This was *not* Trace!

Frantically twisting her head as her back was jerked against his chest, she tried to keep her mouth free of his groping hand. A tiny, strangled cry was all that she had time to emit before her head was pulled so far against the man's shoulder she feared her neck would snap.

"No need to holler. I knowed you wanted me, woman. I knowed it all along."

Addy's mind screamed, "Dear God, Rudy Potts!"

His foul breath was easily detectable though his fingers smashed her nose. She fought for every breath. It was impossible to move without straining her neck, but she struggled as best she could. She tried to kick his shins with her heels.

The movement backfired. When her skirt flounced out, he grabbed the hem with his free hand. She heard the material rip as he yanked it up her leg. He touched her thigh and she jerked until the pain in her head became intolerable.

Terror filled her eyes and he laughed. "Yore a hot'un, y'are. I'll give ya that. An' yore gonna treat ole Rudy real nice, ain'tcha?"

She violently shook her head, or at least attempted to. Again he laughed. "Yore gonna moan an' pant fer me, too. 'Cause if ya don't, I'm gonna tell ole Jubal that pretty boy's been screwin' his wife's kin. What'cha s'pose'll happen to yore feller then? Huh?"

His hand was between her thighs and rippling shivers ran over her skin. "Think a hangin'll be good e'nuf fer pretty boy? Ever seen one? When a man's neck breaks, all of a sudden, his body loses all control. Yep, it does. Ain't a nice sight fer a lady. Yep, think ole Rudy'll go right to his ole friend, Jubal."

The next thing she knew, she was pulled from her

feet. She almost lost consciousness as her neck was twisted and his hand smothered her air. Her back was slammed into the hard ground, but she barely noticed as his hands mauled her tender body.

As her senses gradually returned, she worked her lips, trying to generate enough feeling to open them. Her throat convulsed, but Rudy's hand came back with force, grinding the soft flesh into her teeth until she tasted blood.

A sharp click echoed in the night. Rudy stilled. Addy's eyes fluttered open, though she couldn't immediately focus.

"Get up, bastard, and do it carefully unless you want to lose that pitiful piece of flesh danglin' between your legs."

Tears streaked and burned Addy's scratched cheeks as her eyes filled with all of the love and devotion she felt for her rescuer.

Rudy hissed, "I'll kill ya, Randall. Next time you see me, be ready, 'cause I'm gonna kill ya." The last few words ended in a squeaky whine.

"You're welcome to try. But right now, you an' I are goin' to take us a walk. You won't repeat what you saw the other night, though, will you?" The gun's muzzle dropped another inch and Rudy shook his head. "That's what I figured. Now, get movin'."

Almost as an afterthought, Trace stopped and stared coldly down at Addy. "If I were you, I'd get back to the wagon. No tellin' who else could come along."

That was all. He said not another word to her before he stalked off, pushing a cringing Rudy in front of him.

Addy's mouth opened and closed, but nothing came out. Tears that had barely begun upon first seeing Trace, now streamed down her face onto her bare breasts as she hung her head.

The look in his eyes . . . She would never forget it. The blue had been almost obliterated with the blackness of his pupils. She'd read the hatred and disgust there,

263

and it wasn't directed at Rudy. But why? What had she done? Surely he wasn't *that* angry because she had come to the creek alone.

Loud voices came from the direction of the camp and she hurriedly tried to pull together her tattered clothing. It was imperative she return to her wagon before she was seen in this condition.

Why she even remembered the bucket, she didn't know, but her hands trembled so badly she dropped it, spilling the water over her shoes. She tried to find her way back, but couldn't see through her tears.

The woods closed in around her as hysterical laughter bubbled from her split and swollen lips. From out of nowhere, a dark form appeared. She released the remnants of her dress and held her hands out in front of her. "N-no. Please . . . N-o-o!"

She was caught up into the folds of a blanket as her world shimmered and faded, like a candle flame blown in the wind.

Chapter Seventeen

The rough, scratchy texture of the heavy blanket abraded the bruised flesh of Addy's nearly naked form. As she was lifted easily by a pair of strong, bare arms, she blinked and stared into a dark face with even blacker eyes, that she wouldn't have seen at all if not for their reflection of the stars.

She was on the brink of total physical and mental exhaustion. The instinct to survive warred with her longing to just close her eyes and let what would happen, happen. A shudder coursed through her body, causing her trembling to become more pronounced.

As strange as it seemed, she wasn't as terrified as she thought she should have been. The arms that held her were solid, comforting and, somehow, familiar. The smells emanating from the blanket were reassuring scents of horse and smoke and . . .

Her fingers twitched as she tried to raise her hands and fight free of the person carrying her away. Her chest constricted when she found her arms were trapped to her sides. Taking a breath was extremely difficult.

Suddenly, she started crying. Despair overwhelmed her. She lost the will to care what became of her. What did it matter anymore? No amount of physical pain could hurt her the way Trace's eyes had pierced her heart and his words had shattered her soul. No sympathy, no helping hand, no endearment. He'd criticized her for bleeding in public.

Whoever carried her turned, and headed toward a dense line of foliage. "Wh-where are you taking me?" Her words were strained and softly spoken, as if the answer wasn't really important.

The voice that answered was deep and cultured. "Where no one will find us, for a while."

She sighed and rested her head against the smooth shoulder. A month ago she would have been frightened out of her wits to be so near an *Indian*. "What are you doing here, Eagle Feather?"

"You do not sound surprised to see me."

"What? Oh, I guess not."

"What has happened to you this night, little one?"

A deep chuckle racked through her chest and she nearly choked. "You wouldn't want to know. Believe me."

He finally came to a stop over half a mile from where he'd first wrapped her in the blanket. Addy could see his mustang hobbled nearby in the trees.

"Are you going to abduct me?"

He grinned and she was nearly blinded by the brightness of his teeth. "I do not think so."

"Oh." She moaned when he sat her down on a soft bed of thick grass. "Then why did you bring me here?"

She thought she saw a puzzled frown crease his brow, but whatever expression it was, faded so quickly she would never be sure. His voice was hesitant when he spoke. "I do not know."

The night was warm and beneath the blanket she began to perspire. She started to shrug it off, but remembered her state of near nudity and clutched it tightly beneath her chin.

"You need not fear me, little one. I mean you no harm."

She stared at his black eyes and straight lips. Though he was every inch an Indian, as fierce-looking as any she had ever read or heard about, she had no concern for her life.

"So you've said. But I keep wondering . . . Why did you help me?" As modesty and pride replaced her better reason, she added, "How much did you see?"

He looked away.

"Wh-what did you see?" When he failed to answer, she stood up and paced in front of him, her fingers straining to hold the blanket in place.

"You could have helped me, couldn't you?" Again no reply. She accused, "Why, Eagle Feather? Why?"

She cocked her head to the side to catch his soft voice. "I waited."

"Waited! You would have *waited* and let Rudy . . ."

"No!"

Startled by his sharp denial, she stopped and really looked at him. He gazed solemnly back at her and stated, "It was not right to interfere as long as my brother was present."

Slowly she sank to the ground and rubbed her throbbing temples, uncaring of whether the blanket covered her or not. "Trace . . . was there . . . and never lifted a finger to help me until . . . until . . ."

She couldn't speak, couldn't think, couldn't bear knowing what Trace had let her go through. And she had thought he cared for her, a little bit, anyway.

"I don't understand. Why would he do something like that, Eagle Feather? Why?"

The Comanche had no answers. She fell onto her side and sobbed quietly into the blanket. When she fell asleep, she did so knowing he watched over her. Later, she felt him lift her and she opened her eyes to see he was carrying her back toward the camp.

Before he crossed the creek, she stopped him. "No, it's too dangerous for you to go any closer. I can make it from here."

"The water, it is deep. Your dress . . ."

"Needs to be washed anyway." She placed her hand on his arm and implored, "Please. Go back. I-I need to . . . cleanse myself."

His head dipped in a curt nod. One minute he was there; the next he was gone. She wondered at the intrigue of the man. Yes, man. No matter what she had thought in the beginning, the Indian was very human, and she liked him.

She waded into the chest-deep water and bent her knees until her body was submerged. When she came up for breath, she gasped as the cool liquid ran down her face and neck. At least that was one sure-fire way to momentarily erase Trace from her mind. She wished she could take the creek with her when they left.

It was close to dawn by the time she crawled into the wagon and collapsed on the pallet. Her skin was raw from the scrubbing she had given it, but she could still feel Rudy's rough hands on her flesh. When she closed her eyes she could hear him whining; smell him; feel him; see him; even taste the bitterness of the memory of him on her tongue.

She wondered what had happened when Trace brought Rudy back to camp. What had Trace told the rest of the men, and her cousin?

Turning on her side, she reached down and pulled a blanket up and over her head. Hidden from the world, she was glad now she had made Eagle Feather take his blanket back. He would need it one cold night.

Trace stood hidden at the front of the wagon until she fell asleep. After he had gotten the matter of Rudy Potts settled, his conscience had worried him that Adeline might really be hurt and unable to return to camp alone.

He still remembered the sight of Rudy's hands violating her body. For a while, his anger was directed at Rudy for touching what was his. Hell! How could he care so much for a woman he supposedly hated?

No, he rationalized, he didn't care. He just couldn't stand by and watch. No woman deserved to be treated so cruelly. That was all it amounted to. He would have come to the aid of *anyone* in that situation.

So, where had she been all night? When he had gone back to the creek to check on her, she was gone. He'd searched the camp and couldn't find her. He had gone again to the creek, and even brought back her damned bucket, full of fresh water.

He slammed his fist into his thigh. Water. How many times had he and Scratch warned her about going off alone, especially at night? He had thought she would have learned after her first encounter with Rudy.

He ground his teeth together. Potts had gotten off easy. His only punishment was being banned from the train.

At first Jubal had protested, arguing that they needed Potts to drive a wagon. The dispute fell flat when Trace himself volunteered to drive. He cringed at the thought. here he had been ready to leave . . .

If he had, he would have missed finding the guns and never known Adeline's true character. He took a deep breath to get a grip on his anger. He couldn't afford to lose control — again.

He smiled, but didn't smile, when he remembered Wilkins informing his wife that she would have to drive her own carriage. It had been before the funeral and Delilah had made a most beautiful mourner, though her tears had not been for poor Efren.

Disgusted with himself and the whole rotten outfit, he crawled under the wagon. Even a half hour's sleep was better than none at all. At least Adeline had returned, and seemed none the worse for wear.

Before she dressed the next morning, Addy gently rubbed some more of the salve Eagle Feather had given her into her sore muscles and raw scrapes. She had no idea what was in the greasy concoction. All she knew was that it worked.

Some of the places had almost healed overnight and she wasn't as sore as she expected to be, except for her neck and her lips, where she still felt the imprint of Rudy's cruel fingers.

She dug in her trunks until she found the hateful corset she had abandoned when the weather turned so unbearably hot. Then she donned a dress with long sleeves and a neckline that buttoned so high and tight that she

269

nearly choked. She felt sort of like a knight of old wearing armor, but it lent her a degree of confidence.

She poked her head from the canvas, looking for Rudy before she emerged. If he came near her today . . . Her hands clenched into tight fists. She was so angry, she didn't really know what she would do.

As it was, the only person she saw was Trace, and she was tempted to beat her frustrations out on him. Quickly, before she gave in to the absurd impulse, she ducked back inside until she heard him walk past. Once, he hesitated and her hand covered her heart, more as protection than nervousness.

When he moved on, she hurried out the back of the wagon to get her team. She was almost to the remuda when she saw a sight that stopped her in her tracks.

"Lily? What are you doing?"

Delilah turned a blotchy red face and tear-swollen eyes to Addy, and Addy decided they must look like a matched set of weepy women.

"Oh, that dreadful Efren. Just because he went an' got himself killed, I'm reduced to drivin' the carriage. Can you imagine? Me? Why, soon's you know it, my poor hands are goin' to look as bad as . . . as . . ."

"Go ahead. You can say it, Lily. I know what my hands look like."

"Well, they shouldn't have to, Addy. Neither of us were brought up to be treated like . . . mule skinners. Why, if I could just . . . Oh, Jubal, dahlin', here I am. Are you goin' to help me, like you promised?"

Jubal kicked his lumbering horse toward them and Addy started on about her business. He didn't allow her to get far.

"Well, little lady. You really did it this time. Because of you, your poor cousin has to expose her delicate self to the sun and heat today."

It was on the tip of Addy's tongue to tell him that *she* had suffered and survived, but she bit the retort back, for Delilah's sake. However, she did inform him that, "It is not my fault Efren died. An accident caused your

270

shortage of drivers. Besides, you should have been better prepared for such an occurrence."

He stopped her when she would have walked past him. "Oh, no you don't. You're not gettin' off that easy. It's because of *you* that I lost my best hand last night. If you weren't so loose with your favors, Rudy would still be with us and he could drive your cousin's carriage."

Addy's already pale face completely lost all color. "Still with us? What do you mean? What happened last night?" She had known Trace was angry, but had he been furious enough to kill a man?

Delilah lit up at the prospect of telling Addy the juicy news. "Your Mr. Randall marched poor Rudy right up to Jubal, *demandin'* that my husband do somethin' about a snake low enough to attack unsuspectin' women in the dark. Now, Jubal, bein' sort of judge an' jury on the train, he wanted to know if Mr. Randall had any proof, which, of course, since you weren't around, he didn't. Jubal bein' the fair minded person he is, thought Rudy should be given another chance, but Mr. Randall wouldn't hear of it. A vote was called for, an' poor Mr. Potts was banned from the train."

Addy scowled. She had heard enough "poor Rudy's" to last a lifetime. It was a relief to know that Rudy was alive, yet a disappointment to think his punishment had not been more severe.

Delilah pulled a hanky from her pocket and blew her nose, quite loudly. "Poor man. He'll be out there all alone. Indians will probably butcher him before the end of the day."

Addy thought that sounded fitting, only she hoped they tortured him first.

Jubal glared at Addy. "What's done is done. Just see to it you don't sway your tail around any more of my men. You understand me, little lady?"

Seething, she refused to give an answer to such a demand and spun around to stalk indignantly away. The deep breaths she took caused the corset to irritate the tender flesh on her stomach, and she stepped gingerly,

271

innocently swaying back and forth with each motion of her legs.

With her back to the irate Jubal, she missed his baleful glare while grabbing hold of the top edge of the dratted constrictive thing and shimmying her body to relieve the pressure. It didn't help.

Oohhh! The nerve of Jubal, to suggest she had led that beast, Rudy, to his fate. Why, she'd never so much as smiled at the man.

She was so upset, she wasn't paying attention to where she was going, and was brought abruptly to a standstill when she ran into an unyielding object. She didn't even have to look up to know who it was, for she smelled Trace's special scent.

She lifted her head and stared at the middle button on his shirt, waiting . . . When he didn't say anything, she took a step to the side and walked past him. Her body tensed, and she was on the verge of shaking so badly she was afraid she wouldn't make it as far as her wagon.

Once there, she grasped the sturdy rim of the wheel and dared a look over her shoulder. She covered her mouth, smothering a gasp. He still stood where she left him, his head turned in her direction, though she couldn't make out his features or expression.

For Trace's part, he cursed his inability to move. He'd been lost in his own thoughts when he had bumped into Addy, and had involuntarily reached out to steady her, catching himself just in time. The palms of his hands still tingled and he hadn't even touched her.

God, he was more confused than ever. He had found proof that she was connected to the guns, yet every time he looked into her fragile face, all he could see was her innocence.

He had lain awake all night thinking over all of the possibilities. She had been on the steamer when he left Independence. Since the wagons had traveled far enough for *her* to be the one to find him staked and still alive, they had to have pulled out soon after her arrival.

She *had* to know what was in the wagons. She had said

it was her father's business. Had Wilkins been working *for* her father, or maybe *with* him?

He wanted like hell to give her the benefit of the doubt, but it galled him that he had found crates of guns hidden so carelessly in *her* wagon.

His mind told him one thing, his gut another. He needed time. Time to find out if she was truly the villain he suspected, or an innocent victim. Which made him think, too, of all the "accidents" she had endured.

Someone seemed to be trying awfully hard to get rid of the woman. And he knew her parents had been killed last year in similar circumstances. There were so many questions, but it was too soon to come up with plausible explanations.

Right now, he needed to get his emotions under control and get back in Adeline's good graces so he could continue to watch her closely. He had made a mistake to allow her to see his anger. Now, he would have to work twice as hard to get her to trust him again and not suspect his ulterior motives.

Besides, he still had this damned protective instinct toward her, and his instincts had always been reliable in the past. So, what had gone wrong this time?

He shook his head and walked on to his wagon. At least now he knew about one false bottom. Tonight, he would check out his floor and see what treasures he'd uncover.

The wagon train now followed the Arkansas River, and the mosquitoes were again so bad that the members of the caravan wore more clothing than was comfortable just to protect themselves.

The mules and oxen were restless and hard to handle as blood, drained by various winged insects, dripped down their necks and hides.

Addy was so exhausted she could hardly hold her head up, let alone yank on the reins. At night the mosquitoes beat against the canvas of her wagon like raindrops in a storm.

Scratch had been considerate enough to make her a mosquito bar to sleep beneath — light-weight muslin anchored down on either side by long bars, or heavy pieces of wood, to keep the tiny pests from flying under and bleeding her dry.

She smiled to herself, remembering the way he had shuffled up to her, with his hands behind his back. The old fellow had hemmed and hawed and finally, red-faced and slack-lipped, had produced his offering. It seemed he had traded for the thin material, with her well-being in mind, when a mule skinner camped with them one evening.

Her heart had gone out to the embarrassed man, and she had tried to make it up to him by cooking his favorite meal — boiled turkey gizzards — although she had inexplicably lost her appetite on that occasion.

Suddenly, the mules veered to the side of the trail. The front wheel jolted over a deep rut and she snapped her head up. She pulled the team back into line, then wiped a hand over her eyes before looking guiltily about.

She blinked, sat upright, and blinked again. Off to the right of the caravan, for as far as she could see, were hundreds of brown, shaggy beasts.

What in the world? She had never seen anything like them before. One grazed not thirty feet from her wagon and had two little horns curving from its monstrous head. The hair was so thick she could hardly see its eyes, but they appeared to be small and shiny.

From the shoulders on, the beast's back sloped down and its ribs and rear were skinny and looked almost hairless. She might have been much more frightened if the animals didn't look so funny.

She didn't realize she had stopped the wagon until she heard Scratch's voice behind her. "What in the durn blazes be the holdup, gal?"

She took a deep breath. "Look! Look, Mr. Scratch, at all those strange creatures. What are they? Will they hurt us? They aren't something we have to eat, too, are

274

they?"

Scratch spat, smiled, and patiently waited for her questions to fade to a stop. He remembered the first time he had seen a big herd like that, and didn't blame her for being excited.

"Them's buffler, an' yeah, we eat 'em. Best vittles this side o' Ind'pendence."

She grimaced. "I should have guessed." Then she mumbled, "Anything that can't outrun us, we eat." And these particular beasts didn't exactly look fleet of foot.

"Eh? What's that ya say?"

"Nothing. How come there's so many of them, Mr. Scratch? Why, all I can see for miles is the tops of brown backs."

"Should've seen 'em back in the Thirties, gal. Sometimes, all ya'd see fer a hunert miles an' days on end was buffler. It were a sight ta see."

"How come they aren't afraid of us? Most animals run when they see us coming."

He scratched under his arm and unloaded a wad of slimy tobacco from his mouth. "They be extry dumb, they be. An' they cain't see worth shi . . . squat. They foller they noses. But ya be mighty kerful, gal. Some'un gets'em startled, an' they charge faster'n ya kin yell jackrabbit."

She shivered, seeing how they could be dangerous, just by their numbers alone.

"Better git goin', gal. Ya'll see a mite more o' the critters ever' day from now on, most like."

She was glad. Watching them made the time pass faster.

Several hours later they came to a place called Pawnee Fork, where they would camp for the night. There was a lot of wood and good water. Later, Scratch came by and told her this area used to be an old Indian camping grounds, but now it was mostly used by the traders.

Scratch leaned his elbow against a built-on chest on the side of the wagon and pulled out his sack of tobacco. "Ain't seen the boy lately."

275

She pretended to be very busy mending a torn sleeve on one of her dresses. "He's several wagons up, I believe."

"Don't come 'roun much, huh?" He stuffed the block of tobacco into his mouth and tore off a huge chunk, causing Addy's eyes to widen and her stomach to churn. She never had gotten used to his awful habit.

"He has more responsibilities now, I suppose." It was all she could do to answer, unsure as to whether it was the tobacco or thoughts of Trace that made her nauseous.

"Wal, he ought not leave ya alone."

She stabbed the needle into the material and gave up trying to sew. Instead, she gazed steadily at Scratch. "Look, Mr. Scratch, the less I see of Mr. Randall, the better. I'm not his concern." She smiled sweetly at him. "Besides, you're the only company I need."

Scratch was just about to spit. Her words surprised him so much that he swallowed instead. It took several minutes for him to quit coughing. She rushed over and pounded him on the back.

"Nuf. E'nuf, gal. Ya got my ribs ta rattlin' as it be." Though he continued to sputter and gasp, she could tell she had pleased him. And she was glad. The old man had become very dear to her.

About an hour after Scratch had gone on to his usual card game, she heard someone call her name. She quickly tied a knot in her thread and bit off the end before turning to see who it was.

"Evenin', Adeline."

Her heart jumped into her throat. She swallowed it back down, telling herself not to get excited. After all, they were bound to see each other from time to time. It was a small train.

But she couldn't bring herself to look at him. It was too painful. She had found that out when she noticed that his hair had grown shaggy, still short around the ears and forehead, but longer in the back, where it curled over his collar. His cheeks were also leaner, the hollows deeper.

It was the eyes she couldn't resist, though. She had darted a quick glance and they were that same deep blue. She well remembered how they chilled her that night by the creek.

Finally, though he had only been standing at the edge of the firelight for a few seconds, it felt like hours, and she curtly nodded.

"Still won't speak to me, huh? Can't say as I blame you."

His voice was husky and her blood warmed to near boiling as she recalled how sensual it sounded when whispering to her in moments of passion. She picked up the needle and rethreaded it. Anything to keep her eyes and hands occupied.

"May I sit down?"

"No!" She turned her back to him. "Go away."

He paid her no mind. The next thing she knew, he knelt in front of her. One of his hands covered both of hers and she flinched, trying in vain to pull away. Her heart skipped several beats as her face flushed.

"I don't know what got into me the other night. I've been so ashamed of myself that I haven't found the nerve to apologize. But I had to come. I'm sorry, Adeline. So very, very sorry. Please say you'll forgive me?"

She had to admit it was about the longest speech she had heard from him. There was a sincere quality to his voice that she wanted to believe, needed to believe. But there was something . . . She couldn't bring herself to trust him.

"I will never forgive you, Trace Randall. Not ever. Especially since I found out that you just stood there . . . and watched . . . while Rudy . . . he . . . You could have stopped him so much sooner." She was so close to tears that her nose ran. She sniffed.

Trace was shocked. How had she known he was there? She had been too busy fighting off Potts to notice his presence, he could swear to it.

The puzzlement in his voice lent it the tone of proper

277

chastisement. "I told you, I don't know what came over me. Anger. Jealousy. I don't know. It was like I went crazy for a couple of minutes, then came to my senses. At least Potts is gone and won't bother you again."

She looked up, staring into his eyes. He sounded genuinely remorseful, but . . . "Yes, you did finally step in. I guess I should thank you for that."

"No, you don't owe me any thanks. I just wish that I could have that time back. Things would have turned out differently. I swear." And strangely enough, deep in his heart, he wished he had helped her sooner. The memory of her bruised flesh still tore a hole in his heart, no matter what she might have done.

Burying her trembling hands under the ripped dress, Addy knew she had to make him leave before she reached out and ran her fingers through his thick mane of hair. She wanted to erase the worried frown from his forehead.

"Well, you have apologized. I've thanked you. I guess that's all we have to say to each other."

"All? Hon . . . Adeline, it can't be all. There's too much between us."

Yes, lots of space, but not as much as there's going to be, she maliciously thought to herself. However, his pain, real or imagined, didn't give her the satisfaction she thought it would. "Good evening, Mr. Randall."

He stood and looked down at her. Though she didn't return his gaze, she felt the heat from his eyes roasting the back of her neck.

"All right, for now, Adeline. But this is not the end. I'll keep comin' back until you give in."

"When it snows in July on the Santa Fe Trail."

Chapter Eighteen

During the next several days, Addy learned something new about traveling. When you were not following a river, or crossing a creek bed, you eventually ran out of wood. When you didn't have wood to build a fire, you used the next best thing, buffalo chips.

She was amazed anew. Whoever thought of using manure for a fire? At least it didn't smell as badly as she had imagined.

They did find water. Sometimes it collected in holes in the ground and was as warm as bathwater. Other times, it was yellow and stagnant, but drinkable; at least for the livestock, and humans if they were thirsty enough.

And now she truly saw the West. She'd read of the "vast prairie," but would never have comprehended the meaning of the phrase without seeing it for herself.

The country was flat and rolling, with grass and a few weeds the tallest obstacles to break the horizon. There were no trees, no shrubs, no rocks any higher than the grass. Grass, everywhere.

Delilah had said the scenery was dreary and unusually boring, but Addy liked it. The green carpet was a natural wonder all its own.

If a person really looked, there was a lot to be seen. Lizards, long thin green bugs with long thin legs, bunnies with round white tails, the ungainly jackrabbits, ancient-looking creatures called horned toads.

And of course there were snakes. At night, the men beat around the camping area to rout out hostile insects and snakes. She was more than glad to wait in the wagon until they were finished.

This particular evening, Scratch had shown her how to make buffalo hump stew and it was delicious. The meat was tender and she liked the taste of it more than the wilder flavor of deer or elk. She even managed coffee and biscuits and was feeling quite pleased with herself.

She and Scratch were relaxing around the fire, getting ready to eat, when Trace walked up.

"Howdy, boy. We's fixin' ta fill our bellies. Mite jist as well set a spell an' keep away the wolves."

Addy almost spilled the full pot of coffee. She remained bent over, with her head cocked, hoping Trace would say he'd already eaten.

"Thanks, old man, don't mind if I do. Smells mighty good. You cookin' now, are you?"

Addy slammed the pot back down by the fire. Drops of the liquid sloshed out and sizzled on the hot stones.

"Naw, the gal's taken a turn fer it. Does a right fine job, she does."

Wiping her hands on her apron, Addy handed Trace a cup and plate. "Help yourself." She saw Scratch's frown, but didn't care. She wasn't about to serve the high and mighty Mr. Randall.

She had just taken her first bite of the now tasteless food when Scratch set his plate down and got up. "Wal, reckon ya folks kin finish 'thout me. I got a passel o' harness ta mend. Good vittles, gal."

Addy's mouth dropped open. She started to run after Scratch and beg him to stay, or at least eat another plateful of food. Surely he couldn't have tasted his first. Her softly muttered, "You're welcome," echoed into the quiet space.

"I won't bite, Adeline."

Her hands fluttered above her lap as her plate tipped precariously. "I-I'm not afraid of you." But her words lacked all conviction.

"Aren't you?"

"No."

"Then why are you sittin' way over there?"

"This is where I always sit."

"I see." He rose to his feet and moved to the rock Scratch had vacated near her right side. It was like someone had started a new fire there.

He smiled. "Since I've been drivin', I don't get to see much of you anymore."

She smoothed a wrinkle in her apron. "It's a big disappointment to you, I suppose."

"Yes, it is."

"How is your friend, Eagle Feather?"

His eyes narrowed. What made her ask something like that? "I don't know. Why?"

"Just wondered."

He shot her a sidelong glance. Actually, he had seen Eagle Feather two nights ago. He'd told the Comanche about his findings and about his suspicions of Adeline. His friend had just stared and shaken his braided head. It had made Trace a little angry, to tell the truth.

Now she added more stones to the pile. Her knowledge of Eagle Feather could be dangerous. What if she had already told Jubal about his meetings with the Indian? They would have to be much more careful from here on out.

He tentatively touched her hand. She jerked away as if she'd been scalded. He smiled to himself. She wasn't as immune to him as she pretended to be.

"We'll be at Pawnee Rock soon. Be sure to keep a sharp eye out for Indians."

She quickly met his gaze. "Indians?"

"Yep."

"Y-you mean, like Eagle Feather?"

"Not exactly."

"Uh, what's so special about this . . . Pawnee Rock?"

"You'll see when we get there. It's one of the few places on the journey where you can *expect* trouble."

She was already casting her eyes warily around at the shadows. If Trace was worried about the threat of Indians, *she* should be worried.

"Do you have a gun?"

Her eyes widened with apprehension. "Me? No.

281

Why?"

"Do you know how to use one?"

"No."

He sighed as if resigned to the inevitable, although inwardly he smiled at his good fortune. "Then I'd better show you."

"That's not necessary. I don't have any intention of shooting anyone." She bit her lip with the eerie sensation that he somehow knew she had wanted to learn to use a gun.

"You think a fryin' pan will be enough to protect you if you're attacked?" His voice was hoarse with emotion as he scooted close and probed her eyes for an honest answer.

"W-well, it was once. I . . ."

He looked into the evening sky. A few clouds hovering in the west took on a pinkish hue. "There's still a good hour of daylight. Wait right here. I'll be back in two shakes."

When he had gone, Addy stood up, completely forgetting her full plate of food, ignoring the clatter as it toppled to the ground. She looked one way, then the other, and wrung her hands.

What should she do? She had to get away, but where? Finally, she turned and ran around the end of the wagon, only to bump full into Trace.

"You're anxious to get started. Good."

He took her tiny hand and half led, half dragged her onto the seemingly empty prairie. Tall grass bent beneath their feet. Weeds tugged at her skirt. She tried to reach down and grab the hem with her free hand so she could lift the heavy material.

Trace noticed her difficulties and stopped for a moment. "What would you think of a pair of trousers?"

At her outraged gasp, he sighed. "Well, we can talk about that later. Ah, there's what I was looking for."

Addy had it on the tip of her tongue to inform him she never intended to speak to him again, until her interest was sparked and she tried to see over his shoulder. All

282

she saw was grass waving in the breeze.

Then she nearly fell flat as she stumbled into a dusty depression. It was wide and long and had been completely invisible.

Trace was curt and informative, but his voice was as deep and soothing as a pool of cool water when he leaned near and spoke close to her ear. "Buffalo wallow. It's perfect, isn't it?"

She couldn't help but silently wonder, "Perfect for what?" as she looked around and found she couldn't see out. Evidently, no one could see in, either. Panic assailed her. She didn't want to be alone with him. Not now; not ever again.

"Don't run away. All I'm goin' to do is show you how to fire this rifle."

She eyed him warily, not trusting this considerate side of his personality he insisted on showing her. Who did he think he was fooling, to treat her so abominably one day, or night, and then turn around and expect things to be the same as before?

Well, it wasn't going to work. Not with this lady. She was hurt and angry, and she had always been one to hold a grudge—for a long, long time.

She tucked a strand of loose hair behind her ear and took a step toward him. "I've told you before, I'm not afraid of you."

"Good. So come over here and watch what I'm doin'."

The far side of the wallow was steep, almost like the bank of a creek. He propped up a buffalo skull from a sun-bleached skeleton.

"That's the target." He held up the rifle and opened the magazine, sliding in several bullets, cocking the lever after each one. Then he unloaded the chamber and handed the gun and ammunition to her. "Now let's see you do it."

"What? No. I mean . . . I don't want to."

A deep furrow formed between his eyes. He placed his hands on his lean hips, his muscled thighs outlined perfectly by his spread-legged stance. She gulped and held out her hand for the gun. Her father had given her a lesson or two many years ago. Maybe she wouldn't make *too* big a fool of herself.

She fumbled with the bullets, but managed to follow his example fairly well.

"See? It's not so hard, is it?" He turned her toward the makeshift target and stood directly behind her, leaning over her shoulder. "Now, put the stock here, against your shoulder. Hold it like this. Ah-h-h, that's perfect. Put your finger there. Doesn't that feel good?"

As he positioned her hands, he moved closer, pressing his chest to her back, the front of his thighs to the backs of hers. Her bottom nestled into his groin. His breath whispered into her ear, teasing the loose hair until it tickled the sensitive flesh on her neck.

Her eyes widened. It was all she could do to hold the rifle barrel steady as tremors threatened to rack her body. The impulse to turn around and shoot the maddening man was replaced by the desire to spin in his arms and kiss him — everywhere.

Instead, just when his hands lowered from the gun to slide provocatively down her ribs, she sighted and fired. He recoiled in surprise. "What the hell? I didn't tell you to shoot."

His yelling ceased abruptly when he noticed the bullet had hit its mark. "Hey, I thought you didn't know how to use a gun."

His eyes narrowed. Had he unwittingly stumbled across the evidence he needed to prove she was a deceitful little witch? She had hit the target dead-center.

Addy failed to see the speculative glint in his eyes when she replied, "I don't."

"It damn well appears you can."

Hesitantly, she said, "My father taught me one afternoon when I was very young. It was the only time I've ever held a gun in my life. To be honest, I feel much safer with a frying pan in my hand."

"So do I," he muttered.

"What did you say?"

"Nothin'. Come on back over here. We're goin' to see if that was just a lucky shot, or if you really know what you're aimin' at." Damn it, why did his palms feel so damp? Because he hoped he was wrong?

His palms closed over her shoulders. But instead of positioning her in front of him, he pulled her to him, crushing her breasts to his chest. He didn't immediately kiss her; didn't run his hands down her back; he just held her in a fierce hug.

Her own breath caught in her lungs as he hissed, "God, I've wanted to feel you in my arms for days and days, to know you're real, that I didn't just imagine your soft curves, or . . ." He choked.

Addy stood as still as granite. If she was being completely truthful about the situation, she was disappointed that he didn't go ahead and take the kiss, or force her to endure his familiar touches. Force? She was almost willing to *beg* him.

"I don't know what to do, honey. How can I prove to you that I was a stupid jackass that night?"

His tender, caring embrace was more than proof enough to her, but she couldn't rid herself of nagging doubts. His feelings changed too swiftly, too conveniently. But she was in his arms, and she wouldn't move if her life depended on it.

Taking her acquiescence as acceptance, he murmured, "Aw, honey, you won't regret it. I promise."

More than a little stunned himself by the wild, joyful pounding of his heart, his arms gradually tightened.

The sound of footsteps running to the edge of the wallow broke them quickly apart. Scratch peered into the depression, the muzzle of his rifle pointing between the two startled people. Dead-Eye and Pedro spread out on either side of him.

"By damn, boy, ya near got yore self kilt."

Trace's face colored dramatically. "Sorry. I didn't think to tell anyone we were goin' to have a little target practice for the lady."

Jubal, his face red with exertion, arrived just in time

to overhear Trace's statement. "Target practice? For who?" He pointed to Addy. "She doesn't need to know how to shoot."

Trace cocked his head, wondering why Jubal seemed so angry. What was so wrong with what they were doing?

When the others also gave Jubal odd stares, he backed down, throwing up his arms as he turned to leave. "Go ahead, do what you want. Just a waste of ammunition to me."

Trace looked at Scratch and shrugged. "Well, no harm done. Uh, we'll be through here in a bit."

Once the other men had scowled accusingly and turned away, grumbling beneath their breath, but loud enough so that he would hear their curses, he grinned and turned back to Addy. "Now, where were we?"

His hand shook as he lifted his hat and ran his fingers through his damp hair. He picked up the rifle and held it out to her. She didn't even remember dropping it. Her face was flushed and her eyes burned.

When he once again stood behind her, his upper body was stiff as he held himself away. However, she felt his reaction to her pressing firmly into her buttocks. Her knees went weak and there was a telltale flush to her cheeks.

His voice was strained and husky as he instructed her, "All right, take it in your hands, like that. Squeeze . . . Gently. That's a good girl. Be careful with it."

Her bones turned the consistency of soft butter and her blood boiled through her veins. When she fired, she had forgotten to hold the stock firmly to her shoulder. The recoil knocked her backward. His hands, which had been resting in the area of her hips, reached to catch her and grabbed the first protrusions he encountered.

Her breasts seemed to grow and swell until they fit his palms. Her nipples throbbed, straining for his caress. She arched her back, pressing them firmly into his hands.

Her eyelids drooped seductively as she turned to face

him. She couldn't help it. She wanted him. She needed him to hold her, to love her. She wanted to forget, to forgive.

His breath was low and came in short gasps. "Uh, I knew your first shot was a . . . lucky . . . one. Look. Turn and look. You missed the target by a mile. Guess we'll, uh, have to practice again . . . sometime."

He took the gun and shakily ejected the spent shells before replacing them with live bullets. Then he solicitously placed his hand under her elbow and helped her from the wallow, even as he pondered which shot had been the real indication of her ability with the weapon. Or, would she *have* to know how to shoot to be involved in gun-running? Probably not.

When he left her at her wagon, sleepy-eyed with unfulfilled yearning, he literally ran back to his own bedroll. He slammed his fist into the nearest crate, but the immediate stinging pain did nothing to alleviate the throbbing ache in his groin, or his head.

Where was a deep, cold creek when a man needed one?

Contrary to Trace's apprehensions, the caravan reached Pawnee Rock without incident. Addy had watched it for miles and miles, a huge, dark landmark, all alone, towering above the prairie.

Just like a child who has to climb the tallest tree, or the nearest hill, she could hardly wait to make camp so she could explore the rock.

She slapped at a mosquito. They must be close to the Arkansas River again. Sometimes she had an urge to throw herself in the wagon, cover her head and never come out. The bugs and insects drove her crazy. The sweat and constant dust made her feel as if she would never be clean again.

Her hair was limp and straggly. Her eyes burned. Her nose itched. Her lips were dry and cracked. Freckles had popped out on every exposed inch of her skin. She loved

287

Trace. He didn't want her. And she didn't understand any of it.

Gunfire snapped her from her doldrums. She reached back into the wagon and pulled out the rifle Trace had demanded she carry with her, though he did mention that she should only use it for *show* unless absolutely necessary. They'd had no more shooting lessons since the buffalo wallow.

It was a good thing. She didn't think her body could withstand another "lesson".

Scratch's team pulled up even with hers. He leaned over and shouted, "Ain't nuthin' ta be a'feerd. Boys're celebratin'."

"Celebrating what, Mr. Scratch?"

"Livin' ta Pawnee Rock."

"Oh." She smiled wanly and whipped the mules forward. She wouldn't mind rejoicing over that fact herself.

That evening, she and Scratch walked down the steep hillside after carving their initials in the soft stone. She was surprised by the number of people who had been there and done the same thing before them.

"When did you say that Susan Magoffin was here?"

The old man scratched his chin. "Mind's quittin' me, gal. B'lieve it were '45, or were it '46? She be the first white gal ta reach Santy Fe, she be. Here tell it stirred up some row."

"Have any been there since? White women, that is?" Apprehension clouded her eyes. She could imagine a "row" and it terrified her.

"Prob'ly. Cain't be many, though."

"I-it must have been rough on her. Being the first, I mean."

He moved his tobacco from one jaw to the other, leaving a small lump in the side of his cheek as he said, "That'n traveled right stylish, she did. Her man fixed'er up a carriage fancier'n that o' yore kin. Had a maid 'n a cook. Pampered'er good, he did."

Scratch smacked his lips and spat, leaving his own special mark on the rock. "Heerd she lost a babe."

She shook her head sadly. "Oh, what a shame." It was only natural for her to wonder that if things were rough now, what they must have been like three or four years ago. Mrs. Magoffin must have been a very courageous soul.

"Evenin', Adeline; old man. Carve your initials, did you?" Trace gallantly tipped his hat and her heart did flip-flops down to her toes.

Scratch answered, "Yep."

To keep from wringing her hands like a ninny, she used them as she spoke, pointing, gesturing. "It was so interesting. Why, there was a date as early as 1806. What do you suppose brought people out here? do you think things were different then? Mr. Scratch said there were dates from a hundred years ago, but we couldn't see them because it was getting so dark."

Scratch shrugged and began to hobble on, knowing she could just be getting started with her questions and babbling.

Trace took her elbow and walked her back toward camp. He leaned over and whispered, "Would you like another lesson tonight?"

Her heart jolted. "Lesson? Tonight?"

"If you aren't doing anything else."

"Oh, there are a thousand things that need my attention. In fact, I really must be hurrying on."

"A thousand, huh? That should keep you busy all the way to Santa Fe."

"Yes, probably." She blushed. "Oh, you're teasing."

"A little." He sidled up next to her and ran his finger around the shell of her dainty ear. "When are you goin' to forgive me?"

She sucked in her breath as the heat from his body seeped into her skin. "Wh-when I believe you are sincere."

"Pardon me?" Damn the witch! How could she know? And why couldn't he continue his little charade without being tempted to drag her into his arms and kiss that perfect little mouth until it was pink and moist and pouting with desire as strong as his?

It took all of Addy's will power to keep from swaying and leaning into his broad chest. "You heard what I said. Good night, Mr. Randall."

He watched the gentle rocking motion of her hips as she walked away, and he kicked at the nearest object. "Ow! Damn!"

He flopped to the ground and removed his moccasin to see if any toes were broken. Next time he took out his frustration on a rock, he'd be damned if he weren't wearing boots.

The next week of travel was one of the most tiring for Addy. Once again the trail left the Arkansas riverbed. All she did was walk and cook and collect buffalo chips and walk and cook and work and fall into a restless sleep at night.

But there was a bright spot. Sunflowers. She'd noticed the tall, bright yellow flowers since Pawnee Fork, but there had been so many other things to look at that she had paid them scant attention. Now, watching the pretty blooms sway in the breeze was enough to lighten her sour mood.

Trace had quit stopping by. She saw him now and again, of course, but he only nodded and tipped his hat, then kept walking. Which was fine with her. She didn't want to see him, anyway.

A lonely tear streaked her cheek, burrowing a trail through the fine layer of dust, following its many predecessors. As she had done so often during the past week, she wondered if spiting herself was the right thing to do.

The man had apologized. Heaven knew he wasn't the only one to make a mistake. And what made her think he wasn't telling the whole truth? In many ways she *did* trust him. If there were any danger, she knew she would trust *him* with her life above all others. She would also wither away and die if she continued having to watch him from afar.

She wanted to hear his voice; see his gorgeous smile; smell his clean masculine scent; speak his name; and most of all, reach out and touch him if she so desired.

So, after acknowledging this revelation, what should she do, if anything?

All the while Addy worried over her problems, Trace jounced disconsolately along, absently flicking the tip end of one rein against his knee. He missed Adeline and wished he hadn't handled the situation so poorly.

The more he thought about it, the more he knew she couldn't have had anything to do with the contraband weapons. Or, at least he hoped that was the case. Anyway, he felt magnanimous today, and was willing to give her the benefit of the doubt.

He took a deep breath and let it out slowly. Yes, he felt much better after coming to that decision. But he was restless and needed something to take his mind off the woman, if only for a few minutes.

Glancing into the wagon, his eyes settled on the shotgun suspended between two hickory bows. That was it. When they made the noon stop, he would hunt up a prairie chicken or two, maybe even a turkey. She'd like that, and it would be a pleasant change from buffalo or elk.

His eyes glittered mischievously on the off chance she might need a cooking "lesson".

He remembered thinking later that, as luck would have it, no one cooked at either the noon or evening camp. Black clouds boiled over them from the west. The distant rumble of thunder was heard long before the clouds blocked the sun. Jagged bolts of lightning streaked toward the earth and exploded into a light so bright it hurt the eyes to watch.

Trace was impressed that Jubal had the foresight to circle the wagons early and herd the livestock inside the small blockade. Many trains kept moving, then had no choice but to stay stranded where they were, usually in a long, unprotected line, when the storm broke. On the plains, even a short downpour could make the flat ground impassable.

By the time the wagons were set and everything loose tied down, the wind literally howled, sweeping along dirt and dead grass and debris with every gust.

Trace leaned into the gale, holding his hat on his head as he worked his way over to see if Adeline needed help. When he reached the back of her wagon and looked inside, it took only a second for him to swing up and take the terrified woman in his arms.

She reached for him, wrapping her arms about his waist as if she would never let him go. "I-I was afraid you wouldn't come."

He held her tightly as the storm raged so loudly it drowned out their words and made it impossible to communicate, verbally.

A ghost of a smile curved his lips as he remembered a similar storm and the first night they had made love. She had been scared then too, and had turned to him for protection.

His heart thundered against his rib cage and he drew in deep gulps of sultry air. It was hard to breathe, almost as if the storm sucked away everything in its path, including the atmosphere.

Her fingernails dug into his back when the next bolt hit so closely the ground reverberated. His head dipped until his lips were next to her ear. "Don't be afraid, honey. I'm here. I'll always be here."

He remained bent over, shielding her in the warm cocoon of his strong body. Her hands relaxed and most of the tension drained from her taut muscles. She sighed and snuggled into him.

She was grateful he had come. There were those times when he made her so dratted angry, then he could turn around and be tender and caring when it mattered the most. All except for that one time. Had she been too hard on him?

He was such a strong, dependable, possessive and loving man. Perhaps he *had* been driven by jealousy. The thought wasn't altogether unpleasant. Yes, she could forgive him, for she loved him with all her heart.

Trace had felt the first subtle changes in Addy when she nuzzled her nose into the vee of his collar. Then her fingers drew lines and circles up and over the muscled ridges of his back. At first, he was afraid to move for fear he only imagined the feather-light touches.

He remained perfectly still, though his muscles tensed beneath her evocative caresses. His loins reacted to her gentle ministrations with a fierceness he was hard put to control.

Damn, but he was at a loss as to what to do. His body clamored for release, yet his mind argued that she was frightened and upset. She had gone out of her way to avoid him for days, and he didn't want to risk starting something that might cause her to hate him anew.

Maybe he deserved being put through this hell for acting like such an ogre.

Her soft, sweet voice had the effect of a splinter shoved beneath his fingernail. "Trace, what's wrong? Don't you want me?"

Chapter Nineteen

Addy's soft breath teased his ear. He shuddered uncontrollably as he spanned her rib cage, the heels of his palms pressing the full mounds of her breasts The flickering light from a single candle gave her pale face an almost ethereal glow as he rubbed his cheek to her cool skin.

"Want you?" He took one of her tormenting hands and guided it to the throbbing proof of his desire. "Oh, I want you, all right." His voice was husky and low. "But only if you want me. I mean, if you know what you're doin', and you're not doin' it because you're afraid I'll leave you if you don't. Hell, I don't even know what *I'm* doin' or sayin', how can you?"

His unselfish kindness touched a place in her heart that convinced her, as nothing else could have, that she was doing the right thing.

The kiss she gave him to shut him up caused ripples of sensation to travel the length of her body. She brushed the soggy hat from his head and ran her fingers through his thick, wavy hair.

He gulped when she wriggled firmly into his crotch, and gazed toward the damp canvas overhead as if beseeching help. *"Ahem* — I, uh, think the storm is about over."

"Storm? What storm?" She giggled as his arms tightened playfully about her. He squeezed until she breathlessly whispered, "I give up."

His eyes were set to flame as his lips seared her mouth and eyes and neck. "I'll show you, woman."

Their joining was prolonged by Trace's insistence that he shower each and every part of her body with thorough adoration. She reveled in the delight of exploring his magnificent form without her usual reticence and embarrassment.

He gave in to her frantic whimpers and ended the exquisite torture he inflicted on her body; he entered her, and their coming together was as powerful and as elemental as the wild prairie storm.

When they finally floated back to the reality of the damp wagon and had a chance to catch their breath, Addy lay content with her head tucked against his shoulder, wondering what it would be like to sleep with him for one entire night without having to worry about another thing in the world.

She admonished herself for being so silly. It would be heavenly, and that would make the situation worse.

"Trace?"

"Hmm?"

"What is it you do for the Army?"

He was on guard immediately. "What?"

"You know . . . Why don't you want anyone to know you're a soldier, and why would it be so dangerous if they did?"

"Uh, why? Have you talked to someone about me?" His arm unconsciously tightened about her shoulder until she squirmed uncomfortably.

"Of course not! I promised I wouldn't, didn't I?"

His grin was more of a grimace. "Well, yes, but you are a woman." He began to relax. Maybe her question was innocent, after all.

"Oh, you! Men are every bit as prone to gossip as women, and you know it."

"Do I?" He turned on his side and slid his knee between her legs.

"Yes. Hey! Watch where you put your hands . . . Oh. Oohh!"

Trace closed his eyes and sighed, thankful that he'd diverted her attention. At least now he knew a way to change her train of thought. He didn't mind a curious woman. Not at all.

As quickly as the storm blew in, it drifted away. They made camp where they were, rather than move on in the slippery mud. By the time the sun was up the next morning, they had moved far to the right of the trail to avoid bogging down in the ruts already cut into the earth.

When they stopped at noon, Addy spotted Trace walking steadily toward a nearby hill, carrying a gun. The Arkansas was close by again, and it was good to see trees and shrubs in the background.

Wondering what he was hunting, she lifted the hem of her skirt and ran after him. Strands of loose hair bounced free from the coil pinned at the nape of her neck and tickled her cheek. She breathed the flower-scented air and stopped for a moment, then twirled in the wind, reveling in her renewed health and freedom.

It was the first time she had ventured from the train since the ordeal with Rudy. And it was the first time she hadn't been under the constant surveillance of either Scratch or Trace. They had taken it upon themselves to make sure she didn't leave the wagon without one of them tagging along beside, or trailing suspiciously behind her.

Now that she thought about it, she decided not to follow Trace. Instead, she turned toward the slope leading down to a grove of tall cottonwoods. No one considered the wood good for fuel as it burned too hot and fast, but gathering a few sticks was a good excuse to escape the confines of the caravan for a short time.

She didn't know where Scratch had disappeared to before she left, but she was grateful for the reprieve. It felt good to wander about at her leisure, and no one seemed worried about the threat of Indians, or anything else sinister, along this particular stretch of the trail.

Nearing the river, she didn't stop at the first row of trees, but continued walking. A cool breeze blew off the water and the bugs were not so bad that she couldn't enjoy the outing.

She found a flat rock to sit on, and removed her shoes

to swish her hot, tired feet in the refreshing liquid. A deep sigh left her lungs as she sank her legs in above the ankles.

In the distance she heard shots and wondered again what Trace was hunting. If he were going after elk or antelope or buffalo, he would have taken a horse, so she knew it must be something small like a rabbit, or — ugh! — squirrel.

That was one meal she'd not been able to eat without feeling a pang to her conscience. The little darlings were just too cute.

Several minutes passed while she relaxed and gazed at her reflection in the rippling current. It was hard to tell much in the murky water, but she thought she looked leaner and more mature. Her cheeks were hollow and more defined than she remembered them being when she had left civilization.

She saw a school of minnows and leaned over for a closer look. Just as she ducked her head, something buzzed past her ear. Seconds later, she heard the report of a gun. It was close — very close.

A bullet hit and ricocheted from her makeshift seat. Pieces of rock shattered and stung her legs. Realizing at last that someone was firing at *her,* she fell from the rock and half ran, half crawled to the nearest tree, where she quickly dove head first behind the thick trunk as another bullet chipped off a huge chunk of bark.

Lying prone on the ground, her body quaked so badly she knew she couldn't move again if she wanted to. Her heart thrummed so loudly in her ears that she felt dizzy and disoriented.

Another bullet sliced through the leaves above her head, but she didn't move a muscle. Only her fingers reacted, clawing into the dirt until a fingernail snapped.

Suddenly she noticed how quiet it had become. The only sound was the rushing water, where earlier she had heard birds chirping and the every day, taken-for-granted noises of humming insects and even rustling grass.

A twig snapped nearby and she held in her breath, trying to will herself to melt into the ground. She heard someone shout her name and soon there was a low rumble of approaching runners and murmuring voices.

She saw one pair of boots, then another, as they came toward her. Dirt and mud were caked on the soles, and tiny bits of leather stood out from where they'd been scuffed. She held her breath, wondering if the next thing she felt would be the impact of a bullet in her back.

Trace was the first to burst through the trees. In the next instant Scratch appeared, and then Pedro and Dead Eye. They all rushed to her, yelling questions at once. The air gushed from her aching lungs as she realized the initial threat was over.

She raised her head and answered Trace first. "I-I don't know who it was. I didn't see anyone."

"Gal, ya be all right?"

Her chin quivered and her teeth rattled, but she replied, "I think so."

Trace bent down and put his hand on her arm to help her stand. She didn't budge. She couldn't. Her muscles were frozen rigidly in place. *Scared* was not the word to describe the total, debilitating terror she experienced.

Delilah parted the gathered men and inserted herself between Trace and Addy. "The minute I heard the commotion, I knew it had somethin' to do with you. Come on, dahlin', an' . . ."

"Excuse me, ma'am, but I can handle the situation. Adeline will be fine in a minute or two." To himself, Trace added, "And I don't want you turnin' her into a timid rabbit again."

Addy swallowed. Her eyes stung as she tried to blink. Finally, curling her knees, she raised herself to a sitting position and watched as Trace placed a hand under Delilah's elbow and turned her cousin back in the direction of the wagons, ushering the men along with her.

"Dead Eye, why don't you see Mrs. Wilkins safely back to camp. The rest of you men spread out and see if you can find out where those shots came from and if there are any tracks. The bastard might still be around, so be careful."

Once the area had cleared, he turned back to Addy and held out his arms. "C'mon, honey. Everythin's all right now." Then his mouth quirked and his eyes narrowed. "Except for the fact that you wandered off alone again. Damn it, woman, when are you goin' to get some sense?"

She opened her mouth, but that was the only movement she made. Her eyes darted back and forth from the gun in his hand to his face. All of her doubts raged back full force. She had seen him leave with the gun. Someone had shot at her. Who else could have done it?

Finally, Trace went to her. Leaning the shotgun against the tree, he used both of his hands to literally pry her from the ground.

She flinched away and stood, shaking. Her eyes were round and frightened as she accused, "Y-you sh-shot at me."

Her accusation caused him to take a step backward as he gawked at her in disbelief. "Me? Where did you get an idea like that?"

Then he saw the direction her eyes took as they glanced nervously at his gun and back to his face. "Damn it, woman, that's a shotgun. Whoever fired at you used a rifle."

He began to pace. Tilting his hat onto the back of his head, he rubbed the moisture from his forehead. When he noticed that she seemed to digest the truth of his words and relax a bit, he couldn't stand it any longer and took the steps necessary to close the distance between them. He pulled her into his arms and held her so tightly she could hardly take a breath.

God, he'd almost lost the only woman he had ever loved. And as the reality of that sudden realization bored into his brain, his arms curled even more protectively about her as he nuzzled his cheek into the soft down of her hair. He trembled at the thought of what might have happened to her, and his muscles stiffened with suppressed anger.

Someone was trying their damnedest to kill her. But who? And why?

Sure, he had suspected her of concealing the contraband weapons at first, but now he was certain that she knew nothing of their existence. Someone was trying to keep her ignorant, and it was up to him to keep her safe.

His suspicions had to begin with the train. Her "accidents" seemed to stem from the trip to Santa Fe. He closed his eyes and tried to think. Who hadn't shown up when he and the others had run to check on the rifle fire? Let's see . . . Jubal and three of the others had remained behind.

He shook his head. Jubal's explanation would probably be that he had to stay with the goods. And damn it, that was a valid reason. Besides, he had seen Jubal in camp when he had run past. It couldn't have been him, as much as he would have liked to blame the man.

He pinched the bridge of his nose as a throbbing ache settled in his forehead. From the beginning, the entire affair had had its share of complications.

"Tr-Trace?" Addy's trembling voice was muffled by his soft cotton shirt. "Why is someone trying to kill me?" Though she tried to be calm and to act composed, her voice broke and she nearly sobbed.

A frown drew his brows low as his lids drooped over his eyes. Though it hurt him to see her so distraught, he was also aware of just how inadequate his protection of her had been thus far. He had been unable to foresee the danger and prevent her from being injured. What if he lost her—really lost her?

More gruffly than he had intended, he held her away from him. His hands dropped to his sides as his fingers curled into fists. Frustration was evident in his voice when he finally answered her question. "I don't know who it is. But if I can help it, it won't happen again."

She sniffed as he turned toward the wagons, then she twisted around. "Wait. My shoes." Wobbling slightly, she looked into his face, then quickly to the ground. His eyes held the strangest glow. Instead of being their usual dark blue, they were almost the color of the clear, afternoon sky.

But she was afraid to look into them too long, for fear of seeing them darken with disgust, as they had done several times during the past few weeks.

Disgruntled by the delay, he said, "You sit. I'll go get them." He pointed to a large rock, and she sat. In no time, he was back with her shoes and stockings. Forcing himself to do the gentlemanly thing, he turned his back as she slipped on the soft cotton. However, every once in a while, he managed to snatch a peek, then wished he hadn't tortured himself.

When she reached for the shoes, he pushed her hands away and knelt, taking her dainty little foot in his large, callused hand. He felt the muscles in the back of her calf twitch.

He gritted his teeth as his hand began to work up the back of her knee, seemingly with a mind all its own, then jerked it back as Scratch came limping up. The old man's washed-out gray eyes snapped to life as he glared at Trace. "Found these here shells. An' where a horse be tied. T'weren't no one from the train done it. Tracks led off across the river."

The two men looked at each other, to Addy, and back. Scratch gave a subtle nod of understanding at Trace's determined glare.

Addy drew in a deep breath as Trace rose to his feet. She finished tying her laces, keeping her face hidden from view, hoping they wouldn't detect the moisture in her eyes. She knew what they were thinking, and she loved them for it.

How her heart swelled in the presence of these two men. They had both done so much for her, and had asked for little in return.

Without being aware of it, was she gradually rebuilding the family she had thought she would never have again? Although it gave her a sense of well-being, it was also scary. What if Scratch, too, left her life, as she had

301

this sickening dread that Trace was already wont to do? She'd be devastated.

As Trace and Scratch walked together, heads bent, examining the spent shells, she trailed along behind, a deep melancholy causing her steps, and heart, to falter.

At least she was still alive. Maybe if she put her mind to it, she could come up with a way to keep her newly formed "family" together at the end of the trail.

Several days later, Addy noticed that a general uneasiness had descended on the caravan. She had felt it that morning when she came upon the usually placid Pedro thoroughly cursing his fretful oxen. With the mules, bad behavior was expected, but seldom did the docile oxen act up once the journey was well under way.

Camp was made for the evening, and Addy prepared a meal for herself and her two watchdogs, as she'd come to think of Scratch and Trace. Once the food was simmering, she left it over a low fire and headed for Delilah's carriage. Since they had both had to drive lately, she'd seen even less of her cousin than usual.

She had just reached the end of the Wilkins' carriage when she heard voices from inside. Jubal's was one of them and Addy hesitated—she didn't want to be around him any more than necessary.

But as she was about to turn and leave, Jubal's raised voice resounded clearly. "God damn it, Flo, I . . ."

There was a hushed muttering, and Addy leaned closer. Her guilt at eavesdropping was overshadowed by her extreme curiosity. *Flo?* Who in the world was Jubal talking to? Delilah and she were the only women with the caravan, or so she had thought.

Her conscience dictated that she leave, but she couldn't take the first step. She had to find out what was going on.

She could tell Jubal tried to whisper, but his words still carried out to her. "All right, all right. Quit your naggin'. I'm just tellin' you that I've tried everything. We've got to finish the job any way we can from now on.

302

We're runnin' out of time."

There was another bout of mumbling and she leaned her head against the hard wood, desperately attempting to hear and to make out the owner of the other voice, but the break of worn boards, as if straining under a heavy weight, alerted her to Jubal's approach. She moved away quickly.

Thoughts tripped over themselves, vying for a place of importance in her mind once she knew she had gotten away undetected. The name Flo had her in a quandary. Did Delilah know about her?

And what job needed to be finished before they ran out of time? She thought getting the goods to Santa Fe was the most important thing on Jubal's mind.

Suddenly, she stopped and walked behind the next wagon, turning so she could see the carriage. The door opened and Jubal descended. When he turned to assist his companion, Addy sucked in her breath. The woman following him out was Delilah.

Stunned, she stumbled back to her wagon. She was tired and confused. After a good night's rest, maybe she'd be able to make sense of what she'd overheard.

The next morning, she was awakened from a troubled sleep with the nagging feeling that she was being watched. She batted her eyelids open. She started to scream.

Long fingers clamped her lips to her teeth, smothering any sound. "Sh-h-h. It's only me."

Relief flooded through her as she recognized the voice. At first he'd only appeared as a hulking shadow. Now she could make out his features. There was a glow in his gorgeous blue eyes again, only this time she knew exactly what it meant.

It was the same desire igniting him that burned throughout her own body where his fingers touched her face, where his knee brushed her waist.

When he felt her muscles relax, Trace was loathe to release her, but knew there were more important things to consider at the moment. And it *had* to be important to drive him to pull her from the warm covers rather than joining her there.

"Get dressed. There's goin' to be a meetin' of the drivers and you need to be there. Understand?"

She was groggy, but managed to nod.

"Good. I'll wait outside." His eyes scorched her from the base of her neck to her curled bare toes, even through the thick layer of flannel she'd come to wear every night since the humidity had lessened and the evenings had become cool.

She shivered as she removed the nightgown. The soft material slid caressingly over her flushed skin. She had to shake her head to rid it of the image of his hands taking the place of the flannel.

Just as she was about to lose herself in another erotic daydream, she heard his vibrant voice hiss, "Are you about done in there?"

"Almost." Quickly she put her mind on the task of dressing and in minutes leaned her upper body out of the wagon. "I'm ready, but do you mind telling me what this is all about?"

The next thing she knew, he reached up and lifted her bodily from the wagon. She yelped as her toes bumped the tailgate. "Put me down. You've no right to . . . to . . ."

He put her down all right. Her body slithered down his, their fronts creating a friction that smoldered like ten year old kindling whooshing into flame.

She gulped and stared at the curly hair peeking at her through the open vee of his shirt. He wore a hand-stitched elk-hide vest and she couldn't resist running her fingers over the velvety-smooth hide. Now she could add the new distinctive scent of oiled leather to his already appealing masculine allure.

Trace watched, spellbound, as her brownish-green eyes erupted with golden sparks. His chest tightened as if bound with a drying strip of hide as her eyes branded him there. He flinched when she touched the new vest.

304

He imagined those pink little fingers trailing down his belly . . .

Abruptly, he grabbed her hand and tugged her along behind, as his long strides ate up the uneven ground. She had to run to keep up, her legs tangling in her long, heavy skirt.

Jubal greeted them with a sneer when they finally drew alongside the gathered drivers. " 'Bout time you two decided to join us."

Addy glanced at Delilah and smiled. Before she had gone to sleep last night, she had decided that Flo was probably a pet name Jubal had given her cousin. She'd reacted foolishly. Later, she would find time to talk to Lily. Maybe she could help with whatever chore it was they were worried about finishing.

She winced and looked back to Trace when the hand gripping her upper arm squeezed—hard. Her eyes widened as she heard him say, "You can't take the cut-off. You've got women to consider."

Jubal lifted his upper lip, but it wasn't in a smile. "They're exactly the ones I'm thinkin' of on this matter. Taking the cut-off will shorten the trip by thirty miles. Dead Eye crossed the river. Said the train ahead of us went on through Bent's Fort." His eyes shone with an almost maniacal gleam. "We'll be the first traders to reach Santa Fe. We can name our prices."

Trace argued. "No one's been over the Jornada yet this year. You don't know what you'll be gettin' into."

"Scratch says you know the location of the Lower Spring." Jubal stared Trace straight in the eye, daring him to deny the truth.

"I've been there before." Trace let go of Addy and stuffed his hands into his pockets as if afraid to leave them free to follow his brain's command. "But that doesn't mean I can find it again. You know as well as I do that there are no landmarks out there, nothin' to guide us. The winds blow the sand and things change. And we'll be cuttin' through the huntin' grounds of the Kiowa, Apache, and Comanche."

Jubal shifted to stare out over their small group of wagons. "Yes, yes. I know all of that. It's not as dangerous as it used to be. Several trains cross here every year and most all make it safe into Sante Fe. *And* make it two days faster." He looked meaningfully at his wife. "It'll mean the difference of making enough profit to keep this company goin'."

Finally, Jubal looked at the drivers. "And it'll mean more wages for you men. I say we put it to a vote. How many want to take the cut-off?"

Hesitantly, hands began to raise. Jubal counted and smirked at Trace and Addy. "Seems everyone but you and the other half-owner of the company are ready and willing. That means we'll save your daddy's business in spite of you, little lady."

"All right, men and ladies. We'll stay here today and get everything ready to pull out at first light. Fill every empty barrel with water. Cook enough supplies to last two or three days."

He stopped and raised a fist in the air, then shouted, "We're goin' to be rich, amigos."

Dawn was barely coloring the eastern horizon when the call came to "Catch up!" A chorus of creaking wood, jingling harness and snuffling livestock drifted on the cool breeze.

Addy sighed with heartfelt contentment at the security of the same old routine. The Arkansas had been an easy crossing. The day looked to be clear and bright. All was well. Maybe Trace's worries would come to naught.

As they traveled farther into Mexican territory, she began to look around with dismay. She didn't know what she had expected, but it wasn't this increasingly barren desert.

The caravan plodded across the bleak wasteland, wheeling up clouds of gray dust. Only sparse clumps of grass and the silver tips of sage broke the flatness of the ground. The wagons jolted over every visible, and often unseen, obstacle in their paths.

Other than the usual sounds accompanying the movement of the train, all was silent. No loud shouts or curses drifted along the line. Addy shivered, and couldn't explain why.

By noon her mouth was so dry it felt like wadded cotton. Dust clung to her face and body until she felt she would suffocate. Soon, they would stop and eat and take a drink of water, wouldn't they?

But Jubal pushed them hard. He had to. It would take two, maybe three days of intense, dry travel to reach the Cimarron River. And they had to do it quickly, or perish.

The evening camp was finally made several hours after sundown. As Jubal rode down the line, he made it clear that most of the kegs of water would be used for the animals, who would still not be allowed their fill. The two-legged beasts were ordered to take only a small dipper of the precious liquid with each stop.

By mid-morning of the second day on the Jornada, Addy was already mopping her face with a grimy kerchief. The train had stopped for a water break, and Addy eagerly made her way to the huge barrel lashed to the side of her wagon. Finding the ladle, she removed the lid and dipped the tin spoon inside. She dipped again, and again.

There was a small splash on the toe of her shoe. A feeling of intense dread sickened her stomach. Her eyes traveled fearfully down the wooden barrel, stopping only when she found the small hole.

She dropped to her knees. Gone. The water was gone.

Chapter Twenty

Addy's despair was so great at discovering the loss of the water that she almost forgot the second barrel strapped to the other side of the wagon. She leaped to her feet and ran around the back, nearly tripping over the curve of the big wheel in her haste.

She stopped in front of the keg, her arms held over her stomach to keep it from plummeting to her feet. There was a small, damp splotch on the earth beneath the barrel. Drops of the precious liquid oozed from an inch-long crack near the bottom of the cask.

Feeling drained, much like the seeping barrel, she leaned against the wagon. Jubal's words, shouted early that morning, echoed through her head. "The water for the drivers is on your wagon. Guard it with your life, for that's exactly what it's worth, little lady."

Soon, the crunch of dry grass and disintegrating clods of dirt warned her that the men were coming for their allotment of water. An urge to run and hide caused her toes to dance against the burning soles of her shoes, but she lifted her head and gallantly stood her ground.

A lone tear streaked her cheek as she looked them in the eye and said, "There's a little water left in this barrel." Her voice cracked. "B-but the other one is em-empty."

The men looked at her in stunned disbelief, then with faces screwed with intense hatred for the person they assumed responsible for the loss of their water, they raced toward the opposite side of the wagon like a pack of wolves after a jackrabbit. All but Trace. His voice was husky when he asked, "What happened?"

She shook her head. "I don't know. I waited until the break, like everyone else, and when I came to get a drink, it . . . the barrel . . . was empty. Th-this one still

308

has some water, but it's leaking."

He stepped around her and ran his finger down the cracked stave. Scratch came up to stand at his side. "There be a hole in the bottom o' the other keg. Looks like a knot . . . *fell* . . . out'n it."

Trace narrowed his eyes and nodded. "This one's got a space between the staves that didn't seal. What about the other wagons?"

"We'uns'll find out soon 'nuf. C'mon, boys."

Scratch and the rest of the drivers reluctantly scattered to check the condition of their own barrels just as Jubal and a huffing Delilah walked up with their dippers. Jubal demanded, "What's goin' on here? Where are the men off to in such a hurry?"

Trace stared calmly at the rotund man. "It seems we've got a bit of a problem."

Delilah's eyes went round, but she pushed up to the barrel and held out her dipper. "I don't care about your 'problems', dahlin'. I need a drink, now."

Addy was embarrassed by her cousin's rude behavior, but she took the dipper, then looked askance at Trace, who finally nodded.

Jubal stepped closer. "Now see here, little lady, I'm the wagon boss of this train. If you have any questions 'bout what to do, you ask me." He regarded the barrels suspiciously. "Just what has you so concerned?"

While Trace explained the situation, Addy handed Delilah the water, licking her own dry lips as her cousin greedily gulped the liquid, even spilling some down her chin, forming a muddy spot on her yellow morning dress.

Addy swayed slightly, until Trace offered her his own dipper. "Drink it slowly. It'll have to last a long time."

Jubal consumed his in much the same manner as his wife. His eyes bored into Addy until she shrank against the wagon. "I hope you pay more attention to your responsibilities from now on, little lady." As the rest of the men returned, muttering over their own empty barrels, he added loudly, "It's on your head if these men don't make it to the Cimarron."

Addy's face lost all its color as the men looked at her. She could be the cause of these men dying, just because she hadn't kept a close watch on the water. But how was she to know something like this would happen?

Scratch was the first to ease her fears after the Wilkins' departed. "T'weren't yore doin's, gal. We'uns all lost most our water. Jist have ta make do, be all."

He glanced at Trace and the younger man gave an imperceptible shake of his head. It was as if both knew the barrels had been tampered with, but knew also that it would do no good to raise suspicions and fight among themselves. "The barrels be old, be all. We'uns shoulda checked'em over."

The other men mumbled their agreement and looked sheepishly at Addy as they took their dippers of water. The amount remaining in the barrel would be just enough for a sip that evening, provided nothing happened to it. Once it was gone, there was no more.

Though Addy felt better because of the men's sentiments, they did little to assuage her guilt. She'd never forgive herself if a single one of them suffered on *her* account.

"Couldn't we use some of the animals' water if we need to?" As soon as she asked the question, she knew she had erred. The horrified expressions directed at her actually caused her to flinch.

"Ya got ta understan', gal. Out here, the teams are more import'nt than us'uns. T'hout'em, they's no cartin' them goods ta Santy Fe. An' most o' it be gone now."

"But . . ."

"No use to argue, Adeline. That's the way it is. The way it's always been." Trace took her arm and led her around to the front of the wagon. He offered her a cold biscuit and a piece of the meat she'd fried last night.

She declined, knowing it would only make her thirsty. "What will we do, Trace? What if you don't find that spring, or whatever Jubal called it? Will we all die?"

Trace knew it was a very real possibility, though he

didn't tell her so. Once again he cursed the fates for getting him into a dire predicament. If it hadn't been for his job, and the guns, and one very beautiful, hardheaded tenderfoot, he'd be halfway to Bent's Fort and a cold brew by now.

"We aren't goin' to die, honey. But it will get rough. I won't lie to you." *Very much,* he added to himself.

Addy suddenly preened. He hadn't called her "honey" for ages, and though she was "scared near spitless," as Scratch would say, it bolstered her flagging spirits.

But by the time the wagons rolled again, a state of defeat and utter depression weighted her down. She prayed for the strength to stand up to whatever lay ahead. After finally learning to take care of herself fairly well, and growing into a decently competent pioneer, it would destroy her to break down now and revert to her old ninny ways.

The wagons continued to travel through the late evening. Already, Addy noticed the listlessness of the men and the animals alike. The sky was overcast with high, thin clouds that obscured the moon, making it difficult, if not impossible, to see.

Jubal finally called for the caravan to circle, and she sighed with relief until he shot a derisive glance at Trace and shouted as he rode by, "Don't want to get our guide more lost than he already is, by God."

Trace merely flicked the brim of his hat with his fingers.

The men waited as long as they could to drink their water. They stared reverently at the tepid liquid before taking slow sips, washing it around in their mouths, then swallowing.

Addy followed suit, wishing there was enough to pour over her head to cleanse away even a small area of grime. She couldn't remember going to bed so filthy, at least before she had begun the journey to the fabled "paradise" — Santa Fe.

They were on the trail the next morning before the sun had crested the horizon, to give the animals the advantage of the cool air for as long as possible. She rubbed her eyes, feeling the abrasion of grit beneath her lids.

By midmorning, the mules and oxen had hollows in their bellies and flanks. The men had a sunken look to their eyes. Whenever Addy blinked, dust sifted through her eyelashes. Everyone walked, even Delilah.

Once in a while, Addy looked ahead, caught a glimpse of her cousin, and was surprised by the spry, uncomplaining woman. Was this the Delilah who had bickered so vehemently, was it only yesterday, about being forced to eat dry, tasteless food?

Waves of heat shimmered from the desert floor. Sand filtered through the stitches in Addy's shoes until she limped painfully, unable to take the time to empty her footwear and still keep up with the plodding team. Her strength diminished quickly, and she found herself becoming irritable and cranky, besides jumping at every noise.

Her skin had lost its usual moist resilience and felt pinched, drawing tautly over her bones. It hurt her even to smile. She stumbled with every step.

Trace had given her a small, round pebble before they pulled out of camp that morning, telling her to put it in her mouth when she felt really dry.

She had scoffed at his crazy suggestion then, but now felt willing to try anything, since her mouth felt as dry as the desert they plodded over.

Eyeing the small stone disdainfully, she placed it gingerly in her mouth. Almost immediately the fuzzy feeling on her tongue diminished and she detected a slight moisture. Not much, but enough that she was at last able to swallow.

She became comfortable enough to look around and take in her surroundings. The vast plains reminded her of a far-reaching ocean. Giggling, she swiped a fly from her forehead. Now she knew why Scratch and some of the other men called their wagons ships. Why, if she stood back and looked hard enough, the shape of the

312

wagons resembled boats. Funny, she hadn't noticed it before.

The mules tried to stop, and brayed pitifully when she whipped them forward. Her own steps were short and precise, because she stumbled every time her toes brushed a small stone or clump of grass or ant hill.

It became impossible to look anywhere but at the undulating ground. Only once, when she had worked the pebble around in her mouth so that she could shout at the team, did she manage to lift her eyes high enough to see straight ahead.

She stopped, rubbed her knuckles over her eyes and stared. Was she seeing things? No. It was still there. A lake! A huge, beautiful lake, just ahead.

Excited, she ran forward, past Scratch's wagon, past Pedro's. She almost passed Trace, until she decided she should take the time to let him know about the water. She could share.

"W-wa-water," she croaked, then started running, or what *she* determined was running. Actually, she was barely leaning forward and dragged her feet so that it was easy for Trace to catch her.

His arm shot out and wrapped about her middle, hauling her against him. Her feet continued to move and she didn't take her eyes from the lake, unable to comprehend that she wasn't going anywhere.

"Whoa, woman. Just where do you think you're goin'?"

"Wa-water. Can-can't . . . you see it? A lake. We're saved."

His voice rasped in her ear. "I sure as hell wish it was a lake."

Her head spun around. "Let me go! That's water up there, and I'm going, whether *you* want to or not."

"No. What you see is a mirage. There's no water."

She didn't know how, or where they came from, but she could have sworn she felt tears on her face. There was such a desperate, pleading quality to her voice, that she barely recognized it as her own. "Please, let me go.

313

I've got to get there. I won't be responsible for . . ."

Trace turned her in his arms and pressed her face to his chest while she sobbed and thrashed at him with exaggerated movements of her arms and legs, though the blows she landed were feeble at best. It tore at his heart to hear her cries, yet find no trace of tears on her face.

When she ceased struggling and exhaled a long, ragged breath, he ran his hands over the silky hair that had fallen loose from her bun, and soothingly rubbed her back.

"There *is* water. Why won't you believe me?" She sounded so pathetic, he withered inside.

"I told you, honey. It's only a mirage. Everyone sees them from time to time. Even *I* see it. But don't you think that if it was real, we'd all be running for it, too?"

The logic of what he said made her feel even worse. She raised her head and peered over his shoulder. Yes, it was there. She could see it dancing through the shimmering waves of heat.

"You're *sure* it's not real?"

"Yes."

"I'm sorry."

He touched her dry, sunken cheeks with his finger. "What are you sorry about?"

"For being an idiot."

He chuckled. "But such a beautiful idiot." The urge to kiss her pouting lips was so strong he could hardly restrain himself. He longed to tell her he loved her, and that everything would be all right, whether it was true or not.

But they *were* being watched, and the feelings he had were too new and too disquieting. He turned her back toward her wagon. "Go on, Adeline. We've stopped the caravan long enough."

She nodded and walked dejectedly down the line. Pedro took off his wide, floppy-brimmed hat and inclined his head as she passed. Scratch asked, "Be ya all right, gal?" She sighed and tried to smile as she stumbled by him, but the stiff muscles on her face refused to budge.

314

The rest of the afternoon dragged painfully along. She couldn't help but keep an eye on her lake, but the closer they should have gotten to it, the farther away it seemed. It didn't help her to know that Trace had been right — again.

It was well past dark when they stopped for the night. She couldn't believe they had gone through the third day without finding water. She'd had daydreams about water — cool, fresh water, small streams; large rivers; tiny puddles. Remembering made her nauseous.

The animals were tired and thirsty and restless, and so gaunt that Addy was afraid they would die on their feet. The men were in almost as bad shape, and she was especially worried about Scratch. He had always appeared old and gimpy, but now he looked ancient and even more fragile.

Trace sat alone, with his back propped against one of the wheels, and she went over to join him. "I prayed we would find water today."

"So did I."

"What happens if we . . . don't find any . . . tomorrow?"

"We will reach water tomorrow."

"How can you be so certain?"

He took off his hat and leaned his head back against a spoke. She noticed for the first time just how haggard he looked. She hadn't expected it of Trace. In her eyes, he would always be the invincible hero, strong and sure of himself, just like now, as he spoke so confidently of reaching water.

"We're close to the Cimarron River. Even if we miss the spring, we can dig down in the riverbed and find water. It might be a little thick and chalky looking, and taste like alkali, but it'll keep us alive."

She leaned her head against his shoulder, uncaring that Scratch lay curled in a blanket just beneath the wagon. They had built no fires either night as they pushed as hard and fast as they could straight ahead, taking neither the time nor the energy to search for fuel.

Like herself, no one seemed hungry. Their mouths were too dry to eat anything, anyway.

Inside the closed, dark carriage, Delilah felt beneath the blankets until she found a canteen. She held it to her mouth and took a long drink. "You want more, dahlin'?"

Jubal licked biscuit crumbs from his fingers. "Not now. I've had plenty."

Delilah patted a tendril of loose brown hair back into place. "You know, I almost feel sorry for my poor little 'cousin' and the other bastards."

"Sorry enough to share?"

"Why, dear, I said sorry, not stupid. By the way, wasn't it a shame about all those barrels bein' so old and rotten?"

Jubal laughed and rolled across the blankets to lay close to his wife. "When the boys get here tomorrow, the drivers will be so weak, it'll be like pickin' flies off a dead carcass."

Delilah frowned. "But what if that Randall fella really finds the spring?"

"Aw, he's a blow-hard, trying to impress the pretty Miss Montclair."

"But . . ."

"Not now, Flo. He's the least of your worries. Come on, give ole Jubal a big, wet kiss."

"Wet. Isn't that a glorious word, dahlin'?"

"It'll do. Now, shut up and kiss me."

The next morning Trace helped Addy hitch her team because she was so tired and unsteady on her feet. Her eyes had difficulty focusing. As she returned from a trip to the bushes, she walked stiffly, tottering from side to side.

He understood. He hurt, too. If they didn't find water soon . . . Well he didn't want to think about that possibility. Though it was literally impossible to pick out landmarks in this barren country, he felt there was something familiar about the area . . .

Addy's anxious voice interrupted his musing. "Trace, why are we leaving those poor animals? They'll die . . . I mean, it's cruel." She looked toward a small herd of four or five oxen and two mules that had been cut from the main remuda and driven to one side of the trail.

He sighed. "Some of them are crippled or so worn out that they'll slow the rest of us down. Once we leave, those that can will follow."

"But, what if. . . ?"

"We've got to give them a chance, honey." God, he loved her for her soft, compassionate heart. How could he have ever believed she had anything to do with the guns?

His eyes narrowed as he glanced coldly toward the black carriage and the two Wilkins'. Jubal kissed his wife and then left to find his horse, as Trace watched Delilah start to climb up to the driver's box. She snapped her fingers and stepped quickly back as if she just remembered she had to walk. He wondered how the woman had been able to conserve her energy so well while the rest of them were about to collapse.

Addy found herself thinking the same about Jubal later when she saw the man lean over in his saddle and spit. Her eyes squinted. Surely she had been daydreaming again, or hallucinating. Why, Scratch hadn't been able to chew his tobacco for two days.

Her attention was taken from Jubal when she tripped over an anthill and almost fell. As she steadied herself, she couldn't help but feel sorry for the tiny things. Gazing around at their brown-and-gray world, she wondered where they found their water.

The caravan had traveled about an hour when Trace looked to his left and saw the beginnings of an arroyo. He veered his oxen in an easterly direction and followed the rim of the chasm.

Excitement knotted his guts. If he wasn't mistaken, they were only another hour or two from the lower spring. His high spirits were short-lived, however, when he happened to look down the line in time to see Adeline

317

fall.

The team seemed unaware they had lost their driver as they continued to plod on, ceaselessly following the wagon in front of them. Scratch had pulled his wagon in behind Addy's, but he was trudging painfully on the far side, his eyes downcast.

Trace had difficulty stopping his team. A breeze had picked up and the animals must have gotten their first scent of water. Nevertheless, he fought them to a stand-still, set the brake, and rushed to Addy.

He lifted her upper body and rested her head in his lap. Gently, he shook her. "Adeline, you've got to wake up. Please." She stirred as he shook her again. "Come on, honey, we're almost there."

"Hhmm?" Her eyes fluttered open. "Go on. Go on without me."

"Huh-uh. You get up right this minute." Panic edged his words. If she didn't get up, she would lie there and die. He'd seen it happen before, under similar circumstances.

"Leave me, like those poor beasts this morning. If . . . if I can . . . I'll catch up."

He stood up abruptly. Her head fell into the dust before she could catch herself.

"All right, if that's the way you want it." He grimaced at the serene smile curving her mouth. Her eyelids dropped closed.

"I told you from the beginnin' you'd never make it to Santa Fe. You're nothin' but a born an' bred tenderfoot. Scratch took a likin' to you, but you'll break his heart, an' won't give a damn, will you? Go ahead, lay there an' die."

A sudden gleam of inspiration lit his worried expression. "Yep, Jubal knew what he was talkin' about. Delilah is a stronger woman. She's quite a trooper, you know? Look at her, back there yellin' at her mules. Yeah, you stay here, tenderfoot. We don't need a woman we have to mollycoddle along."

It was the hardest thing he'd ever done, turning his

318

back on Adeline. But he'd seen her eyes pop open, had watched the muscles in her arms twitch. He wanted to, but knew he couldn't help her. If she was to get up and find the strength to handle her team, she had to do it with her own grit, and God alone knew she had plenty of that, or she wouldn't have survived this far with all the adversity she'd had to put up with.

He kept walking until he reached his wagon. Hatred boiled in his gut for whomever was responsible for doing this to Adeline. His fist slammed into the side of the wagon. The pain was a welcome relief to the insistent churning in his stomach.

Under the guise of unwrapping the reins from the brake, he glanced quickly back. She was on her feet, though a bit wobbly. Relieved, he turned back and soon lost track of her as he had to concentrate on controlling his animals as the scent of water became stronger and stronger.

Before long, the remuda thundered past, with the outriders close behind, trying to turn them back. It was no use. There was water somewhere ahead, and the animals were crazy with thirst.

Every once in a while, he thought he caught a glimpse of tracks off to the right — wagon tracks. Could Dead Eye have been mistaken? Perhaps the other caravan had cut off at a different crossing. If so, Jubal would not be happy to discover they were still behind in the race to Santa Fe.

A few minutes later, Trace could see the winding depression of the Cimarron riverbed. As he expected, it was bone dry. He steered his team to the left and soon saw the thick thatch of dark reeds that concealed most of the spring. He couldn't stop the ripple of elation that threatened to buckle his knees. He had done it. He'd led them to water.

The loose oxen and mules had already found the shallow pool, which caught some of the gushing water before it overflowed and disappeared into the porous soil below.

In less time than it took for him to grin and tilt his hat

319

to the back of his head, the bubbling end of the spring disappeared beneath a rush of flailing arms and legs as the men dove headfirst into the water. Trace searched for Adeline. When he couldn't find her, he turned to stare at the line of wagons continuing, driverless, toward the spring.

Addy was there, stoically unhitching her team so they could drink unfettered. He thought his heart would break when she then turned and staggered to the water, collapsing in a heap of skirt and petticoats. Quite daintily she dipped in her cupped hands and drank slowly, a sip at a time, as he had taught her when she'd been injured.

And he had thought she was a tenderfoot. Not anymore. She was every bit a trail hand, and very much a lady. As he knelt beside her and thirstily gulped down his first swallow, his stomach grumbled and he laughed. He'd do well to follow his woman's example.

Addy looked curiously at Trace when he laughed, but she was too busy washing the dust from her face and neck to take the time to find out what was funny. As disheveled as she felt at the moment, she wasn't sure she wanted to know.

It took over an hour for everyone to drink their fill and for Jubal to decide to make camp a quarter of a mile west of the spring. It was a sensible decision, as the buffalo gnats would devour them alive any closer to the river.

The wagons had barely been assembled into a reasonable camp when Scratch hobbled up to Trace and pointed across the dry river. Just visible were what appeared to be a band of Comanche scouting the train.

"Go tell the men. Have them take cover under the wagons."

As Scratch hurried off, Trace hunted up Adeline. He discovered her taking a sponge bath in the back of her wagon. She gasped and snapped her head up when she heard his swift intake of breath. He felt like a schoolboy caught snatching the teacher's apple.

She wore her petticoat and chemise, so was modestly

320

attired, but she grabbed for her blouse when he snapped, "Dress yourself and come to my wagon. There's trouble coming."

Her eyes blazed, but she closed her jaws on a scathing retort and nodded. He backed out of the wagon, angry at himself for losing control every time he got near her. He hadn't intended to yell at her but, damn it, anyone could have burst in and caught her nearly naked. What was the woman thinking, anyway?

As he stomped away, Addy fastened the last button on her blouse and quickly tucked it inside her skirt. She smiled as she thought of the flare of desire in Trace's eyes when he'd bulled his way, unannounced, into her private domain. Oh, he had covered it quickly enough, but she'd seen it, nonetheless.

It made her almost giddy to think that as terrible as she must look, he still wanted her. Now, if she could only *keep* him interested.

Even as she plotted, she hurried. One thing she had learned, when there was trouble brewing, you didn't stop to argue over how dangerous it might be, you just obeyed the orders given for the safety of all concerned.

She had almost reached Trace's wagon when movement from across the river caught her eye. Stopping in her tracks, she stared wide-eyed at the spectacle of painted warriors and decorated ponies. Sunlight glinted off the barrels of rifles and from the honed edges of lance tips.

As the thin, vaguely familiar leader raised his rifle in the air and whooped, she couldn't move. She stood mesmerized by the powerful sight of the surging horses and the whipcord-lean bodies that straddled them.

Chapter Twenty-one

Trace lay beneath his wagon, the barrel of his rifle propped against the dead root of some long departed bush. He kept an eye on the gathered assembly across the dry riverbed while wishing Adeline would hurry.

He sighed with relief when he caught sight of her swishing skirt, but ground his teeth together when she suddenly stopped.

"Adeline! For God's sake, come on."

Still, she stood unmoving. He dipped his head to see her white-faced and open-mouthed, staring.

Just as he started to crawl from his place of concealment to fetch her, he heard the warning yells. He rushed to knock her to the ground, then threw himself on top of her, sighted the gun and fired at the scrawny brave in the lead. The bullet went true.

Trace tugged Addy under the cover of the wagon as he watched the renegade pitch forward to wrap his arms around his pony's neck. Another round-faced savage rode up beside the injured man and grabbed the reins to the frantic horse's bridle.

The rest of the drivers had taken their places and were firing into the melee of spinning animals and shouting men. Soon, the charge was halted and the attackers retreated as quickly as they had advanced.

Jubal came running, shouting, "Damn you! Damn you to hell!"

Dead Eye joined him, slapping the wagon master firmly on the back. "S'all right, boss. They ain't done a lick of harm."

Jubal sputtered, "Well, uh, well, in that case, I think we, uh, deserve a reward. Just so happens, I have a fresh jug. Uh, come on, men, and we'll toast to your quick thinking and good eyesight. We showed the, uh, bastards, didn't we?"

"Shore did, boss."

Everyone but Trace and Addy followed after the swaggering Jubal. Trace had pulled a muscle in his thigh when he jerked back under the wagon, and he rubbed it as he scolded, "Damn, woman, just when I begin to think you've learned a little somethin', you go and try to get yourself killed. Why in hell did you just stand there?"

She blinked and looked him square in the eye. "It was strange. I thought I recognized that Indian in the lead. I know it's impossible, but all I could do was stare at him."

Trace didn't berate her further. Now that he thought about it, there was something . . . And the second man had grabbed at the horse's bridle. Comanches didn't use bridles. They tied a thin rope to their horse's lower jaw.

Pushing his hat to the back of his head, he scratched his forehead. He didn't like the way things were shaping up. If Eagle Feather were close by, he hoped the Indian sought him out, soon.

He shook his head and took Addy's arm, helping her out from under the wagon. "Let's go find the others. We could both stand a tot of that whiskey, couldn't we?"

She looked at him with grateful eyes and nodded, but he wasn't through with her yet. "And if you *ever* do somethin' foolish like that again, I'll turn you over my knee and paddle your pretty little backside. You hear me, woman?"

She smiled. "Yes, dear."

Flustered by the first endearment he'd ever received from her, and unable to tell if she was serious or teasing, he snapped. "Well, that's more like it."

Later in the afternoon, Addy saw Trace staring at her. There was a glint in his eye that reminded her of the old Trace, the man she had known before the incident with Rudy Potts.

She frowned. It had been a long time since she'd thought of that horrid creature. A shiver raked her spine. How she'd like to put him from her mind forever.

Then Trace gestured and pointed toward the spring. A big grin curved his lips, for there, coming very slowly but steadily, were three of the oxen and the two mules they had left behind.

She clasped her hands together and closed her eyes. Oh, she knew they'd had to destroy some of the animals along the way, especially those that broke a leg, or became otherwise injured so badly it was inhumane to prolong their suffering.

But she had never been able to rid herself of the notion that she was somehow to blame for the loss of all the water, though in her logical mind, she knew it wasn't true. Still, it was a relief to see that most of the animals had straggled in to camp.

By midmorning of the next day, though, any respite she had blessedly experienced was long gone. Even as they traveled to the side of the river bottom, the awful buffalo gnats found them.

She swatted and slapped until her flesh was red, and still the pests penetrated the tender areas of her ears and around her hairline. Blood welled from several bites along her neck, and her white hanky came away spotted with red every time she wiped her face.

At least the leaky water barrels had been repaired and all were full. Now and then she would drop back and ladle some out, dampening her cloth as she walked and swatted, walked and slapped.

Trace had promised that with two days' good travel they would reach Middle Spring at a place called Point of Rocks. He said there were pools there and that she might even take a bath.

Just the thought of immersing herself in clean, clear water was enough to take her mind from even the most persistent winged insect. Let them do their worst, for tomorrow evening, she would be clean again. As she scratched her scalp, she knew the time could not come any too soon.

They made camp early that evening, as the men had to go down to the riverbed and dig in the sand to find water for the livestock. She hadn't really believed Trace when he had told her about it earlier, but even as she watched, the whitish liquid seeped up to slowly fill the deep holes.

It looked extremely unpalatable to her, but the animals didn't seem to object as they were led by teams or separated into small bunches in order to drink their fill.

The terrain had become sandy and rough, and as they hurried the next day to make the campsite, Addy thought her insides would jiggle and bounce and turn upside down.

At the noon stop, Trace showed her a huge jutting bluff in the distance, saying that was Point of Rocks, and that they would be there well before dark. Anticipation built all afternoon as she dreamed of her coming bath.

That was why she was so disappointed when he stopped his wagon and walked off the trail, disturbing a horde of huge, vociferous black birds. As the caravan drew to a halt, other drivers joined him. The birds circled overhead, reminding her of the day she had found Trace.

She tapped her fingers impatiently against the reins, watching the men shaking their heads and poking around some black-looking objects scattered among the bushes and tall grass.

Her curiosity finally got the best of her, and she started climbing from the wagon just as Delilah bustled by. "What's the delay, dahlin'? I thought your friend knew where we were goin'."

Addy shrugged. "They've found something up there. I was on my way to see what it is."

Delilah narrowed her eyes and tapped her chin with her fingernails. "Well, I guess we'd better have a look."

They had almost reached the intensely absorbed men when Trace happened to glance up and see them coming. Immediately, he rushed over and blocked their path.

"Sorry, ladies, but this is as far as you come."

There were black smudges on his hands and his moccasins sent up a black cloud of dust as he walked.

"Whatever for, Mr. Randall? We just want to see . . ."

"No! You don't want to see. Take my word for it, and go

back to your wagons. We'll be leaving in a while."

"Trace, what is it? Why does everyone look so . . . sad?"

Addy had been watching the men and noticed that their faces all held the same downcast expression. All but Jubal. She couldn't exactly put a name to what was on his face, but she certainly wouldn't say it was *sad*.

Trace sighed, took off his hat and ran his fingers through his hair, leaving dark trails through the thick strands as he did so. "It's the other wagon train. Evidently they didn't go on by Bent's Fort after all."

Addy shuddered. What she was seeing was the burned wreckage of the wagons and, perhaps something much more gruesome. "Are . . . the people. . . ?"

"They're dead."

"Well, for Go . . . *goodness* sake, dahlin', let me go to my husband. Maybe I can be of some help."

Trace nodded resignedly. If the woman insisted on seeing what was left of the bodies, then by all means, he would let her go. However, he put his hand on Addy's arm, detaining her from following her cousin. "I'm serious, Adeline. You don't have any business over there."

Addy gulped. He was right, she didn't, but she was leery of appearing squeamish or afraid. "But . . ."

"Come on. I'll walk you back to the wagon."

She looked over her shoulder as he turned her, in time to see Pedro and Dead Eye lift something bent and charred. Delilah was near and quickly covered her mouth. Addy's own stomach churned at the stench of the place, and she meekly allowed Trace to take the decision out of her hands.

She remembered the three men back at Council Grove and how they had spoken of finding the remains of a burned train. At that time the occurrence had seemed so distant that she hadn't given it much consideration. Now, seeing it first hand, gave her a fresh understanding of the destructiveness and tragedy of the situation.

She sat in the back of her wagon, mending a few tears in her petticoats. All the while she pictured in her mind the horrid details of finding and burying the poor souls from

326

the ill-fated caravan.

Were the Indians, who tried to attack them the other day, also responsible for the burned train? If so, she was glad so many of them had been wounded by the withering barrage of bullets from their own well-defended position.

She shuddered to think of what might have happened if they had been caught before finding the water. The men would have been like helpless babes, tired and thirsty and barely able to hold their heads up, much less a heavy weapon. And it was lucky Trace'd had the foresight to position the men strategically beneath the wagons.

Addy didn't sing at the short ceremony conducted at the burial. Under the circumstances, it was decided that they should proceed to Point of Rocks with all haste.

Now, when she thought of the forthcoming bath, it took on more meaning than just a cleansing of the body. It would represent a cleansing of her soul as well, as she prayed for those lost, and gave thanks for their own relatively unscathed journey.

It was a rather subdued group that circled the wagons a mile or so out on the flats, away from the overhanging cliffs above the water.

Once the teams were unhitched and things fairly settled for the evening, Addy caught up to Trace. "How come we camped way out here? I had counted on taking that bath you promised."

His eyes scanned the distance between the wagons and the steep rocks, watchful as the men drove the livestock over to water. They all wore several pistols and each carried a rifle.

"As you saw earlier, this is a favorite ambush site for the Utes and Apaches and whoever else might decide we'd make fair pickins. At least out here where it's flat, we can see them comin'."

Her face reddened. "Oh, yes, that really makes a lot of sense. But . . ."

He leaned close and whispered, "Don't worry. I'll see to it you get that bath."

She lifted her chin and turned her head when he gave

her a lazy smile. Deep inside, her stomach fluttered and her blood sang excitedly through her veins. Instead of finding herself embarrassed or affronted by his suggestiveness, she could hardly wait for the time to come.

What would her. . . ? No, who cared what her friends thought. Things were different here; she was different now. She flashed him a saucy grin and walked back toward her wagon, glancing back once to see if he was watching.

He was. Trace had all he could do to keep from running after the sassy little wench. The natural sway of her hips and the cocky tilt of her head did more to excite him . . . He stretched the tension from between his shoulders. He was tempted to show her what her teasing was good for, even if it was unconscious. But he could wait. And when he took her over for that bath, he might just join her.

Scratch ambled up and frowned at the gleam in Trace's eyes as they both watched Addy climb inside her wagon. His weathered face contorted into a scowl as he quickly looked about the camp, glad that no one else had seen the two young people's unwitting display.

He shook his head as he realized they probably weren't even aware of the emotions *he* so easily discerned on their faces.

Taking out his knife, he whittled a sharp point on the end of a willow branch he carried. "Did I hear mention o' the gal takin' a bath?"

Trace cursed under his breath. Whoever said the old man was hard of hearing was sadly mistaken. "She's been beggin' for a week or more now. I told her this would be as good a place as any."

"Uhm-huh. Better'n most. Want I should take'er over later?"

"No! I . . . I mean, I can do it. I've already made the time and it's no bother."

Scratch cocked his head as his lively eyes studied the young man. " 'Member what I told ya? I be holdin' ya respons'ble . . ."

Trace held up his hands. "I know. I know. And I told you I wouldn't hurt her."

There was something in the way Trace said the words this time that was different from the last time Scratch had been subjected to them. And there was a soft, warm glitter in Trace's eyes as he, also, recognized the change in his tone.

Though it was undetectable beneath the hair covering his lips, Scratch grinned. "See ta it ya don't. I'm usually a right peaceable chap." He tested the point on the stick by drawing a drop of blood on the back of his hand. "Don't take much ta violence, ya know?"

Trace grimaced. "Oh, yeah, I know."

It was late when Trace finally went to Addy's wagon. The sun had set. The moon had yet to make an appearance. As it was, they'd just have time to walk to the spring before full darkness descended.

He knocked at the tailgate. "Adeline, you ready?"

When she suddenly poked her head through the canvas, he leaped back. Damn, but he'd been as anxious as a pregnant cat all evening. He didn't know why. He'd seen her take a bath before, had even done the bathing himself when she was hurt.

She hesitantly handed out a bundle for him to take, and he felt better, observing her own nervousness. Maybe she wouldn't hold it against him if he made a total jackass of himself.

As they started off across the open prairie, she kept glancing warily back and forth over her shoulders, hoping no one from the train had noticed them leaving together. She had been looking forward to this time with Trace, and she didn't want anything, or anyone, to spoil it.

Even in the twilight, the tall cliffs and thick-growing bushes made the spring seem more like an oasis in the middle of the desert. It was so beautiful that it took Addy's breath away.

With one hand on Trace's arm and the other across her heart, she walked slowly, almost worshipfully, to the edge of the nearest pool. "I-I've never seen anything quite so lovely."

Trace glanced around, as if seeing it for the first time.

329

Then his eyes fastened on her delicate profile. Her cheeks were cast with a rosy glow in the fading light. "Yes, it is, isn't it?"

He led her to a small pool that was almost entirely surrounded by rocks and greenery. It was perfect for bathing. He knew it was deep and that it would still be warmed from the sun.

Placing her bundle on a flat stone, he turned to leave. "I'll be on the other side of that bush. If you need . . . anything . . ." He nearly choked. "Just give a holler."

She smiled sweetly. He noticed the top two buttons on her blouse were already loose, and swallowed whatever else he was going to say with great difficulty. Knowing he was walking on eggshells with her these days, he fled from her presence, tripping over a loose stone and causing quite a clatter.

"Damn!"

Her melodic, "What's that you say?" caused him to bite into his tongue. "Aw, hell."

Addy smiled a devious smile. Everything was progressing perfectly.

She knelt by the pool and trailed her fingers leisurely through the water. Heavenly. Then she slowly unbuttoned the rest of her blouse, letting it slip casually from her shoulders and off her arms.

Scooping up a handful of water, she raised her arm and let the liquid trickle down to her elbow to drip back into the pool. Another scoop she splashed on her face. She arched her neck. It ran in tiny rivulets down her chin and throat to soak the clinging silk chemise.

A muffled groan eddied through the small enclosure and she nearly laughed out loud. If she had planned it, it couldn't be better.

She stood up and unfastened her skirt, slipping it and her petticoats provocatively over her hips and down her long legs. Stepping from the puddle of material, she stood silhouetted in the moonlight, wearing only her pantaloons and chemise.

Her long, languorous sigh echoed in the stillness as she

330

arched her back and stretched her arms above her head. She could have sworn she heard a muttered, "For God's sake, get on with it," and she closed her eyes in blissful contentment.

She discarded the chemise slowly, one lace at a time, but the minute the pantaloons hit the ground, she stepped into the soothing water, wading carefully over the slippery stones until she stood on the bottom with the water lapping teasingly at the crests of her lush breasts. Water droplets sparkled like diamonds on her arms and chest as she lay her head back and dampened her hair.

A frantic rustling came from the bushes along with a strangled, "Damn it to hell," as a pair of pale legs ran to the edge of the pool. Water splashed and waves rippled toward her before she was crushed in a hug so tight she was afraid her ribs would crack.

Pretending to be startled, she whispered loudly, "You fiend, put me down. My guardian is behind that bush. Help . . ."

Firm, moist lips halted her outcry, then whispered against her like a breeze ruffling downy feathers, "Guardian, hell. One more minute of your torturous little game and I would've been ready for a lunatic asylum."

"Game? I have no idea what you are babbling about, sir."

His mouth caressed her cheeks, her eyes, her nose, and nibbled down her neck. "Sorry, but I don't believe you. Is this what you were wantin'?"

He cupped her breasts in his palms as her hands spread over the tops of his shoulders. His tongue laved the tip of each nipple until she squirmed to get closer, fitting her hips to his, cradling his hardness between her thighs.

He murmured, "Do you like this?" as his hand slid sensuously around her body to cup her buttocks.

She sighed, "Oh, yes."

He lifted her up until she wrapped her legs about his waist. The tip of his manhood slid into her velvet cleft. "Now do you admit this was all your doin', little minx?"

"Oh-h-h, yes-s-s-s-s."

Words failed them both as a magical rhythm took over their bodies. Waves undulated the crystaline smooth surface of the pool to lap against the sheer face of the cliff wall. Short drawn breaths drifted on the faint breeze to be diffused into the shrubbery.

When all was quiet once again, Trace slowly lifted her until he could carry her over to sit on a smooth rock to dry. He frowned when she shifted and he was forced to sit beside her, although it pleased him that she refused to release her embrace.

"Are you happy?"

His eyebrows shot up. "I think that's supposed to be my question."

"Well, are you?"

"Uh, yes."

"Pardon me?"

"Yes, damn it! I'm happy, satisfied, content and anythin' else you can think of."

"Good." She snuggled her nose into the base of his neck, thrilled to feel the quickened beat of his pulse. It *was* good. She had to keep him off guard, and excited.

He frowned. "Good? That's all? Just good?"

"Uhh-huh." His smooth skin beneath her cheek felt wonderful, as did the flesh against her breasts and hip. He was tough and strong, yet soft and gentle. An intriguing combination in a soldier.

From out of nowhere, she asked, "Why weren't you wearing your uniform when you left the boat that morning?"

He scowled and stiffened. "Uh, I'm on leave. Why?"

"You looked handsome in dark blue. It matched your eyes."

He released his breath. "Well, thanks. And I think I would be remiss in my duties if I didn't tell a certain woman just how beautiful she is."

She ran the fingers of one hand through the thick hair at the nape of his neck. "You're quite a charmer."

He nuzzled his nose to hers. "As are you."

"I wish we could stay here like this forever."

"So do I." And he meant it. There were so many uncertainties ahead of them, and he had no idea how things would work out between them when his suspicions concerning Jubal and maybe even her cousin, or his questions about her father's true business, were finally revealed.

"I wish it was possible to stay here all night, honey, but it's best to get back to camp before everyone scatters to their bedrolls. We might have to answer to some ugly questions, otherwise."

She was tempted to inform him that it was within his realm of capabilities to make an honest woman of her soon, but she bit her tongue to keep stating it.

The evening had been wonderful, almost too wonderful, and there was no sense in ruining it. Besides, she had another worry on her mind she wasn't quite ready to discuss with him yet, if ever. It would depend on what happened within the next few weeks, and how he continued to treat her.

"Do you need help dressing, honey?"

She coyly batted her eyelashes. "Yes. But . . . You'd better not. We might never leave."

He laughed and tenderly slapped her bare bottom as he headed for the clothes he had so hastily discarded in the bushes. "You're a wanton little minx."

A sadness crept over her features as he turned his back. The rotten shame of it was that he was right. She was wanton, where *he* was concerned.

They walked quickly across the prairie, and were almost within the line of wagons when Scratch stepped out of the shadows. "It's 'bout dad-burned time ya showed up!"

A sultry voice spoke from behind Scratch. "Why, there you are, Addy, dahlin'. I was goin' to ask you to join me for a late bath, but from the looks of you two, I'd say you were way ahead of little ole me."

Chapter Twenty-two

Addy's mouth gaped, then snapped shut. Her cousin knew . . . Perhaps they did look . . . Even Scratch suspected . . . She trembled violently. Delilah sounded so smug, it hurt her physically.

Trace stepped between the two women before either had a chance to cause further harm. This was all his fault. He should have been more cautious, paid more attention to the time.

To Delilah he said, "Yes, Adeline's been to the spring. I stood watch while she bathed, then she kindly washed my clothes while I took my turn."

He failed to add that the reason his clothes were damp was that he'd been so busy watching Adeline dress that he accidentally dropped his own garments into the water. As Delilah's frown eased somewhat, he was pleasantly surprised that his quick explanation might actually work.

Only Scratch glared at him.

Delilah grudgingly said, "Forgive me, Addy. I shouldn't have behaved so childishly. I do apologize."

Addy opened her mouth, closed it and opened it again before she finally stammered, "I-it's all right, Lily." She looked down at the way her wet clothes clung revealingly to her body. "I-I forgot to take a towel. And . . . I can see how you might have thought . . ."

Trace intervened before Addy said too much. "Now that we've got that all settled, do you need someone to go with you to the spring, Mrs. Wilkins?"

He blushed as Delilah gave him a thorough once over beneath her lowered lashes. He could see how she appraised him. He was thankful that the others hadn't noticed. It was beyond him how a sweet, gentle woman like Adeline could be related to such a woman.

"Thank you for the offer, Mr. Randall, but my husband will escort me. Maybe another time."

Trace backed off a step. "Pardon me, but I must've given you the wrong impression. I wasn't goin' to accompany you, Scratch was."

For a brief moment, hatred flared in the hauty woman's eyes, but it was Scratch who ruffled up like a banty rooster with its hackles raised and sharp spurs extended, fighting mad. Trace winced under the look the old man shot over, for daring to volunteer him for such a distasteful chore.

"Well, my thanks to both of you . . . gentlemen . . . but I'd best be gettin' on. My Jubal worries about me so. See you tomorrow, Addy, dahlin'."

Addy only nodded. She had been transfixed by the exchange taking place between Trace and her cousin. At first she had wondered if there was some attraction drawing them together. Jealousy consumed her at the thought that Trace could look at another woman after the glorious love they had made only moments ago.

Some of the pain was still evident when she said, "I-I think I'll go to . . . bed now. Goodnight, Mr. Scratch. G'night, Tr-Trace."

She stumbled over his name and felt very insecure until he looked at her with eyes that set her blood to boiling. Then she smiled. A sudden, powerful surge of love caused her to tremble.

Solicitously, Trace put his arm about her shoulder, drawing her close to his side. "Are you cold, hon . . . Adeline? That's the second time I've seen you shiver."

Warmth suffused her and she thought she'd never see another cold day as long as she had Trace near. All the time she'd thought he had been looking at Delilah, he was keeping an eye on *her*. She felt like she could sprout wings and fly, she was so happy.

Beaming at both of the men, she bubbled, "No. I'm quite warm, actually." And in her best imitation of Delilah's southern accent, she intoned, "Would you 'gen'lemen' care to escort little ole me to my wagon? It shuah is daak out heah."

She fairly floated as they each took one of her arms,

and dreams of the future dared to find their way into her mind.

By the time the caravan reached a place called Willow Bar, Addy was sorry she hadn't decided to keep a journal of all the events that had happened and the places she'd seen.

Looking in the distance, she was surrounded by sharp buttes, flat-topped mesas and a jumble of arroyos carved throughout the years by numerous flooded streams. She eyed it all warily, for she knew they would have to cross that wilderness, dubbed the Cimarron Breaks.

And it turned out to be every bit as rough as she had imagined. Going down the steep inclines, she just knew that sooner or later the heavy wagon would roll right over her poor team.

On the climb up, the beasts strained and lunged for every inch of ground, throwing sand and rocks every which way from beneath their hind quarters.

It took two days to travel the twelve miles of the Breaks, since it was often necessary to hook extra teams to haul the wagons. Addy's ears fairly rang with the shouts and curses of the drivers and, much to her surprise, she found that now *she* joined in when her mules needed extra encouragement.

What a relief it was to be on the open plains again. Addy couldn't get over the change in the countryside since crossing the Arkansas River. Instead of a thick carpet of green grass and tall trees, the grass grew in sparse clumps, and if there were trees at all, they were short and stumpy.

She made a face when she went over plans for the evening menu. There was plenty of meat, meat of all kinds, but the remainder of the meal seemed to always consist of hard tack and beans. More and more often she had that dreaded nightmare of Boston and food, food of all varieties, baked, broiled, sauteed . . .

At the next camp, she went in search of buffalo chips. Traveling in the open, wood was nonexistent.

The chips were spread far apart so she had to walk quite a distance. She had gathered one good arm-load when she bent to pick up a fat patty and unearthed a huge, hairy spider that waved all of its long legs at her. She screamed and dropped half an hour's worth of work as she ran backward.

Her heel caught on a root. The next thing she knew, she landed smack on her bottom on the hard ground. In falling, she flipped another chip. Just beside her hand crawled a long, ugly thing that must have had at least a hundred tiny legs.

She screamed again and scooted sideways until she could scramble to her feet. She started to run, but her skirt snagged in a sagebrush. The more frantically she fought, the more entangled she became.

Realizing she was too far from camp for her shouts of help to be heard, she bit her lower lip, whimpered under her breath and gradually ceased her wild motions.

She closed her eyes and took several deep breaths. When she raised her lids, she discovered that she was all right. None of the unspeakable creatures had come charging after her. In fact, when she drummed up the courage to flick her eyes around to look, the long, leggy insect seemed to be working as hard to dig itself into hiding again, as she was trying to escape it.

And now that she actually *looked*, it was beautiful. Bands of brown and yellow and red circled its body. Sheepishly glancing over her shoulder toward the camp, she was grateful no one had heard her screams and come to her "rescue." How embarrassed she would have been if Trace had seen what had frightened her.

But as she carefully regathered her lost chips, she avoided the depression where the spider had hidden. She may have developed a new appreciation of *some* of nature's creatures, but that didn't mean she had to like, or be close to them.

After supper, Addy went in search of Trace or Scratch. During the meal, she had forgotten to ask about the colorful insect, and was certain one of them would know what it was.

She walked the entire circle of wagons asking after them, but no one had seen them. Worried now, she happened to look toward the remuda. There they were, standing about halfway between the stock and camp, seemingly in deep discussion.

Just as she started toward them, they turned and headed in her direction. Leaning back against the nearest wagon, she waited. The day had been so tiring that she propped herself between the wagon and wheel and laid her head back against the wood. Standing as she was, and wearing her old brown wool dress, she unwittingly blended perfectly with the shadows.

As the two men approached, they had their heads together, whispering softly. She started to step into the open and stop them when she heard Trace ask, "And you've looked in all the wagons?"

Scratch's raspy answer was, "Yep, ever durn one. Like to got catched more'n oncet."

She frowned. Scratch caught? Doing what?

"And they were all the same?"

"Yep. They be guns an' whiskey hidden in all of'em."

Scratch spat and leaned closer to Trace. It was all Addy could do to make out the rest of what he said. She tilted her head to hear better, admonishing herself for the knots in her stomach that kept her from telling them she was there.

"How'd ya figger it out?"

"Stumbled over a loose board in Adeline's wagon."

Addy stifled a gasp.

"Hell, ya say! When?"

"Remember the night Rudy Potts was thrown off the train? That afternoon."

The old man scratched his beard. "Ya don't reckon the gal be in on it?"

Addy didn't need to hear more. Everything started to make sense now. Trace's uniform. Information of guns and whiskey. Her vivid recollection of the look of hatred on his face when he found her that night. His expression

338

had had nothing to do with Rudy's attack at all.

And now she knew why he'd been so nice, even loving, toward her lately. He wanted to be around when she let it slip about the guns. Her stomach turned over and she covered her mouth. Dear Lord, *guns*. In *her* wagon. Why? Where had they come from? What was going on?

It seemed her world suddenly cracked and shattered into bits before her. She slipped slowly and cautiously along the side of the wagon. Because she was concentrating so hard on escaping, she missed the rest of their conversation. Inch by inch, she worked her way to the end of the wagon.

Trace stared at Scratch. "I can't believe you said that old man. You're her biggest champion."

"Didn't say *I* reckon'd she be. Asked if *you* reckon'd on it."

Trace had learned his lessons the hard way and sidestepped when Scratch spat. "No, I don't think she had any idea of what's goin' on around here."

"Ya be right smart, boy."

Trace put a finger to his lips. "Did you hear that?" He turned and caught a glimpse of movement out of the corner of his eye.

Scratch grumbled, "Whoever it be, be wearin' a skirt."

At that moment, a shrill woman's laugh echoed from the center of camp. They recognized it as Delilah's immediately.

Trace pulled at Scratch's leather sleeve as he ran in the direction he'd last seen the movement. "By God, old man, it must've been Adeline. How much do you think she heard?"

Scratch huffed along behind the younger man. "I'd stake my wages t'weren't what ya said 'bout believin' in'er. Godspeed, boy." He rumbled to an unsteady halt to watch as Trace sped ahead while he stood, helpless, heaving for breath.

Addy ran until she thought her heart would burst. She could hear footsteps close behind her. Her legs churned faster, until her muscles ached and burned and her throat felt raw.

Suddenly, ahead, she saw the Wilkins' carriage and Jubal's big sorrel horse tied to a wheel. She sent a prayer of thanksgiving heavenward and slowed her pace enough to approach the horse without scaring it.

She assumed it was Trace following, for whoever it was, was certainly persistent. As she neared the horse, her eyes blinked closed and her heart sank. It wasn't saddled. There was no time to lug over a saddle.

Walking directly to the horse, she held out her hand, speaking in what she hoped was a calm, soothing voice. She untied the animal and used the wheel spokes to help her mount. For a moment she floundered, half of her hanging off each side, until she finally threw her leg over and scooted up behind his withers.

Barely settled, she heard Trace's voice only a few yards away. "No, Adeline. Don't! Let me . . ."

She drummed the horse's sides with her heels and leaned as low over his neck as she could with her skirt and petticoats bunched up around her hips. For the hundredth time, she wondered how she could have been such a fool. She'd never known loving someone could hurt so much.

Sure he wanted her to come back. He would tell her lies and she'd believe them, idiot that she was. But she wouldn't give him that chance, not again.

The wind in her face felt good as it cooled her flushed cheeks. She turned the horse westward toward the line of mountains she'd been watching the past few days. She didn't know what she'd do once she got there, but at least she would be far away from Trace, and she'd have a chance to think.

The farther she rode, the darker it became. The ground was uneven and rocky and the horse stumbled badly. She finally slowed it to a trot, then a walk, as it had been so long since she had ridden astride that she felt like the wishbone of a chicken breast, pulled first one way, then the other, until she thought she would split up the middle.

The night was so black that she couldn't tell if she was going straight west, or riding in circles. Eventually, the only thing that made her *think* she was traveling in the right direction was that it felt as if the horse were climbing uphill, and something sharp and scratchy, like a branch, scraped against her leg.

When she sagged over the horse's neck and the insides of her thighs felt raw, she still continued. When she couldn't hold herself upright, and slipped to the horse's side, causing him to shy and almost throw her, she stopped.

Getting off was agony in itself. Once her feet were planted firmly on the ground, she had the eerie sensation that she was disembodied from her legs and floated dizzily in the air. Her sore ankle throbbed with pain.

For one fleeting moment the layer of clouds parted, allowing the moon to shine around her. Ahead, she saw a sparse assortment of short, fat trees whose branches sprouted from the trunks all the way to the ground, providing no shelter.

Just before the clouds boiled together once more, she spotted one irregular tree that was bent, with a trunk that curved back toward the ground. Any protection was better than none, so she hurried to it while she could.

After tethering the tired horse, she crawled beneath the limbs, carefully avoiding the sharp, pointed needles. Her entire body ached and she groaned as she tried to curl into a shape small enough to fit the small shelter.

How she wished she hadn't run off without thinking of food or a blanket or even a coat. She did manage to tuck her feet beneath her petticoats, and pulled her skirt up to cover her arms.

She tried not to think about how thirsty she was, or how she regretted passing up the hard tack at supper. Damn Trace Randall! Why couldn't he trust her? Why couldn't he have asked her about the guns? And how could a man make the kind of love he did with a woman he hated?

341

Tears welled in her eyes and rolled down her cheeks. She caught one on her tongue. It was salty, but moist, and it helped, until she decided to think about anything besides Trace.

All that formed in her mind were more questions. Questions about why the guns and whiskey were on her father's wagons; about who put them there and where they were taking them; questions concerning Jubal and her cousin that were driving her crazy.

When the sun hit her eyes the next morning, she blinked and drowsily batted open her lids, unaware at first of where she was and why her bed was so dratted hard.

A horse "whuffed" nearby and stomped his feet. She pulled the cover off her cheek and turned her head. Pain shot up her spine, and she was surprised to find that the "cover" was her skirt.

Everything from the past evening came flooding back. She gingerly raised her hands to massage her throbbing neck and forehead. It took a while to sit up, and when she did, she caught her hair in the branches of a prickly pine tree.

Hungry, thirsty, aching and generally out of sorts, she yanked at the pins in her hair until it fell loose and she could free herself. Curses streamed from her mouth as she stiffly crawled from under the tree. She sighed, ashamed of herself.

The horse seemed genuinely glad she was awake and giving him attention, and that lifted her spirits. She was grateful to have him for company for, otherwise, she knew she would have been terrified, all alone in the wilderness. And she was scared.

In the back of her mind, she grudgingly acknowledged that it was thanks to Trace and Scratch that she'd had the self-confidence and the ability to survive this far. She could have still been sitting timidly inside the wagon, afraid to take a step out. But that was *all* she could concede in that beast, Trace's, favor.

When she finally managed to mount the horse, she

thought she might faint from the pain. The insides of her legs were chapped and burned and she had to scoot awkwardly around to pull a layer of petticoat between her flesh and the animal's hide.

He took right off when she nudged his sides and, for a minute, she almost thought he knew where she wanted to go. She shook her head. Impossible! The horse just felt good and was anxious to stretch his legs.

As she rode over one hill after another, the trees grew thicker and taller. She was hopeful of finding water in one of the arroyos.

The sun shone directly overhead, then dipped in front of her. No water. Her stomach complained noisily. The sorrel pulled on the bridle every time she dozed, trying to nibble on grass or weeds.

Suddenly, it raised its head and whinnied. She almost lost her precarious seating as his big body vibrated with the call. He started walking faster. She tugged on the reins. No response. She yanked harder, but he bowed his neck and pranced sideways.

She tried to reason with him. "You don't want to do this. You don't know where we're going, or who might be up there, boy. Stop, you hardheaded son of a jack-ass!"

He did. She sighed. But when she raised her head and looked around, she sucked in her breath and tried to turn the animal about. She kicked and pulled. He refused to budge. Her shoulders slumped, but she held her head up, chin high, as she gazed at the threatening line of riders strung out in front of her.

"Well, well. Looky what we got here, boys."

"Hey, what's she doin' with the boss's horse?" The voice was high and nasal, and Addy shuddered with recognition, though she wouldn't look him in the eye. She couldn't. She was too busy staring at the ragged group of Indians; well, some were Indians and some were white men dressed as Indians.

Then Rudy's words penetrated her brain. He had asked what she was doing with Jubal's, the boss's, horse.

343

It hadn't been her imagination. The horse had known where he was headed after all.

Dear Lord! She slid from the traitorous animal's back and nearly fell to her knees when her legs momentarily refused to support the weight of her body.

As soon as she felt the blood circulating again, she awkwardly made a dash for the nearest trees. Whoops and shouts followed her. She ran, stumbled and ran again.

Hoofbeats trampled the ground around her. Someone rode in front of her, bumping her with a horse's shoulder. She spun back. Another rider yanked at her hair.

A gunshot rang out and she ducked to the ground. She hid her head under her arms, praying that if they were going to kill her, they would get it over with quickly.

The riders stopped circling. Everything went quiet. Then she heard a voice that sent her heart reeling to her throat.

"Get away from her. Now!"

She peeked through her fingers. The first thing she saw was an Indian holding his bleeding arm. Her stomach churned and she felt light-headed.

"Back off, all of you. Adeline? Can you get up?"

Tears filled her eyes as she staggered to her feet. It suddenly didn't matter that she had run away from him. She couldn't even remember the reason. The important thing was that Trace had come for her. Once again, he had saved her life.

Without thinking, she started running. She tripped. Trace took his eyes off the renegades for a second to see if she was all right.

She staggered and watched, horrified, as Rudy brought up his rifle and fired. The bullet took Trace in the shoulder and he lost his grip on the gun. Another renegade shot, and Trace crumpled from his horse.

Addy stumbled and went to her knees, though she struggled to get to Trace. She couldn't believe her eyes.

344

She crawled toward him. He lay so still, so bloody, so . . . lifeless.

The sound of more horses and men climbing the hill alerted the ragtag band that there were other men following the one that was down. A bullet thunked into the ground in front of Rudy's horse.

"C'mon, men. Let's get out of here. Someone grab the woman, an' bring the boss's horse."

She hardly knew when a thick arm grabbed her around the waist. Her head spun every direction as she refused to take her swollen eyes from Trace.

He had followed her. He had tried to save her. He was dead. It was her fault. All her fault.

Chapter Twenty-three

Addy was dazed, despondent, and barely cognizant of her surroundings. They had been riding for hours and hours. She was long past pain. Since losing sight of Trace, nothing equaled the hurt that had pierced deep into her soul.

Whatever fate had in mind for her at the hands of these filthy, cowardly renegades, she deserved. If it hadn't been for her reckless behavior, Trace would be alive and joshing with Scratch back at the wagon train.

Her stomach roiled as her captor fondled her breast for the hundredth time. She closed her eyes. Her chin drooped to her chest. The beast's stubbled chin scratched the sensitive flesh on the back of her neck as he slobbered kisses at the base of her ear.

She couldn't find the will to care. And that revelation presented quite a shock. Though she had been meek and shy as a young girl, she always had a sense of self-worth about her, until now.

A greasy-smelling Indian, wearing nothing but a grimy loincloth, rode up to grin lewdly and point and make crude gestures at the hand at her breast. Her eyes drifted to the ground, dull and lifeless, as she tamped down the nagging little voice that whispered, "Don't let them do this to you, ninny. Show them you have pride and dignity."

But that larger part of herself, that portion that had died along with Trace, refused to be taunted. Nothing they could do, or say, would ever hurt her again.

The only thing that kept her alive and willing to go on, were the few glimpses she caught of Rudy Potts. The desire for revenge welled so deep inside her that nothing else seemed of any consequence. Somehow, some way, she would kill that snake of a man and, then . . . Then?

She inwardly shrugged. Then . . . it didn't matter. She was as good as dead, anyway.

It was late that afternoon when the small band finally stopped. Addy had given up the battle and slumped against the huge man's chest.

And, blessedly, it had been a while since he had paid any attention to her.

She heard the rustle of clothing and creaking leather as the men dismounted. Soon, Rudy's whining voice came from the general direction of her left knee. She didn't bother to look at him.

"How's our 'guest' doin', Freddy?"

"Huh. Woman no fight. No holler. No fun."

One of Rudy's hands spread over her thigh. She flinched. It was the most responsive thing she'd done all day.

"Hand her down, an' I'll find a place to make'er *comfortable.*" Rudy snickered and the hairs on the back of her neck tingled. Her hands clenched, but she didn't have the energy to lift her arms. Frustration gripped her heart. How would she find the strength to kill him?

Once he had her in his arms, he shifted her away from one shoulder. Addy thought it felt like a layer of padding under his shirt, probably a bandage. Too bad it was so far from his heart, if he had one. As he walked, she took a vague interest in her surroundings, mostly an assortment of board shacks and ragged tepees, all in a state of ruinous disrepair.

As he stopped in front of one of the sturdier-looking hide tepees and bent to step inside, she decided that the time was as good as any and clamped her teeth into the fleshy lobe of his ear.

Rudy yelled and literally threw her inside the dark, smelly interior. She put one hand over her nose to block the foul stench while struggling to her feet. She scrambled toward the doorway, but he was too fast

Grabbing hold of her flying hair, he yanked her head around and backhanded her across the face. Her neck

347

snapped backward, and he let her fall to the dusty floor.

"Serves you right. I been tryin' to be good to you, but you just won't let me."

He jerked her hands above her head and bound them to a round stake in the center of the cleared area. "That'll keep you for a while." Before he left, he reached down to rip the bodice of her dress all the way to her waist, exposing her bosom to his glassy eyes.

She warily studied his face until she saw drool forming at the corners of his mouth, then resignedly closed her eyes. Her time would come. Soon, it *had* to be soon.

"You're prime, woman, prime. Ain't got the time just now, but you'll be here when ole Rudy gets back, won't you?" He tied her feet before leaving, and his mad giggle echoed in the rank air. She gagged.

Quickly testing her wrists against the leather binding, she tried to wriggle her hands. They were tied so tightly that the strap bit into her skin and her eyes watered. No matter how hard she tried to convince herself she couldn't feel pain, she did — over and over again.

Several fires flared in the camp. The flickering light reflected off the dark hides enclosing her shelter. Once she had gotten somewhat used to the sickening odor of animal and human sweat and excrement, she worked up the nerve to inspect her 'cell'.

Her eyes widened. Stacked around the walls of the tepee were crates and sacks of supplies similar to the ones packed in her wagon. There were also bolts of cloth and a plow. Trade goods. But what were they doing in the middle of a renegade. . . ?

Suddenly, the horrendous spectacle of charred ashes and blackened bodies popped into her head. The massacred wagon trains. She was willing to bet every ramshackle cabin and tepee in the camp were filled with goods taken from those unfortunate traders.

A surge of white-hot rage rippled through her system. This was something else Rudy would atone for. Rudy *and* his 'boss'. Right behind the enraged anger, though, came a shivering bout of dread.

She had stolen Jubal's horse. Rudy recognized it and called it the 'boss's' horse. In a way she wasn't surprised to find out the worst about Jubal, but what of Delilah? Was her cousin an innocent victim? Or part of the nightmarish scheme? One way or another, she would find out the truth before she died.

Her eyes blinked closed. She tried to swallow past the raw constriction of her parched throat. It was hard to remember how long it had been since her last meal or drink of water.

She must have dozed, for when she next opened her eyes, the campfires had died down to smoking embers. The Indians and their white cohorts laughed and shouted, staggering drunkenly about the entrance to her shelter.

A nudge at her feet caused her to groan. Someone untied the thong around her ankles. As circulation returned to her feet, pinpricks of pain shot through her soles and toes.

A hand lifted her head and a canteen of acrid water was placed against her lips. She could hardly swallow and the water dripped down her chin as she choked.

"That's all for now. Just a drop or two. If you make ole Rudy real happy, I might decide to let you have more later."

She stared at him with blank, unseeing eyes, or so she hoped. He grumbled under his breath and she heard, then felt, a knife and ungentle hands removing the remainder of her clothing. Her first instinct was to shrink inside herself and clamp her knees together, but her legs were so numb they wouldn't move, or she couldn't tell if they did. And she couldn't feel her arms any more, either.

She closed her eyes and prayed, "Please, Lord, let me live to have one chance at him. That's all I'll need." It wasn't exactly reverent to beg for an opportunity to murder a man, but, under the circumstances, she truly believed God would at least understand her motives.

She heard the rustle of clothes being hastily removed

and the soft thunk and smell of dust as the garments hit the earth near her head. The air left her lungs in a startled gasp as he slithered over her until his face was even with her breasts. She struggled beneath the weight of his body and screamed.

"That'a way, bitch. Let'em know how much ole Rudy pleases his women."

Addy's face contorted, unable to believe what she was hearing. He talked like his taking her by force would be something she should enjoy and look forward to every time he attacked her. He actually thought he was giving her pleasure. She had to choke back vomit. He was sick, twisted.

Suddenly, there was a noise at the entrance to the tepee. Addy jerked her head around, a faint glimmer of hope shining in her eyes. Trace? No. She had to remind herself he was dead. He had saved her many times before, but not tonight, not ever again.

Even Rudy's face turned a mottled shade of red, along with the rest of him, as he moved to pull on his trousers.

"My apologies for catchin' you at such a . . . awkward . . . moment, my friend, but I need to speak with you, outside. Now!"

"God'amighty, boss. I can't leave now. Give me two minutes, one even. That's all I'll need. Promise." Rudy's nasal whine rose in pitch as he frantically begged.

Jubal Wilkins had the effrontery to tip his hat and wink at Addy. "You looked mighty good with a man a'tween your legs, little lady. Wish I wasn't in a hurry." He snapped at his henchman, "Come with me, Rudy."

Jubal turned on his heel and ducked out of the entry. Addy heard her captor curse.

Rudy whined, "Damned sonofabitch. All his fault . . ." He snatched at the rest of his clothing and shot a quick look at Addy. "Maybe it's for the best. We'll have a humdinger of a time when I get back. You'll see." Seeing the revulsion in her eyes, he experienced renewed vigor in his loins and puffed out his thin chest.

He became so engrossed in hurrying after Jubal and

keeping his back turned to Addy while he buttoned his breeches, that he never noticed when his knife fell from its scabbard. Addy held her breath. Would he leave without retrieving it? Her chest felt as if it might burst when he stomped from the enclosure without another glance.

She quickly dug her heels into the ground and scooted her body upward to relieve the strain on her arms. The knife had fallen near the stake. If she could only get enough feeling in her fingers to pick it up . . . She flexed the muscles in her arms and winced as blood slowly began to circulate.

Wriggling her wrists, she had to stop for a minute when it felt like her fingers would shatter, but she kept working, bending them methodically, painstakingly.

Voices came clearly from the far side of the tepee and she quit struggling, thinking that Jubal and Rudy had returned. However, when they continued to speak, she strained her neck and saw a long slit in one of the hides near where they stood. Evidently, they hadn't realized her proximity.

She continued working toward the knife, as noiselessly as possible, and still listen.

"Damn it, Potts, I near threw a fit when I learned you brought the woman here. That Randall fellow will be on our tails quicker than . . ."

Rudy giggled. Addy flinched at the gruesome sound. "Mr. high'n mighty Randall's not gonna bother us, boss."

"What? How do you know . . . ?"

"He's dead. Shot him first myself."

She could even hear Jubal's indrawn breath. "God damn, Rudy, you knew we needed him alive. We have to know if he's the man Black Crow left for us to find."

"But you said you never saw no sign."

Jubal snorted. "That damned woman wasn't supposed to get there ahead of us and trample all over the place, either."

"One way or the other, he needed to be got rid of. An'

we done it."

Addy's eyes burned with tears. Jubal was responsible for Trace being staked out that day and, more than likely, for the murder of Trace's friends on the stagecoach. Her head throbbed from everything she had learned in just that one evening.

The tips of her fingers brushed a bone handle and she nearly yelped with relief—and pain. Her wrists burned and she felt a dampness beneath the thong. A little later, she was surprised to find that as her blood soaked the leather, it gave, just enough that she stretched her fingers and prodded the knife closer.

She sucked in her breath when she realized it had been quiet for a long time. Where were Jubal and Rudy? Then she sighed as they resumed talking at a different location, but still close enough that she could hear.

"What about the woman? What'll we do with her?"

"Ah-h-h, Rudy . . . Once Miss Montclair is taken care of . . . everything will be ours."

Addy had known Jubal didn't like her, but she was flabbergasted by the satisfaction she heard in his voice, the near exultation.

"She don't know a thing, does she, boss?"

Jubal laughed. "She's even more gullible than her stupid daddy."

He mentioned her father just as she sliced the sharp blade through her bonds. Before she could really think about the meaning of his statement, boots crunched on the gravel outside the entry. She held on to the leather thong with one hand, making it appear she was still tied, while hiding the knife as best she could in the other.

"You'll bring the men in three days?"

"We'll be there."

"Good. Come at daybreak. There shouldn't be any resistance without Randall to give the damned orders."

"Better not be. We're gettin' a mite short-handed, thanks to him."

The next thing Addy heard was the closing of the flap

352

when Rudy entered the tepee. He walked over and stood looking down at her. She thought she saw a brief flicker of regret in his eyes, but it was gone in one blink.

"Told you I'd be back, didn't I?"

As he shed his clothes, her body tensed. She was tempted to get up and run, but was afraid to trust her arms and legs. Most of the feeling had returned, but she was so weak from hunger and thirst that she only dared to hope that she would have the strength to do what was necessary when the time came.

Right now, though, she needed to get information from Rudy. Her flesh crawled with the sensation of a horde of leggy spiders climbing over her when Rudy knelt, naked, beside her.

"Ain't never seen a woman with skin so soft." He ran his hands up and down her body in wonder. She shuddered.

"Feels good, huh? Just wait till I get inside you."

Her voice cracked when she tried to speak. She swallowed and tried again. Finally, Rudy grunted and reached for the canteen. After several gulps of water, she was able to drink without choking it all back up. She didn't have to try very hard to sound pitiful. "Wh-what's going to happen to me, Mr. Potts, R-Rudy?"

He frowned and put the water away.

"Jubal wants me dead, doesn't he?"

"Well . . ."

"I don't know why. I've never done anything to hurt him." She sobbed and clenched her fists to keep from slapping away his hands as he continued to feel and touch her. She could almost see his demented mind working, and knew when he came to the conclusion that she wouldn't live long enough to repeat anything he told her, anyway. Her heart dropped to the pit of her stomach, then rose to wedge in her throat. Did she really want to know . . . ?

"Jubal's not like ole Rudy. Ain't satisfied with what he's got." He winked.

"Uh, pardon me?" What was the man getting at?

353

Rudy shrugged. "The boss likes his money. Figured makin' the fast dough by tradin' with the Mex's be the easiest way to get it."

She tried to keep her voice soft and husky as she concentrated on his words, not his hands. *Don't feel what he's doing. Listen. Ask your questions,* she scolded herself.

"What does that have to do with killing me? He'll get a good portion of our profits."

His hands reached her hips and for a moment she was afraid he wouldn't answer. Her fingers tightened on the knife.

"He wants *all* the profit. He found out how much your Daddy made with one summer's haul, an' he had to have the business. Just ain't satisfied."

Addy trembled from head to toe, but not from Rudy's questing touch. The color drained first from her face, then from her entire body. She felt cold and clammy. "Are . . . are . . . you saying . . . that Jubal is . . . was responsible for my . . . parents' . . . deaths?"

He licked his slobbery lips and ran his tongue around her quivering breasts before he sat up and looked into her damning eyes, then to the flap at the door. "Look, I'm gettin' tired of all your yappin'. I'll tell you this, an' then you better keep ole Rudy happy. Jubal won't like . . . Well, won't make no dif'rence, no how, I reckon."

His Adam's apple bobbed in his throat. "Jubal figured with your folks outta the way, you'd stay back in Boston an' never find out what happened, least not before you met up with an accident all your own."

"Oh . . . my . . . Lord. All those things that happened to me weren't 'accidents'."

"You're a mighty hard woman to kill, that's for sure."

This time she couldn't control the shrillness in her voice. "What about Delilah? Did she know about this?"

But Rudy was through talking. He flopped on top of her and bile rose in her throat as she thought of what he intended to do. Then she thought of how he had shot Trace, deliberately pointing the gun and pulling the trigger.

Her arm sockets were stiff and sore, but gradually, slowly, she moved her arms from over her head. She was especially careful with the hand that gripped the knife. With her fingers still slightly numb, she concentrated solely on keeping her knuckles bent and her grasp firm.

Rudy cursed and pinched her thighs cruelly when her knees instinctively drew together. He raised up and would have slapped her, only he saw the reflection of a solitary flame off a shiny blade.

His arm flew up and deflected her thrust. She brought the knife down hard and it sliced deep to grate along the bone. He screeched and savagely twisted her wrist with his uninjured hand. The knife thudded to the ground as his blood dripped over her chest.

"You bitch. You damned bitch. Can't be nice to you. Can't do nuthin . . ."

She closed her eyes. The effort had sapped her strength, and it had not been enough. She had failed.

All at once, the weight of Rudy's body left her. There were sounds of a brief but intense struggle, and a strangled gurgle.

Her eyes snapped open and she sat straight up at the sight of bare, stocky legs standing within touching distance.

"Are you unharmed?"

She gulped and raised a hand to her fluttering heart at the sound of Eagle Feather's voice. All she could do was nod and blink. A thrashing sound came from just beyond his feet. Afraid to look, but drawn nonetheless, she turned her head.

Rudy gave one last kick and lay still, lying in a pool of his own blood. She inhaled deeply and turned quickly away.

Eagle Feather stepped away and rummaged through the stacked wares. When he came back to her, he shook out a woolen blanket and wrapped her safely within its confines.

As he gently picked her up, she rested her head on his solid shoulder. It felt good to be with a friend, even if that friend was an Indian, and especially *this* Indian friend.

Her slight form vibrated as his deep voice rumbled in his chest. "I thought white women took great pride in hiding beneath layers of cloth. Yet every time I lay eyes on Randall's woman she is as naked as a Comanche infant."

She knew his words were intended to lighten her spirits, but the mention of Trace brought fresh tears to her eyes. It was strange, she thought, she hadn't even had a chance to really cry over the loss of her love.

"Eagle Feather, there is something I have . . ."

He shushed her as he warily stepped through the slit she'd seen in the back of the tepee. Now she knew how he had gotten inside without being noticed by either herself or Rudy, or the renegades still lounging around the dying fires and passed out on their bedrolls.

Once they were away from the camp, she tried again to tell him about Trace, but he spoke first. "There is someone who is anxious to see you, little wildcat, but for now you must close your eyes and ears."

She looked into his sternly chiseled features. "I don't understand . . ."

Gunfire broke the stillness of the night. Screams and terrifying Comanche yells erupted throughout the small clearing. Ducking her head, she prayed that none of Eagle Feather's people were hurt or killed. She came to the sobering conclusion that she brought nothing but bad luck to everyone she touched.

He carried her into a thick growth of pinon pine and juniper, to stop in front of a lean-to of sorts, with a roof and back of small branches tied together with rope and strips of leather. Rumpled blankets lay atop a bed of pine needles.

She could easily see the fierce scowl on his face, even in the darkness, and wondered why he was so worried. Was he, too, thinking of the warriors that battled to save her? Of course he was. How stupid of her to think otherwise.

The muscles in his arms jerked as he lay her on the blankets. Quickly and gracefully, with little movement, he piled her lap with a soft leather bag filled with what she assumed to be water, also bits of jerky and hard tack.

Bless him! Trying to drink, eat and talk at once proved to be impossible. By the time she looked up to thank him, she was startled to see that he was already gone.

The intensity of the battle diminished, though every once in a while she still heard sporadic gunfire and bloodcurdling yells. No wonder people were so frightened of the Comanche. All one had to do was hear them, and it set a person to shaking in their boots, or shoes, or whatever they wore.

Once she had her fill of food and water, it was more and more difficult to hold her eyes open. She nodded, and was about to lie down on the soft blankets when she thought she heard something.

Her eyes flew open and her hands searched until she found a large rock. If it was one of Rudy's men, they wouldn't take her again without a fight.

She recognized Eagle Feather. Her muscles relaxed and the rock fell unnoticed from her limp fingers. He and another Comanche walked slowly, supporting an injured man between them. Her heart went out to the poor fellow as tears spiked her long lashes and her eyes drifted closed.

Chapter Twenty-four

Addy's rest lasted only a few minutes. She stirred groggily when Eagle Feather unceremoniously dumped the person he'd been bracing onto the blankets.

Her eyelids peeped open when the fellow groaned. She slanted her gaze warily in that direction. She frowned and blinked, blinked again and fought an arm from beneath the blanket to rub her eyes. Her voice squeaked, "Tra-Trace?"

No, it couldn't be! She had seen him shot down. She had to be hallucinating. That was it. Like the mirage in the desert.

She looked anxiously at Eagle Feather. He stood in all of his majestic splendor, arms crossed over his chest, grinning broadly.

Suddenly, her heart took wing and she launched herself at Trace. There was a muffled groan when she landed in a tightly wrapped bundle on top of him. She hastily regained her composure enough to squirm back and be content with just touching him, running her finger over his pale cheek.

He was certainly real. Her voice quavered, "I-I thought you were d-dead."

His hand covered hers. "For a while there, I felt like I was." He cleared his throat. "When I saw the bastards take you away, I was afraid . . ."

Trace found he couldn't put into words the demoralizing fear he had suffered as the renegade pulled Adeline from the ground and slung her onto his horse. Debilitating rage and shock from his wounds had kept him from racing after them. "Did they . . . hurt you . . . badly?"

She looked up at Eagle Feather, then shook her head. "I'm fine. Just a little hungry and thirsty and tired."

Scooting closer to him, her eyes searched his lean body. He was alive. All of the grief she had suffered, believing him dead . . . The man she loved. The man who suspected her of smuggling guns and whiskey to . . .

Her thoughts were interrupted and her eyes widened, abruptly halting their inspection when she found a dirty, blood-stained bandage tied about his shoulder. "I knew you were hurt. I saw you shot—twice."

He ran a finger over her bruised cheek and grimaced as Eagle Feather sank down to sit cross-legged in the opening of their shelter. The Indian had such an intent expression on his face that Trace nearly laughed.

"One bullet grazed my shoulder. The other hit the pistol I had tucked into my waist band and knocked the wind out of me. I guess I did lose consciousness, cause I don't remember much until my friend"—he pointed at the Comanche—"turned me over and asked if I was goin' to nap all day or go the hell after my woman."

Addy blushed. Until Trace, himself, said something about it, she wasn't sure she would *ever* really be his woman, as much as she dreamed and hoped it was so.

"Then you weren't hurt, real bad?"

His tanned face turned darker, tinted with red. "Naw, just lost some blood, is all."

Her eyes took in the deep lines on his face, evidence of the pain he fought to hide. Knowing he would never admit to weakness, and determined not to humiliate him by fussing, she nodded and said, "I'm glad," though her voice trembled.

Eagle Feather's glance touched her. She shrugged. There was approval in his eyes as he rose fluidly to his feet. "You will rest. There are things to attend to. We will see about leaving in the morning."

Addy knew that he meant their going depended on how she and Trace and any of his wounded warriors felt by morning. She was grateful to the fierce-looking Comanche for his kindness and insight. The Indian was truly an individual worthy of *anyone's* respect.

Suddenly, in the silence after Eagle Feather's departure, she remembered what she had learned of her mother's and father's death. The Indians weren't responsible at all. Her hatred and anger had been mistakenly directed at Indians in general, and she had been wrong.

A tingly sensation ricocheted down her spine. She glanced over to find Trace watching her.

"Where were you, honey? You looked a million miles away." He shifted and held out his arms. "I probably don't look or smell much nicer than an old buffalo bull, but I'd sure like to hold you. Please? I need to touch you."

Her heart melted as she happily complied. It must have cost him a great deal to *ask* her to come. She snuggled against him, feeling safe and secure in his arms.

Once he held her close to him, her eyes began to fill with moisture. Then the pent-up emotion overflowed as if a dam had burst deep inside of her. She gulped and stammered, divesting herself of the horrendous pain, as she related the events and happenings of the long hours she spent in captivity.

She told him of the foul deeds Jubal and Rudy had instigated and sobbed until his shirt and the edge of her blanket were soaked with tears.

He hugged her until they both groaned from squeezing too many aching muscles and bruises. "I'm so sorry you had to go through all of that, honey. God, if they had hurt you . . ."

She couldn't help but wonder if he had felt the same way about seeing her abducted as she had felt about his being shot. Did he really care as much as he said, or was he continuing to use her?

She stiffened in his embrace. "Trace, why did you come after me?"

A muscle jerked in his jaw and his belly knotted. "I had to. When Scratch and I saw you runnin' . . ." His grip on her became iron hard. "We assumed you had heard *part* of our conversation."

360

From the mutinous look on her face, they had figured correctly. He had to proceed cautiously. He
couldn't risk losing her again. "You ran before you
heard everything we had to say."

"I heard enough." She jerked her eyes away from his
compelling blue gaze before her insides turned to flowing lava. By all rights, she shouldn't care *what* he had to
say. But she tilted her head, to make sure she heard
every word.

"No, you didn't. You didn't hang around long
enough to hear me tell our friend Scratch that I knew
you didn't know anything about the false bottoms on
the wagons, or that they contained contraband."

His fingers grasped her chin so she had to look at
him. "And you didn't wait to hear Scratch say that it
was a good thing I didn't suspect you, or he'd tan me
good and hang me out to dry with the rest of the
mangy hides he's collected."

She knew he was teasing, and tried hard not to
smile. "Really? You think I'm innocent?"

"Honey, I *know* it." In so many more ways than that
one, he thought, as he kissed her on both cheeks and
then on her perfect bow-shaped mouth.

She pulled away. "So you didn't come after me just to
. . . use me again?"

He hesitated. She struggled. Her energy ran out before his. He held her tight as a long sigh hissed through
his teeth. "So, you had that figured out? Yeah, I did
take advantage of you, at first, when I wasn't sure what
to believe, but not for the past few weeks. Honest to
God!" As if sensing what she needed to hear, he added,
"And I've never made love to you believin' you were
guilty of anythin' more than bein' a hell of a beautiful
woman."

It was the conviction in his voice and the sincerity in
his deep, dark eyes that convinced her he told the
truth. If he would only tell her *how much* he cared, for
she knew he must, everything would be perfect.

Trace closed his eyes. He was tempted to say the

words that seared his brain and choked in his throat whenever he looked at her. But he was reluctant. If he asked her to stay with him, and she accepted, he would be putting her life in danger again.

This was not an easy land, and he had seen it take its toll on too many women. Did he have the right to ask her to take that risk? It was something he would have to think about, though he wondered if he would have any kind of life at all without her.

As she lay wrapped in Trace's warm embrace through the night, Addy studied the handsome features she loved so dearly. Though she had been shocked and hurt when she ran from the train, she had never stopped loving him.

In her heart of hearts, she believed that he loved her, too. She just didn't have the slightest notion of how to go about getting him to admit it.

Determination hardened to a defensive gleam in her hazel eyes. By the time they reached Santa Fe, she would hear the words "I love you" from the stubborn man's lips. He might not mention marriage, but she *would* hear those important three words. Yes, she would!

Trace awoke the next morning to see portions of Adeline's bare back peeking from beneath the blanket. She had clutched the cover to her all night, like a child holding a magical charm.

He sucked in his breath at the flawless, ivory perfection of her skin, then frowned when he saw a dark purple bruise along the curve of her rib cage.

"Adeline?"

She started, and lost hold of a corner of the blanket as she turned over. He saw a creamy shoulder and a hint of rounded breast before she snatched it back into place.

He gulped. "Uh, I thought you said you weren't hurt."

She hunched the blanket up around her neck. "I

362

wasn't."

Reaching out, he pulled her closer. "What are you hidin' under there?"

"Nothing."

"Now, Adeline, you don't . . ." He accidentally caught the blanket under his knee as he leaned forward. The hand he placed on her shoulder slipped, pulling the cover down. He gasped. She was completely naked.

Then he cursed and gently touched her bruised skin. She shrank back, but he caught her and crushed her to his chest, though he took special care not to hurt her. "Those bastards. I wish we had killed every one of them."

Her voice was venomous when she exclaimed, "The worst one is dead."

"Rudy?"

She nodded. "I saw. I must have gotten to the tepee right after you left."

She shuddered. "I tried to kill him. I planned how I would do it, and I . . ." Her voice shook as she tried to suppress another outburst of tears.

He ran his fingers through her hair and held her head to his shoulder as he rocked her back and forth. "Go ahead and cry, honey. Let it out. I'm here. You're safe now."

She did cry, for what seemed like hours to Addy, a lifetime of horror to Trace. He'd never heard a woman cry with such gut-wrenching sobs. He vowed she would never have to cry again as long as he was around to . . .

To what? What was he thinking? He couldn't live in Boston. He hated it in the east. Here he was free, to be his own kind of man, to have control of his life.

He owned a ranch near Santa Fe and fully intended to settle down on it once this matter of gun-running was over. He'd won the land in a game of monte from Governor Armijo in '46. Of course, he'd never told anyone that bit of information. He just acknowledged it had been given to him after doing the governor a certain favor.

He sighed with relief when Eagle Feather approached, carrying an armload of goods. "I told your woman I would find something for her to wear. There was little of value."

Addy leaned away from Trace and sniffed, giving the Comanche a watery smile. "Thank you."

Watching the easy camaraderie between the two most important people in his life caused a quick surge of warmth, and also a tinge of jealousy, to course through Trace. God, he wished he knew what to do.

He was still staring into space when he heard a grunt and a giggle. His head snapped around to see Adeline modeling a pair of long johns and a plaid flannel shirt whose hem fell well below her knees and whose arms hung so long he couldn't even see her tiny hands. He grinned.

"Mighty fetchin', woman. She'd be the height of Boston fashion, wouldn't she, Eagle Feather?"

The Indian grunted, but his black eyes twinkled with amusement.

Addy twirled in front of them. "At least when we reach the caravan, I'll . . ." Suddenly, she stopped and covered her mouth. "I forgot. Dear Lord, I almost forgot . . ." Her face drained of color as she clenched her fists and stomped one dainty foot.

"What did you forget, Adeline?" Trace shot his Comanche friend a long-suffering look, as if to say he'd made a terrible blunder, maligning a woman's sense of fashion.

But the last thing on Addy's mind at that moment was how she might look. "Rudy and Jubal . . . They have it all planned. Rudy's going to lead an attack on the wagon train in . . ." She counted how many days it would be now. It seemed a week had passed, rather than just one awful night. She guessed it was still "in three days."

The two friends looked at each other, their visages

suddenly grim. Then their eyes lit up at the same time.

"You thinkin' we oughta keep that rendezvous?"

Eagle Feather nodded.

Trace reached over and gave Addy a hug. "Damned right!" She blinked, wondering what she had done to deserve the embrace, wishing she could do it again.

By early morning of the third day, Addy was painfully glad that things were finally about to happen. Another day of torture around the perturbing Trace, and she would pull her hair out.

She had never been so physically aware of a man in her entire life, and so frustrated at doing anything about it. She had teased and tantalized and come right out and flaunted herself at the man until she was embarrassed by her outlandish, uncharacteristic behavior.

At least once, she was sure she had seen him clench his fists and grit his teeth to keep from touching her, but why? What was stopping him? The one time she had been brazen enough to actually throw herself at him, they had been completely alone and, still, he shied away.

She shook her head and sighed just as Trace and Eagle Feather rode up beside her on top of the hill. Below, the train was camped at a spring, and thin spirals of smoke rose into the hazy sky.

As Trace reined in close, his body was as taut as a bow string, and not just from worrying about what would happen in a few minutes. It was Adeline who caused him to be as jumpy as frog legs in a frying pan.

Every time he turned around, she smiled a secret little smile, or sent him a look that seared his guts, and he was certain she was completely unaware of how sultry and seductive she appeared. Oh God, and when he had caught her almost naked, taking a sponge bath last evening . . .

He wiped sweat from his forehead. Never had he wanted a woman so badly, yet he had refused to take her, for her own good. For the first time in his life, he used a woman's feelings and well-being as a standard by which to judge his actions. And he was dying! Mentally and physically.

Eagle Feather looked over expectantly and Trace blinked, clearing his foggy brain. Oh, yeah, his mind had wandered again, as it did far too often of late.

"Adeline, you know you have to wait here. Once it's all over, I'll fire three shots in the air as a signal for you to come down."

He leaned sideways in the saddle and glared at her. "Do you understand? *You wait here!*"

She smiled sweetly and he cursed. Quirking his lips at Eagle Feather, he threw his hands in the air.

Eagle Feather said, "Perhaps we should tie her to that tree. We will return when it is safe."

Addy gaped when Trace's eyes flared as if he thought the suggestion a marvelous one. "You wouldn't dare!"

Trace's eyebrows rose and significantly lowered.

"All right. I'll stay here. I'll wait until you big, brave men have everything under control." Her lower lip jutted out and she huffily crossed her arms over her bosom.

Trace's eyes closed as he took a deep breath.

Eagle Feather asked, "Is that your word?" while shooting his longtime friend a curious glance. He seldom saw Trace Randall lose his assurance and self-control around a woman.

Addy immediately got off her horse and stood, irate, out of their way. "Yes, I give my word. I promise. Are you satisfied?"

Trace grabbed for her horse's reins and spurred off down the hill, calling over his shoulder, "Now I am."

She fumed and stomped the ground, then stood with her hands on her hips and smiled. How she loved her arrogant, reckless soldier. Suddenly remembering the reason for his mad dash, she ran until she had a good view of Trace, the thundering Comanches and the peaceful-looking wagon train.

Trace held up his hand and eased the pace of the

366

charging Indians. Some of the drivers had heard their approach and reached for their weapons, but the Indians were almost upon the wagons before he heard Jubal shout, "We're being attacked. Be quick men."

When Trace spotted Scratch amongst the panicked group of men trying to put together some semblance of defense, he held up the barrel of his rifle. There was a white flag attached to it.

About that same time, Scratch recognized him and hollered, "Hold your fire, boys. Hold your fire."

As they had previously discussed, Eagle Feather halted his warriors a short distance from the wagons. Trace rode forward, the white flag in front of him.

Scratch came from between two wagons. "Trace, boy? What be ya up to?"

Trace looked toward the startled Jubal, who was raising the muzzle of his gun. "I wouldn't, if I were you."

To Scratch, he said, "We're just payin' a little social call." He dismounted, leaving his horse ground-tied behind him, as he stepped over a wagon tongue and into the camp, moving cautiously toward Jubal. "You *were* expectin' visitors, weren't you?"

Jubal's wild eyes searched the empty hills, then settled anxiously on the suspicious faces gathering behind Trace. "Uh, I don't know what you mean. We were going to pull out in a few minutes, just like every mornin'. What . . . ?"

Scratch shook his gray head. "We'uns been tryin' ta git ya up an' 'round fer a good spell. Why ya been stallin'?"

Jubal backed up a step. There was a frantic look in his eyes, and his huge body jerked spasmodically. "My . . . wife's feeling poorly. Needed to give her some time, is all."

Down the line, a carriage door swung open. "Jubal, dahlin', I cleaned the . . ." A head of perfectly coiffed brown hair stuck out for a moment. "Excuse me, I didn't . . . Oh . . . Oh-h-h." The door slammed shut as she quickly ducked back inside.

Trace advanced on Jubal. "Jubal Wilkins, I hereby arrest you in the name of the United States Government for tradin' stolen Army rifles and illegal whiskey to the Indians. And for the destruction of two known wagon trains and the murder of all those connected with the trains."

He took a breath and tapped the end of the rifle barrel in the palm of his left hand. He had to keep his hands busy doing something, or he'd strangle the slimy bastard.

The drivers muttered between themselves and asked Scratch if what Trace said was true. Scratch started to explain about the false bottoms in the wagons, when there was a commotion amongst the waiting Comanches and Addy ran into the center of activity, panting for breath.

Trace had no chance at Jubal as she stopped directly between the two men. In a second, Jubal grabbed her from behind, holding his forearm across her neck, squeezing until she gagged.

"All right, Randall. Looks like I've got the better hand now. Drop that gun!" He pressed his arm tighter. Addy's eyes bulged. Her fingers clawed at his sleeve, but her defense was as effective as a kitten spitting at a grizzly bear.

Jubal repeated, "Drop it, or I'll break her neck."

Addy stopped struggling when she saw the look of utter defeat on Trace's face. Lord, would she never learn? She closed her eyes, thinking, knowing she had gotten herself into this situation, and it was up to her now to get out.

She reopened her eyes, feeling responsible for the indecision and despair warring on Trace's features as he bent to lay down the rifle. He would never forgive her for breaking her promise. Her fists clenched. She could explain. He had to listen.

But first, she had to get free of the horrid man choking her to death. She raised her right forearm. Swaying her hips as far to the side as possible, she aimed for the only area on Jubal's fat body that she could reach and hurt. Her fist swung down—hard.

Jubal roared. She ducked out of his hold, fell flat on the ground, and squirmed through the dirt and dust to get out of the way. Jubal swung the muzzle of his gun toward Trace just as Trace rolled and came up firing.

Jubal's gun went off, the bullet striking harmlessly into the ground as he slowly fell to his knees, then pitched forward to lie, face down, on the ground. He didn't move.

Addy got up and ran to Trace, wrapping her arms about his waist, rubbing her cheek thankfully against his chest. "I'm sorry, Trace. So sorry. I couldn't stand it up there, not knowing . . . I didn't mean . . . Please forgive me."

Trace looked over the top of her head and motioned for Scratch. When the old man walked up, his face wreathed with curiosity, Trace pried Addy loose and gave her over to Scratch.

Walking as if in a trance, he went straight out to Eagle Feather.

Addy covered her face with her hands and sobbed quietly as Scratch gently led her to the wagon. She had done it now. She had broken her word, and more importantly, needlessly risked lives. If Trace never spoke to her again, it would serve her right.

Trace trembled violently by the time he reached his friend. His face was devoid of color. His eyes wide, their usual brilliant blue, faded to almost gray.

"God, I can't take any more of this. The damned woman is goin' to be the death of me, or me of her."

Eagle Father stared solemnly into Trace's tortured eyes. "What do you want to do?"

"I *want* to throw her on the ground and make mad, passionate, glorious love to her every time I see her. But that's not the problem."

"You love her."

"Hell, yes, I love her. She's the most beautiful, spir-

369

ited, intelligent, well, maybe not intelligent, spunky, uninhibited woman I've ever known."

"You would have her change?"

"Change? Damn it, no. It's taken two months for her to lose her prim Boston society manner. I hope she stays just the way she is."

"So?"

Trace paced in circles. "So, what? What are you tryin' . . . Oh. Damn." He grinned. "Life with that woman would never be dull, would it?"

Then the smile faded. "I can't do it, my friend. I vowed I'd never go back east, and I can't ask her to stay here. Look how many times I've almost lost her. One of these days, I won't be so lucky. No, I can't be responsible for her gettin' hurt, or maybe even killed."

"Perhaps you should let *her* make the choice, my brother."

Trace shook his head. "Huh-uh, I've made up my mind."

Chapter Twenty-five

A short time after Trace's confrontation with Jubal, Addy sat in her wagon, still very shaken. Trace remained with Eagle Feather and the Comanches, leaving her to wonder and worry over what would happen between them when they next met face to face.

As she changed out of the long johns into a presentable dress, she overheard some of the drivers debating whether to bury Jubal's body or leave it to the buzzards. She wrinkled her nose, personally opting for the buzzards.

Thinking of Jubal reminded her of unfinished business. She took a deep breath and climbed down from the wagon on her way to the black carriage.

"There you are, Addy, dahlin'. I was hopin' you'd be here. I just can't believe everythin' that's happened this mornin'." Delilah sniffed pitifully and dabbed a lace handkerchief at her red, puffy eyes.

The woman sank onto a log that had been rolled next to the fire. She daintily fluffed her skirt and peeked through her damp lashes at Addy. "Isn't it just too awful, what that dreadful man did to my poor Jubal?"

Addy felt the tender flesh on her neck where her cousin's *poor* husband nearly choked her to death. "Well, I can't say . . ."

"Oh, I heard what all went on, but I can't believe it, Addy. I just can't believe my dahlin' man could do such horrible things." Delilah's eyes teared and she choked on a sob.

Taking a seat beside her cousin, Addy's heart went out to the distraught woman. Seeing Delilah's tears made her feel guilty for thinking that Delilah could

371

have had any knowledge of Jubal's nefarious activities. Why, the dear thing was no more than an innocent victim, like herself.

"You really loved Jubal, didn't you, Lily?"

Delilah's dull brown eyes sparked with deep emotion. "Yes. I adored him." She swiped the wet streaks from her cheeks. "He came in to my life when I most needed a friend, and more."

"Oh, Delilah, why didn't you ever answer my letters? I begged for you to come and stay with us in Boston."

"Uh, I . . . Sure, but I would have been imposin'. Besides, I got along. Just fine." Her eyes shifted to the wooded hillside and the deep, deep arroyo running along its base.

Addy patted Delilah's shoulder. Things could have been so different — for both of them. "Lily, just what did you know of Jubal's business dealings?"

Delilah sighed. "Not much, really. He made several successful trips to Santa Fe for your father. He enjoyed his work. That's about all."

"Did he ever mention the cargo he traded on those trips?"

"Oh, uh, no. I imagine it was much the same as what's packed on the wagons now."

"Very probably." Disgust was evident in Addy's voice. How she wished she'd had the chance to talk to Jubal about her father and the business. She knew her parents would never have condoned smuggling guns and whiskey to the Indians, and it hurt that Trace and Scratch thought otherwise.

Delilah's eyes narrowed at Addy's flippant remark. "What are you sayin', cousin, dahlin'?"

Addy swallowed. "This will be a shock to you, I know, but your . . . Jubal . . . had my parents, your aunt and uncle, murdered so he could take over the trading. And Rudy Potts was hired to k-kill me." She shivered anew at the grizzly thought.

Delilah gasped. "No-o-o!"

"Oh, yes. I can't believe I was so naive and stupid.

He actually thought that I was such a prim little city girl that I would never have the courage to leave Boston to check up on him."

She clenched her fists. Just thinking about Jubal's high-handed arrogance made her angry all over again. Suddenly, she glanced at Delilah. "And you did everything you could to help him convince me to stay, didn't you?"

"Of course, dahlin'. I knew this was no place for you. I think I was right, too." She innocently pleated a fold in her full skirt, pressing the material against her thigh.

Addy's brow wrinkled. In a way, maybe Delilah *was* right. There were times when she had been lucky to come out of a situation alive. Yes, she had misjudged her cousin, and it lightened the burden on her heart.

Delilah stood and walked toward the hill. "You don't think your Mr. Randall will hold my husband's doin's against me, do you?"

Addy also got to her feet and held a hand out toward the other woman. "I'll talk to him, but he's a very fair man. I'm sure no one will have any hard feelin's."

"I hope so. I just feel so bad about everythin'." Her voice shook as she continued to walk.

Addy stared at Delilah's back and was about to turn back when she remembered something. Hesitantly, she followed her cousin. She needed to get the answer to one more question. It was silly, but it would put her mind to rest at last.

Delilah walked quickly and was near the arroyo when Addy caught up. For some reason she would never be able to explain, Addy called out, "Flo!"

The other woman stopped and twirled about. "Ye-e-es-s." The one simple word faded to a guttural hiss as her lips compressed.

Addy frowned as the heretofore annoying suspicion took deep root.

Delilah put a hand to her breast. "My goodness, dahlin', you startled me. Wherever did you come up with such a name?"

"If you didn't recognize it, why did you stop and answer me?"

"Uh, I, uh, knew it was your voice and stopped to see what you wanted. Why?"

There was the possibility that Delilah told the truth, but Addy didn't relent as she came closer. "I heard Jubal call you by that name. At first, I thought it was a nickname, but now . . ."

Addy's eyes rounded as Delilah's face, or Flo's, or whoever she was, contorted into a vicious snarl, causing Addy to take a step backward. Delilah's eyes narrowed, and Addy could almost see the woman's mind working as she darted cunning glances about the area.

Addy didn't want to show her sudden fear, but stumbled as her heel caught on a loose stone as she took another backward step. Delilah had a crazed, desperate look in her eyes, and it dawned on Addy that she was alone with the woman, and at quite a distance from the camp and any form of help.

Perspiration beaded her upper lip and soaked the palms of her hands, but she held herself still and erect. "Just who are you, really?"

A maniacal giggle was her answer.

The ground Addy stood on was soft and shifted beneath her feet. She looked down to find the arroyo had widened and she was near the edge of a steep precipice. The earth was gradually giving way beneath her. Quickly she stepped to the side, to find herself against her cousin, who now pulled a knife from beneath her skirt.

It had been strapped to her thigh all along, and Addy now knew why the woman had continually fooled with her skirt, obviously reassuring herself the weapon was still there. She gasped when the sharp tip bit into her neck.

"I've waited a long time for this *cousin*." To the doubt in Addy's eyes, she responded, "*Half* cousin. I had you fooled, didn't I, dahlin'?"

"But, Delilah?"

"Oh, yes, the pampered little Delilah, the apple of my daddy's eye. I'm afraid she's no longer . . . with us. Isn't it sad? My precious half sister and her precious *daddy* are burnin' in Hell where they belong, you know."

"I don't know what you're raving about." Addy's voice was high and strained. "My uncle was a wonderful man."

"Ha! Wonderful? He refused to acknowledge his illegitimate daughter. I wouldn't call that nice." Her upper lip curled and Addy shuddered. The knife pricked her skin when she gulped.

"All you had to do was die quietly, an' Jubal . . ." Tears pooled in the corners of the woman's eyes. "My dahlin' Jubal an' I would have been on our way to California with more than enough money to start a new life. Everythin' would have belonged to the last Montclair, little ole *Delilah*."

"Th-then you knew about my parents and . . . Jubal?"

"Why, certainly. It was *my* idea. An' your dahlin' pappa was so-o kind to play right into my scheme. His only mistake was in tryin' to stop . . . Well, that's all water under the bridge now, isn't it?"

Horrified at learning the real truth, Addy could only stare at . . . Flo. She was bragging about killing her parents and her cousin Delilah, and who knew how many others? Addy felt sick, truly sick.

Addy nervously shifted her feet. Her footing was becoming more precarious by the second, and she tried to move away from the ledge. It was over sixty feet straight down to the bottom of the arroyo.

All of a sudden, a strong gust of wind nearly toppled them both, and Addy used that moment to grab for the knife. Her fingers clenched around Flos' wrist and wrenched, but the other woman was larger and stronger.

A voice in the back of her mind screamed *No!* She would not die! Not at the hands of this demented woman.

Thunder boomed menacingly near. Addy flinched even as she struggled. Wind whipped her skirt, tangling the material about her legs until she could hardly move. Her hands were stretched over her head, holding the knife less than a foot above her chest, but her knees quaked as more and more of the dirt crumbled beneath their combined weight.

Lightning flashed and Flo suddenly jerked upright as Addy's fingers lost their grip. She looked up into such a feverishly deformed face and eyes that her heart stopped beating. She'd never seen such hatred focused on anyone before. The force of it literally pinned her to the ground.

The hair on Addy's body stood on end. Her feet slipped down the incline. She felt herself falling. A second jagged bolt of lightning split the heavens and Addy gagged at the nauseating odor of burning hair and flesh even as her hands groped for, and finally found, protruding roots anchored in solid earth.

Her arms felt as if they would soon wrench from their sockets as she hung there, sobbing. Her toes sought a foothold, but she knew her strength was failing and any moment she would plummet to her death.

Then fingers as firm and hard as steel cables wrapped about her wrists. Drops of water as large as stones beat upon her face when she tried to look up.

"Hold on, honey. I've got you. Just hold on!"

The desperation in Trace's voice was frightening. She again fought to save herself, with her feet and legs and knees, until she felt her body rising, inch by slow inch.

It rained so hard the dirt turned to mud in an instant, making the ground slippery and hard to maneuver for them both. Then Eagle Feather's large, stocky body loomed above her and with one hefty jerk, he and Trace together brought her to safety.

She threw herself into Trace's arms, burying her head in his shoulder. Soon a churning in her stomach caused her to push away and she stood shaking, her arms wrapped across her stomach.

As the sickness gradually passed, she looked into the cloud-shrouded sky. Her eyes closed. The rain washed her hair away from her face and blended with her tears.

"Honey?"

She licked her lips and slowly opened her eyes. She questioned, "Deli . . . my cousin?" At least the latter was *half* true, she guessed.

Trace glanced at Eagle Feather, then back to her. There was regret in his eyes. "I'm sorry."

Her chin fell to her chest as the air left her lungs. She still felt and heard the horrendous crackling sizzle as the lightning had struck her half cousin's body. No matter what the woman had done, no one deserved such a terrible death.

As she straightened and glanced once again into the raging heavens, it was as if the rain cleansed her soul. She wasn't afraid any more. A deep peace settled over her as she gazed into Trace's taut features.

"Are you all right, honey? I tried to find you, but didn't see you until the storm broke and . . ." He choked. He'd always have nightmares from the sight of the knife descending toward Adeline, and the heat of the lightning as it . . . A shudder shook his stalwart frame.

He took her in his arms and held her tenderly to his breast. Her stomach gurgled again and he turned her toward the security of camp. "Come on, tenderfoot. Let's get you into some dry clothes."

With his use of the endearment, Addy sighed and knew she had been forgiven. Tension drained from her body as she leaned into him for support.

Eagle Feather stepped in behind them until Addy stopped and held out her hand to him.

Chapter Twenty-six

Later in the afternoon, the storm passed and the sun once again shone brightly upon the quiet caravan. A troop of Mexican soldiers arrived to escort the train the rest of the way to Santa Fe.

Eagle Feather and his warriors took some of the soldiers on to show them where the stolen goods from the burned-out trains were hidden, before continuing on to the Comanche encampment. Addy had bid a tearful goodbye to the handsome Indian, sad at heart because she didn't know if she would ever see him again.

The decision had been made to wait until morning to continue on, and Addy was grateful. She swallowed as her stomach turned upside down, and pressed her hands over the queasy area.

As naive as she was, she had a feeling her lack of "monthlies", and the early morning sickness she had experienced of late, pointed to only one thing. She was carrying Trace's child.

A tear rolled down her cheek. What would happen once they reached Santa Fe? He had been so loving and kind, yet had never mentioned a word concerning a future together.

Too, he was such an honorable man, if he knew she was pregnant with his child, he would insist on "doing the right thing." She didn't want him to feel forced into a marriage he didn't want.

Sometimes she would catch him watching her, and swore she saw a flame of desire burning in his eyes, and perhaps something more. Something she probably only imagined because she wanted it so badly.

"Trace sat on the bench beside Adeline, shaking the reins at the tired mules. In another hour they would top the ridge overlooking Santa Fe.

For the past few days he had sought the courage to ask her to stay with him, to marry and build a new life, even raise a family. But fear gripped his insides. What if she turned him down, or left without so much as a backward glance?

His fingers held the leather so tightly his knuckles were white. Then again, what if she said yes? What if he couldn't protect her? God knew, he'd done a damned poor job of looking out for her so far.

"Trace?"

His head snapped around. His eyes lit with surprise, then pleasure. She was so beautiful.

Minutes dragged by before she said anything. He hated himself for suddenly becoming tongue-tied and unsure of himself.

She cleared her throat. "I-I guess we'll be in Santa Fe soon?"

He tapped the end of a rein against his thigh. "I guess."

"How long will it take to trade the goods and prepare for the return to Independence?"

He sighed. Damn it all, she was already anxious to leave and they hadn't even gotten there yet. "A couple of days."

"Will you be going back . . . with me . . . us?" She plucked at the non-existent lint on her skirt.

"No."

She jerked as if she had been slapped. That was it? Just *no?* Her heart pounded so violently she could hardly breathe. She fought to hold back the deluge of tears that threatened to pour down her flushed cheeks.

Trace clawed at his collar. It felt as if a thousand lances pricked his flesh whenever he looked at her. If only he could make up his mind. Should he ask her, or not? What would be best for *her?*

When he stopped the caravan at a spot overlooking the village of Santa Fe, Trace couldn't help casting leery glances at Addy. What if she didn't like it? After all, she was a lady, used to the luxuries of city living. The life he could offer was a long way from her fancy Boston upbringing.

Sitting sadly next to Trace, flinching every time he brushed her arm or thigh, Addy was taken unawares when he suddenly pointed and said, "There she is. Santa Fe."

She squinted and blinked. At first all she saw was a long, seemingly empty valley. She blinked again. Was that it? Where she had expected to see buildings and streets, she barely made out drab outlines of mud walls and dirt tracks, so well did it all blend in the countryside.

Disappointment welled inside her. *That* was Santa Fe? Paradise? For two months, through hardship and disaster and uncertainty after uncertainty, she had looked forward to arriving in a spectacular city. If there had been streets paved with gold, she would have been less astonished.

"Well, uh, what do you think of her?"

She sensed the tension in Trace and plastered a smile to her lips. "It's . . . it's . . . different . . ."

He sighed and patted her hand. "Wait until you see her up close. It's hard to tell much at this distance." His heart plummeted to his feet. She hated it.

Addy heard the shouts and cheers from the rest of the men. Hats were thrown into the air. Some of the drivers danced a jig. She took another long look and shook her head. What was it about Santa Fe that inspired such jubilation?

Almost four hours later, Trace turned the wagons into a large square, what he called a plaza. Trees were planted around the area to provide travelers and townspeople a cool place to rest.

He pointed out the governor's house, a long, low building that ran one full side of the plaza with a wide portal across the front. Addy's head spun as she studied the other sides, too. One consisted of a large church and several homes. Along the other two were stores and private dwellings. All had a portal, inviting customers and friends to walk in the shade.

They had to wait for the goods to be examined and taxed before the trading began. Trace stood off to one side under a tree. She left the wagons to join him, but was hailed by American officers and their wives from the nearby Fort Marcy. She was welcomed effusively.

Trace watched her closely and was delighted to see her blushing prettily when she later approached him. He was so proud of her. And he began to realize why he had never fully understood the meaning of the word *love* until he met Adeline Montclair.

His voice was deep and trebled when he repeated a question from earlier in the day. "Well, what do you think?"

She tilted her chin. "It's wonderful. I've never seen any place quite like it." Oh, how she wished he loved her. She could stay here with him forever.

"It's nothin' like Boston."

She eyed the plaza for perhaps the hundredth time. "No-o-o, it might be even better." She took a deep breath and spoke before she thought. "*You're* not in Boston, Trace."

Her eyes widened as a furious red suffused her face. When had she turned into such a brazen hussy? Then she thought a minute, and raised her head. Since she had taken the initiative to leave Boston. Since she had crossed the Jornada and come out alive. Since she had helped deliver her father's goods safely to Santa Fe.

She felt good, and proud, and somehow sensed that her parents would be very happy with the woman their "tenderfoot" daughter had become.

Trace was too stunned to say a word. Had she meant what she said? If so, would she consider. . . ?

His fists clenched and a muscle along his jaw spasmed as he asked, "Ah, what would you think about . . . stayin' . . . here?" He licked at his parched lips, not daring to take a breath.

She trembled all over. She thought — hoped — she knew what he was saying, but had to be sure. "Here? But . . . what would I do?"

His eyes looked everywhere but at her, desperately seeking an answer. "Well . . . you could . . . Damn it to hell! Marry me!"

She cleared her throat. "What?"

He took her in his arms, unmindful of the scene they might be creating. "You heard me." His mouth teased her ear. "If you don't hurry and say yes, Adeline Montclair, I'm goin' to whallop your backside."

She smiled so brightly she rivaled the sun. "My, how could a woman resist such a romantic proposal as *that?*"

He squeezed until the breath hissed from her lungs as she huskily answered, "Yes! Yes! I'll marry you."

So jubilant he could hardly stand still, Trace was still plagued with doubts. "I don't know, I'm afraid . . ."

She reached up and put her finger on his lips. "There's something very important that we haven't said yet."

He sucked in his breath. Damn! Here it came. There was a condition. Could he live with it?

As if reading his mind, she told him, "I love you, Trace Randall. Wherever you are, that's where I belong." Her eyes shone with a happy moisture. A smile lit her face with an ethereal glow.

He blinked, then frowned. Had he heard her correctly? "But your home . . ."

"Is with you."

Suddenly, he hugged her and buried his face in her long, luxurious hair. "God, honey, I love you. I was afraid to hope you would consent to staying in such an unsettled country."

She placed her palms on his cheeks and stared into eyes the color of the morning sky. "I love it here. I love the wildness and the beauty." She removed her hands and twisted them in front of her. "What are your thoughts about a fa-family?"

"Of course we'll have a family. A big one. Why?"

"Would you rather start with a boy, or a girl?"

"I don't care. Whatever we have, when the time comes . . . Wait! Surely you. . . ? Are we?"

She nodded. If his arms crushed her any harder, she would break.

"Dadburn it, if'n I'm not gonna be a gran'pap."

Trace jerked so hard that Addy squealed. "Damn you, old man! I'm goin' to tie bells to your buckskins."

"Wal, ain't I?"

Addy looked helplessly about the busy plaza, but no one paid them any mind. "Yes, Mr. Scratch, you are."

"Crissakes, we got us'uns some cel'bratin' ta do."

Addy crossed the fingers of both hands behind her back. "First, Mr. Scratch, I've been doing a lot of thinking and, if Trace agrees, I'd be grateful if you'd take over the management of . . . my . . . business."

It was hard for her to think of her father's hard work and accomplishments coming solely to her. Solely. Her family was gone. She hadn't even known her real cousin Delilah.

But, as she looked closely at the two men hovering near her, she discovered the pain wasn't nearly as great any more.

"I'd be plumb proud ta think ya'd trust me ta do ya a good job, gal."

Addy winked at Trace. "When you get back from checking with the office in Independence, I wouldn't be a bit surprised if you don't call us 'partners' next spring."

Scratch fairly beamed through the frosted hair coating his seamed features.

Trace placed his hands tenderly on Addy's cheeks. "Do you have any idea what a happy man you've made of this lonely soldier?"

She rubbed the tip of her nose and grinned. "I certainly hope so, dear. After all, aren't we in *Paradise* now?"